THE

DONOVANS

VOLUME I

A.C. ARTHUR

THE DONOVANS
VOLUME I

A.C. ARTHUR

AN ARTISTRY PUBLISHING BOOK

PLEASURED BY A DONOVAN, Copyright © 2012 by A.C. Arthur
First Edition: 2012

HEART OF A DONOVAN, Copyright © 2013 by A.C. Arthur
First Edition: 2013

THE DONOVANS, VOLUME I © 2013 by A.C. Arthur
First Edition: 2013

www.acarthur.net

This book is a work of fiction. Characters, names, locations, events and incidents (in either a contemporary and/or historical setting) are products of the author's imagination and are being used in an imaginative manner as a part of this work of fiction. Any resemblance to actual events, locations, settings or persons, living or dead, is entirely coincidental.

ISBN 10 – 0615827357
ISBN 13 – 978-0615827353

PLEASURED BY
A
DONOVAN

PROLOGUE

Eleven Years Ago

"He makes me sick," Victoria snapped, heading into the lecture hall where the legal contracts class was always held.

"Who? Ben? He's gorgeous and he's rich as hell. I'd sleep with him in a heartbeat if I had the chance." This was Grace Monroe, a 23-year-old second year law student with her mind more focused on getting laid and finding the perfect husband to settle down with. (In Grace's mind, "perfect" meant rich and good looking.) Getting her degree in law was actually just her backup plan. Grace didn't like hard work, clearly evidenced by her lackluster grades.

Victoria Madeline Lashley was the exact opposite. "Hard work" should have been her middle name and "goal-oriented" her nickname. She knew what she wanted and planned to get it without anyone's help, especially not from some arrogant, stuck up rich boy who was skating through law school on his good looks and family name.

"You can have him. He'll never make it as an attorney because he doesn't care about anyone but himself."

"And parties. Don't forget Benjamin Donovan is always the life of the party," Grace said, in her own world as she gazed at the guy they spoke of.

He was about five feet eleven, or maybe he was six feet. Who knew and who cared? His skin was the exact color of a Hershey bar, plain, no almonds. His eyes that same milky brown color. And his smile, well, he always seemed to be smiling. A fact that both perplexed and pissed Victoria off.

Then there were his clothes…no, that was enough. Benjamin Donovan was not all that. And when she walked past him, her chin up, back rigid, she hoped he got her message that she could care less about him or the great car he drove or the way his smile made her insides tremble.

⌇⌇⌇⌇⌇

She had a funky attitude, but sexy as hell eyes. And that's what really counted, because the eyes really said all that he needed to know about a person. They were gray, like gunmetal, or maybe a little lighter. Her skin always looked so smooth and creamy, like freshly churned butter. And her body…damn! That's the only word Ben could come up with to describe Victoria Lashley. But then again, she had a jacked up attitude that made her one of the most hated girls in school. Still, he couldn't resist looking at her.

Getting up from the seat on the back row that he loved to occupy, Ben walked down the aisle a bit until he came to the row where she and her only friend, Grace, sat. With a nod to Grace while Victoria was searching for something in that huge bag she always carried, Ben switched seats with her friend.

"Need help finding something?" he asked, his signature smile already in place when Victoria looked up at him.

There they were, those eyes, cool and flinty. He loved when she looked at him, felt like he'd been captured, and waited anxiously for her to reel him in instead. A little line appeared between her eyes as she frowned at him.

"Your seat is in the back, playboy," she quipped.

Even her voice—just husky enough to be sexy—turned him on. Ben tried not to be offended that she was the first female to cut him down at every turn. Even on days he wasn't trying to hit on her and was only speaking to be polite, she still shot him a frosty glare or icicle words he swore would cut if he were a lesser man.

"I like this seat right here."

She rolled her eyes. "Lucky me."

The class started and Ben only halfheartedly paid attention. Good grades came easy to him, almost too easy some said. But he'd been that way all his life. Much to his older brother Max's dismay, he rarely ever had to study, but still maintained a perfect GPA. The fact that this female was shooting down all his moves was probably karma for being so blessed in the realm of education. That's something else Max would say.

Ben on the other hand, was always an optimist.

CHAPTER 1

"Oh, this is my jam!" Ebony Reece yelled as she turned up the car radio and rocked her body to the thumping bass of the song.

It was Thursday evening, one more day until she could start her weekend. Her family was having a huge cookout on Saturday for her twin cousins who had just graduated from Spellman. Whenever her family had a gathering, whether it was a cook-out or dinner or even a brunch, it was like a party. Her Aunt Gemma would cook every piece of meat they were allowed to eat, while Gemma's younger sister Shan would prepare salads galore. Her Uncle Pete would guard the grill, flipping burgers like Ronald McDonald had taken lessons from him. Tabby would be on the music, speakers blasting old school hits with a few new school songs for the younger folk thrown in. It promised to be a great time and Ebony couldn't wait.

For the last three weeks, she'd been working late hours, spending most mornings running between the courthouse and the office while Ben worked the Ramone Vega murder case. She'd been working at Donovan Law, LLC for the last four years and absolutely loved her boss Benjamin Donovan because of his laidback attitude and ferocity in the courtroom. Normally, Ebony loved to watch Ben work his defensive magic in the courtroom. He was a dynamic litigator who charmed jurors with his warm smile and charismatic demeanor. He was also fine as hell in a suit and even better looking when he came out of his jacket as he wore down witnesses until they were admitting who they'd slept with back in high school. He was virtually unbeatable in court.

Until the Ramone Vega case.

Ben hadn't been sure about this one and Ebony felt bad for him. They'd done everything they normally did, bombarding the district attorney's office with discovery and suppression motions on a daily basis. They'd impeached expert witnesses before the prosecution even had a chance to put them on the stand. But there had been something more, something Ben felt he couldn't ignore.

"It's in his eyes," Ben had confided in her one night when they were at the office late. "He killed those people. I can see it in his eyes."

Ben had seemed shaken after that, and when she'd left him at the office that night she'd wanted to call his brother or one of his cousins to come over and check on him. But in the morning he was back to normal, ready to fight for a man's innocence he didn't even believe in.

But that was all over now.

On Tuesday the jurors came back after three days of deliberations—they were deadlocked. A mistrial was declared and Ramone Vega walked out of the courtroom with a smile on his sadistically handsome face.

Ebony's voice escalated as she tried to hit the same high note the as singer on the radio. She'd always wanted to be a singer and had believed in her talent until she realized believing wasn't paying her bills. At the same time, having a day job to make ends meet didn't have to kill the dream. She sang louder, convinced she could hit Mariah Carey's highest notes. Her solo was interrupted by the loud blaring of a police siren and the subsequent flashing of red and blue lights.

"Shit!" she cursed and immediately turned her music down, pulling over to the side of the road as signaled by the authorities.

Ben had already cleared about a half dozen speeding tickets for her with his friend down at the police station. He was going to be pretty pissed if she got another one. Ebony took a deep breath and tried to prepare herself to be nice and cordial, something she didn't do well most of the time.

She sat up a little straighter and pulled her shirt down just a tad, squaring her shoulders so her assets were on full display.

When the tap came to her window, she pressed the button to roll it down with one long-nailed finger and was already preparing her smile. The grin slowly disappeared as she looked into the eyes of a killer.

It never failed. The second he got to the door and was about to leave, his cellphone rang. It wasn't the office because he'd let Ebony go about an hour before he left himself. And if there was one thing he knew for certain about his legal assistant, it was that when he said it was quitting time, she took those words to heart and made a fast escape for the front door. She was planning to party no doubt, because Ebony had a very high-spirited personality and didn't bother to hide it, not even when she was at work.

Ebony was in her late twenties and had been with his firm for the past four years. Mrs. Jefferson, his first assistant/office manager had been there when he started the firm five years ago only to retire a year later when her daughter gave birth to quintuplets and needed help. Ebony was efficient, intelligent and nosy as hell. She talked a lot and loudly, took long lunches and harassed a good portion of their clients. But she was the best fit for the firm. Clients knew not to play with Ebony. When she called them about their payments, they paid or risked her going off on them. She typed faster than anybody Ben had ever known—even with nails that looked as long and sharp as weapons—and the office was superbly organized, right down to the blue-only pens she purchased from the supply company. There was no argument that she was an invaluable asset to the firm.

But that didn't stop her from getting on Ben's nerves at least three days out of the work week.

"Ben Donovan," he answered, stopping in front of the door.

"This call is strictly a reminder. Dinner at Aunt Bev's this Sunday at five. That's two days from today. Don't even think about using me as an excuse should you not attend."

Ben only smiled. Max was so damned serious.

"Good to hear you've got my back, big brother," he quipped, clenching the phone between his ear and his shoulder while he opened the door and closed it behind him.

"Well, since they believe I'm my brother's keeper, I was told to remind you again."

He had missed the last few get-togethers, Ben admitted to himself. But he'd been in trial—a very high-profile murder trial, at that. He'd barely had time to breathe or hit the gym or anything else he liked to do for fun. Now that the case had been declared a mistrial, he was seriously thinking about a little vacation, maybe a couple days on some lovely beach where he could swim until his muscles ached, then sleep until late morning and eat until he couldn't move. That was Ben's idea of the perfect vacation.

"I'll be there," he said.

The Donovans were a close-knit family. Even though they were stretched across the United States, they still kept in close contact with each other. That was something bred in them from generation to generation. Ben remembered his father telling him that their great-great-grandfather Elias Donovan said there was nothing more important than family, not business and definitely not money. Only family survived. Ben believed that wholeheartedly and normally never missed a function.

"You okay?" Max asked after Ben had been quiet for a few seconds.

Ben had just climbed into his car and was staring through the front windshield at a piece of paper that wasn't there twenty minutes ago when he'd parked.

"I'm fine," he finally replied, still deciding whether or not he was going to reach for the paper. "Just trying to get to the gym before it gets too crowded."

"You and that gym. It's like your second home," Max told him as if he didn't already know this.

Slipping on his Ray-Ban Aviator sunglasses, Ben reached for his seatbelt. "It's good for my health," he told his brother. He left out that it was an excellent way to work off stress and to keep his mind focused on the important things in life since the field of work he'd chosen wasn't the most calming.

"If you say so," Max said. "Stop by and see your niece sometime. She's growing like a weed. You probably won't even recognize her."

That thought made Ben smile. Max and his wife Deena had adopted a beautiful baby girl from a small town in Brazil. Max and Ben's mother Alma, along with her business partner Noreen Lakefield, ran a nonprofit agency called Karing Kidz which facilitated adoptions for children in North and South America. The girl's name was Sophia and she was the absolute apple of Max and Deena's eyes. She'd also wrapped her Uncle Ben around her baby finger so tightly he just about beamed each time he saw her.

"I'll recognize her and she'll definitely recognize her favorite uncle. Tell Deena I said hello."

"Will do. Be safe."

"Will do," Ben agreed, disconnecting the phone. When he'd tossed it onto the passenger seat, he gave in to curiosity and reached for the piece of paper on his dashboard.

THINK AGAIN
Route 215, Exit 11

It was typed and cryptic and the headache that had been sluggishly hanging around since about ten o'clock on Wednesday morning began pounding immediately, as if to say, "I'm back!" Ben had no idea what the address was referring to, but he knew the meaning of the two words.

As Ben drove, an earlier conversation from the day played in his head. It was something he'd planned to forget, to ignore and file away with other crazy incidents in his life as a defense attorney.

He'd been walking to his car, going down the steps to the underground garage across the street from his office building. It was well-lit on both floors but like traveling through the gates to the White House to get a car in and out, which was the reason he'd chosen this lot instead of the above ground one a half block down. His shoes clicked rhythmically across the concrete as he pulled his key from his pocket and disengaged the automatic locks. The headlights flashed on and off as the sound of his alarm being disabled echoed throughout the space. He was about a foot away from his car when the man stepped out and stood in front of him with arms folded over his chest.

He wore an expertly tailored single breasted suit in a milk chocolate brown hue. His thick, inky colored hair was combed back and generously sprinkled with a glossy sheen. A burnt orange complexion, dusky brown eyes and lips that spread into an eerie smirk topped off his appearance. He was almost a perfect match for the witness description of the person who'd climbed into a gray Lexus after leaving the house of Congressman McGlinn and his wife the night they were brutally murdered.

"I didn't get a chance to thank you for a job well done," Ramone Vega said in his heavily accented voice.

The car was a perfect match for the one made in the witness statement that had been suppressed at trial. Disregarding that thought, Ben decided to take the hand Vega extended to him. They shook as he said, "No problem. It's my job."

Vega nodded. "I guess they'll want a new trial."

They did. Ben already knew that. He'd known the second Julius Talmadge, the assistant district attorney on the case, had slammed his briefcase closed and stomped out of the courtroom. He also knew because they'd already served him with a motion stating their claim.

Ben only nodded.

"We'll be ready for them the second time around, huh?" Vega asked with a chuckle.

Ben did not laugh.

"I won't be representing you at the new trial," he told him, and kept his eyes trained on the other man's.

Vega didn't look shocked, only annoyed. "I pay my bills with you, man. So what's the problem?"

"I can take or release any client I want. That's in our retainer agreement. You paid me for this charge and this trial date. I represented you. I am not obligated to retry this case for you."

"Don't do this Donovan." The sentence had been simple enough, its tone meant to be a warning.

Ben shook his head. Something about Vega had always bothered him. No, it wasn't something, it was guilt. The man was as guilty of murder as Ben was innocent. And knowing that, he couldn't effectively represent him, he *would not* represent him.

"It's already done. You need to find yourself another lawyer and fast. I'm sure the prosecutors are going to push for a speedy trial."

Ben had started to walk away.

"I want you on this case," Vega said, his accent almost gone, his voice deeper, deadlier.

Ben didn't like having his back to the man as he walked the rest of the distance to his car. When he was at the driver's side door, he opened it and tossed his briefcase into the back seat. He looked up at Vega who had turned and was watching him intently.

"I won't work on this case. And I'm not going to change my mind."

He'd climbed into his car and pulled off, headed for the Justice Center where he could file his own motion to strike his appearance. Out of the rearview mirror he'd watched Vega reach into his jacket pocket for his cellphone. When he turned toward the exit, Vega had still been standing there, looking at him drive away.

Ben hadn't given a second thought to what the man might have been thinking or doing. He'd just been glad to have this case behind him.

Now he wondered if it really was.

CHAPTER 2

This was her life, Victoria thought, checking the full length mirror behind her closet door. Her black suit was classic, stylish and functional all at once. The skirt scraped a few inches above her knees; the jacket, when buttoned, creating the perfect hour-glass figure. She looked professional and serious, her dark hair cut into layers that fell in soft waves past her shoulders. As for jewelry, she wore stud earrings that were practically invisible and her school ring on her left ring finger. Simple and to the point. That's how she liked to keep things.

One last turn to the side showed off her legs in four-inch Alexander Wang peep toe ring pumps. Her gaze lingered on the shoes a second or two longer as she acknowledged her one true obsession. Some women loved ice cream, or handbags (that was Grace). She even knew a woman who was obsessed with fragrances. She worked in one of the offices at the Justice Center and Victoria developed a headache each time she passed the woman's desk, the scents were so strong.

Victoria loved shoes. That wasn't a crime. And these had been a splurge for her, seeing as they cost a good chunk of her pay checks. Still, she figured she didn't party, drink, gamble or otherwise waste the money she made. In fact, she paid bills for herself and her retired mother. Naomi Lashley refused to move into a senior home and refused even more sternly to move in with her daughter or let her daughter move in with her. She was a proud, independent woman and had raised Victoria to be the same way. That's why her daughter didn't argue with her, but did what she could to make the pension check her mother received from the Clark County school system stretch as far as it could.

Not that Victoria was getting rich off her salary as assistant district attorney in Clark County. It definitely wasn't the paycheck that kept her going to work each day. Victoria would say a passion for the law, fighting for justice and the night of her sophomore dance were the driving forces behind her career choice. And she didn't regret them one bit.

She loved her work, felt it was more rewarding than money and privilege could ever be. So what she rented her house instead of purchasing a condo or home of her own. Her car, a 2010 Honda Accord, was a serviceable and attractive vehicle that she could comfortably afford. That's the word Victoria would use to describe her life, comfortable. And she was just fine with that.

A half hour later she parked her car in the garage and used the walk-thru to connect to the Justice Center where she worked. While taking the elevator to her floor, she spoke to co-workers who were both happy and downright pissed that they had to be there. She never could figure out why more people weren't thankful to have a job, even if it was one they didn't particularly care for.

Victoria loved her job. Prosecuting criminals was exhilarating and liberating to her, especially since her father's senseless murder more than ten years ago. Victoria had promised herself that she'd seek justice for all the innocent victims in the state of Nevada. After graduating law school she'd filled a law clerk position for Judge January and on his recommendation was hired two years later by the Clark County District Attorney's office. It had been another two years since she'd been practicing, going to court to prosecute felony trials. Today, however, she didn't have anything on her docket. Her day would most likely be spent reading over upcoming cases.

Walking into her office, she said a warm good morning to Evelyn and Roxanne, the two secretaries who manned the reception area for the felony trial division.

"Good morning, Victoria. No calls," Evelyn said with her daily smile.

Evelyn was a thirty-something year old woman—African American, married, three kids, a dog and a cat—who had been with the district attorney's office for more than ten years.

Roxanne spoke with a movement of her lips but no sound. She was on the phone. Again. Twenty-two years old, African American, and as mature as one of Evelyn's middle school kids, Roxanne had a lot to learn about working in a professional environment. She was going to college, but hadn't yet selected a major. Victoria figured that could be attributed to the fact that she didn't want to do anything besides talk on the phone and hang out with her friends. If her father hadn't been a district attorney for forty years and pulled some serious strings for her, she wouldn't have this position. There were days when Victoria wished he hadn't pulled those strings.

Proceeding down the short hallway, her steps muffled by the worn carpeted floor, she passed two offices with doors closed—other ADA's hard at work first thing in the morning? That may or may not have been the case. Her office was the third on the left. Walking inside she dropped her bag on the chair that sat near the door and moved to her desk, where she slapped her purse down.

"Did you hear?" A female voice interrupted Victoria's morning ritual before it could even begin. "Jules had Ramone Vega indicted again."

Grace had also gotten a position at the DA's office. Hers came complete with a husband who was a judge in the traffic division. Even though Grace's dream had been to marry rich enough so she didn't have to work, she seemed to really love Clinton Ramsey. And she was actually a pretty good attorney when she cared enough about the case to prosecute it thoroughly, which wasn't all of the time since she basically thought it was a waste of time for them to prosecute criminals who would be let back out onto the street for one foolish reason or another.

"Really?" Sitting in her chair, Victoria switched on her computer, then swiveled to reach for the strings that would close the blinds to her window.

It was a gorgeous, sun-blazing, temperature-rising day in Las Vegas, but the sun's beams were a bit too bright for her this early in the morning.

Grace was nodding as she gave Victoria the bag that she'd removed from the chair where she was now preparing to sit.

Grace was also seven and a half months pregnant. Standing was not a good idea for her at any time of day.

She folded her hands, resting them on the bridge of her protruding belly. "Grand jury convened first thing Wednesday morning. Indictment was filed just before the clerk's office closed last night. Jules is happy as a jaybird."

"Wow," was all Victoria could say at the moment. She looked at her watch. It was barely 9:30. "That was a first degree murder case, a witness statement but no witness to testify and no prints on the gun. But Vega's a known criminal. He's Pena's hit man, everybody knows that. I can't believe that jury refused to convict him. Damn."

"You said it right there. Vega is well known in this area. There're more people out there afraid of him and Louverde's gang than there are in this entire city. Who's going to find him guilty and risk retaliation?" Grace asked dryly.

"Even if he's a drug-dealing killer?" Victoria couldn't believe it. This man had a wrap sheet as long as both her arms put together. He was dangerous, cocky as hell. He belonged behind bars. "You think Jules is going to retry the case himself?"

Grace began fanning herself, the wispy bangs of her blond frosted hair lifting with the effort. She looked completely miserable, Victoria had to admit. Her once pert nose was now pudgy and always red at the tip. Coupled with her light brown complexion, she looked like Rudolph the red-nosed reindeer even in the midst of summer. She was always hot, so there were no sleeves in her black dress, which fanned out into a full skirt beneath her heavy breasts. Once Victoria's shoe-shopping buddy, she now wore ballet flats, though she often kicked them off and put on her house slippers.

"He doesn't have a choice. The Mayor and the DA will be on his ass if he doesn't."

Victoria nodded. "True."

Two seconds after that acknowledgement Julius Talmadge III, head of the Felony Trial Division, was standing in her doorway.

"I need to see you in my office. Now."

Then he was gone. Grace shrugged and braced her hands on the sides of the chair in an attempt to pull or push herself up. With a chuckle Victoria was up and around her desk. Reaching out she grabbed Grace's hands. "On three," she prompted.

Grace nodded.

"One. Two. Three!" She pulled and Grace basically pushed all her weight forward until Victoria took a couple steps back with Grace coming up to her feet. "Girl, you can't last much longer," she said as Grace let her hands drop to her side and tried to catch her breath.

"I know that's right," she said. "Now get on down that hall and call me the minute you come out of his office."

She waddled out of the office and Victoria took a deep breath. Heading towards Jules' space felt like walking to the principal's office.

❧ ❧ ❧

Of all the things in the world he could have said, Victoria would have never guessed this would be it.

"You want me to handle the new murder trial?" she asked, befuddlement clear in her tone.

"That's right. Enter your appearance. File it and hand deliver along with a stack of discovery motions to that cocky ass defense counsel at the end of the day. I want a new trial date ASAP and I want Vega picked up again and held on a no bail status."

She'd taken her legal pad and pen with her into Jules' office and was scribbling furiously as he talked. He, unlike her, had not closed his blinds, so the glare shot across the room and landed right on her bright yellow paper, making everything she wrote look like blurry lines.

"What were the specific grounds for the mistrial?" she asked.

"Because he's got a cocky, rich attorney who thinks all he has to do is smile at the jury and they'll believe whatever he says," Jules spat, contempt dripping from his every word.

Most prosecutors didn't like defense attorneys. That was nothing new. But Victoria had a feeling this went a little beyond normal camaraderie. "Is that what the jury said?" she asked cautiously.

Jules could be very temperamental when he was working a case. He could also be a bit cocky and on the better side of being an asshole himself, so she was taking his comments about defense counsel with a huge grain of salt.

He responded by slamming both of his palms down on his desk. The keyboard shook and his pencil holder tipped over, spilling its contents onto the blotter. But Jules' dark gaze stayed fixed on her.

"I just meant..." she started to say, but stopped when he began shaking his head.

"He's got a silver spoon stuck up his butt and thinks that makes him invincible. The jury said they couldn't reach an agreement. Half of them thought Vega was guilty and the other half thought innocent because that damned attorney gave them some bogus alternative scenario in his closing."

Victoria nodded. It sounded to her like defense counsel had done his job. But she wasn't about to say that to Jules. "And the problematic defense counsel is...?"

"Benjamin 'I'm the King of the World' Donovan," he said with pure, unadulterated disgust.

Normally, Victoria made a valiant attempt to be on Jules' side whenever possible, just because they worked together and an allegiance to the justice system should come before personal opinions. This time there was another reason entirely to stand on the man's side. As he'd said the name, Victoria's insides did something weird. If she'd been standing she might have faltered. Instead she tapped her pen against the pad and vowed that this was going to be the best case of her career.

CHAPTER 3

Henry and Beverly Donovan had recently moved into a sprawling estate on almost two acres of land in the Queensridge area of Las Vegas. To call it a home sometimes seemed an understatement with seven bedrooms, ten baths, eight oversized car garages, an elevator, a home spa and basketball courts. Not to mention the glorious views of the Strip and luxurious golf courses. It was more like a resort.

As Ben drove through the east side gate, he circled his convertible Infiniti G37 around the stoned driveway and pulled into the garage behind the black Navigator that he knew belonged to his brother Max. All the family should be here today, at least all of the Las Vegas Donovans. Their family stretched across the United States, taking the Donovan name and legacy along with them.

Uncle Henry was the second oldest of the six Donovan brothers born to Dorethea and Isaiah Donovan. Together with Aunt Beverly, Uncle Henry had three children—Linc, Trent and Adam. Ben's father was Everette and he was Uncle Henry's younger brother. Ben's mother was Alma and she was his favorite person. Henry and Everette were the only two Donovan brothers currently living in Las Vegas. They'd all been born and raised in Houston, where Isaiah's father and uncle had started an oil company that became the seeds to their multimillion dollar empire. Some of the brothers remained in oil as they grew up, expanding with the company and building their families in other states. Others, like Bruce and Reginald, used the Donovan name and their strong work ethics and good business sense to branch out into the media industry and were based in Miami. There was also Uncle Bernard, who'd shifted his interests towards marketing and advertising and had his own firm in Seattle. Uncle Albert had been the only one to stay in Houston, still running Donovan Oilwell in the same vein as his grandfather. Even though the Donovans were spread across the world, they were still a close-knit family, constantly keeping tabs on each other and trying to get together at least once a year.

"I see you decided to join us this time," Camille Donovan said, stepping out of her husband Adam's SUV and smiling at Ben.

He quickly moved to her, leaning in to kiss her offered cheek. "I've missed a few gatherings, I admit. Don't shoot me."

"Not me, but Ms. Beverly might." She talked while opening the back door and reaching inside to undo the car seat where Josiah, their four-month-old son, sat.

Adam came around the truck, his hand outstretched. "You know we were about to come out to Agosta Luna to get you."

Ben took Adam's hand and the cousins hugged. He laughed at his cousin's threat to come out to the development where he lived, but Ben knew it was no joke. His cousins, with his brother leading the pack, would have done just that.

"No need. I'm here now," he told him.

"He's getting big," Ben said when they all walked towards the house. He was looking down at the baby seat that Adam now carried. Josiah was the best of his parents, with Camille's creamy mocha skin and Adam's deep brown eyes. When he lifted one chubby hand and swiped at one of the toys hanging from the handle of the seat, Ben couldn't help but smile. Babies did that to him. They made him want, to yearn, to think about something he was beginning to realize might never happen for him.

"Whoa, the gang's all here," Trent Donovan said when the three of them walked through the house, coming out onto a covered patio filled with people.

The sun had just begun to set and warm golden light bathed the entire area, pouring through the columns out onto the lush green grass. A few feet away was an enormous pool and just beyond that was Uncle Henry's private golf course.

Ben walked onto the patio, instantly finding his mother and kissing her on the cheek. "See, I'm still alive," he told her.

Alma hugged her son tight. "Good thing. I didn't want to have to come down to that office and grab you up."

Ben laughed.

"I told you she was looking for you." That was Max speaking as he wrapped an arm around his wife, pulling her close.

Deena Lakefield had swept Max off his feet more than a year ago, bringing the man out of his dark past and giving him a bright future. Sophia cooed in the walker just beside the lounge chair they both sat in.

Another family, he thought with an inner sigh.

"I heard there was a mistrial," Everette said coming up from behind and slapping Ben on the shoulder.

"Hey, dad. Yeah, mistrial was declared on Tuesday morning. Just before I left the office yesterday the DA had a slew of motions delivered. I haven't even looked at them yet," Ben said, taking a seat and the bottled beer offered by Trent, who had joined them in their corner of the patio.

"Wow, they didn't waste any time," Trent said. "What were the grounds for the mistrial?"

Trent wasn't a lawyer, but he was a professional private investigator and an ex-Navy SEAL. He knew his way around the criminal element of the world just as Ben did.

"Jury couldn't make up their mind, especially after one of the jurors suddenly became pro-defense. The judge didn't think sending them back to deliberate another day or so was going to help, especially since the DA was making some sounds about jury tampering," he said, not particularly happy to be discussing work at a family function. But if there was anyone he could talk to with the hopes of being understood, it would be Trent.

His cousin nodded, rubbing a hand over the growing goatee he was cultivating. "Vega's got a reputation,"

Ben nodded. "I know."

"So how are you going to get him off this time?" Max asked.

"Why would you try to get him off this time?" asked Tia, Trent's wife.

Tia was an ex-supermodel, but she still looked like a very current supermodel to Ben. Long legs, gorgeously toned body and a face that should be classified as a lethal weapon. She was madly in love with Trent and their son Trevor, hence the reason she was now only a part-time model.

"It's my job," he said with a shrug, knowing instinctively it would spark more conversation.

His family was very supportive of his career choice, each and every one of them. Now the direction in which he'd decided to study law had come as a surprise to some, but Ben did not want to sit behind a desk all day reading boring contracts or negotiating corporate legalities. He wanted to make a difference.

"Vega's not a good guy," Tia said solemnly.

"You may be right," Ben stated. "But everybody deserves a defense."

Trent rubbed his wife's shoulders, more in an attempt to tell her not to push the issue than to comfort. "And he's going to get an excellent defense with Ben on his side. I came down to the Justice Center a couple days of the trial and caught you in action. Pretty good, little cousin."

The words filled Ben with pride. Affirmation that he was doing a good thing was always welcomed. Even thought he had no intention of representing Vega again. Somehow, Ben knew if he'd said that, the door to even more questions would open.

"Enough talk about business," Alma said. "I want to talk about the upcoming family reunion."

And so the conversation shifted, with the women making plans and the men trying to keep their mouths shut for fear of suggesting the wrong thing.

When they figured they were no longer needed, a few of the cousins moved into the den where the pool table was located. Linc took the liberty of racking the balls while Adam went to the bar and began pouring himself a drink.

"FYI," Max said coming into the room and giving Ben a friendly slap on the back of his head. "Mom's got some woman she wants you to meet."

Ben groaned while the others laughed.

"The only remedy is to find your own woman," Linc offered.

Linc had been the first of the Triple Threat Donovans to cave into marriage with the lovely Jade. They now had twin daughters, Torian and Tamala, and lived in their own lavish home a few miles from the Strip, where Linc's Gramercy Casino was located.

"I don't want to be set up," Ben said, grabbing a stick and moving to the end of the table.

"But it's been too long since she's seen you with a date. You know how she gets," Max told him.

"It's your fault, getting married and having a baby," Ben replied to Max. Then he lifted his stick and pointed around the room. "It's actually all you guys' fault. Getting married is like an epidemic in this family now."

"Nobody's getting any younger," Adam added with a chuckle.

"Donovans do fall easily, but when they do, they fall hard," Linc said with confidence.

Trent leaned over the pool table, lined up his shot. "He's right. Once you get a taste of the right woman, you're not gonna want to let her go. Marriage keeps her there forever."

Ben was already shaking his head. "Have you checked the divorce rate lately? Marriages aren't lasting as long as they used to."

"That's because people are rushing in with blinders on instead of marrying for love," Adam told him.

Of the bunch gathered here, Adam would be the one talking about love, even though Ben had no doubt all of his cousins loved their wives implicitly. Donovans were just loyal like that. But the others weren't the wearing-feelings-on-their-sleeves type of men.

Offhand Ben wondered what type of man he would be, or what type of woman he would possibly fall in love with. As he took a sip of his rum and Coke, a picture of a female flashed before his eyes. He immediately began to choke.

"Can't handle your liquor, little bro?" Max asked, clapping him on the back.

Ben covered his mouth and tried to catch his breath. Visualizing Victoria Lashley when he was thinking about the woman of his dreams was not a good thing.

Hours later, after they'd eaten their share of barbeque and grilled corn (Ben's favorite), the Donovan family all sat on the back terrace still talking, kids falling off to sleep and enjoying each other's company.

Ben hadn't wanted to leave and had actually contemplated staying the night. He'd missed his family, missed their easy conversation and unwavering connection. For some reason he felt like he needed that now more than ever. Later that evening he would cling to that fact and swear he was having a premonition.

His cellphone chimed and Ben reached along his belt to pull it from the holder.

"Ben Donovan," he answered, his normal greeting no matter who might be calling. Had he known who was on the other end he might have said something differently, not that it would have mattered.

"Ben, it's Noah. I've got some bad news."

Ben stood immediately, walking off the terrace and over the grass towards the pool. Noah Hannity was a homicide detective; he was also Ben's sparring partner at the gym and a friend from college. The fact that they generally operated on the opposite sides of the law didn't stop them from being close friends. Outside of his family, Noah was the only other person Ben trusted in this world. So if Noah said there was bad news, Ben took him seriously.

"What's up?"

"I'm sitting at my desk holding a piece of paper in my hand. The paper has your name and address on it," Noah told him immediately.

Ben inhaled slowly, let the breath out quick and asked, "So what does that mean?"

"The piece of paper was found in a car that had been run off the road. Or driven down into a ditch is more like it. There was also a body." Noah paused.

"Okay, there's a car and a dead body. What else, Noah?" A sick feeling had already settled in the pit of Ben's stomach. Waiting for Noah to drop the rest of this news on him wasn't going to go well. He needed it all right now.

"It's Ebony, Ben. She's dead."

Ben cursed and it must have been loud because behind him he heard a lull in the conversation being had by the rest of the family. He walked a little further down towards the pool.

"What the hell do you mean she's dead? She was just in the office yesterday. Are you sure?" His temples had once again begun to throb. This seemed like second nature to him, at least for the last six months.

"One shot above her left eye. Two behind the ear," Noah sighed. "I'm sorry, man, but it looks like a hit."

"Fuck!" Ben cursed and pinched the bridge of his nose.

"I'm concerned about this note with your home address."

Through clenched teeth Ben said, "I should have been more concerned about the note I received yesterday evening."

"What? You got something to tell me?" Noah asked.

"Yeah. But I can't talk here. I'll come in."

"Okay, bring your note with you. I'll be in my office."

"I'll be there in about twenty minutes," Ben said before disconnecting the call.

"What is it?" he heard before he could even turn around.

It was Max and Trent. They'd been the ones chosen to come and see what was going on. Luckily they were also the first two he would have gone to with this. Ben wasn't stupid enough to try and keep secrets from his family, at least not from the men in his family. The females, well, he dealt with them on a situational basis. And this situation he definitely didn't want them to know about.

"Ebony's been killed," he said, the words leaving a sour taste in his mouth.

"Ebony? Your assistant?" Max asked.

Ben nodded.

"How? When?" Trent questioned.

"I don't know when. But she was shot." Ben took a deep breath and kept his gaze focused on Trent's. "It was a hit," he said solemnly.

Trent stared at him steadily. "Were you threatened?"

Ben slipped his hands into his pockets, his lips drawn in a tight line. He would have never brought this up because he hadn't taken it seriously himself. Foolish, he knew, considering who he was dealing with. But now, since he'd made the first move, Ben would be damned if he sat back and waited for him to make another one.

"Yesterday, after I was served with the papers from the DA, I decided not to represent Vega again. I drafted the papers to strike my appearance and was on my way to file them when Vega met me in the parking garage. I told him about the new trial and that I wouldn't represent him. He wasn't happy. I didn't give a damn. So I left. I filed to strike my appearance a half hour later. Another two hours of work then I let Ebony go home around 3:30. I left the office at 5, went straight home to change, then went to the gym."

"Did he threaten you?" Trent asked again, his brown eyes already growing darker, broad shoulders squared like he was ready to fight.

"Goddammit Ben! This thug threatened to kill you!" Max yelled.

"No. He didn't say those exact words. And keep your voice down," Ben told Max. "You want Mom and Dad to know this? I didn't think it was a big deal. I'm a public figure, dammit. If he touches me, he'll be on death row."

"You're giving him too much credit, Ben. Vega doesn't give a damn who you're related to or how well you're known in the criminal arena. He's a killer, remember?" Max was not happy.

Ben wasn't either. And he hadn't seen his brother this angry in he couldn't remember how long.

"I just didn't think anymore about it. Until last night," he said.

"What happened last night?" Trent asked.

"There was a note in my car. It said 'think again' and it gave an address. I thought about Vega briefly before I went to bed, but then I let it go. He's an ass, a pompous ass."

"And he's a killer," Trent stated solemnly. "You know he's a killer and that's why you declined to represent him again, isn't it?"

"I'm a defense attorney, Trent. It's my job to represent criminals," Ben said, sure of his words, his job, his goals. What he wasn't sure of was what would happen next.

"I'm heading down to the station to compare my note with the one Noah found at the crime scene. I need you to tell mom something, but not the truth. Just that I had to go take care of some business or something," Ben said to Max.

"She's gonna know something's wrong," Max argued.

"They're all going to think something is wrong. Especially since I'm going to the station with you," Trent said.

"That's not necessary," Ben told him. "I can handle going into the police station alone. I'll call you guys later and let you know what happened."

"You'll go to the police station with me standing by your side. I'm not arguing with you Ben. I should be kicking your ass for not calling me last night with this information. But I'll save that for later."

"Trent, it's not that big of a deal. It's nothing for you to get involved in." But Ben wasn't sure of that. Ebony was dead. Vega had been serious. And Ben shouldn't have thought otherwise.

"For you to have gone through all that schooling, you're not all that smart. Go to your car. I'll meet you in the driveway." Trent had already turned to walk away, so Ben couldn't argue his case further.

Trent was and would always be a warrior. He craved a good fight and fought with the elite training of his kind. Ben, on the other hand, fought with his own training. He wasn't a Navy SEAL, but he was no slouch either. He was in impeccable physical shape and had called boxing a serious hobby for at least ten years. In his line of business, he'd also thought it prudent to take lessons at the gun range and was licensed to carry a concealed weapon.

He simply wished he could have protected Ebony.

CHAPTER 4

Ben and Noah moved in silence up the walkway leading to the house on Portage Lake Court. The sun was blazing down on the rock covered front yard, palm trees looking as if they were as parched as Ben felt.

When he and Noah had met last night, they'd talked about what their next steps were. It was very likely that Vega was responsible for Ebony's death. The two notes he'd left said he was aiming to intimidate Ben into representing him once more. Ben's stance was the plan wasn't going to work, nor was he going to cower in some safe house until Vega's new trial had concluded. Their first step, however, was to talk to Ebony's family. Ben felt like he at least owed them that much and Noah refused to let him go alone.

Noah knocked on the door, squinting as he looked towards Ben, who pushed his sunglasses up on his nose. "You should invest in some of these," he told Noah.

Noah shook his head and gave a dry smile. "Not on my salary."

Ben smiled in return. Noah was about his size and build with a light bronze complexion, completely shaved head and hazel eyes that women seemed to fall for. He was a good looking man with his head on straight, but he was still walking the bachelor path right alongside Ben.

An older woman answered the door. She couldn't have been more than five feet tall, with her graying hair pulled into a messy bun. She wore a colorful housedress and ruby red lipstick that made her very light complexion look a little pasty.

"May I help you?" she asked in a voice that, to Ben, sounded tired.

Her eyes were red-rimmed and puffy from crying and Ben felt like a piece of crap for coming here during this time, regardless of whether or not it was the right thing to do.

"My name is Benjamin Donovan. Ebony was my legal assistant," he said to her.

She nodded her head, her eyes filling with tears. "Yes. Yes. She told us all about you. Come on in."

Ben stepped inside first, Noah following right behind him. It was warm inside the house, almost as warm as it was outside. Box fans blew furiously from their perch in the two living room windows. More dry air was circulated by an upright fan located in the kitchen, which they could still see in the open floor plan of the house.

"This is Detective Hannity." Ben introduced Noah when the woman had led them through the living room to the dining room. She motioned for them to take a seat at a table that looked like it was on the brink of collapse from all the cakes and bowls and jugs of juice sitting on it.

"You investigating what happened to my girl?" the woman asked after she'd taken her own seat, one meaty elbow propped up on the table as the other arm reached for a tissue.

"Yes ma'am," Noah said. "Do you know if she had any boyfriend issues?"

Noah would proceed with the investigation as if they didn't already have a suspect; that was as much to throw off Vega as to appease the family. If they thought the police knew who committed this murder and wasn't doing anything to pick the guy up, there would definitely be some outrage. Ben knew that because he'd been feeling it ever since last night. The difference was Ben knew how the justice system worked, what could and could not be proven in court, what would make or break a case. He knew because he'd used those techniques for the past few years to rise to the level of success he enjoyed. Or at least he'd enjoyed until last night.

"Her boyfriend was here yesterday, first thing in the mornin', cryin' his eyes out just like the rest of us. Aunt Mae'll tell you that once she stops crying for the loss of her only daughter," another woman said. She was just a little taller than the lady she'd referred to as Aunt Mae and had hair the color of a fire engine, stacked on top of her head like a curly beehive.

"Alright, can you tell me his name?" Noah asked, pulling out his notepad.

"Ernie Forrester. He works down at the gas station three blocks over. He ain't do nothin' to Ebony. Word on the street is it was gang related," she continued.

"Stop that foolishness, Jasmine. All that's gossip and you know it. Ebony ain't have nothing to do with gangs. And neither did Ernie. He did his time and he was walking straight now."

"So Ernie had been in jail?" Noah asked.

"I remember Ebony mentioning that to me when he got out. She wanted to find out how his record could be expunged," Ben added. "He'd been in for eighteen months on an attempted robbery charge."

"He ain't steal that car. The girl he was messing with before Ebony got mad because he was with Ebony and called the police, told them he took her car. But her cousins drove that car down a ditch so she could collect the insurance money."

Ben wanted to say "wow." But then again, he didn't. He'd heard stories like these more times than he wanted to count. Most of his clients had girlfriends who had families who came up with schemes to get away with everything. Ben had turned his head away from all of it, declaring it had nothing to do with his case so he didn't want to know. It was activity that he couldn't stop even if he'd tried.

"Okay, I'll talk to Ernie. Anybody else Ebony say she was having trouble with?" Noah continued.

Mae shook her head, tears pouring out so fast Ben couldn't help but go to her and put his hand on her shoulder.

"I am so sorry for your loss, ma'am. So very sorry," he told her.

Mae rocked back and forth, moving her head slightly to acknowledge she heard his words, but she was too upset to speak her own. He looked over to Noah, who closed his book. "I can come back later and talk to you."

"Her name's Maeretha Reece," Jasmine added. "And I'm Jasmine Lynch, her niece. Me, my brother Harold and Ebony's two brothers Bunk and Jay live here with her. We were all here Friday night waiting for Ebony to come home so she could drive us to the market to get more stuff for the cookout."

"We couldn't celebrate with the twins after we heard the news," Mae finally choked out. "I'm sorry but I can't do this now. I gotta get to the funeral home and make the arrangements."

"Please, Mrs. Reece, I'd like to take care of the arrangements," Ben offered. "If that's okay with you?"

"You mean you want to pay for everything? Ebony said you was a rich one even without having to represents those criminals," Jasmine replied, looking Ben up and down.

That sounded like something Ebony would say.

"You go on to the funeral home, pick out whatever you want and have them send the bill to me." Ben reached into his back pocket for his wallet and pulled out a business card. "Give them this and tell them this is where they can send all the bills."

"Hmmhmmm, rich just like Ebony said," Jasmine commented.

Ben ignored her, stuffing his business card in Mrs. Reece's hand. "And if you need anything, Mrs. Reece, anything at all, please don't hesitate to call me. Ebony was like a little sister to me. She was a wonderful employee and I was very proud of how much she'd grown in the last four years. I also want you to know that I'm going to do everything in my power to see her killer brought to justice."

"How are you gonna do that? He might call you to represent him?" Jasmine asked snidely.

Ben resisted the urge to tell her to remain quiet, even though she wasn't under arrest.

"I think we should go now," Noah spoke up. The way he was looking at Jasmine told Ben he wasn't pleased with Jasmine either. Noah was most likely considering taking the girl outside for a word or two. And that wasn't going to end well.

"I am also sorry for your loss, Mrs. Reece. Here's my card as well. If you think of anything that might help us in the investigation, please give me a call."

Noah shook her hand after he'd given her the card.

"I'll walk you out," Mrs. Reece said, wiping her eyes once more.

"There's no need," Ben said.

"Yes there is," she insisted. "Death don't give a reason to be rude."

When they were at the door, she grabbed Ben's hand, holding it tightly in hers.

"Ebony wasn't afraid of anybody. She didn't care who it was or how big a gun they carried, she said they were living and breathing just like her. The cop that came by the other night said she fought hard. I feel good knowing my baby didn't go down without a fight. I didn't raise her that way."

Ben nodded. "Ebony was definitely a fighter."

"You find him," she said adamantly, her watery eyes looking from Ben to Noah. "Both of you work hard and find that bastard that took my baby."

Her bravado was lost then as she began crying. Ben wrapped his arms around her, holding her tight, closing his own eyes to keep from crying.

"We will do everything we can, Mrs. Reece," Noah told her.

"You have our promise," Ben added.

CHAPTER 5

Three Weeks Later

The courtroom was already full with citizens, either eager to watch what they thought was a vicious killer sentenced to death or another victim being forgotten by the state.

For Ben, it was a coin toss. He knew this case inside and out, knew Ramone Vega as well as the victim—Congressman Theodore McGlinn and his wife Myrna. The Congressman and his wife had been executed, both shot three times to the back of the head. The Congressman had been stripped of his clothes, both of them lying face down on the floor of his home office. Nobody had heard a sound, no gunshots, nothing. A woman in the cafe a block away from the Congressman's house claimed to have seen a gray car speeding around the corner around the time of the murders. She'd gone to the police station the next day, sure about fulfilling her civic duty, and signed a statement. Her name was Alayna Jonas and two weeks later she was gone.

Ben's defense had been to simply plant the seeds of doubt. The state didn't have a lot on their side to prove Vega did the murders. All Ben had to do was present more evidence that said maybe he didn't. And it had worked, that first go round. He wondered if Vega's new attorney would take the same tactic.

The letter Ben had received along with the one found at the scene of Ebony's death were circumstantial evidence. Nothing else was found at the scene, so pinning Ebony's murder on Vega seemed like a repeat of the congressman's trial. And that meant the DA's office wasn't jumping to file charges. Instead they were hoping by using the easily brilliant and certainly attractive Victoria Lashley, they would be able to put Vega in jail this go round.

That's precisely why Ben had decided to sit in on the preliminary hearing. Vega had hired another attorney, just as Ben had advised. And he hadn't contacted Ben since that letter on his car. But with Ebony's death, Ben knew Vega hadn't forgotten about him. It didn't seem plausible that his only motive for killing Ebony was that Ben wouldn't represent him. Then again, murderers rarely had good reasons for killing people. At least that's what Ben thought. He'd thought long and hard over the last couple of weeks about what other reason Vega could have had. All he could come up with was retaliation, which pissed him off even more. In all his years working as a defense attorney, Ben had never endured violence from any of his clients, whether or not he won their cases. If Vega wanted to be the first, so be it. The man obviously had no idea who he was dealing with.

Upon entering the courtroom, his gaze automatically went to the prosecution table. She was already there. He should have known she would be.

They were in front of Judge Leontine Mercer, who was known around the Justice Center as the Bitch on the Bench. She was a fifty-something year old African-American woman who'd been married five times and loved bossing men around as much as she loved cutting females down. She was also a known animal hater. It seemed there was no species on this earth that could please this woman. And she was notoriously strict about how her courtroom was run.

She could be expected on the bench at exactly 9:30, and for whatever attorney that wasn't already at the table waiting for her arrival, Ben could only pray for their survival.

It was a good thing Victoria Lashley was punctual. She was also kick-you-in-the-gut beautiful, fierce in the courtroom and sexy as hell. This was a combination she'd refined over the years and Ben had kept tabs. The question for him wasn't so much as why, as it was what he planned to someday do with all the information he'd gathered on her.

As he moved to take a seat on one of the back rows, the door behind him opened once more. Franz Melmer strolled in wearing a black pinstriped suit, dazzling black and white pointed toe shoes, a black shirt and bright white tie. He looked like a member of the mafia instead of a defense attorney and Ben knew why. If the jury were enamored by his flashy dressing and smooth talking, they were likely to miss key testimony and find his client not guilty. It was a lame attempt at influencing the jury. Unfortunately, it worked more often than not.

"Mr. Donovan, I'm surprised to see you here," Franz said with a bright toothy smile that came off more as a smirk that Ben tried to ignore.

Ben accepted his hand for a shake. "Good morning, Mr. Helmer. Just thought I'd sit in on the hearing before I have to be in another courtroom."

"You could have been sitting at the defense table," he said as he continued eyeing Ben suspiciously. "I wondered why you discharged a client in the middle of a trial."

"The trial I was hired to try was over," Ben replied. "Besides, I'm sure you'll do a great job heading up your own defense team."

Franz always worked with a team of younger attorneys. They actually did most of the work while Franz put on the performance. He had billboards and television commercials that also showed his acting abilities. Concentrating on all that promotion, it was no wonder he needed a team of attorneys to do the actual trial for him. Said attorneys had also come into the courtroom heading straight for the defense table.

"We'll get the job done," Franz said after turning to shake the hand of one of his team. "Sit tight, you might learn something."

Ben didn't even bother with a retort. It wasn't worth it. He was just about to take his seat when Vega entered the courtroom, his own entourage following closely behind him. One of the beefy wrestler-type men spotted Ben and taped Vega on the shoulder. Vega's gaze met Ben's.

And held it.

"All rise," the courtroom clerk announced.

Vega turned away first and Ben watched him head to the defense table.

When they were instructed to be seated, Ben caught sight of Victoria. He was now staring into more illusive eyes and the anger that had roiled through him at the sight of Ramone Vega dissolved into something hotter and much more primal, much more dangerous.

❦❦❦

Finally, she could breathe a sigh of relief.

Victoria walked out of the courtroom first. Her files were in a box her law clerk would bring back to the office later. What she needed to go over tonight was in her bag. But she couldn't stay in there a second longer. He was driving her crazy. "He" being Ben Donovan, the arrogant and still fine as hell defense attorney sent to her right from the devil himself. Okay, that was probably overreacting, but dammit, why was he here?

Initially she'd been excited about this trial. Then she'd found out he'd backed out—afraid of going against her! A naïve possibility, but she hadn't wanted to consider another reason. And just when she'd resigned herself to not having to see him, he showed up.

He'd been in court this morning, at least for the first half of the hearing. At one point, when she'd stood to hand an exhibit to the clerk, she'd allowed her gaze to sweep the entire courtroom. He was no longer sitting on the opposite side, back row, fourth person. He was gone.

And for the next hour and a half of the hearing, she'd felt relief.

Now she was feeling a bit of confusion mixed with the swirl of adrenaline being in front of a judge usually gave her.

Ramone Vega was a killer. There wasn't an ounce of her that didn't believe that. His attorney, Helmer, was a self-centered ass who loved the media about as much as he loved cream-filled donut. He would make this trial a circus, she was sure. There were already a crowd of reporters and photographers waiting outside the courtroom for them.

With her briefcase in one hand, Victoria lifted another arm to shield herself from all the microphones being shoved in her face. Cameras flashed and she blinked rapidly. Questions were fired at her and all she replied was, "No comment."

At some point, Jules or the DA would have a press conference. She'd be required to attend but she wouldn't talk. She never did. Her legs moved swiftly toward the elevators where she jabbed a finger into the button, praying it could tell she was desperate and hurry up. A few seconds later she figured she should be partially thankful that part of her prayer was being answered, except it came with a price.

"Back up, back up," he said in that loud, commanding voice he had.

She'd heard it a couple times over the years as she'd walked past a courtroom that he was in. And yes, she'd sneaked a peek at those times because she couldn't resist the temptation. This, however, was a different circumstance and he was no longer across the room from her. No, this time Benjamin Donovan was standing right beside her.

The elevator door opened and he moved her inside with a hand to the small of her back and a little push.

"She said no comment, people. Can't you take a hint?" was his parting shot as he held a hand up to stop a reporter who was bold enough to try and board the elevator with them.

Thankfully the doors finally closed and Victoria leaned against the back wall. "Thank you," she murmured without looking at him.

"You're welcome," he said. "It's going to be worse when the trial actually starts. Maybe you should see if someone could sit second chair with you, preferably a man that can put some distance between you and the attorneys."

What? Did he really just say that?

Victoria took a deep breath, let it out slowly as she looked into the eyes of the man who had haunted her dreams for longer than she could remember. And yes, she meant haunted, because Ben Donovan was not the man for her, not the man she should be dreaming about, or secretly wanting. He just wasn't.

"I don't need a bodyguard," she replied in a frosty tone.

He didn't even flinch at her words. She'd actually had men flinch when she'd said things to them, usually when she was turning them down from some pitiful line they'd tried to use on her. But she should have remembered Ben Donovan wasn't the flinching type. Instead he smiled.

"Not a bodyguard, just somebody to deflect some of these people. I know the DA's office has a spokesperson. Maybe she could come down at the end of each trial to make a statement so they won't hound you."

"I can take it," she said, then saw that the destination of the elevator had not been selected.

She moved forward to do so, but that meant brushing past him. And when she did...oh, why the hell did she have to do that.

"I'm just trying to help," he said, looking down at her.

Victoria looked up. She had no other choice. No matter the swirls of heat soaring through her body at the contact. Disregarding the flare of arousal at the simple scent of his cologne, she took another breath and refused to even blink in the midst of her discomfort.

"I didn't ask for your help."

He nodded. And still smiled, that amenable smile that always came across as too attractive to ‧ really be condescending. God, she did not like this man. Or at least, she did not *want* to like him.

"You didn't. But I like to look out for my colleagues and my friends."

"We're not friends."

"We could have been."

If she weren't such a bitch. He didn't say it but the words were clear in his eyes. It was okay, she could take it. What she couldn't take was what a man like him could do to her in the long run.

"This is my floor," she said when the elevator doors opened. Then, because she wasn't totally oblivious to what he was trying to do and how much sense his words had actually made, she paused, looked over her shoulder and said, "I'll call the administrative office to see about having a spokesperson on hand during the trial."

He didn't say another word, which he could have and which she actually expected. He simply nodded. And as she walked away, hearing the elevator doors close behind her, she thought about his smile and how it made her feel like forgetting all the promises she'd made and following the signals her body had given her for the years since she'd known him.

In the end, she wouldn't do that. The promises were more important, the person she'd made them to holding a much bigger piece of her heart than Ben Donovan ever could.

CHAPTER 6

Tonight was bingo night for Naomi Lashley. Sure she lived in Las Vegas, had lived there all her life, so there were definitely more lucrative games she could play for money. But bingo was fun and it was affordable. She didn't have much and had learned to deal with much less after Porter's death. But she was content and that was all that mattered. She wished she could say the same about her only child.

Victoria was even more beautiful today at thirty-one years old than she had been when she was three minutes old. And she was just as stubborn as she'd been when she was three and sat at the kitchen table for the better part of six hours refusing to eat brussel sprouts.

"I'm not going to play bingo," she said with exasperation.

She had brought a plate of grilled tilapia and macaroni and cheese into the dining room that she kept impeccably clean along with the rest of her house and taken a seat. Clearly, she wasn't planning on leaving this house tonight.

"I have briefs to read and motions to go over. I don't have time to sit with you and Bobby Witkee while you battle it out at bingo."

"Bobby never beats me," Naomi said, holding her head high and reaching over to pinch off a piece of fish. Sticking it into her mouth, she moaned. "You're getting better, this is good. And Bobby cheats, the lying fart."

"Really mom? You were a teacher for thirty years. That's the best you could come up with while I'm eating?"

"I wanted to say something else, but I thought I was being tactful. You work too much," Naomi said with a wave of her hand.

"There's no such thing," Victoria replied. "When you have a job, you do it. Remember you told me that."

Naomi nodded. She had told her daughter that the day she graduated from law school. "You also have a life you need to lead and so far, you're not doing that. What you are doing is sitting in this house buying shoes like there's no tomorrow and getting older everyday."

"Mom! That is not something you should remind someone of. Do I remind you how old you are?"

"No. Because no matter how old I am, I'm still your mother. I've also had sex in the last century. What about you?"

Victoria groaned. Her mother's candor was unlike any other she'd ever known. Whatever Naomi Lashley thought, she said. Depending on who she was speaking to, she would adjust her tone and wording accordingly, but she would always share her honest opinion.

"Sex is not the answer to everything," Victoria said with a sigh. She was fairly certain she was correct in that assessment, but she did remember sex as being enjoyable. Sort of. At any rate, she was not going to discuss this with her mother.

"Maybe not, but it's great recreation. Why do you think I keep playing bingo with Bobby when I know he cheats?" Naomi asked matter of factly.

Victoria choked, putting her hand over her mouth because she wasn't sure what she'd put in wouldn't come flying back out. Naomi just waved her hand at her again. It was one of her favorite moves. It meant, *You're wrong and I'm right, get over it.* She wore a dark purple velour jogging suit, crisp white tennis shoes and her freshly dyed auburn hair pulled back into a ponytail that made her look about twenty years younger than she was.

"You keep right on sitting here reading your files and prosecuting your cases while cob webs grow—"

That was it. Victoria raised a hand. "Enough! Mom, I'm eating."

"Alright, whatever you say. I'm going," Naomi continued and stole another piece of Victoria's fish. "I'll call you tomorrow."

Her mother leaned over to kiss Victoria's cheek. "Have a good time," she told her even though she knew it wasn't necessary. Bingo was...probably like sex to her...great recreation. And on some days, some of those long, dark days, Victoria envied her mother for her vivacious spirit, for her zest for life and her tenacity in living on even after her husband had died.

"Oh I will, and I'm going to win me some money."

"If you need anything..." Victoria said, getting up out of her chair to walk her mother to the door.

Naomi opened the door, then turned to Victoria. "I don't need anything. And if I did, I would get it myself or I would ask my wonderful daughter. Now go eat your food before it gets cold."

With a nod and a heart full of love, Victoria watched her mother move swiftly down the walkway to the little red Prius she'd just bought even though there had been nothing wrong with her old car. "Sometimes you just need to shake things up," Naomi had told her.

Closing the door, Victoria shook her head. Her mother was always shaking things up.

⁓⁓⁓⁓

Two hours later, Victoria had long since finished her dinner but was still sitting at her dining room table, reading the Ramone Vega file. She'd read this file at least twenty times in the weeks since it had been assigned to her. But today in court, she'd lost two key motions to Helmer and his glamour squad. The witness that gave her statement two days after the murders was still missing. City cops had no idea where she was and were reluctant to even consider calling in the FBI. Alayna Jonas was her name and she was nineteen years old with a three- year-old daughter who was now being raised by her grandmother. They hadn't said it, but the cops figured she was dead. Victoria didn't believe that. She didn't want to believe it.

It was almost 11:30 when Victoria yawned. Then yawned again. Four times in immediate succession. Slamming her palms down on the table, she sighed. "Alright, I get the message."

Standing, she didn't even bother to pull the papers back into the file because she'd simply pull them out again in the morning when she had breakfast. She did, however, take her glass and napkin with cookie crumbs on it to the kitchen. Coming back out, she switched off the lights in the dining room and walked through the living room to get to the front door. She'd just double checked the locks when she heard the glass crashing. To her credit she didn't scream—Victoria hated screaming and screeching or any of those overly played out female reactions to fear. Instead she gasped, clutched a hand to her throat.

More glass shattered, scattering across her living room floor as her entire front window caved in. She took a step, thinking to get to either her cellphone or her house phone, but the room filled with smoke. Her eyes watered as she coughed and fell to her knees, chest burning with the pain of not getting enough air. She hacked and crawled on hands and knees, praying she could avoid most of the glass, moving by memory to where she knew her purse was.

Silence seemed to invade the space along with the smoke, but there was no more crashing glass and the lights were still out. Fumbling, she knocked her purse onto the floor and had to flatten her hand over glass to find the phone that had fallen out. When it was in her hand, she pressed the ON button and hit 911. Throat burning, she was just able to give her name and her address before she collapsed to the floor, eyes closed, tears streaking her face.

ᕰᕫᕰᕫᕰᕫ

"A call just came in. Units are heading to Victoria Lashley's place. Suspected vandalism," Noah spoke into the phone as he climbed into his truck. He wasn't a beat cop and this wasn't a homicide. What he was and was damn proud of was a good detective. And as such he had a gut feeling this was no suspected vandalism. Victoria Lashley was in court this morning with a notorious killer. An attack on her tonight was no coincidence.

"I'll meet you there," Ben answered immediately.

Noah figured as much. There was history with Ben and Victoria. Well, not exactly history, more like "the one that got away" syndrome, and his good friend was even better at denying it. But Noah had no doubt that Ben would do exactly as he'd said. He would be at Lashley's place, probably before him.

❧

She lived in a quaint little house on the corner of Commitment Court in North Las Vegas. Ben knew because he'd made it a point to know everything there was to know about Victoria Lashley. He called it one of his hobbies; anybody else who'd known would most likely call it stalking. The drive from his place to hers would normally take about thirty minutes. Tonight, with the information he'd just received and riding his Ducati 1199 Panigale motorcycle, it took him fifteen.

He drove his bike with intensity and focus that he only used when he was in the courtroom or the boxing ring. It gave him a powerful and unbeatable feeling that couldn't be matched. Tonight, as the dry night air whipped over his face and he made that last turn onto her street, he realized he didn't feel unbeatable. He felt angry as hell, a rock-like sense of dread settling deep in his stomach.

Cop cars were pulled up in front of the house along with an ambulance. As he parked his bike and secured his helmet, he looked up to see a stretcher being pushed from the house. He was off the bike and across the lawn in about thirty seconds, only to have an officer's hand clamp tightly on his arm.

"Hold it buddy, this is a crime scene," the officer said in a gruff, just about rude voice.

Ben jerked his arm away. "First, I'm not your buddy. I'm Ben Donovan and I'm here to see Ms. Lashley."

"I don't care if you're the King of goddamned England," the officer had started to say.

"Hall, let him go," another deep voice ordered from behind Ben.

"He's with me," Noah told the younger, obviously more inexperienced cop who then looked at Ben and took a step back. His glare was still lethal, his right hand resting on his side arm.

Ben didn't waste another second with the cops or their egos. He pushed by and had to run a few steps down the walkway as the paramedics pushing the stretcher had it almost to the ambulance. He came up beside it, seeing first blood and cursing loudly.

"What are you doing here?" her voice was thin, a little shaky. Ben hated how it sounded.

"I came as soon as I heard."

Her hair was a wispy mess, her eyes swollen, red, tearing. There were flecks of blood on her face and more on her hands and coming through the knees of her sweat pants.

"Why would you have heard about this? About me?" She was obviously confused and obviously in pain as she winched when he touched her face to wipe away a piece of glass.

Not wanting to keep her on the street longer, holding up treatment, Ben shook his head. "I'll meet you at the hospital," he told her.

"Why?" she asked again, but he'd already signaled to the paramedics to take her away. He was headed back to his bike when Noah looked up and Ben signaled him over.

"What happened? What do you know?" he asked as he put on his helmet.

"She told the 911 operator before she dropped the phone that she'd just locked her doors when she heard the window breaking. Tear gas followed and she fell to the floor."

"Tear gas? Who uses tear gas to break into somebody's house? And why didn't they try to come in afterwards?" Ben asked.

Noah nodded towards the house to the left of Victoria's. "Neighbor heard the noise when he was taking his trash out, said there was a car parked across the street." Noah took a step closer to Ben and whispered. "A gray Lexus."

Ben cursed and started his bike. "I'm going to the hospital. Call me when you wrap this up."

He hadn't waited to hear Noah's reply.

CHAPTER 7

"Who are you?"

The woman garbed in all purple and a familiar scowl asked him this the minute he pulled back the curtain to the space where they were examining Victoria.

"I'm Ben Donovan, ma'am," he said, clamping down on his anger and the urgency to see Victoria because he suspected this was her mother.

They had the same complexion and high cheekbones. Her hair was a different color, but he didn't believe that was natural. It had probably been as dark as Victoria's years ago. And she was looking at him the same way her daughter had earlier today in the elevator.

"I didn't hear a doctor before that name, so what are you doing back here?"

She'd narrowed her eyes as she glared at him, taking a step closer. Ben tried for charm.

"I'm a colleague of your daughter's, ma'am. I just came to make sure she's alright."

"A colleague? How did you know she was here? I just got the call about twenty minutes ago. I don't see why they would call someone from her job so quickly."

He could see where Victoria got her skepticism.

"Ben?" Victoria whispered from the bed. "Mom, let him in."

Her mother looked at him like she had more questions, but moved to the side so Ben could get past. Ben felt her eyes on him as he moved closer to the bed. The term "watching him like a hawk" felt like an understatement. His neck felt it was burning because he knew her eyes were fixated on him.

"How are you feeling?" he asked Victoria.

Her face, normally a very light complexion, was red and splotchy. The gray of her eyes seemed a little muted as red and puffiness surrounded them. She was no longer crying or tearing up, which was good because seeing that had given Ben an unexpected jolt.

"I'll be okay. The burning in my eyes has ceased a bit." She coughed and Ben hurried to the table beside her to pour a cup of water. He handed it to her and she drank deeply.

A few seconds later she closed her eyes and took a deep breath. "I'll be fine," she stated firmly.

Ben nodded. "I know you will. I talked to the doctor. They're going to keep you until morning."

"What? No. I can't stay here. I'm just fine. I'm going home," she protested and tried to push at the sheets on the bed.

"You are not," her mother came to the other side of the bed, pulling the sheets back up and tucking them tightly beneath her arms. "If the doctor says you need to stay, you'll stay."

The feisty older woman met Ben's gaze with tight lips.

"Your mother's right," he said, looking down at Victoria. "Besides, your window needs to be fixed before you can go back home."

"Right, they broke the entire front window," she said with a sigh.

"That's a big window," her mother said. "Kids play too seriously now days."

Ben wondered if he should tell them it wasn't kids. He wondered if Victoria had seen the Lexus before the windows were broken out. Later, he would also wonder why it was he felt like bringing Victoria to his house to stay with him.

"You're working a really high-profile case," he began, figuring it made sense to at least alert Victoria to the possibility of what might be going on. To be forewarned was to be forearmed, he believed. Besides, he already had plans for her protection.

"The police are going to want to investigate the scene a little more closely than they would if it were just a classic case of vandalism," he finished.

"But it *was* just a classic case of vandalism, wasn't it?" her mother asked.

"This is my mother, Naomi Lashley," Victoria said by way of introduction. "Listen, I really don't think police investigation is necessary. I'm sure it was just kids driving by and playing a prank." Even as she spoke those words she didn't believe them, but Ben didn't need to know that.

"Like a gang initiation prank?" he asked with a tilt of his head.

"Yes. No!" she almost yelled.

"Look, I don't want to upset you." Ben moved closer, touching a hand to hers. "I'm not saying definitively that it wasn't vandalism. I'm just saying that in light of the case you're handling, the police are going to take more precautions. And you should take more precaution."

"Do you think there's a hit out on her?" Naomi asked.

"No. No. Nothing that serious," Ben said, but inside he knew it was that serious. There was already a person connected to this case that was missing. Intimidating a DA wasn't something that would scare Vega and his crew.

"I am not being intimidated," Victoria replied seriously. "The police can investigate all they want. First thing tomorrow morning I'm going home and then I'm going back to work. I still have a case to try."

Ben nodded. He'd expected nothing less from her. Naomi stood beside her daughter, holding her hand with a serious look on her face. But she was afraid. Ben could tell.

"Thanks for coming by Ben. Even though I still don't know why you showed up in the first place."

And that was her way of telling him he could leave. Ben wasn't going to argue with her, not now. Besides, he'd come here to see that she was okay, and she was. Now, he'd go home and take care of the rest of this business.

"I'll see you in court," he told her. "It was a pleasure meeting you, Mrs. Lashley."

Naomi only nodded to him as he walked out of the room. She still watched him carefully, knowingly. Ben smiled at the thought when he was headed for the elevators. If Mrs. Lashley had any idea what he thought of her daughter, she wouldn't have just given him the evil eye, she probably would have punched him out.

⸎

"You did what?" Trent asked, his eyes about to bulge out, his fingers flexing at his sides.

"I sat in the courtroom at the preliminary hearings yesterday. I saw Vega," Ben told him.

"Why would you do something so stupid? And why would you do it all alone?" Trent stood, pacing the length of his office.

He moved with very controlled steps, hands at his sides as he thought about strategy. Everything with Trent was about strategy, either divide and conquer or ambush and kill. The SEAL mentality was something he'd never lose entirely. Especially when he thought one of his family members was in danger.

"Look, I wanted to show the guy that he cannot intimidate me. Sending me some note as a message that he can do to me what he did to Ebony is cowardice. If he wants me dead, I want him to know I'm not hiding."

"He doesn't want you dead. At least not yet."

The low, raspy voice belonged to Trent's former captain, Devlin Bonner. Devlin had just returned from Miami where he'd been helping Ben's cousins Sean and Dyon Donovan keep their magazine. Now, he was in Vegas, supposedly visiting Trent, but Ben knew it was something else. Devlin had left the Navy SEAL program a year after Trent, but they'd still worked together on special op assignments here and there. At least they had before Trent had married Tia and they'd had a son. Now Trent ran D&D Investigations with Sam Desdune and went home every night to his beautiful wife and child. As for Devlin, Ben had a feeling he was having a harder time breaking free of his soldier mentality and the world of hand-to-hand combat.

"Vega's a professional hitman. He could have you killed in the blink of an eye, the same way he did with your assistant. Sending you the note was a warning alright, but it was a playful one. The minute he gets serious about taking you out, you'll know it. Same goes for that prosecutor," Devlin continued.

He sat in the corner of Trent's office, the one with the least amount of sunlight from the open blinds. He was a dark-skinned man with steely eyes that resembled pieces of onyx. The scar running in a jagged line from his left ear and across his jaw to stop just before his top lip made him look angry and dangerous, even when he wasn't trying to be angry and dangerous.

"Wait a minute. He's not going to get the opportunity to kill Ben because Ben is going to start taking precautions," Trent interrupted.

"I'm not going to hide, Trent."

Trent shook his head. "You know I'd be the last person to suggest something that ridiculous. What I am saying is that you need to start thinking like a criminal to protect yourself."

"He's right," Devlin added. "Vega likes people to take him seriously. If he's called in on a job that means the job is serious, whether it be about drugs or money, it's important enough to bring in the top of the line to make sure the job gets done right. He was sent to kill the Congressman and his wife, there's no doubt about that. But the former prosecutor could never figure out why. Do you know?"

Ben immediately shook his head. "Client confidentiality. I cannot divulge anything I know about that case."

"Even if it gets you killed," Trent replied skeptically.

"I'm not going to compromise the career I've built for this guy. Besides, I don't know for sure there was a reason he was hired to kill the Congressman. I don't ask those types of questions."

"Really?"

Ben nodded. "It's a lot easier to defend a client when you don't know if he's guilty or not. And believe me, I didn't want to know what Vega was doing or not doing."

"You just wanted to get him off?" Devlin asked with barely masked contempt.

"Everybody is entitled to a defense. It's my job to defend until proven guilty. I take a lot of pride in my job."

Devlin didn't move a muscle. "And I take a lot of pride in mine. If Vega so much as steps on a blade of grass in front of your house, I'm shooting his ass. One quick shot to the head," he said, making his fingers into a mock gun and pointing them to his own head. "Dead and done."

Ben believed every word Devlin spoke.

"You need security."

"I do not need or want a bodyguard," Ben said adamantly. "But what I came to see you for was some protection for Victoria. If he's toying with her to get to me, I don't want her hurt."

Trent leaned against the edge of his desk, muscled arms crossing over his chest, and nodded. "I figured as much. I'll assign someone to her. But let's think about what you just said. Why would Vega toy with Victoria to get to you? There's no connection between you two other than this trial. Right?"

Ben had been thinking about that all night. Vega could simply be after Victoria in an attempt to make her drop this case. But that wasn't her call. She could ask to be removed from the case, but the DA would still prosecute. They wanted Vega behind bars. So there had to be another reason he'd ordered someone to her house last night—because Devlin was absolutely right about one thing, if Vega wanted Victoria dead, she would be.

Ben didn't like how that thought made him feel.

"We went to law school together," he told Trent.

"Did you sleep with her?"

"No," was Ben's adamant reply.

Trent narrowed his gaze on his cousin. "But you wanted to?"

Lying wasn't an option. It wouldn't get them anywhere and Trent would still know. Donovan men knew how to appreciate beautiful women. When he'd come into the office, Trent already had a file on Victoria Lashley, including her very attractive DMV photo sitting on his desk.

Ben shrugged, not ready to let his cousin know that he'd always thought of Victoria as the one that got away. Or the one he'd never been able to catch. "I was interested."

"And she wasn't? Why?" Devlin asked.

"Don't know. Guess the old Donovan charm is slipping."

Trent chuckled. "Never that. There must be another reason. When's the last time you've tried to take her out?"

"Law school," Ben admitted. "Look, I like to limit my rejection to first and second helpings. After that, I kindly move on. But since we're both attorneys, I've seen her a lot over the years either in court or at lawyer functions with the bar or other entities."

"Doesn't sound like anything that would interest Vega," Devlin replied.

"That's exactly what I was thinking. So right now we don't know why Vega killed Ebony or why he sent me the note to let me know where her body was. And we don't know why he's messing with Victoria," Trent said.

"Right," Ben nodded. "So let's go with what we do know. Vega killed Ebony, else how could he have sent me the note telling me where the body is? Vega wasn't happy that I wouldn't take his case again. Vega wasn't happy to see me in the courtroom. And Vega is definitely connected to what happened at Victoria's. The gray Lexus is proof of that."

"So, he's definitely aiming at you. He's pissed that you wouldn't take his case and attacking you from all directions. Does your police buddy knows all this?" Trent asked, rubbing a hand across his chin.

"Noah's a good guy. We went to college together. He's solid," Ben said, knowing where Trent was going with his question.

"Solid cops get bought off all the time," was Devlin's reply.

"Noah's helping me with the case," Ben argued.

"But he hasn't made an arrest even though he knows about the gray Lexus being at two crime scenes and about the note Vega allegedly sent to you telling you the location of a dead body?" Trent asked. Then he waited for Ben to answer.

But Ben didn't have an answer.

"Vega's a slippery character. I had a hell of a time planting enough doubt in the first jury's mind. The missing witness I think was key. If Victoria doesn't find that witness, she's not going to have much luck. In the meantime, if Noah comes up with more to connect Vega to Ebony's murder, that's another charge they can go after him on," he told them.

"And possibly lose," Devlin stated. "Vega needs to go down hard and quick, just like he takes people out. The justice system may not prevail on this one."

Ben had stood, tired of this meeting and the issues running through his mind. "Let's just stick with the justice system for now. That's what I do."

Devlin stood also. "Well, you know what I do."

Ben nodded. "Yeah, I know and you do it so well you scare me half the damn time."

The corner of his mouth twitched and Ben knew that was as close as he was going to get to a smile from Devlin Bonner.

"Devlin's going to keep an eye on you and we'll set something up for the prosecutor. You and Noah work the justice system and I'll work the back end to see if there's any loophole we need to fill to make sure this guy goes down once and for all. That sound good to you?" Trent asked.

"Sure," was Ben's half-hearted reply. He didn't want to know what lengths Devlin and Trent would go to in order to take Vega down. And he wanted to trust the justice system that he loved so much, but as he walked out of the offices of D&D Investigations, he had to admit that his faith in that system had begun to waiver.

And that hadn't just happened with these latest events. Ben had been wary of the justice system doing its job right around the time he got wind of what might be the reason the Congressman and his wife had been killed.

CHAPTER 8

Victoria had a headache. She'd had one since last night, since right before the tear gas came flying through her living room window like a scene from some television crime drama.

She'd been discharged from the hospital around noon, after a long night of nurses interrupting her each time she tried to drift to sleep, checking everything from her temperature to how many fingers she could see in front of her. For all the interruptions and the headache they'd failed to treat, she could have come home last night.

Upon release, she'd had to deal with her mother, who in all her well-meaning, overprotective, overbearing and just generally hovering nature, pushed her headache to another level. The level which had her right eye twitching—an action added to the still bloodshot look she was sporting in both eyes. After three hours of Naomi's picking up this, moving that, telling her this, warning her about that, asking her about…him, she'd finally left. And Victoria had breathed a sigh of relief.

Her living room window had been fixed by the time she arrived home. She hadn't asked why or by whom, because she knew. But she was too tired to deal with it. Dinner hadn't gone well, even though Naomi cooked perfect lasagna each and every time. Her stomach was having its own issues, separate and apart from the hospital stay and the tear gas.

Finally when even work held no appeal, Victoria had taken a long bath and was just about to climb into bed to do…what? She had no idea. She had a sinking suspicion sleep was also going to be an enemy tonight. Especially when the door bell rang.

Cursing would seem cliché, so she didn't bother. Stomping down the steps to show her irritation would be childish and would most likely jack her headache up to even higher heights. As she walked to the door, déjà vu had her halting and she gritted her teeth—because she couldn't find anything wrong with that action. Taking a deep breath and reciting the first line of the 23rd Psalm in her head, she opened the door.

Then sighed with relief.

And frowned with confusion.

"What are you doing here?"

"You keep asking me that," Ben replied.

She sighed once more, weary from last night, this morning, tonight... "Because you keep showing up where you don't belong."

"I keep showing up where I'm needed."

The laugh that escaped her sounded more like a nervous chuckle, one that sent slithers of pain to her temple. "I do not need you Ben Donovan. For some reason you have this demented belief that you are God's gift to this world. You've always had it. Some thought you would grow out of it. I knew you never would. Your kind never does. You're no longer a part of this case, and yet you show up in my courtroom. Some insane vandals attack my house and you show up. Now I'm trying to go to bed, to get myself together for work tomorrow and you show up again. Why? Just tell me why?"

He'd stood perfectly still the entire time she talked. Everything about her was gorgeous, but there was more. So much more beyond her physical attributes. In the eyes that had always intoxicated him, Ben saw fatigue and a little fear. It was with that in mind that he stepped into the doorway, into her personal space. Another woman might have stepped back, but not Victoria. She stood her ground, tilting her head back slightly to keep eye contact with him.

"Because I can't stay away from you," he told her honestly.

Victoria was smart, graduated fourth in their class in law school type of smart, and she was tenacious and decisive. She had integrity oozing from her pores and unhappiness creeping up her neck to settle—as he presumed from the twitching of her eye—in her temples, creating one hell of a tension headache.

"What you've done has plagued me for years, Victoria. I have absolutely no explanation for why I can't stay away from you or what you're doing with your life. None at all. But here's what I can tell you—I really like looking at you. And last night when I looked at you lying on that gurney, blood freckling your face, I wanted to kill someone. That makes me believe that my fixation with you has taken a really big step, one I can no longer ignore."

She shook her head. "You're crazy."

It was Ben's turn to laugh and since she had yet to tell him to get out of her house, he closed her front door, secured the locks. "I've been called a lot of things before. Crazy's not one of them, but I'll accept it."

"I meant what I said," she told him, "I do not need you here."

"Humor me then. I just want to make sure you're alright."

Folding her arms over her chest, she looked at him with impatience. "I'm fine."

"You're tired."

She nodded. "Yes, I am. That's why I was about to go to bed."

"Have you had dinner?"

"I tried but I wasn't really hungry," she said without thinking, then snapped her lips shut. He almost smiled, but that would have certainly irritated her more.

"You should eat. Taking pain medication on an empty stomach is not a good idea."

"I haven't taken any pain medication and don't plan to."

"Then how do you expect the headache to go away?"

Ben had already walked through her living room and was moving through the dining room when she caught up with him.

"I didn't tell you I had a headache and, wait a minute, where are you going? This is my house, Ben. You don't rule here."

"No, I don't," he told her. "And believe me, the last thing I would do is try to rule over you. I'm just trying to help, so it would be nice if you decided to relax and let me do that."

"People allow help when they need it and…"

"I know you don't need me," he finished. "Again, I'll ask that you just humor me. Maybe I'm the one who can't sleep until I know for sure you're okay. So if I can feed you and medicate you and tuck you safely into bed, maybe I'll feel better and I can go home and go to bed."

She tapped her foot on the floor in her fluffy white slippers. He noticed, not for the first time but again, that she wore a nightshirt, a purple nightshirt that skimmed her knees and nothing else.

"If I eat and take an aspirin, will that be enough to appease this guilt trip you seem to be on?"

Inwardly Ben smiled. It wasn't easy for her to give in. Later he'd give himself a point for achieving that magnificent feat. Right now, he sensed it was more to get him out of her hair as soon as possible than anything else.

Giving credit where it was due, she was absolutely right about one thing. He was guilty. So guilty he'd almost choked on it all day while he'd tried convincing himself that coming to see her was a very bad idea.

"You cooked?" he asked after he'd moved into the kitchen to see a dish of something wrapped in foil on top of the stove.

"I forgot to put that away. She would have a fit if she saw that," Victoria said.

"'She' meaning your mother, I presume?" he asked even though he'd figured on the answer. Her kitchen was small compared to his, but definitely homelier with its warm beige walls and friendly yellow curtains. There was an island in its center with a vase full of fresh flowers, a stack of cloth napkins and two placemats that matched the checkered pattern of the curtains.

Victoria nodded. "She loves to cook. Lasagna's her specialty."

Lifting the foil from the dish and inhaling deeply, Ben replied, "And it appears she does a great job. How about I heat us both up a bowl?"

While he was salivating over the lasagna, she'd already moved to the cabinets—light oak polished until they practically gleamed—and had two plates in her hand as she looked over her shoulder at him. "Right, because both of us need to eat to ensure that I'm alright."

Ben shrugged, not in the least bit offended by being caught. "My mother always told me never let a woman eat alone."

She smiled.

And the tense atmosphere that he'd walked into dissipated. His gut had also suffered what seemed like a terrific sucker punch at the sight, but he chose to ignore that.

⌒○⌒○⌒○

"So you're a mama's boy?" she asked while she sat back in the chair watching him devour his second helping of lasagna.

He didn't look like he had a big appetite. His body was fit, muscled, toned to the point where he looked absolutely delicious in his clothes, whether dressy or casual. The khakis and black t-shirt he sported tonight looked as if it had been painted on his sculpted chest. He was gorgeous.

Victoria liked to think she was a realist. She didn't believe in fantasies, didn't indulge in meaningless fairy tales. The fact that Ben Donovan was an attractive specimen was a given. She could admit that and not feel an ounce of guilt. And before thirty minutes ago, she would have firmly believed he was an arrogant, egotistical ass most of the time. Now, however, she was seeing another side of him.

"I wouldn't say that. I adore my mother and so does my brother. She dotes on both of us, even though we're adults. My dad just shakes his head at the three of us most of the time. I'd say we just love each other a lot. Kind of like you and your mother."

She'd watched him talk, watched his lips move over shockingly white teeth, the muscles in his jaw tick as he took another spoonful of food. His eyes were dark, almost black, but still held a warmth she hadn't considered he possessed.

"My mother and I are very close," she admitted. Never in her wildest dreams had Victoria thought she'd be sitting in her kitchen talking about family with Ben Donovan. "Especially since my dad died."

"I'm sorry about that," he told her, and she got the sense he knew exactly what had happened to her father. Why he would know didn't make sense, but then again nothing about this man was adding up into the neat little column she'd placed him in.

Shaking her head, she said something else that surprised her. "Tell me more about your family."

He took a drink of the iced tea she'd poured for them both. "We have a very large family. Some of us are here and some are in Washington, Texas, Miami. We're all spread out," he told her. "But we get together at least once a year to catch up."

"Like a family reunion. I've never been to one of those before." And making that statement made her realize she really wanted to.

"Your family doesn't get together?"

"It's just me and my mother. She has some family back east, but we rarely hear from them, let alone see them."

"Family should always keep in touch," he said earnestly.

"Your family is not like most," she said, reaching out to pick up her own glass even though she didn't want to take a drink. She just needed something to do with her hands.

"I could take you to a family dinner if you want. That'll prepare you for the reunion. We can be a bit overwhelming," he told her and took another bite of food.

She did take a drink then and looked at him with consideration as she put her glass down on the table. "You're very presumptuous."

"Really? I'd call it optimistic," he said with a smile as he swallowed the last bit of his food.

His skin was the tone of tree bark, smooth and alluring. Her fingers tingled as she thought of rubbing them along his biceps, over his strong shoulders.

Shaking her head, she resisted closing her eyes to get the visual out of her head. "No, you presume too much. If you wanted me to go to your family dinner you would have asked me and hoped I'd say yes. Instead, you tell me that I'm going like it's already been settled. Presumptuous."

He laughed. His head tilted and a deep, full-bodied sound filled her kitchen. She was certain that had never happened before.

"You've always been so intense. Every question has an answer, every answer an explanation. Sometimes things just are, Victoria."

"Not without a reason," she added, shaking her head. "So what's your reason for being so presumptuous? You came over here tonight expecting what, to get lucky?"

"Whoa? Where did that come from?"

"I'm just getting the small talk out of the way. I mean, you've been here for almost forty-five minutes now. You've eaten, I've eaten, we're talking, so what's next? I have to ask since I know you think you know the next step."

He shook his head. "I came here to check on you. This dinner was an added bonus and I'll be sending your mother a bouquet of her favorite flowers tomorrow to thank her."

"You don't know her favorite flower," she said sarcastically.

"Touché, but I was going to ask you before I left. And just for the record, I know you're favorite flower."

"You do not."

"Gerber daisies," he said without even looking up at her.

She would never let him know how sweet those two words sounded to her. Instead, she asked, "How?"

"No, it's not a presumption as you would like to think. You have a vase full of colorful Gerber daisies sitting right there. I just made a logical conclusion."

She looked at said vase, wanted to frown, but didn't want to lower herself that much. Instead she drummed her fingers on the table, an act that normally annoyed the hell out of her when Roxanne did it at work. Now it soothed nerves that had quickly become frazzled.

"How did you know what they were called? You don't strike me as the flower kind of guy."

"I should be calling you presumptuous since you seem to think you know all about me. My mother likes flowers so I make it a point to send her favorites at least once a month. Calling the florist on a monthly basis puts you smack dab in the middle of the flower business."

"And your mother likes Gerber daisies?"

"No. Tulips. But they're not in season all year, so sometimes I have to switch it up. That's how I know what Gerber daisies are. She likes them too, and they're very cheerful."

"They are and I'm not having sex with you."

He'd been just finishing his tea and choked just a little.

"No," he said when he put his glass down. "You're not. At least not tonight. You're tired, I'm tired after all this good food and you need time to recuperate."

"I mean ever, Ben. I'm not sleeping with you ever."

He waited a beat, seemingly contemplating what she'd said, then nodded. "Okay."

"Is that it?" she heard herself ask and wanted to bite her tongue.

"Yes. That's it. Thank you for dinner," he said, standing and taking his plate to the sink. "I can wash these up before I go."

"No, thanks. I'll put them in the dishwasher."

"Good. I want you to get to bed as soon as possible." He breezed right by her and was on his way out of the kitchen when she finally stood from the table to follow him.

"Are you angry?"

He turned and she bumped right into him since she'd walked fast to catch up with him. "I'm not a child, Victoria. Something else to scratch off your list of misconceptions about me."

"I didn't mean to blurt it out. I just meant that this wasn't going to lead to sex. We're colleagues, as you told my mother. We're not...anything else," she said for lack of a better term.

He reached out a hand, traced a finger along the line of her jaw and Victoria held her breath. He was close to her, very close. Her heart hammered in her chest. He was so close and she was so...what? What did his closeness do to her?

"We're not anything else...yet," he whispered, then dropped his hand from her face and turned away.

He was unlocking the door before Victoria could get her feet to move again.

"Lock the doors when I leave. The windows have locks already installed. Keep a dim light on down here when you go up and sleep well," he told her as he walked out.

She grabbed the door handle and watched as he walked down the three steps that led to her door. She wanted to say something, to correct him, admonish him, something.

"Goodnight," was what she heard falling from her lips and felt like biting off her tongue the minute she did.

He stopped, turned back to face her and grinned. "Goodnight, Victoria."

Closing and locking the door, Victoria slowly leaned against it, letting her head drift back as she whispered a word she'd never thought would apply to herself. "Idiot."

CHAPTER 9

Fear was not an option for Victoria. It was one of those things she'd boxed up and stuck in her mother's attic along with her father's belongings. He hadn't been afraid, even when those robbers had approached him and stuck the gun in his face. Porter Lashley had never been afraid of anything, and he'd instilled that in his only daughter.

"If people know your fears, they'll have a tool to manipulate you with. Fear makes you weak. Show no fear and you maintain the upper hand."

Sitting at her desk at almost noon, two days after her home had been violated, Victoria remembered those words. She heard her father's voice as if he were standing right in the room with her, and she wanted to cry. At night sleep evaded her and by day headaches taunted her. Thoughts of Ben Donovan steadily crept forward to fill the in-between times.

He wasn't what she thought he was. At least she'd begun to give some credence to him being a normal guy. Except he was still rich and privileged and didn't need the job he did, the job that allowed a man like Ramone Vega to walk free. She understood the justice system and knew that everyone was entitled to a good defense. Ben gave above and beyond a good defense for all his clients, and was actually one of the best defense attorneys in Clark County. And a few weeks ago he would have been the attorney she planned to beat in court. But he'd stepped out of the case. She wondered why?

She also wondered why he'd continuously turned up in her life. No, there was no need to wonder about that because it was a question she'd always known the answer to. There was something between them, a sort of thunder and lightning type of reaction: He strutted like a boastful peacock and she struck like an angry eel. And yet they couldn't seem to stay away from each other. To counter that, she'd tried to head him off by stating she wouldn't sleep with him. He hadn't seemed phased. That had intrigued her.

Enough so that yesterday she'd been expecting him to show up at her door or at her office. She'd even stayed downstairs longer than usual under the pretense of working after she'd had dinner with her mother, waiting for him to come knocking on her front door. But he hadn't. That had her wondering too. Until now, she felt like a bundle of contradictions, like her normally cut and dry go to work, win a case, start over again life seemed a little out of control.

And then there was the fear.

She was trying to keep it at a minimum, trying like hell to not let the thought of Vega seeking some kind of intimidation towards her take hold. He was a killer, she knew this. So he could have her killed without a second thought. But she was still here working on a way to convict him. "Why" was a question that she didn't want to explore, yet she couldn't help thinking about. And feeling what she felt.

"If you're thinking about this case that hard we're in for a conviction," Grace said as she made her way into the office.

"When does your maternity leave start again?" Victoria asked instead of replying about the case. Talking about Grace and the baby was a much better idea.

Grace shook her head, her ponytail waving behind her. "Not until my water breaks. Clinton says I should stop now but I'm trying not to use any of my vacation time. Besides, things are heating up around here," she said, rubbing her hands together. "You know Karl Maddow, down in economic crimes division, he and Roxanne are dating. Now ain't that some mess? Roxanne's clearly ten or fifteen years younger than that man."

Victoria nodded because Grace could always be counted on to take her mind off things. She hadn't told her about the incident at her house, hadn't wanted to worry her so close to the end of her pregnancy. Luckily, the scrapes to her face from the glass were small and were easily hidden by make-up. And as she watched Grace continue to talk in the animated way she did with everything, she realized it was a good decision. Grace would have wanted to come right over after hearing what happened. And then she would have wanted to come over the next day and now, instead of telling her the office gossip, she would have been questioning Victoria about her locks and security systems and whatever else came into her mind.

"So anyway, Jules wants you to wrap this case up quick. He's putting in for a transfer out of the felony division and doesn't want this hanging over his head."

"What? It's just another case. He's had at least a dozen mistrials he hasn't even bothered to retry. What's so special about this one?" As Victoria asked the question, other questions she'd been mulling over as she'd reviewed the file took hold.

"Probably all the media attention," Grace replied with a shrug of her shoulders. "I think the transfer thing is a front. Clifton says he's already filled out the ballot. He's going to run for DA."

"Really?" That was certainly interesting. The district attorney's position was a public office where one had to be elected to fill it. Jules wanted to enter the world of politics and he needed the murder of a congressman and his wife to be cleared up before he did. Very interesting indeed.

"Who do you think will take his place?" Grace asked at the same time there was a knock on the door.

Grace was sitting close to the door and they'd both assumed it was someone who worked at the office. She reached out and turned the knob to let them in.

Victoria wasn't sure which one of them was more shocked to see Ben Donovan standing there.

"I apologize if I'm interrupting," he said, stepping slowly into the office.

Grace shifted in her seat, a smile spreading quickly. Across the room Victoria felt that warming sensation sifting throughout her body that was only incited by this man.

"You are most definitely not interrupting, Mr. Donovan," Grace replied. "You don't remember me do you?" she asked when he turned from staring at Victoria to look at her.

"I do," he, said reaching out a hand to shake Grace's. "I've had a case or two with you over the years and we graduated from law school together. You're Grace Ramsey."

Grace took his hand, her smile brightening as she cut Victoria a quick look before returning all her attention to Ben. "I sure am. It's nice to see you out of the courtroom, Ben."

"Likewise," he told her, then nodded towards her protruding belly as he released her hand. "You don't look like you'll be in the courtroom much longer."

Grace chuckled and rubbed her stomach. "No. More like the delivery room."

Ben smiled.

Victoria almost cursed. Instead she closed her legs as tightly as she could beneath her desk, praying this rapidly spreading heat didn't make her look flushed.

"I'm sure Ben didn't drop by to hear about having babies. So what does bring you by?" she asked, clearing her throat immediately.

He turned slowly, pushing the jacket of his black suit back and slipping his left hand into his pant pocket, gave her that sinfully sexy smile. The one she dreamed about, grew wet at imagining, and despised all in the same breath.

"Actually, I love children. So I'm always pleased to see a pregnant woman. However," he continued before she could interject, "I wanted to talk to you about something."

"Well," Grace added quickly, planting her hands on the arms of the chair and pushing herself upward. "That's my cue to leave. Call me later," she told Victoria and made the fastest exit out of her office she had in months.

"So now I know how loyal you are," Ben said, taking the seat Grace had just vacated.

Grace had also closed the door behind her, which seemed to have sucked all the breathable air from the room now that it was just her and Ben. He wasn't smiling now, instead looking seriously fine as he adjusted his paisley print tie, smoothing it down so that his strong hands moved lightly over his chest and abs.

Okay, you really need to get a grip, she admonished. *He's just a man.*

But Victoria knew that simply wasn't true.

"Grace and I have been friends a really long time. She's like a sister to me."

Ben nodded. "I see. So when's the baby due?"

"In about three weeks,' she answered before she could catch herself. It really wasn't any of his business. "Why are you here?"

"You like asking me that, don't you?"

"Not really. It's kind of getting tiresome. Then again, you keep popping up, so what else am I supposed to do?"

"I was in the courthouse. Motion to suppress hearing in Judge Leontine's courtroom," he informed her.

So he had an excuse to be in the courthouse today. That didn't lead to her office.

"Her courtroom's all the way down the hall," she replied.

"It's not that far," he countered, then held up his hand as if to call a truce. "I came to see if you had plans for lunch. Is that better?"

Hell no!

Though her inner voice was screaming, warning alarms blaring in her head, Victoria nodded. "Honesty is always better," was her reply.

"I'm glad you feel that way because there are a few things I want to ask you about your investigation into the Vega case."

Victoria shook her head. "The answer to that request would be no. I'm not giving defense counsel information on my case."

"I'm not his lawyer anymore."

"Still not going to discuss my case with you."

"Even if it might involve the incident at your house?"

Victoria paused. She hadn't wanted to think that, had in fact, been pushing that very theory out of her mind for the last two days. "It was random vandalism. Teenagers." Even as she spoke those words she knew they weren't true.

"What teenagers do you know own tear gas?" he asked pointedly.

"Gang initiation," she offered hopefully.

"Then why didn't they come inside? Gang initiations usually involve some type of robbery or a murder. Thank goodness neither of them happened that night. But something did and I'm not willing to let it slip through the cracks because somebody's afraid to put two and two together. How about you?"

Now he looked like a defense attorney. He'd leaned forward, resting his elbows on his knees, staring at her as if he wanted to say more. And she, instinctively, felt like saying he was badgering the witness. Instead she sighed.

"I thought about that, but I dismissed it. If Vega wanted to hurt me, he would have. He doesn't do warnings. You should know that."

He was quiet a moment and Victoria wondered what was going through his mind. He sat back, rubbed a finger over his neatly trimmed goatee.

"He's changing the game," Ben stated matter-of-factly. "And that's all I'm going to say about this here in your office. We can go right across the street and grab some lunch and talk more, without probing ears."

"This is my office, the place where I work. So if we're going to discuss my case—"

"We're not discussing your case, *per se*. We're discussing a possible connection. And I'd think you of all people would know about the reported leaks in this office."

Victoria remained silent. There had been talk in the last couple of months about confidential information from the DA's office getting out to the press. Hell, the Vega mistrial and new trial date had been on the local news before she'd even signed the entry of appearance. So while she wasn't thrilled about having lunch with Ben, she recognized the importance of finding out all she could about the attack on her house. Especially if it involved Vega. And who better to know the man then the lawyer who'd gotten him off a capital murder case.

"Fine. One hour," she told him, then stood to pull open her lower left desk drawer and retrieve her purse.

"You won't regret it," he said once he'd stood and held the door open for her.

She'd given him a half smile in return as she passed through the door, while her mind screamed that it was already regretting this decision.

CHAPTER 10

Ella's was a quaint little diner about a block away from the Justice Center. Most of the courthouse staff came here for lunch as well as police officers and some of the construction crew that were working on the building two more blocks down. So it was extremely crowded when Ben and Victoria walked in.

He could tell instantly she was rethinking her agreement to come here when they walked up to the hostess and what he presumed to be a few colleagues spoke to her. The fact that they were all men made Ben a little uncomfortable, a feeling he tried to nip quickly and quietly in the bud. Victoria was not his woman, no matter how much he may have wanted her to be. Yes, even after all these years, all the times she'd rejected him, Ben still wanted this woman. It was undeniable and as he'd told her, inevitable.

They were led to a booth snuggled tightly between a long row of seats and the chatter of at least fifty people surrounding them. After ordering their drinks, they were finally left alone with menus and the silence that drifted between them.

"I usually have the hot pastrami on rye. How about you?" he asked by way of getting her to relax again.

She was extremely uncomfortable around him. Now, for the most part, Ben attributed that to attraction. Yeah, that might seem arrogant, but he felt pretty sure it was true. He was a Donovan after all; he knew when a woman was attracted to him, no matter how much how much they might deny it. But Victoria had admitted it, just two days ago. He'd told himself when he decided to go to her office and take her to lunch that he wasn't going to play in that direction. He had some serious concerns about her case and her safety that had to come before anything personal.

"I don't like to eat a lot at lunch. Especially if I'm in trial," she told him.

She kept looking at the menu. Ben figured she knew basically what was on there because he did and he didn't work right up the street. Again, this was a part of getting her to relax. His comments about the event at her house had made her nervous, rightfully so. He didn't want her walking the streets scared because then she wouldn't be alert, and whatever Vega was trying to pull would be much more successful if Victoria were off her game in any way.

"You're not in trial right now. The trial doesn't start until next week. So you can splurge. How about having pastrami with me?"

"And have heartburn all afternoon? No thanks." With those words came a little smile and Ben felt the tension in his shoulders relax a bit. He liked it so much better when she smiled.

She continued to study the menu, then said, "I think I'll stick with soup."

"Chicken."

"No. French onion," she replied.

He chuckled. "I was calling you a chicken for not having the same sandwich I am."

She lowered her menu then and the right corner of her mouth lifted in a part smile, part smirk. "You are hilarious."

"I've been told I have a great sense of humor," he quipped and closed his menu, setting it to the side.

"I'm sure you've been told a lot of things that have helped inflate your ego."

The waitress came with their drinks and they gave their meal orders. Taking a sip of his soda, Ben sat back against the booth. "You have a very low opinion of me, don't you?"

Victoria also took a sip of her drink, then folded her arms and rested them on the table. "You have to know about your reputation, Ben. Everybody has an opinion of you and the rest of the Donovan family, for that matter."

"I don't care about everybody's opinion. I'm talking about yours. You've always thought low of me, even back in law school. Why is that?"

She shrugged one shoulder, the tip of a gold hoop earring bunching between her ear and the collar of her pale blue blouse. The color looked really good on her as it made her complexion seem brighter, her eyes more poignant.

"In school I thought you were a spoiled rich boy, getting by on his looks and too lazy to use his brain," she said as simply as if she'd just given the weather report.

"Ouch," he replied and actually shirked back as if she'd slapped him. Of course that was overreacting, but he had to admit the words, coming from her, stung.

She held up a hand. "That was what I thought of you eight years ago."

"And now that's changed? I sure hope so."

Another kind of shrug this time with her head moving, her lips curling a bit at the ends. "Kind of," she admitted reluctantly. "I know this is probably going to come back to bite me in the butt later, but you're a phenomenal defense attorney."

He smiled, couldn't help it. Even though he sensed it had taken a lot for her to admit that to him. "Well, thank you very much. You're an excellent prosecutor."

"Thank you," she replied.

"And on a personal level you're a very attractive woman. But I think you already know that."

"Thank you, just the same." Then she sighed. "I thought we weren't going to do this."

He knew exactly what she was talking about and had just reminded himself of why he was here with her today. Still, what was between them seemed to have a mind of its own. "Do what? Get to know each other better? Who told you that?"

"Ben. We're colleagues."

"We're a man and a woman. Can you deny that?"

She shook her head as the waitress picked that moment to arrive with their food. For the first few minutes, they ate in silence. Then she spoke.

"Why throw tear gas through my window?" she asked using a napkin to wipe around her mouth.

"Scare tactic," Ben answered a question he'd asked himself repeatedly in the last few days.

"But how was I supposed to connect the incident to Vega? Nobody came in, no note was left. It could have been anyone."

"Your neighbor said they saw a gray Lexus parked across the street from your house. Exactly seven minutes before the window was broken." He let those words hang a second, watched as she considered them and nodded his head the moment she picked up the clue he'd wanted her to.

"No. He wouldn't use the same car he used in the commission of a murder."

"There are a couple things I know about Vega that wouldn't take me into the fine area of attorney/client privilege if he were still my client. If you think I'm arrogant you haven't seen anything yet. He's cocky as hell and walks around like he's the king of the damned world. He believes he's invincible, so there's no need to fear being caught."

"He thinks he's invincible because you keep getting him off whenever he commits a crime," she snapped.

Ben remained silent a moment because he probably deserved that shot, at least on some level. "I represented Vega in two cases. A drug case and this murder. Yes, I got him off on both. That's my job."

"That you do by choice without a second thought as to who you're letting back out onto the streets to do whatever they want."

Her words hit a spot in him. Ben paused before speaking again. "Then it's your job to make sure he goes to jail this time."

"Are you planning on helping me do that?"

Ben knew what his job was. He also knew the ethical lines with which he'd never thought he'd cross. But he wasn't the one who'd crossed the line, Vega was. And because of that, Ben had the wherewithal to end his representation of him. It would have stopped at just that, Ben was certain. But Ebony had been killed and Victoria's home invaded. Vega had run headlong over the line and landed right in Ben's backyard. To him, those were fighting words, and next to law, boxing was Ben's favorite past time.

"I've got someone looking for Alayna Jonas. She's the key to your case," he informed her.

"The cops think she's dead," Victoria stated, pushing her plate to the side.

"And so they've stopped looking for her. But if she's dead, where's her body? Vega likes recognition. If he kills someone, he leaves them for everyone to see." And sometimes he leaves a note, like a signature. Ben kept that part to himself.

"You think she ran because she knew he'd come after her."

Ben nodded.

"But she left her daughter unprotected. What kind of mother would do that?"

"The kind that has a lot of information. Killing her daughter would only enrage her, possibly enough to have her talking faster than they could shoot her. As long as she's alive, her family is safe because what she knows means more to Vega than another dead body."

Ben had thought long and hard about this. He'd even considered that Vega could have gone the opposite route and killed all of Alayna's family as a way of keeping her quiet. But that would have gone against instructions from the person who'd hired him to kill the congressman and his wife.

She considered his words. Her brow furrowed slightly, he'd seen that look before. "You work the opposite side of the law than I do. Why tell me all this?"

He finished chewing the last bit of his sandwich, swallowed and wiped his mouth, all the while watching her closely.

"I want Vega in jail for the rest of his life, or I just might kill him myself."

⌒⌒⌒⌒⌒

The afternoon hours flew by as Victoria stayed closed in her office, pouring over the entire police file and prosecution file on Ramone Vega. She knew where he was born, where he went to school until ninth grade, the first man he'd shot and the first woman he'd raped. He was a vicious character, a heartless killer that would let absolutely nothing come between him and his money.

He was born Jose Ramone Vega to Conchita and Raphael Vega, Mexican immigrants who came to the United States in the early seventies and ran a fruit stand off the local highway. Reports told a story of stark poverty and endless teasing in Vega's elementary years. Sometime in middle school he'd met up with Salvatore "Big Sal" Peña. Joining Big Sal's gang had been the turning point in Vega's life, and before he'd hit his sixteenth birthday he was Big Sal's lead enforcer.

Now, at almost forty years old, five feet eleven inches tall, two hundred and thirty-five pounds, Vega's name carried more clout than the local law. He and Big Sal ran the streets with an iron hand, one that wouldn't hesitate to slit the throat of anyone who crossed them.

To put it mildly, this case was huge. It was highly publicized and more dangerous than any case Victoria had ever tried. And that made her heart beat a little faster as she sat back in her chair, looking around her office at all the spread out papers and letting out a sigh.

"Can I do this?"

The words came out on whispered breath but seemed to echo in the small government office she called home from nine to five.

Of course she could do it, she told herself. She had no choice. This was her job, bringing justice to the same streets that had taken her father's life was the goal she'd been working towards all her life. It was everything to her, and the stems of fear taking hold deep inside weren't going to win. She could get a conviction on Ramone Vega. She *was* going to get a conviction on Ramone Vega, no matter what the cost.

Three chimes that sounded like half a bell toll sounded and jolted her almost out of her chair. It was her cellphone signaling she had a text message. Only it seemed she could never find that phone. Picking up folders and moving aside stacks of paper, she didn't stop until a minute or so later when she found it practically buried on her desk.

Dinner's at six.

"Crap!"

She was running late. To appease Grace and to hopefully head off all the questions she knew would undoubtedly come her way if she'd declined, she'd agreed to dinner with Grace and Clinton tonight. In the next fifteen minutes she'd performed a partial clean up of her office and a vague organization of the Vega file. Tossing the police reports from the congressman's murder into her briefcase, she grabbed her purse and headed out.

Thirty minutes later, Victoria had showered and changed into jeans and one of her favorite pairs of pumps and headed to the prestigious single family home development of Judge and Mrs. Clinton Ramsey.

"Besides my wife, you've got to be the sexiest prosecutor in Clark County," Clinton said, kissing Victoria on the cheek as he welcomed her into their home.

"Don't let your wife hear you talking like that. She's liable to hurt us both," she joked right along with him.

Clinton was a tall, slim man with strong arms and an even stronger temperament. Lawyers and defendants alike feared the moment they learned their case was being heard in his courtroom. More traffic citations were paid through Clinton's verdicts than any other traffic court in the county. And he loved his wife to pieces. Victoria could hear it in his voice each time he said her name, could see it in his eyes whenever he looked at her. It was that all encompassing love that was meant to last forever. The love she'd seen between her parents. The kind of love she feared she'd never have a chance to experience for herself.

"She's gorgeous and she knows it. Besides, you're her best friend so you know you'd have to look good too for her to tolerate you," Clinton continued while walking towards their den where Grace was no doubt sitting in her favorite chair, feet propped up and the television tuned in to whatever reality show she was currently addicted to.

"You're right about that. Grace has always been stuck on fashion's glitz and glamour." And she loved the shoes Victoria was wearing, had often offered to buy them from her. So when Victoria entered the den, she didn't think anything of the first word to slip from Grace's lips.

"Bitch."

"I love you too, dear," Victoria said waltzing her four inch fuchsia peek toe heels right over to her friend and kissing her soundly on the cheek.

"Sit down. Clinton's cooking on the grill. We have about ten minutes to talk alone before he comes back with the food," she told her pointedly.

"Make that fifteen. I'm going down to the cellar to get a bottle of wine," Clinton said, rubbing a hand over his wife's belly before leaving the room.

"That is one fine man," Grace said, watching her husband walk out of the room.

"And he's going to be a great father," Victoria noted. "You're so lucky."

"You could be lucky too if you'd stop being so picky all the time," Grace snapped.

She was indeed sitting in the antique rocking chair Clinton had bought her for her birthday three months ago. The seat cushion had been hand-sewn for her in a bright yellow satin material. She'd changed out of her work clothes to a loose fitting maternity dress that hugged her swollen breasts and flared out softly around her girth. Her hair was loose at the moment—Victoria didn't figure that would last long as Grace's body temperature shifted in ways that alarmed Victoria each time she witnessed them. And the woman still managed to look absolutely beautiful.

"I know you are not calling me picky. Who had her ten point husband criteria typed and framed by our twentieth birthday? And if I'm not mistaken, you never once swayed from that criteria when you were dating."

Grace nodded. "But at least I dated. When's the last time you've been out with a man?"

"Just this afternoon at lunch to be exact," Victoria replied automatically.

"Ah ha! I knew it. You and Ben Donovan are dating. If I could jump out of this chair, I'd come over there and shake you for not telling me."

"If you jump out of that chair, Clinton's going to be heading to the delivery room instead of to the wine cellar." Victoria laughed as Grace had actually shifted in the chair like she meant to move all that body with any sort of swiftness.

Most likely uncomfortable and a little winded, Grace sat back in defeat. "Don't try to change the subject. What happened at lunch and when are you going out with him again?"

"We talked about work and we're probably not going out again." Victoria reached onto the end table that separated the sofa from Grace's chair and snagged the remote. She began channel surfing as she knew Grace's total attention was now on her and what she wasn't telling her.

"The minute after I deliver, you and I are going to fight," she heard Grace snarling. "What do you mean you're not going out again? I told you years ago you two made a cute couple."

Victoria sighed and flipped past an infomercial. "We're so totally opposite. He's rich, I'm not. He's defense, I'm prosecution. He's all glitz and glamour while I'm...I'm—"

"A little on the glamour side with your three hundred dollar shoes and high-end salon treatments," Grace added.

She shook her head. "That's no comparison to the women he's probably used to dating." She'd seen some of those women pictured in newspapers with him at his family's many charity functions on the rare occasions the society pages drew her attention. Ben and his cousins were known for their dating prowess. She recalled that several of them had since married and seemed to live normal committed lives now. Still, the last thing Victoria wanted was to become one of the growing number.

"He's wanted you for eight years. And he still does. I could see it clearly in his eyes today. How long are you planning to ignore that?"

"'That' is purely physical. And you know Ben's the type to want what he can't have, just for the thrill of the chase."

"How do you know that? He seems like a decent guy to me."

She turned to Grace and stared incredulously. "How do I know? You've seen the stories in the paper. I know because you live and breathe the society pages. You've even been to a couple of the Donovan functions with Clinton. So you've seen them all in action, in person."

Grace was shaking her head and Victoria looked away from her back to the television.

"What I saw was a close family dedicated to giving back to the world some of what they have. Clinton has even played golf with Henry and Lincoln Donovan. He says they're good, stand-up guys. They just have a lot of money."

Her finger pressed the channel button so hard that the pad was beginning to hurt. The verbal exchange between her and Grace added to the tug of war going on inside her head.

"I really don't want to discuss this," she told Grace. "Ben is who and what he is and that has no effect on me."

"Uh huh. You keep right on telling yourself that," Grace said. "In the meantime, tell me what work you talked about, because as you stated you're both on opposite sides of the legal table."

"That's the weird thing," Victoria replied immediately, because this was something she felt comfortable talking to Grace about. "He thinks the witness in the Vega case is still alive."

"Who? The girl? But nobody's seen her in almost a year. The cops don't hold much hope of finding her."

"That's what I told him. But he said he has someone looking for her."

"Why would Ben Donovan have someone looking for Alayna Jonas when he no longer represented Vega?"

"Exactly."

"More importantly, why tell you?" she asked with overblown drama and a lift of her arched eyebrows.

Victoria shrugged that question off and was relieved when Clinton came into the room with a tray of two filled wine glasses and one glass of milk—which Grace detested.

Victoria didn't want to talk about why Ben was giving her information on Vega, not with Grace anyway. Actually, she didn't want to talk about work or Ben Donovan any longer. For tonight, she wanted to relax and enjoy spending time with her friends. That was something good in this world—friends and family. Not death and betrayal, two things she prayed wouldn't knock on her door anytime soon.

CHAPTER 11

It was after 10 by the time Victoria parked her car and walked up the walkway to her house. A light breeze ruffled her hair, which had lost all its curl and now lay flat past her shoulders. In her hand, her keys jingled as she walked, thinking of the lengthy baby name discussion she, Clinton and Grace had over dinner.

From the house two doors down, Yoda, Mrs. Graham's bichon frise, was yipping loudly in front of their open living room window. She could hear him as if he were right on her own steps. Leo Mack, her next door neighbor, had his blinds closed, and probably didn't want to see anything else after he'd seen the car the other night.

She took the six steps leading to her door one at a time, tired from the day's work and more than ready to get a hot shower and climb into her comfortable bed. But when she looked up at her door, Victoria's heart stopped.

A single piece of blue tape held a sheet of paper in place just beneath the peep hole on her door.

She swallowed hard, kick-starting her brain to send a message for her to take a breath. She closed her eyes and breathed a tremulous sigh. Opening them again only proved she still had perfect vision as her optometrist had told her just four months ago at her last exam. When she figured standing and staring was as pointless as the fear rippling up and down her spine, she reached forward and pulled the paper from the door.

BE CAREFUL OF THE COMPANY YOU KEEP
805 Agosta Luna Boulevard

She read the typed message once more before her eyes fell to the bottom half of the page where a picture had been printed. A picture of her and Ben Donovan having lunch at the diner earlier today.

Victoria knew exactly where Agosta Luna was and who lived there. She was down the steps and climbing back into her car before she could think of a reason not to go.

❧ ❧ ❧

It had been a long day, made into a long evening by the meeting Ben had with Noah. Trent and Devlin had been able to tap the phones at Ethel Jonas' house.

"There's a guy sitting on the house in a black SUV," Noah had told Ben as they'd sat in his car just outside the city limits.

A defense attorney meeting with a homicide detective wasn't totally strange, but they didn't want to bring any unnecessary attention to the side investigation they had going on.

"There's a shift change around 10 pm, but other than that the SUV doesn't move. I can't put cops on the house without an official investigation going on."

"But there is an official investigation going on into these murders," Ben had interjected.

"I'm working the Ebony Reece murder, not the congressman's," was Noah's comeback.

Ben nodded his agreement. "That's why I gave Trent the go ahead to do whatever was necessary to find Alayna. He's got a wiretap on the phones in the house and eyes on that same SUV as well as the house."

"Cool," Noah said with a nod. "We need to find her soon. Trial starts next week."

"And Vega's getting antsy. That's why he tried to scare Victoria."

"I don't know about that one," Noah said.

"I do and I don't like it. So the sooner we get this SOB, the better," he'd said and come home.

He was bone tired and a little hungry. He'd just trudged up the steps and was in his bedroom unbuttoning his shirt when his doorbell rang. Before he could even curse at whoever was daring to come to his house at this time of night, the person was banging on the door as if their life depended on him answering it immediately. Taking that into consideration, he headed down the steps and to the door, pulling it open ready to yell. Then he saw her and all coherent thought fled from his mind.

Bathed in the light that illuminated the alcove leading to his front door, he saw her eyes glittering with emotion—exactly what emotion he'd revisit later. She stood with one hand planted firmly on her hip, one leg slightly forward. On said legs were black jeans that looked as if they were made especially for a woman with this figure, long legs and curvy hips. Her top was intriguing as well, fitted and consisting of some shiny feminine material. It hugged her breasts, and its thin straps tempted him to the point of distraction. And those shoes—Ben didn't have sisters, but he did have cousins and they considered themselves well-versed in the area of fashion. And the shoes Victoria was wearing were definitely of the kick-a-guy-in-the-gut-sexy variety. Hot pink, high heels, peep toe—that's all that really mattered as he swallowed hard and tried even harder for composure.

"Victoria," he managed finally.

"What the hell is this?" she asked and before he could answer, thrust a piece of paper so close to his face he couldn't begin to read what it said.

"Ah, it looks like a piece of paper," he said with a slight chuckle.

She made a motion with her hands that he swore looked like she was about to attack, and he reacted instantly by grabbing both her wrists and pushing them down to her sides.

"Is this some type of joke? If so, it's not funny!" she yelled up at him.

Ben had stepped forward, pulling her so that she was flush against his body. He looked down into eyes that he could now see were filled with rage.

"I don't know what you're talking about, but I'd be happy to take a look at whatever it is you have in your hand and offer an explanation if I can."

"Oh, I'm sure you can. Let go of me," she told him, her voice considerably steadier.

He released her, stepped back inside and signaled for her to do the same. She eyed him, not suspiciously, but definitely warily. She was afraid to come into his house, even though she'd driven all the way over here. It was possible she hadn't thought she'd need to come inside. Questions could be asked from anywhere. But not with Ben.

He closed the door and when he turned back to her, caught her looking around. She would be interested in how he lived, but she'd never admit it. That would be like somehow admitting that she liked him or was interested in him, two things she'd tried valiantly to hide over the years.

"I found this on my door when I came home. I want you to explain it. Then I want you to stay away from me and away from my case," she said when she turned to him abruptly, the shield of disinterest back in place.

Ben walked to her, taking the paper she'd thrust forward from her hand. He read it and cringed, first with a cold shiver that moved methodically through his body from head to toe in record time. And then with rage.

"Was there anyone around your house? Any cars you didn't recognize?"

"No," she insisted. "And I'm still waiting for you to tell me why I'm receiving this. It's your address and a picture of us."

"I can see that," he mused, then moved in, touching her elbow. "Let's sit down."

"I don't want to sit," she said, pulling her arm from his grasp.

"Well, I do." He actually needed to or he just might go out and try to find Vega himself. Instead, Ben walked through the living room into his den, across the deep cranberry colored carpet to the back bar that occupied the shortest wall.

He put the note down on the bar, gently, as if it might rip if he balled it up and pitched it into the trash like he wanted. No, he would keep his composure, that's what he always did. No matter what.

The first drink went down fast, two fingers of whiskey. Hot and potent, stinging his throat and warming his chest. The second, same type, same amount, slightly harder punch.

"It's Vega isn't it? He knows we're talking about him," she said walking into the room, her legs perfectly balanced on those heels that looked killer high.

"I don't like that he's turned his attention to you. I don't like it at all."

She waved a hand. "Then you should have thought about that before you suggested lunch in a very public place."

"He'd already shifted to you. The moment you walked into that courtroom, he decided to go after you."

"But he's not coming after me. I mean, a note on my door, tear gas in my window, all just scare tactics?" The questions were clearly bravado, because her voice shook.

Ben rubbed a hand down his face, moreso to break the contact of her intense, fearful gaze, than anything else. He took a deep breath because this was new territory he was about to venture into. New, but inevitable.

Leaving the comfort he'd found at the bar, he pulled out one of the chairs to the dining-room table he rarely used and sat down. "Come here," he told her.

She didn't move.

He wasn't surprised.

"Please, come here and I'll answer all your questions," he tried again, resisting the urge to snag her by the waist and pull her down onto his lap. From there he would hold her tight, so tight she might not be able to take a breath, but she would certainly feel him completely covering her. Sheltering her, protecting her, because that's exactly what he planned to do.

"I don't like being watched," was what she said and still did not move. "I don't like having to look over my shoulder and wonder where that asshole might be."

Ben sat back in the chair, let his palms rest on his thighs. "You don't like being afraid."

She licked her lips. They'd probably been heavily glossed a few hours earlier. Now they were their natural tone, glistening slightly after the sway of her tongue over them.

"Fear is not an option," she replied and took a step closer.

Her hips swayed with her movement, a motion that had his penis twitching.

"If people know what you fear, they can manipulate you with that knowledge." Her voice had lowered slightly, her approach continuing.

She was coming to him, enticing him along the way. And damn, his hands itched to touch her.

"I will not be manipulated and I will not be scared away. I'm going to prosecute the hell out of this case and I'm going to put Vega's coldhearted behind in jail."

There was only a slight elevation in her voice and her breasts jiggled as she stopped in front of him, those feisty pink shoes leading her right between his legs.

"I won't let him manipulate or scare you, Victoria. I can promise you that." Ben had to keep talking to keep from reaching forward, from touching the thighs that looked so full and so soft even beneath the denim.

She chuckled then and tossed her hair back. "I'm not just talking about Vega," she told him about a second or so before she leaned over and swiped her tongue across his bottom lip.

⸎

This wasn't what she came here for. Then again, maybe it was.

Victoria wasn't even going to deny that she'd been thinking about Ben all evening. Even though for a while she and Clinton had managed to keep the topic of conversation on anything but him and this case, Grace, in all her candid glory, had managed to circle right back to him. She thought they made a cute couple, thought Ben could relax Victoria a bit, thought she'd love his family once she let go of her misconceptions. And when Clinton had gone to the bathroom, she'd made a point to go into how sexy he was, how his body screamed "great-in-bed."

After seeing that note and that picture of them looking so comfortable at lunch, she'd driven here without delay or doubt. She'd known the address on the note was his because Grace knew the realtor who'd shown him the house a year ago. The realtor was so happy to have made the huge sale to a Donovan she'd blabbed immediately. And as rumors are usually spread, Grace had raced to tell Victoria. As for Victoria, she didn't repeat the information, but she hadn't forgotten it either. Now she was practically straddling him in a chair in the middle of his dining room. It was unprecedented.

And when his tongue snaked out to touch hers lightly, it was like lightening streaking through the sky. She pressed forward hungrily, accepting the swift pressure of his mouth against hers, the needy exchange that had her breasts swelling, nipples hardening.

His hands went immediately to her waist, his palms slipping down to cup her bottom in a tight grip. She moaned into his mouth, heard the distinct groan of a man on the edge. When he tore his mouth away, nipping the skin along her chin, down to her neck with teeth and tongue, Victoria couldn't help but gasp loudly. One of his hands had moved in a northerly direction by then, slipping beneath the rim of her top, the pads of his fingers rubbing warmly over her skin. It had been far too long since she'd felt the deliciousness of arousal, the intense waves of passion rippling through her body. And truth be told, she'd never felt either emotion quite like this.

"I'm going to make love to you all night," he said in a tone that had gone from its normal sexy timbre to a deep guttural rasp that stroked every nerve ending his kisses had already exposed.

That's when she noticed his shirt was open, his chest exposed. Dark skin was smooth, cut into perfect pectorals and sculpted abs. Her hands went there, had no other choice really, fingers moving shakily over his skin.

"Yes," was her breathy response, because really there was no other possible reply.

This was what she wanted. This was the reason she'd driven here without a second thought. She'd come to him when she probably should have gone straight to the police. She'd come to him and that was all that mattered right now.

"Not here. Not like this," he said, pulling his mouth away from her.

When she opened her eyes, letting them focus again, she saw his eyes had darkened, his lips slightly parted as he struggled for breath the same way she did.

"Upstairs, in my bed," he whispered, his hand coming up to cup her face. "Is that okay with you?"

She nodded. "That's okay with me."

Backing off his lap, she stood and waited for him to join her. Her heart startled a bit when he took her hand. It was a simple enough action, and after the heavy duty kissing and groping they'd been doing probably seemed a little on the chaste side. And yet, a fluttering started in her chest, slowly slithering down to settle into her belly.

Ben led the way out of the dining room, back through the living room towards the stairs. Luckily she'd looked around earlier, saw the lavishly decorated bachelor pad that screamed like a page from GQ. For now her gaze couldn't be torn away from the man in front of her, the way his jeans cupped his bottom, his thighs. The confident strides he took and, oh yes, the soft grasp by which he held her hand.

The upstairs hallway walls were flanked with pictures. They passed them and two partially opened doors, turning to walk through the third door on the left. A light was already on in this room, his bedroom. The king sized bed and plush dark brown carpet gave that fact away. Looking straight ahead she could see out to the Vegas night. Ben let her hand go then and walked across the room, pulling a string that drew custom blinds closed, casting a dimmer scene in the room. On his trek back he removed his shirt, tossing it so that it fell over the arm of a leather chair.

Victoria shifted, then let her hands grasp the hem of her shirt, about to pull it over her head.

"No," he said coming to stand in front of her quickly. "I'll do it. In here."

He had her hand again, this time walking her to a door across from his bed. After he touched a pad on the wall, recessed lighting showed his master bathroom, decorated in deep greens and soft browns. A sunken tub caught her attention, to be followed by the man that turned the knobs to run water into same. When he returned to her again, it was to lift her shirt slowly over her head.

"I've dreamed of this day for far too long to let it go fast," he said.

When her shirt was lying on the marble counter top beneath the mirror and next to the sink, his fingers whispered over the line of her neck.

"I want..." he began, then shook his head. "No, I need to see every inch of you."

He cupped her breasts in the strapless bra that held them high. Reaching around to her back, he undid the clasp, pulling the bra away to sit next to her shirt.

"Beautiful," he whispered, his gaze fixated on her breasts, his thumbs rubbing over her puckered nipples.

"Ben..." she gasped his name as her knees shook. She didn't know how much longer she would be able to stand upright with his intense perusal and electrifying touch.

"Shhh. It's okay, I've got you," he said taking a step closer, his hands moving to the button of her jeans. "Look at me, Victoria."

She did, and what she saw was a desire that most likely mirrored her own.

"We're going to be so damned good together," he told her before he leaned forward to kiss her lips.

Victoria nodded and whispered, "So damned good."

When he'd removed her jeans and panties, taking her shoes off and shaking his head at them before placing them on the floor close to the door, he stood again and stared at her.

"I knew you were fine. But now that seems to be an understatement."

Victoria took a step to him this time, reaching for the button on his jeans. "Maybe I'd like to see if you're as good looking as I've always thought."

He stood still while she pushed his jeans and his boxers down his hips and stepped out of his shoes so she could push them all the way off. He was gorgeous. That had been seen easily when he walked the length of the courtroom dressed in a suit. Or when he began his rebuttal and had to come out of the suit jacket. Even tonight, when she'd seen him in jeans and a shirt, he'd looked exceptionally enticing. But now standing here completely nude, there wasn't really a word to describe him. If someone had passed her a thesaurus she still wouldn't find an adequate enough description. Everything about him screamed perfect, just as she'd always thought. For a minute, she figured he was too good to be true, but he reached for her then. She felt the tingles of desire sifting up and down her spine and knew instinctively this was real. He was real and she was right here with him.

"Come on," he said when they'd both stared their fill and led her to the tub.

He washed her slowly, gently, methodically she thought. Each touch designed to nudge her excitement another notch. When he touched between her legs, she sighed and pressed closer to him. He'd grinned, that all-knowing I-know-I'm-the-ish grin he had, so she felt the need to get back at him. Using the bar of soap, she built a thick lather in her hands, then slipped them over his length. After only two strokes he was moaning, his eyes closing and Victoria's chest poked out with pride. Two could certainly play that game.

"Enough," he groaned grabbing her wrists and rinsing them both off without another word.

He'd dried her with a thick, fresh-smelling towel, then escorted her back into the bedroom. Going to his nightstand he pulled open a drawer to retrieve a condom. With quick motions he sheathed himself then looked up to find her staring at him.

In her mind she thought, "This is it." Her heart hammered in her chest as she looked at the large bed, then turned back to look at him. Ben pulled the towel she'd held around her, letting it fall to the floor. Then he grabbed her by the waist, lifting her so that her legs wrapped around him.

"Now," he growled, taking her mouth in a hungry kiss, tongue and teeth included.

The initial thrust was so quick, so potent, Victoria gasped, her nails digging deep into the skin of his shoulders. He was pumping before she could take her next breath and all she could do was sigh and hold on. When he finally let her fall back on the bed, her thighs were quivering, chest heaving. She reached for him immediately and he was there again, planted firmly inside her so perfectly she might even begin to believe they were meant to be together.

He moved slow, plunging deeper, holding her tighter than Victoria had ever been held before. In return, she held onto him, unwilling to let go of this foreign feeling coursing through her body. The room was bathed in light and the sound of their bodies mingling, their voices moaning. Her legs lifted of their own accord and he reached back to lock them just above his hips. Pushing up slightly, he changed the angle of his entrance and proceeded to drive her delirious with desire. It was when she felt herself slipping, the control she normally kept on a tight rein drifting slowly and surely out of her reach, that he said her name.

"Victoria. Open your eyes and look at me. I want to see your eyes when I come."

The words didn't make sense to her, hadn't been words she'd heard before. But she did as he asked. She looked right up at him, felt the tensing of his thighs and the decisive fill of his penis deep inside her. She gasped and let go, let all her worries and inhibitions where this man was concerned drift happily away on the tidal wave that culminated in a fantastic orgasm. He followed suit with a tense look on his face, a gasp and a deeply moaned, "Damn!"

CHAPTER 12

"The letter looks just like mine," Ben told Noah as he talked on his cellphone in the hallway just outside his bedroom.

Victoria was still asleep in his bed.

He'd done just as he promised and made love to her all night long. It was almost dawn when they'd both admitted getting some sleep might be good since they had work in a few hours. But Ben hadn't slept. He'd held her in his arms and waited until her breathing had steadied and he was sure she rested before slipping out of bed and giving Noah a call.

"I don't like you keeping evidence at your place," Noah told him. "Maybe you should bring them down here."

"There's a leak at the station, Noah. You know that. How else did Vega's men show up at every location the cops tried to hide Alayna Jonas? He's got cops on payroll as well as politicians."

"You keep saying that, which leads me to believe you're holding something back. What really happened between Vega and the congressman?" Noah asked for about the millionth time in the last couple of weeks.

Ben squeezed the bridge of his nose, shaking his head even though he knew Noah couldn't see him. "I'm not talking about the congressman's murder. I'm talking about Vega's killing Ebony and now turning his attention to Victoria. I won't let him touch her!" He'd been trying to keep his voice down, but his emotions were fierce.

"Don't forget he's got himself a little fixation with you as well. I gotta tell you, Ben, it doesn't make sense to me. Why's Vega so intent on getting to you?"

"Because I didn't take his case," Ben replied.

"That can't be all," was Noah's retort.

And he was right, Ben thought with an inward sigh. He wasn't telling Noah everything and the biggest reason was guilt, plain and simple.

"Look, you can take her letter to dust for prints but I doubt you'll find any but mine and hers. Then I want it back to keep with mine." The one he had locked in the safe beneath the bar in his dining room.

"And then what? Either she has to get a conviction or we need to get some concrete evidence to bring this bastard down."

"Or I could just kill him," Ben said, and was struck by how serious that statement was for him.

"You're not a killer," Noah replied seriously.

Ben inhaled deeply. "I'll do whatever it takes, Noah. Whatever it takes to keep her safe."

"That's my job. You just tell her to win this damned case."

The reply was emphatic and Ben wanted nothing more than to relay it to Victoria just that way. But because he was an attorney as well, because he knew the case was only as good as the jury panel selected, he wouldn't say that to her, wouldn't put that kind of pressure on her, not again. He realized that maybe he'd been hard on her in the diner and he'd told her she had to win the case.

"I'll drop the letter off to your house after work," Ben told him.

"Actually, I think it might look better if I picked it up from another location. If he's watching her, he's watching you. Let's not give anybody any unnecessary ammunition. How about you take it to your cousin and I'll stop by his office to retrieve it."

"Sure. I can do that." Even though he knew that would lead to even more questions.

Trent was no fool. He knew Ben was keeping something from him as well, something that involved this case. It was only a matter of time before his cousin pushed for the answers he wanted, or simply went out and found them himself. Hell, knowing Trent, he'd probably already started to look for the answers on his own. A fact Ben knew would lead to even more trouble.

"We shouldn't be seen together," Victoria stated the moment she emerged from the bathroom.

When Ben had returned to the bedroom, she hadn't been in the bed. He tried not to be disappointed by that, but realized it was already after 7 and they both needed to get ready to head into their offices. He'd already moved to the closet to retrieve his clothes for the day and was just deciding whether or not he should join her in the shower when he heard it shut off.

In the next seconds, as he sat on the side of the bed waiting for her, he wondered what this morning after confrontation would be like. Would she have regrets? Would she curse him out? Would she be nervous or embarrassed? None of those reactions mattered. Ben could deal with them all. What he couldn't and did not want to see was that lace of fear that had shimmered through the alluring depths of her eyes when she'd shown up on his doorstep.

The door opened, light pouring into the bedroom, and she stepped out. Her words came before she took another step, taking him only slightly off guard.

"You might be right to some extent," he conceded. "But I have no intention of keeping the fact that we're together now a secret."

She shook her head, wisps of hair that she'd combed back into a smooth twist brushing over her forehead. "I don't recall saying we're together."

Ben stood then. He wore only his boxers as he crossed the small length of floor to stand in front of her. "You didn't. But I'd think our actions last night speak louder than your words this morning."

She lifted both hands, stopping his next forward step, planting her palms firmly on his chest. "This will have to wait, at least until after the trial. I can't afford to be distracted, and if Vega's following us both around, neither can you."

He clasped her wrists, brought her hands up to kiss the backs one at a time. "Partially correct again."

"Ben," she started.

"Look, I see where you're coming from. But we've got to find some common ground here. I've waited, we've both waited, a long time to see where this thing between us is going to go. I'm not thrilled about the idea of waiting longer."

"Now is just not a good time. I still don't even know why Vega would send me this note or how you're connected besides the fact that you used to represent him. It just doesn't add up."

With a sigh, because he knew he'd have to do this sooner or later, he led her to the bed where they both sat.

"I told Vega I wasn't going to represent him on the second trial, the day you served me with the new trial notice. He wasn't thrilled with the idea."

"Did he threaten you? Because if he did, we can have him arrested on those charges as well?" she asked, real concern etching her face. The face that was free of any makeup and even prettier than he could have imagined.

Ben shook his head. "That's the thing, he didn't threaten me that day. He gave some half-assed type of warning, but he didn't threaten me with any real conviction. He watched me leave with a sort of smirk on his face and then I didn't hear from him again. Until later that evening." He took a deep breath and ran both hands down his face.

"There was a note stuck on my windshield when I left my house to go to the gym. I'd seen Vega maybe three hours before at the parking lot across from my office. I was on my way to the courthouse to file my motion to strike appearance and he was there."

She kept a serious face, even though her shoulders sagged just a bit at his words. "A note like the one I received last night? What did it say?"

"It was an address. I ignored it. The next day my assistant was found murdered. Her body was at the location on the note."

"My god, Ben. I had no idea. Why hasn't Vega been arrested for her murder? Have you given the note to the cops?"

Ben was already shaking his head. "I have a friend that's a detective. I told him about the letter and I told my cousin who is a private investigator. I don't want to take it to the cops officially until we have enough evidence to charge and convict Vega. I don't want his ass slipping through any loopholes this time."

"Did he slip through a loophole the last time? Is that how you got him off?"

She didn't say it, her voice didn't give away any hint of belief to what she was saying. Still, Ben was offended. When he turned to look at her, it was to find her staring intently at him. She looked the same, but there was something more. Her beauty was deeper this morning. It wasn't as stark and as assaulting as before because he'd actually gone behind that layer with her. Last night, as he'd slipped in and out of her, Ben had felt something he'd never felt with another female. Each time she said his name, rubbed her hands over his body, let her lips be taken by his, a tightening had increased in his chest. For one brief second as they'd lay waiting to fall asleep, he'd imagined that tightening being her fist around his heart.

Linc had warned him that when Donovans fell, they fell hard. He hadn't tried to deny that fact before; he just hadn't experienced the fall yet. Until now.

"I tried the case I had. I countered the evidence Jules presented and I implored the jury to find my client not guilty. They couldn't decide. So despite how it might seem, Victoria, the mistrial wasn't a win for me either."

Her head nodded slightly as if she understood his rationale. "Do you think he killed the congressman and his wife?"

Ben didn't answer immediately. In fact, he looked away from her.

Victoria's fingers were soft, her grasp firm as she turned his chin until they were face-to-face once more. "You do, don't you? You think your client is a killer."

Ben pulled away and stood. He walked over to the window but didn't open the blinds. Victoria's car would be parked out front. His car was in the garage. If Vega were watching, if one of his men were watching, they knew she was here.

"He's not my client anymore," he said, moving from the window to the nightstand where he'd laid his phone. He picked it up and hit speed dial.

"Yeah. Victoria's going to need an escort home. Right, you were already on it." He sighed and disconnected the phone, then turned back to her.

"Who did you just call and why do I need an escort?"

"Look, Victoria, there's a lot going on here. A lot that you don't know."

She'd stood now and had folded her arms across her chest. "Then tell me so I will know."

He didn't immediately respond. Didn't know where to possibly begin.

"Oh. I see." She was nodding and Ben was feeling regret at the same time. "You get to know everything. You get to tell me what you want when you want and I'm supposed to follow your lead. I'm supposed to take all your information and try this case. I'm not supposed to ask questions or do anything to help in this situation at all. Am I correct?"

"You're not correct," he told her. "Not entirely."

"Okay, well, let me just clarify this situation for you Mr. All Mighty Donovan. I do not now nor have I ever needed your help to win a case. I can get a conviction on Vega without any of your top secret help. And as far as this 'thing' between us. Consider it an itch that has been thoroughly scratched. Should it resurface for you I suggest you look elsewhere for relief."

She'd spoken and turned to storm out of the room before Ben could say a word. What he did was curse, long and fluently at the mess he'd made of things in the span of about twenty minutes.

By the time he made it down the stairs, Victoria had already found her purse and was looking around in the dining room, moving things out of her way, not giving a damn whether she broke something in the process. She was so angry at him. No, she was pissed at him and angry at herself. What had she been thinking by coming here? How had she thought he could help the situation when he was the one who had created it? Even though she hadn't known that then. Whatever. Now she wanted to find that note and get the hell out of this house!

"Victoria, listen, it's not what you're thinking," he said from behind her.

"It is exactly what I'm thinking. Exactly what I've thought since the beginning. You like to control everything as if it's your job to run everybody else's life. Well, I'm not a part of the Ben Donovan harem or fan club and I certainly don't walk to the beat of your drummer. Where the hell is my letter?"

"I took it and I'm going to give it to my friend the homicide detective today. He'll test it for fingerprints, then return it to me."

"To you? For what? You're not investigating this case or any case involving Vega for that matter since you backed out of his trial."

"I'm still working on the case," he said, solemnly folding his arms across his chest.

He still wore only his boxers and still looked way too attractive to ignore. But Victoria was determined to ignore him. Her sanity depended on it.

"Why?" she asked simply. "Tell me why you still have your hands in this or I swear I'll go to the police with everything I know."

He took a step towards her, then stopped. A muscle in his jaw twitched, his eyes going a deep dark color that looked almost lethal.

"You go to the police and you'll be dead by the end of the day. I think Vega has someone on the inside at the police station. I also believe he killed the congressman and his wife and Ebony Reece, my assistant. Now," he continued slowly. "I need for you to prepare for this case like you normally would. When I find Alayna Jonas, I will bring her to you. Her testimony will convict Vega and he'll go to jail."

She shook her head because it still didn't make sense. There was more he wasn't telling her. Ben Donovan would not do all of this just so she could get a win under her belt.

"You know why he killed the congressman, don't you? You know there's more to this case than what's been reported, but if you expose the truth others will be hurt. Others who you either care about or need to protect to save your ass."

He didn't speak at all and the quiet of the room seemed to engulf them.

"Are you involved in this somehow, Ben? Before I say or do another thing where you're concerned, I need to know," she told him in a voice that to her ears sounded quiet, still.

"What I know could get a lot of people in a lot of trouble, myself included. Is that what you wanted to hear?"

"Dammit!" she swore and despised herself just a little more at this point. Not only had she ignored her brain and followed her body into his bed, now she was putting herself in the direct position to become an accessory to heaven knows.

"I haven't broken any laws, if that's what you're thinking. But I do have information that could be detrimental to a lot of people. I'm just trying to do the right thing, in the right way. I'm asking for your help."

He'd come to stand right in front of her by now. She didn't know exactly when he'd moved or why she hadn't backed up or did something to get away from him. But now it was too late. He was standing there, his arms were extending, his palms cupping her face.

"I need your help, Victoria. And in return I will keep you safe. I won't let Vega touch you," he whispered.

"I don't know how I can help you when I don't know what you're hiding. And I'm not afraid of Vega."

"I don't want you to be afraid of him, Victoria. I want you to trust me," he told her earnestly.

He pulled her closer and when she thought he would have kissed her, he didn't. He touched his forehead to hers, holding them together as if the possibility of them separating was too painful to comprehend.

CHAPTER 13

"Are you out of your mind fraternizing with the enemy?" Jules came screaming into Victoria's office about twenty minutes after she'd arrived at work.

"Excuse me?" she'd said, setting down the pen she'd been writing with and letting her hands fall flat on her desk.

His tie was crocked and hanging around his neck more like a noose than an accessory. Sweat peppered his brow and his cheeks were ruby red. She'd seen him flustered during and after his trials before, but nothing like this. Still, she remained calm, or she gave the impression that she was remaining calm.

"What the hell are you doing having lunch with Donovan? This damn picture is all over the papers. Do you see the headline?" he asked as he tossed the folded newspaper onto her desk.

DEFENSE AND PROSECUTION TEAM UP FOR A SECOND SHOT
AT ALLEGED MURDERER

Crap!

"It was just lunch," she replied stoically. "I am allowed to have lunch."

"Not with defense counsel from the biggest case in this office at the moment," Jules yelled back.

"He doesn't represent Vega anymore."

"Right, that's what the record says. But how do you think this looks? How do you think this makes our office look? No answer? I'll tell you. It makes us look like a bunch of incompetent jackasses, running around grasping at straws to try and get this guy locked up for good! And I don't like it. I don't like it at all!"

"Are you finished?" she asked, still using the calm voice that he couldn't tell was about to break. "Because if you are, I'd like to address this situation from my point of view."

Jules didn't say anything, just waved a hand in her general direction. An action she considered rude, as rude as his yelling and this entire out-of-control rant he had going on.

"How I try this case will depend on the evidence and witnesses I have to work with. I do not now, nor have I ever relied on help from outside counsel to do my job. If you think I'm not doing my job accordingly, file a report and have me removed from the case. But do not come in here questioning my integrity again."

Jules was her immediate supervisor and wanted to run for DA. And if that depended on her vote, he was most likely never going to sit in that office. Victoria loved her job and she did it well. What she would not do is be disrespected in the process. If that meant she would lose the job she loved, then so be it.

He'd stopped pacing and stood right in front of her desk, flattening his palms over the files she had and leaning forward so that he was closer to her face. "What did you talk about at lunch? What did he say to you and how long have you two been seeing each other?"

Did he not just hear what she'd said?

"What I do on my personal time is none of your business," she replied coolly.

"You little bitch! Do you know how important this case is? Do you know what's at stake here?"

He was visibly shaking now, the sweat that had been just beads now running in rivulets down his cheek. He looked like he was about to have a heart attack right there in front of her.

"I'm going to ask you to leave my office." She was so angry she shook on the inside.

Jules looked like he was about to say something else but Victoria stood, putting her hand in his face to stop him. "I'm only going to ask you that one time. Next I'm going to call security and file a formal complaint against you for verbal assault. Now. Get. Out!"

Jules snatched his hand away from her desk, pulling the files and their contents with him to fall in the floor.

"If you mess this up, I swear I'll hunt you down! I'll hunt you and I'll—"

"You'll what?" she inquired. "Say it right here, right now so I can call the police."

"Just wrap this case up and get the conviction!" he yelled, finally pushing the door back so hard the knob went straight through the cheap drywall that separated one office from the other.

When she sank back into her chair, the inner shaking had broken through. Her hands shook and her heart hammered. Not out of fear but out of fury. She'd wanted to wrap her hands around Jules' fat neck for the way he dared to speak to her. Her temples began a dull throb as she realized she wanted desperately to do something else. She wanted to call and tell Ben what had just happened.

"You can't ignore my calls if I'm standing in your face," Alma Donovan said about five minutes after she walked into Ben's office.

Ben had been reviewing the statement of charges for one of his drug clients and had vaguely heard the bell to the front door chime. His office building was secure: Everyone had to sign in and show identification at the front door before the guards would call upstairs to let him know who was there to see him. He hadn't received a call, and had been so focused on his work he had barely realized someone had come into the office. Considering the current circumstances, he should have been on higher alert, but he also knew that there was a plainclothes guard standing right outside of his office door as well as Devlin, who was no doubt close by. The guy really was like a shadow, one you never saw until you absolutely needed him. Both of them would have seen his mother and not bothered to stop her entrance.

Alma Donovan wore one of her signature business suits, this one in a pale pink color, the jacket with short sleeves and the skirt with some type of flourish at her knees. Under her right arm she clutched a leather purse in a pearl white color that matched her shoes and the pearl choker at her neck. She looked like a professional, which she was since she was the president of not one but two non-profit companies.

"Hi Mom," was his reply to whatever she'd just said to him. She was standing at the end of his desk with one hand on her hip giving him that glare that said, "You are so in trouble".

"Don't 'Hi Mom' me," she started by slapping her purse onto the end of his desk and yanking one of the guest chairs closer so she could sit. "I've been calling you and calling you since I saw the paper this morning and haven't received an answer yet. Not even a response to my text messages. And that's just rude Benjamin. One hundred percent rude to not respond when there's no real reason why you cannot."

"I'm working, Mom. I have cases to try, clients to represent," he told her, knowing full well that excuse wasn't going to fly with her. "And actually, I have an appointment in a half hour." Ben looked at his watch, then back up to his mother.

He loved her dearly, had never met another woman like her. And lying to her went against everything he'd ever believed in, but if she asked him about that Vega case he couldn't tell her what was really going on. Ben didn't have any idea how she could have found out since only Trent and Max knew. But both of them were married and could have easily told their wives under that full disclosure rule that came with the marriage vows. One of the woman would have definitely wanted to tell Alma.

"Then you have thirty minutes to tell me exactly what's going on between you and that pretty little prosecutor you had lunch with yesterday."

She spoke so matter-of-factly Ben had to do a double-take before getting the full jist of what she'd said.

"How did you know I had lunch with Victoria Lashley?" he asked, giving her his full attention now.

"Everybody in town knows that was a perfect picture of the two of you smiling at lunch. I told your father we should frame it since we never see you with your females."

Ben didn't mean to be rude, but his fingers moved quickly over his keyboard as he pulled up the local newspaper and searched for the picture his mother referred to and...dammit!

He'd thought he'd held that curse in as he slammed back in his chair. But the way Alma's eyebrows raised, her lips stilling, said he'd mumbled it aloud.

"Sorry," he said.

"I take it you didn't want people to know you were dating her. I can see that since she's prosecuting that case you just finished with. But listen son, the heart does not take politics or any of these other prejudicial things in mind. It wants who it wants and there's not a whole lot you can do about changing that."

"We were just having lunch, Mom. We were discussing our work. It wasn't really a date," he told her and felt good about that being basically the truth.

"You could probably make other people believe that, Benjamin, but not me. A mother knows these things." She paused then, watching him as if he didn't need to say a word for her to know exactly what he was thinking and feeling.

"But you already know how you feel about her. You know but you're not sure about her feelings. Is that it?" she asked.

Ben looked down at his mother's hands, clasped neatly in her lap, the sparkling diamond wedding ring set on the left hand and a jewel encrusted anniversary ban on the right. Those had been symbols of his father's love for his mother, but Ben knew Everette and Alma's love went much deeper than jewelry. Just as he'd watched his Aunt Beverly and Uncle Henry show how much they loved and respected each other by staying in a healthy relationship and keeping their family close. His cousins had wives, loved unconditionally, protected with a fierceness Ben hadn't felt before. So his mother was absolutely correct, he knew how he felt about Victoria, had known for quite some time now.

"We met in law school," he began. "She's still too hung up on the Donovan reputation to see what a great catch I am," he finished with a smile that had his mother responding likewise.

"She looks like a really smart girl. I'm sure she'll come around."

"I hope so," he replied, still leaning on the honesty fence. "But we both have work and that's a little distracting right now."

Alma nodded. "You got out of that case just in time. That man's no good."

"I know. I'm thinking now I should have never agreed to represent him in the first place."

"No," Alma shook her head adamantly. "Don't do that. The past is in the past for a reason. It's over and done with, regrets are a waste of time. You did your job and you'll continue to do your job."

Ben leaned forward, let his elbows rest on his desk, his fingers a steeple at his chin. "But what if the job I'm doing is all wrong? What if I shouldn't be helping criminals get off?"

"When you first came to us and told us what you planned to do with your law degree, your father and I asked you if you were sure. You said you were sure, that you wanted to be one of the people who gave hope to the hopeless, who helped those others thought were helpless. And that's what you do, Ben. You give people what they're legally entitled to in this country, a right to a fair trial and unbiased legal representation."

"But at what cost?"

"Only at the cost you burden yourself with. If you don't do this job, someone else will. Someone who's not as good and not as honest as you are. Is that what you want?"

"I want to feel good about what I do and the people I'm helping. Ramone Vega is not someone I can say that about."

"Not everybody's guilty," Alma replied with a knowing smile.

Ben grinned. "Man, I must have been some kind of advocate for defense attorneys. I remember saying that too."

"You're an advocate because you believe in what you do. Don't let one bad apple dissuade you from your calling. And don't let circumstances keep you from the woman you love."

Hours after his mother had left the office, Ben was still thinking about her words. For all that he and probably any grown-up hated to admit that their parents were right, Alma normally was. Today had been no different. Ben wasn't quitting his job; he just wasn't going to represent scum like Ramone Vega anymore and let said scum keep him from doing what he knew was right.

With that in mind, he picked up the phone and made one of the toughest calls of his career.

CHAPTER 14

The text had come about five minutes before Victoria pulled to stop in the parking spot in front of her house. It had been an extremely long day and she'd worked extra hours in the hopes of preparing herself for next week's trial, all while still fuming at the audacity of Jules and the way he'd spoken to her.

She was tired and hungry and not really looking forward to at least two more hours of reading, writing and preparing. But Ben was sitting on her front steps, a bunch of colorful balloons tied to her railing. Victoria grabbed her briefcase and climbed out of the car, pressing the alarm button on her keychain to lock all the doors and enable the alarm.

Walking up the walkway without smiling was difficult. He looked like a delivery guy, dressed in faded blue jeans and a fitted black t-shirt, motorcycle helmet painted in bright red, black and silver between his legs. His beard was thin and freshly trimmed, casting a dark and dangerous look to his facial features. Then again, she'd never seen a delivery guy with a diamond encrusted Cartier watch on one wrist and a top of the line racing bike as his mode of transportation.

"Working late?" he said as she came closer to the steps.

She lifted her briefcase and sighed. "Upcoming trial."

He nodded knowingly. "Got time for a break?"

"Not really," was her instant reply. "You on your way to a birthday party?"

He smiled and stood up, his entire six plus feet towering over her even more as he stood two steps above her.

"I thought they looked more cheerful than flowers," he told her while untying the balloon bouquet from the railing. "Do you like them?"

Victoria couldn't help but smile when he thrust all the balloons right in her face. "I like them alright," she commented while swatting them away. "But I'd like to get into the house so I can put my bags down."

"Here, let's do an exchange," he offered.

Ben stepped down, taking her briefcase and her purse and giving her the strings tied together that kept the balloons from taking a sky ride. Victoria was still smiling as she moved up the steps and unlocked her door.

"By the way, I forgot to thank you for having my window fixed," she told him when they'd both walked inside and closed the door behind them.

She let the balloons go and they all disbursed, heading right to the ceiling, blues, greens, yellows and reds floating in a happy circle around her living room.

"No problem. I wanted to install a security system on the house but I wasn't sure if you were a homeowner or not."

Victoria didn't believe him for one second. If Ben knew about the incident with the window in the first place, before she'd even been taken to the hospital, and knew enough to get it fixed without her consent, she was sure he knew that she was only renting this house.

"Right. Well, thank you for not doing that. I'd like to make that choice on my own," she told him anyway.

He nodded, placing her bags down by the entryway into the living room. "So why don't you go up and slip into something comfortable and come for a ride with me?"

"A ride?" she asked startled. "With you? On your bike?"

"Unless you want me to carry you. I mean, I can, but I think you'd have more fun on the bike."

He was too good looking for his own good. And too smooth. Already her tired bones felt relief even though she hadn't done anything to relieve them. The heaviness in her shoulders felt lifted as she stared back at his cheerful gleam. He looked like he didn't have a care in the world and it was starting to feel like it might be contagious.

"Give me five minutes," she said, turning away from him to head up the steps.

She was halfway up the steps when he yelled, "I'll give you ten while I make this phone call." Ben moved deeper into the living room, standing by the window that had recently been repaired. "Yeah," he said when Devlin answered. "We're heading out for a ride."

"You think that's wise considering the circumstances?" Devlin asked.

"I think it's necessary," was Ben's quick response. He couldn't stay away from Victoria. And if they were in the house together they'd certainly find a very physical way to pass the time. But their thoughts would inevitably return to the obvious.

"Ace picked up a tail on her this evening. White minivan parked four doors down."

Ben frowned, looking down Victoria's street. "Where are you?"

"I circled the block after Ace texted me. You were still sitting on her steps like a lovesick puppy. So I pulled up behind the bastard as he parked. Tags run back to an auto dealership owned by Peña. My bet is there's a rookie behind the wheel trying to earn his stripes. She's his first job."

"It'll be his last," Ben swore.

Dev agreed. "Go for your ride. I've got your back."

"Where's Ace?"

"I'll tell him to stay on the house until you get back."

Ben could see the white minivan down the street. The windows weren't tinted so the two men sitting in the front seats were clearly visible, definitely amateurs. They wore dark sunglasses and black baseball caps and a part of him hoped like hell they made a move on Victoria tonight. He hadn't had a chance to get to the gym in the last couple of days so adrenaline buzzed along his system like an addict needing a fix. He'd beat the hell out of them with his bare hands.

"Where's Trent?"

"He's following up on your earlier call to City Hall. If everything pans out, we might have this situation under wraps before the trial starts on Monday."

Ben nodded, one hand gripping the cellphone at his ear, the other clenching into a fist at his side. "That sounds good to me."

"And if not—" Devlin replied, purposely letting his words drift into the silence.

"I'm ready," Ben stated slowly, lethally.

"So am I," Dev replied.

"You're ready for what?" Victoria asked from behind him.

Ben clicked off his cellphone, stuffing it back into the case at his hip. He turned to face her and had to swallow quickly before speaking. She wore jeans again, these as form-fitting as the others she'd had last night. Her t-shirt was navy blue with tiny rhinestones edging the neckline. On her feet were black Timberland boots that looked way too sexy to be functional. Her head was tilted slightly as she arched an eyebrow in anticipation of his answer.

"I'm ready for our ride," was his reply.

She was skeptical, he could tell, but she brushed it off. "Well, let's get this over with. I'm starving."

Moving closer, he took her hand and led them to the door. "So I'll entertain you then I'll feed you. Deal?"

Going through the door ahead of him, she turned back, resignation clear on her face. "You've got a deal."

⁘⁘⁘⁘⁘

The warm breeze felt like heaven against the bare skin of Victoria's arms and cheeks. It had been years since she'd ridden on the back of a motorcycle, and truthfully the last ride was nothing to write home about. But this one, she'd known the second he'd suggested it, would be memorable.

It was with Ben, after all.

Her fingers tingled as she'd wrapped her arms around his waist and held tight. He drove with speed and agility, like this bike was actually an extension of him. It moved right along with his body, the power thrusting against her thighs and buttocks. There was a freedom here. A strange sense of weightlessness that made everything else seem insignificant. Laying her cheek against his back, she embraced that feeling, let it engulf her and prayed she could hold on to it just a little bit longer.

Time had seemed to stand still except that the sun had almost finished its descent as the bike came to a slow stop. Victoria heard the engine silence and felt a shift as he put down the stand. She thought he would get off immediately, but he sat there, his hands falling from the handlebars to cover hers at his waist.

Even that felt good. It felt safe.

And that made her more nervous than she cared to admit.

She pulled her hands away and maneuvered herself off the bike. Her fingers tingled she suspected from the loss of warmth after touching him. In response she thrust them into her front pockets and walked a few steps. They were at some type of canyon. She hadn't been paying attention to where he'd been driving, which really was unlike her. But this was an open space, desert-like with its dry dirt ground and parched palm trees stretching skyward.

The view was magnificent, capping the tops of the buildings that decorated the infamous Strip. The city skyline looked like the tiny depictions captured inside snow globes. There were no fake white flakes to accentuate the scene, just the silky haze of dry heat settling over the surrounding land. It would be quite breathtaking, if the man who'd brought her here hadn't already stolen her breath.

"We're safe here," she heard him say from behind. "Nobody followed us."

"How do you know that?" she asked, not that what she was thinking had anything to do with someone following them.

In the serenity of the ride or from being close to this man, she wasn't sure which, she hadn't thought about their current situation. Which just proved how being around him was throwing her off balance.

He removed his helmet, placing it on the handle bar before swaying a leg over the bike stand.

"Remember I told you my cousin's a private investigator? Well, he's assigned someone to watch us until this situation with Vega is over."

"Oh great," she said, shivering even though it was anything but cold. "So I'm being watched by even more people?"

"Just for your protection," he added, but the words gave little consolation to her whirling emotions.

Victoria simply nodded. It was no use arguing this with him. He acknowledged early on that he felt she needed protection. And in light of who they were dealing with, she wasn't foolish enough to deny it.

"Right. Protection."

"They won't find us here. And if they did they'd have to get through Dev and his crew first. So you can relax."

She probably could have if he hadn't come up behind her, touching his hands to her shoulders.

"I'm not good at this," she heard herself admitting. It was like that with him. She said things she shouldn't have, did things she never thought about doing.

"Come on inside and you can tell me what you're not good at."

Inside? Victoria turned around again and was face to face with him. She was about to say there was no inside to go to, but just over his shoulder, about thirty feet away, there was a little cabin. It almost looked out of place, as if it had been dropped down in the middle of the desert by mistake. Then again, there was a quiet appeal to the mostly wooden structure enhanced by intricate stone work that could use some cleaning.

"You're really cute when you're baffled," he said, tweaking her nose, then gathering her hand in his and walking towards the cabin.

Once they were inside she pulled her hand from his as he closed the door, then took a few steps away and reached for something she prayed was a light.

"I don't like being baffled," she admitted and continued to look around, trying to soak in her surroundings this time.

"Does that mean you don't like being cute?"

She wasn't totally shocked to see him standing right in front of her, a lit lantern held between them. The grin on his face should have been expected. It shouldn't have slid along the base of her spine like a soft touch, causing ripples of pleasure to float through her body.

"You like being cute enough for both of us," she said with a sigh. "Ben, what are we doing?"

The small room was further illuminated by another lantern Ben seemed to know exactly where to find. The kitchen wasn't modern by any means, but she could see where repairs were being instituted. A brand new stainless steel refrigerator was squeezed into a tight nook in the corner. The wood was dark, cherry maybe, and looked to be in good condition. That and the stone work outside was probably why the dwelling was being rehabbed as opposed to demolished.

"I don't know about you but I needed a break. From the office, the cases, everything. I'm thinking of taking a long vacation really soon. In the meantime, I just wanted to unwind a bit. I bought this place about a year ago because I like the open space to be able to ride."

He moved as he talked, getting down glasses from a cabinet whose handle looked as if it would fall off the very next time someone pulled on it. The refrigerator was fully stocked from what she could see, but he opened and closed it so quickly, grabbing two bottled waters without any thought at all.

"I meant what are 'we' doing?" Victoria smoothed her hands over her hair. She'd pulled it all back when she'd changed her clothes, but was sure the wind from the ride had ruffled it to a perfect mess. Not that she was worried about her looks. She was more worried about her state of mind. "I thought we were going to wait until after this case to do whatever it is we started last night. Then I come home to find you on my steps holding enough balloons to cheer up the entire pediatric wing at the hospital."

"Did they cheer you up?" he asked when he'd finished filling both glasses with water and pushed one towards her.

He sat at the small round table and nodded towards the only other chair in the room for her to do the same.

She sighed and took a seat, moreso because her legs were feeling a little watery being on solid ground after the long ride. "That's not the point."

Ben took a long drink, then set his half empty glass down. "It's precisely the point. If something cheers you up, or makes you happy, you should just go with it. Don't question it because they'll be plenty of time for questions later."

"Who told you that?"

He shrugged. "Figured it out all by myself."

Ben didn't grin this time, although she fully expected him to. The finale to his charming words was always a dashing smile. This time he looked at her seriously.

"There's enough going on to keep us both stressed. I wanted a moment without all the worry and concentration to relax and enjoy life."

"And you had to pick me up for that?"

For the first time in a very long time Ben looked agitated. The carefree guy she thought she knew looked as if there were more going on inside his mind except plans for the next good time.

"Why are you so distrustful?" he asked. "Who broke your heart?"

She clamped her lips down tight. That wasn't a question she expected, nor was it one she thought she could easily answer. How could she tell him it wasn't what he thought? That it wasn't some guy that she'd fancied herself in love with then found out he was the scum of the earth. That her track record with men was severely less decorated than his with women.

"It's not about my heart being broken. I can handle heartbreak." That wasn't a lie. Hadn't she handled her father's death like a champion? Sure she had. That's what all her teachers had told her when she'd come right back to school the day after the funeral.

"I bet you believe you can handle anything," he told her, almost as if he were reading her mind.

"I don't think I'm invincible, if that's what you're trying to say. I'm just confident. I know what I want and how I plan to get it." And she didn't need Ben Donovan trying to tell her differently.

"That's fair," he said with a nod.

Then he reached for her hands. She wanted to pull away but they'd been resting on the table and she didn't really feel like being difficult. For the first time in Victoria's life, she was thoroughly confused. The right way to act or thing to say wasn't naturally on the tip of her tongue. And for her that was very problematic.

"I'm just not sure this is the right time for us," she admitted and figured the truth was probably the best way to go. "There's so much other crap going on."

She'd given him her hands and loved the way they fit perfectly into his. His fingers rubbed over her skin and she looked down to see them intertwined. They looked like they belonged.

"We make the time right. We make the rules," he said seriously. "I'm not giving Vega anything, not my job, my life, my happiness, nothing. And neither are you."

His words had been said with such conviction, the deep timbre of his voice rubbing over her body like warm oil. He expected her to say something to that or maybe act some sort of way. Victoria was almost positive he didn't expect what she said.

"I want you to make love to me, Ben. Right here in your little cabin," she said after a moment's thought.

She hadn't really expected them herself. The words didn't sound like anything that she'd ever said in her life, anything she'd ever thought of saying before. But as they'd slipped from her lips, Victoria knew they were the exact thing she wanted to say, that they were her true feelings, and hadn't she decided to go with the truth?

"Ask and you shall receive," he whispered, keeping one of her hands as he stood from his chair.

It only took a step and a half before he was standing right in front of her, pulling her to her feet.

"This time won't be slow. It can't be," he told her as he stared down at her, his eyes darkening with desire.

She licked her lips, swallowed deeply, and let her body press willingly into his. "I didn't ask for slow. I asked for right now."

❧❧❧

Victoria didn't think her feet had touched the ground, or at least she hadn't felt any ground beneath her as Ben led her into a bedroom that seemed much larger than the size of the cabin had appeared. Clearly it stretched long and beyond what could be first seen upon driving up.

Measurements, room sizes, furniture, rehab projects, all of that was forgotten the second Ben's lips touched hers. His lips covered hers, his tongue stroking along her own, everything else slipping away like puffy white clouds on a bright summer's day. His hands ran up and down her body, slipping beneath her t-shirt to coast along bare skin. Her own fingers tightened over his shoulders and down his back. She pressed against him, needing to be closer, to feel as if they were one.

It was strange, this longing feeling, to her. Like she needed him more each time she saw him. The attraction to him had grown over the years, along with her resolve to steer clear of the attractive playboy. Only now Victoria couldn't let her mind rule, not in this case. There was definitely something between her and Ben Donovan, something that was proving a lot stronger than anything she'd ever faced in her life. They kissed as if they'd been doing it for years, a moan slipping through her lips as his tongue now traced a heated path along her jaw line. She arched her back, letting him lift one leg up to wrap around his waist.

"I love the feel of you in my arms, the taste of you on my lips," he whispered along the line of her neck.

"I do too, Ben. Oh god, I do too." It was a wanton admission, an honest one, and when he lifted her into his arms and then turned to gently lay her onto the bed, her body screamed for more.

He removed her boots first, then her socks, cupping one foot in his hand and lovingly kissing her toes. He rubbed along the length of her foot, kneading his thumbs into her arch. Waves of pleasure seemed to float from the tip of her toes up to her ankle, spreading through her calves to her thighs and ultimately settling in a heated pool of desire at her moistened center.

"Whatever I can do, whatever I can say is all for your pleasure, baby."

His breath was warm, tickling her skin. His tone was deep, slightly commanding and damned enticing.

"I never thought it would be like this," she whispered breathlessly, her fingers clenching in the sheets beneath her.

"Always, baby. It can always be like this."

It was a promise one that clenched around her heart like tightened fingers. When he moved up her legs continuing to massage the tired muscles there, she could do nothing but moan. Deftly he undid the snap at her jeans, unzipped them and began pushing them over her hips. She lifted to accommodate him and had to catch her breath when he snagged her bikini at the same time, leaving her completely bare from the waist down.

This wasn't like last night's intimate session. It was still hot and made her heady with desire, but there was more. The difference was her and how her body was even more sensitive to his touch. So entranced in the memory and the anticipation of their joining once more, she hadn't felt him spread her legs wide or noticed that he'd dipped his head low until it was too late.

Ben kissed her most intimate part the same way he'd kissed her lips, with intense fervor and experienced flare. Her thighs shook as he licked along the plumped folds of her center. She moaned because it was the only thing left to do. Her body felt heavy with desire, sinking into the cushiony softness of the bed. When he lifted her thighs onto his shoulders, pulling her into him like she was a decadent dessert, she fell completely apart. Tremors of pleasure coursed through her body.

Her eyes were glazed seconds later as he pushed away from her to remove his own clothes. She watched as he stripped, her eyes absorbing and memorizing every gloriously dark-skinned inch of him, from his taut pectorals to his sculpted abs. When he pushed his jeans over his hips, his boxers going south with them, she gulped. Ben Donovan was a magnificently built specimen with muscled thighs, a gorgeous ass and further endowments that made him an excellent candidate for a Playgirl centerfold. She grabbed the edge of her shirt, pulling it over her head quickly, unable and unwilling to keep her desire for him at bay.

"Take off the bra," he instructed, and she sat up, reaching her arms behind her back to do as he requested.

"Cup your breasts in your hands."

He was watching her, his hooded gaze sending spikes of heat straight to her nipples where he stared. She put her hands to her breasts, cupped their weight and let her thumbs rub over her nipples.

Ben licked his lips.

"Squeeze harder."

As he spoke, his hand went to his rigid arousal, grasping its length with all the power the man exuded.

Of their own accord, her legs spread open and one hand slipped down her torso. Victoria had no idea what she was doing. She wasn't a stranger to pleasuring herself, especially with her demanding work schedule, but she'd never in all her life imagined she'd be performing such acts in front of a man.

"Lay back and show me," he virtually growled, coming closer to the bed. "Show me now."

She lay back against the pillows, one hand still massaging her breast, the other slipping through the damp folds of her center. She opened herself and gasped at the hungry look covering Ben's face as he climbed onto the bed with her.

"I like what I see," he murmured, still stroking his length.

She sighed. "I like what I see."

"Then take it," he told her, coming onto his knees, positioning himself between her legs.

The hand that was on her breast retreated and she extended her arms, reaching for him.

"Take it," he told her again when he released his length. She sat up slowly, licking her lips as she spotted the glistening bead of arousal at his tip.

Her mouth watered when she took him in both her hands, rubbing from the base to the tip. He sucked in a breath and she trembled, dipping her head to lick away the droplet of pleasure. She moaned as his fingers scraped along her scalp, his hands tugging insistently against her head. She kissed him as he'd kissed her, loved his masculine scent as it permeated her nostrils.

When he'd finally had enough of her blissful torture, Ben pushed her mouth away from him. He'd never been addicted to any type of substance, but had to believe that this was what withdrawal felt like, the clenching in his chest and deep sense of loss he was now experiencing.

She hadn't said slow. Had only commanded that she wanted him. He couldn't wait to give her what she wanted and, sinking his thick length into her waiting center, he could do nothing more than whisper her name.

With her ankles resting on his shoulders, Ben pumped into her mercilessly, searching desperately for the intense release he knew was stored inside. Below he watched as her breasts jiggled with his ministrations, her mouth was agape, her eyes focused on him. She gave as well as she received, pumping with his strokes, touching her nipples once more, enticing him as he loved her.

Loved her.

The words echoed around in Ben's mind as the feel of his erection delving deep and slipping out slowly, being grasped by her hot and wet walls, lulled him along the path to complete abyss.

She whispered his name, lifted her hips, gnashed her teeth as his fingers grasped her buttocks. He wanted more, so much more and pulled out of her quickly, twisting her into another position. When she was up on her knees, her delectable bottom facing him, Ben wanted to scream. No, he wanted to come deep inside her. His body strained with the effort of holding back, just a few moments longer.

"Take me," she whispered when she'd turned to look at him over her shoulder.

He didn't need to be asked twice as he slipped inside her from behind. She pumped back immediately, thrusting her hips until they'd found a beautiful rhythm, one that incited the delicious sound of their bodies joining.

Ben held tight to her hips, loved the feel of her surrounding him, the tingling that had begun at the base of his spine. When she tensed beneath him, calling his name loudly, Ben couldn't fight it any longer. It was intense, moreso than he'd anticipated and it was delicious, addicting, invigorating. They came together in a maelstrom of moans and tremors. Hearts pounded as they shifted and he pulled her into his arms. Ben held her tightly, his chin resting on the top of her head as she wrapped her legs and arms around him. She pressed against him, fitting them together like they'd been born attached, like this was where and how they belonged.

As they both struggled to catch their breath, Ben thought it was true. This was where they belonged and this was how they were meant to be. Together.

CHAPTER 15

"Why'd you become a prosecutor?" Ben asked when they lay in the dark, listening to the absolute quiet that surrounded them.

"My father was killed when I was fifteen. He was coming to pick me up after the sophomore dance. He parked his car at the corner of the school instead of coming to the door—I'd requested he do that. Anyway, he stepped out of the car to smoke a cigarette when he was approached by a guy. Robert Fulgham was his name. Fulgham demanded my father's money and his car keys. My father gave him his wallet, but not his keys. Fulgham got mad and shot him. Point blank range, three times straight to the chest. He died before the paramedics could arrive."

She stiffened slightly in his arms as she spoke, but her voice remained calm and decisive, as if she were giving an opening statement.

"You're really good at your job. He would have been extremely proud of you."

"My mother would say he was always proud of me, no matter what." She took a deep breath, then let it out slowly. "I have to believe I'm doing some good in this world or his death is in vain."

Silence filled the air again as Ben thought about her words. "I became a defense attorney because I wanted to help those that others discarded. I wanted to be the voice of those whom everyone had already decided did not deserve to be heard. So I get up every morning and head into the office, taking drug cases and murder cases and more often than not, traffic cases. And I try each case as if my client were being faced with the death penalty because I think each one of them deserve a zealous defense. I don't ask about their guilt. I make my case from the notion that they're innocent."

With one hand tucked between his head and the pillow, the other running fingers up and down her arms, Ben paused and thought about his next words. It would be his first time making this admission out loud.

"Vega was my first mistake."

"Because you believe he's guilty?" she asked.

"I know he's guilty," was his reply.

She waited a beat and so did he.

"This is totally off the record, Ben. I would never use anything you tell me in our personal life in the courtroom."

He believed her. He trusted her. Otherwise they wouldn't be here.

"Three weeks before the first trial, just as I was about to start working on the case, I received a call. They wouldn't say who they were, just that they worked in the mayor's office and had some information about my case. Naturally, I wanted to know what it was. I don't like surprises in court."

"Surprises are never good," she agreed, shifting slightly so that she was now laying on her side, her cheek pressed to his bare chest, one leg tossed over his.

"Exactly. So I agreed to meet with this person. We met at my brother's casino. Lots of witnesses for me if it turned out I needed it. He was an older guy, balding, sweating. We talked in the men's room of all places."

"Cozy," she quipped, which made him laugh.

He felt that telling her was the right thing to do.

"Mayor Radcliffe is the father of Alayna Jonas' baby. Congressman McGlinn had an affair with her last year as well, so there was an apparent discrepancy as to who the real father was. Alayna was in love with the congressman and so she wanted it to be his. She'd just left the congressman's house after telling him and his wife that she planned to go public with the baby scandal when Vega arrived. The mayor had paid Vega to kill Congressman McGlinn. Myrna McGlinn was just a casualty since she was there."

"Wow," she said, letting out a whoosh of breath. "Damn, Ben. How did you continue to represent him knowing all that?"

"How could I not? He was my client. Innocent until proven guilty. All I had was this sweaty bald guy's word taken in the men's room of a casino. Not exactly the most credible evidence and I didn't have a lot of time to investigate its viability."

"Why not ask for a postponement?"

"The state had requested two prior postponements. I vehemently argued at the last one that my client's right to a speedy trial was being sacrificed at the state's whimsy. There were going to be no more postponements. Besides, I needed Alayna to back all this up. Either her or Mayor Radcliffe and I knew that wasn't about to happen. But she was gone. Which meant I didn't have anything either way. I tried the case I had going on my client's account of where he'd been and what he'd been doing that night."

"And there was a mistrial."

Ben sighed realizing this wasn't what she really wanted to hear, but knowing that she needed to hear it. "Think about it, Victoria. The state has no real case against Vega. No weapon and no eyewitness."

"Alayna signed a statement," she argued.

"But she's not here to be cross-examined, or to even verify that she signed that statement. Her statement means nothing. Nobody can place Vega near the crime scene, nor can anybody prove that Vega and McGlinn had ever even met. I know you know all this."

The sound of her releasing a shaky breath said she did indeed.

"So what now? I try a losing case and Vega continues to haunt you because he somehow knows what you know?"

She was very smart, there was no doubt about that. "Yeah. I think Vega knows. I tried calling the informant on his cell but I didn't get an answer. The name he gave me when I asked was a fake. Nobody by that name has ever worked at the mayor's office. Trent's tracing the number but I'm not real hopeful. It would have been common sense to use a disposable phone. But I should have at least gotten his real name."

"You can't get information that he wasn't willing to give," she said. "And thinking of what you should have done isn't going to help us now."

She was right and he'd already been down that road with himself. Moreso the night he found out Ebony was dead. But the one thing that was always true about the past was that you couldn't erase it, no matter how hard you might want to.

"Probably not," he admitted. "But I went to see the mayor earlier today."

"You did what?" she asked, bolting up from the bed.

"I have to make this right. I still believe everyone deserves a fair trial and I believe I'm a damn good defense attorney and that's why I declined to represent Vega again. But he's bringing all this right back to my door. If he had simply walked away and let his new counsel handle his case, I would have been okay with that. The information I had was hearsay. It couldn't be corroborated. But he couldn't walk away. He had to show me who he really was. He killed Ebony."

In that moment, Victoria saw something she never in a million years would have guessed she'd see on Ben Donovan. Guilt. It weighed on him like a hundred tons of steel, in his eyes, his shoulders, even in the way he breathed as he'd said those words. This was personal for him now, very personal.

"And if that wasn't bad enough, he started coming after you. I can't let him get away with that. So I have two choices, get him legally or get him illegally."

"Ben," she said, placing a hand on his chest. "Think about this rationally."

He nodded. "I have, Victoria. Believe me, I don't want to lose all that I've worked for and I definitely don't want to disgrace my family in any way. At this point, I just don't want anybody else to be hurt because of the decisions I've made."

He was about to say something else when his cellphone rang. She watched him reach across the bed to retrieve the pants he'd dropped to the floor soon after they'd made it to the bedroom. He took the call.

She thought about everything he'd said and couldn't believe it. This was like something off a television show. It couldn't be real. The mayor and the congressman sharing a woman, a baby with a father who most likely would never publicly claim it and the infuriating fact that murder seemed to be the easiest answer to all of these supposed intelligent adults. It was heartbreaking and senseless.

"We gotta go!" Ben's words jolted her out of her thoughts.

"What? Who was that on the phone?"

"It was Devlin. He followed us from your place. When he figured out who was tailing us, he distracted them, then circled back to come up here to keep an eye on us. One of his men just spotted Vega's infamous Lexus heading this way."

"How does he know that and where are we going? There's nowhere to go out here." A fact that wasn't reassuring right about now.

"There are some back roads," he told her as he was already off the bed and tossing her clothes to her. "Besides, we'll have a head start and Dev and his guys will stay between us and them."

She talked as she dressed. "So we're running from Vega?"

Ben shook his head. "I doubt he'd chase us himself. He's had guys following both of us. My guess is that my little meeting with the mayor ended with him calling Vega to finish the job, so he'll send his flunkies to collect us and bring us to him."

Her mouth went immediately dry, her heart pounding so fast in her chest it was almost painful. "So now he's past intimidating us. He's going to just kill us?"

"He's going to try," were Ben's words before he pulled open a drawer and lifted a gun into his hands. "I'm betting he won't succeed."

This motorcycle ride was different from the first. There was no romance here, no closing her eyes to inhale the scent of the wind. Ben had hurriedly placed the helmet on her head before donning his own and climbing on the bike. They took off without Victoria seeing anyone, anywhere. If there was a threat she hoped they made it out before it arrived.

Ben drove for what seemed like forever until finally he pulled to the side of the highway and took out his cellphone.

After he talked for a few minutes, he slammed it back in its holster and stood with his hands on his hips.

"Trent made us a reservation at a hotel. He wants us to lay low for a couple of days."

"What? I can't lay low. I have to work."

"Vega's got men everywhere. The hit on both our lives is official, especially since he knows that we're together. If you go back to your place, you're as good as dead."

She must have looked like his words had scared the crap out of her because Ben sighed, then took a step closer to where she still sat on the bike.

"Look," he said, placing his hands on her shoulders. "I'm not going to let anything happen to you. This is going to be over soon, I promise. But for right now, I need you to go along with the plan."

"And what exactly is the plan, Ben? How long are we going to be in some hotel and what happens to the other people in our lives until then? What about my mother?" she asked, refusing to let her voice depict how the thought of losing another parent upset her.

"I'll take care of it. All of this is going to work out, Victoria. I promise you."

She'd promised her father she'd be the best she could be and that she'd make a difference. If Vega killed her, that would obviously be a promise broken. She had to live and so did Ben, because for all that she still wanted to deny it, he was slipping closer into her heart. It wasn't intentional. She'd fought it for years. Now, with her eyes blurring with tears, the night sky hovering like a heavy blanket over them and Ben standing close to her offering her his protection and his own promises, she couldn't lie. She was falling in love with him.

As if that weren't enough, Victoria was also pretty damned pissed off! If he weren't so cocky and arrogant Ben would have gone to the police with all this information sooner. He would have gone to the judge and had himself removed from the first trial because of new evidence. And that evidence could have convicted Vega on the first go round then they wouldn't be in this predicament.

Her temples throbbed at the thought and she came to the conclusion that it was useless. Anger had always been a useless emotion for her. In this case, just as with her father's death, it wasn't going to change the past. What was done was done, all she could do was look to controlling the future.

About an hour later, they pulled into the parking lot of a hotel. Ben rode his bike to the back of the lot and slipped between two black SUVS. She didn't move until he got off the bike and removed his helmet. He reached for hers and helped her off the bike. Her thighs were sore, her butt flat out hurt. She was hungry and she was tired. This wasn't her home and she didn't know when she'd sleep in her own bed again. Complaining was futile. This was the situation and she would need to suck it up and deal with it. Besides, she was so exhausted she thought that right about now, any bed might do.

The driver's side door of the SUV to their right opened and Victoria jumped. Then she cursed because fear had begun to take permanent residence in her mind. Ben touched a hand to her shoulder for reassurance. She was surprised that it actually worked.

"It's okay. This is Devlin Bonner," he said, introducing her to the tall menacing looking man that had stepped out and now dwarfed her in height and width.

"Dev, this is Victoria Lashley."

"Nice to meet you, ma'am," he said in a deep drawl that had her tightening her fists at her sides and releasing them slowly.

Another man came up behind her.

"Let's get you inside," he said in a voice just a little less deep. He was big too, not bulky and beefy like the guy named Dev, but tall and broad, definitely some type of soldier and definitely fine as hell.

"I'm Trent Donovan," he said to her, then reached for her arm. "I'll get you inside safely."

Devlin and Trent, along with two other guys who'd come out of the SUVs, made a circle around her and Ben and led them into a side employee entrance of the hotel. They walked fast down a flight of stairs, then through a short hall where they boarded the freight elevator. The men stayed around them in a tight circle and Ben held her hand with a death grip.

Their room was on the very top floor, all the way down the end of the hall next to another exit door. Trent swiped the card through the lock, but she and Ben weren't immediately allowed inside. The two other guys went in first, then came out with stoic looks on their faces, small devices in their hands with green lights flashing across the top bar.

"It's clear," the light complexioned guy with the sprinkle of freckles over his nose said. That was the only normal looking trait this guy had. His head was completely bald, his eyes an eerie shade of...gold? She probably would have deduced they were hazel if she wasn't so tired and overwhelmed by hit men and going into hiding.

The second guy was of the same big build as the rest of them, his eyes dark and ominous, his skin a tawny shade that, along with his ink black hair, gave her the impression he was of Latino descent. She was sure they'd said their names at some point, or maybe not. Maybe they were so secretive that they weren't supposed to tell her their names. But Trent and Devlin had. They were Ben's relatives she thought. At any rate, her mind was whirling with facts and accusations and limitations and possibilities. Her legs wobbled when she walked and she felt at any minute she'd collapse and embarrass herself in the midst of all this mess.

"Come on inside," Ben told her. Then he placed a hand at the small of her back for support. Again, he seemed to know what she needed and offered it without question.

"Rio's going down to get some food. Burgers and fries good?" Trent asked, looking at her.

Victoria nodded, then spoke. "That's fine." Then she looked around the room. "There are too many doors," she said absently.

Trent nodded toward the doors as he spoke. "Bathroom, clothes closet, utilities closet—ironing board, etc.—adjoining room door. We booked both rooms so you don't have to worry about nosy neighbors."

"Oh," she replied, then felt foolish for noticing in the first place.

"So what happened?" Ben asked the moment the door closed behind the one named Rio, the Latino one.

The freckled one—Devlin called him Ace when he gave him his assignment—stood outside the door on guard. Trent had gone to the window, drawing the curtains closed before sitting on the edge of the table. Devlin stood in the middle of the room, arms folded over his chest like he was some type of super hero.

"Radcliffe wasn't impressed by what I had to say," Trent told Ben. "He denied everything, then threw me out of his office. But my bug had already been planted. Not ten minutes after I left he used his cellphone to call Vega. Dev had already run a skip trace on his phone and linked it to our mainframe at the office. The call is recorded."

"Sonofabitch!" Ben cursed, walking across the room with his back turned to them all. "I should have said something sooner."

"And you would have been dead sooner," Dev replied without hesitation. "Or at least they would have come after you sooner. You're the justice guy, so it stands to reason you wanted proof first."

Trent nodded. "He's right, Ben. Don't beat yourself up about this. You played the hand you were dealt. Without concrete proof against Vega you knew he'd walk again. Keeping quiet kept you alive longer."

"And now what?" Ben yelled, spinning around to face them. "Now he's after Victoria too! I've involved her when I could have handled it myself."

Trent shook his head, but Victoria touched a hand to his arm indicating she could talk for herself.

"Jules involved me the moment he handed this case down. He was adamant that I take the case, that I be the one to beat you. So I took it. I walked into this with my eyes wide open." Even if what she'd been seeing when she walked into this situation was more along the lines of ultimate victory against the man who just could not stay out of her dreams.

"Really?" Trent said, rubbing a hand over the light goatee at his chin. "Julius Talmadge. He's planning to run for public office, isn't he?"

"Yes," Victoria replied, a bit taken aback by the swift change in subject. "He's already put in his official application to be on the ballot. So he needs this case. He needs a big win under his belt," she said and instantly thought of the erratic way he'd been acting in her office earlier today, or yesterday she figured since it was well past midnight.

"And he's desperate to have Vega jailed before he gets elected?" Trent continued.

"It's a big case for the city," Ben told him. "I had a couple of higher ups give me a call during the first trial. The head of police for one. He wanted to know how I could sleep at night trying so hard to get Vega acquitted."

"Of course the cops would feel that way," Trent said almost absently. He'd begun rubbing his fingers over his chin.

"Not exactly," Dev added. "Didn't Alayna Jonas disappear while in protective custody, which was spearheaded by the police?"

"Correct," Ben said, folding his arms over his chest.

Victoria loved when he stood like that, with his legs slightly parted, his face grim with concentration. He struck that pose a lot in the courtroom and it never failed to arouse her.

"That's why Noah and I were convinced there was a leak," Ben finished. "Nobody should have known where Alayna was besides the two detectives assigned to take shifts with her and their commanding officer."

"Do you know who they were?" Trent asked.

"Hamlin, the chief, was the commanding officer since this was a political hit. The two detectives were Richley and Alvarez, both veterans of the force. Noah and I both came up dry trying to figure out where the leak was. But knowing there was one is why I didn't turn both the notes over to the cops."

"Where are the notes?" Victoria asked as she'd sat on the side of the bed watching and listening, wondering how all these pieces fit together.

"I have them in my office," Trent replied. "Noah dusted them for prints, came up with none besides yours and Ben's."

"I never gave the police my fingerprints. How could he know they were mine?"

"He matched them to the majority of the prints lifted from your house the night of the attempted break-in," Trent told her.

Victoria nodded, wondering when she'd become one of the victims versus her usual job on the other side of the law. This all seemed to happen so fast and to be spun so completely around her she could hardly breathe. But there was something missing. A huge piece of this puzzle wasn't available to them and until they got their hands on it—or her—they'd still be in danger.

"I think they're all working together," Ben said finally, his voice deep, strong, serious. "There's one circle of corrupt individuals all covering each other's backs. That's how Vega keeps slipping through the system, that's why he can kill and walk away. They're protecting him."

Devlin nodded. "I think you're right."

"The question is why?" Victoria asked, following Ben's train of thought.

"Money," Trent answered. "It is the root of all evil, right? If everybody keeps the other's pockets lined, they can all remain powerful and rich without being caught. I'm going back to my office to start tracking the money going in and coming out of some of these accounts."

"I'll work the computer, map out their political connections," Ben added.

"I'll stay on security. Noah just texted me that he's sitting on your mother's house personally," Dev said to Victoria. "The lovely chief of police will be attending a function with the mayor tomorrow night, so all available officers are on security detail for the convention center, the mayor and the chief."

"Leaving Vega free reign to hunt us down without anybody knowing until it's too late," she added. They were definitely all connected.

"Ace, Rio and I will stay here with you tonight. Tomorrow we move again," Dev said, heading for the door. "Keep the door locked, don't open the curtains and don't answer the phone. If I need you I'll call your cell. You do the same for me," he told Ben, who nodded in agreement.

Rio did some timed type of knock and Dev let him in. Victoria had no idea how the man knew Rio was even on his way up. Then again, he'd probably texted him too since Devlin had continued to hold his cellphone in his hand the entire time they'd been talking.

The food smelled heavenly, and while Victoria wasn't normally a fan of processed take-out, her mouth had already begun to water at the smell of hot French fries and a juicy burger.

"Ace is going to stay at the door. I'll guard the front desk," Rio told Devlin and waited for his approval.

Devlin nodded. "I'll watch the back. Call me when you two are up and ready in the morning," he told Ben.

"We'll be up early. We need some things from our houses if we're going to be gone a few days," Ben added.

Victoria nodded. "I need my laptop and some clothes and I need to call my friend. She's expecting her first baby and if I don't show up for work, she'll worry. I don't want her worrying about me."

"Who is she?" Trent asked with concern. "They might already know about her."

Victoria's heart plummeted. "No," she whispered.

Ben was across the room in no time, sitting on the bed beside her and taking her hand. "She's Grace Ramsey, assistant DA and wife of Judge Clifton Ramsey."

"Damn!" Trent cursed. "If Vega figures that out, they're definitely in danger."

"Or the judge is already on his payroll," Devlin commented blithely.

"No!" Victoria protested immediately. "Clifton's not like that."

"Okay, I think that's enough for tonight," Ben spoke up. "In the morning we'll figure out how she can contact Grace without causing too much of an issue. I've known Grace Ramsey for years. She's not involved in this."

Devlin obviously wanted to press forward, but a nod from Trent stopped his idea.

"If anything changes, you call me right away," Trent told Ben, clapping a hand on his shoulder.

The two men stared at each other a moment, and to Victoria it seemed like one hell of an emotional bond. They were family, so that would be expected, but this seemed a little more intense, like they both recognized the danger and hated it equally.

"I will."

Devlin walked up to Ben and gave him a very curt nod. "I'll be right out back."

Ben mimicked Devlin's nod and their gazes locked. There was no physical contact, but the bond here was strong too. Devlin would die for Ben and for anyone he cared an ounce about. She could see that in the big man's dark eyes, could read it in the ready-for-war stance he kept at all times. And she couldn't help it, she admired him for that type of loyalty and devotion.

She admired each of the men who would circle around to protect her from a coldhearted killer.

CHAPTER 16

An hour later, Victoria and Ben had eaten and with more than a little trepidation climbed into the king sized hotel bed. During the meal, neither of them had spoken of the current events. In fact they hadn't spoken much at all. Ben wasn't sure what was going through Victoria's mind and he wanted to get away from what was going through his.

He had no idea how things had become so screwed up. In all the years he'd dreamed of being with Victoria, he'd never thought they would end up like this. In some hotel laying in a strange bed unable to think of anything else but their safety. For that alone he wanted to strangle Ramone Vega.

"I'm not afraid to die," she said, snapping Ben completely out of his own self-pitying thoughts.

"What?"

She pulled the sheets up and flattened her hands over her chest, which he assumed she was doing by the sounds made. The room was dark as they'd already turned off all the lights.

"I've never been afraid to die. When I saw my father lying on the sidewalk, blood seeping from his chest, the one thing I remember clearly is the most peaceful look had come over his face. He'd never looked like that in life. So I took comfort in the fact that he was in a better place. Then my mother told me that death is as natural as life and that no matter what we did during the in-between time, it wouldn't change the final outcome. My mother's very candid about things like that."

Ben couldn't help it. Despite the subject, he chuckled. "I like your mother."

"Most people do," she said with what he imagined to be a smile.

"I won't let you die," he said seriously. "That's not an option."

"I know this sounds strange considering what I've thought of you for so long. But I won't let you die either, Ben. I just won't."

He reached out a hand, knowing that it would find hers eventually, just as eventually they'd found each other. Intertwining his fingers with hers seemed natural enough. Sliding across the bed to be closer to her did too. When Victoria turned on her side and let her head fall against his shoulder, he prayed that would be a natural reaction for her, one that would last for years and years to come.

It was a couple hours later when Victoria woke up to use the bathroom. She slipped from beneath Ben's warm embrace, hating like hell that she had no other choice. Stopping on her way to the bathroom, she peaked out the window, grabbing the curtain in her fists and pulling it apart only slightly. Their view faced the back parking lot. Devlin's black SUV was parked in the same spot as it was when they'd arrived hours ago.

Finally making it to the bathroom, she was washing her hands when she heard the soft hum of a cellphone vibrating. She assumed it was hers since she'd hung her jeans and t-shirt in the bathroom. It was bad enough she had to put these clothes back on for a second day; no way was she going to sleep in them too. Besides, she and Ben had already been intimate. There was really no need for modesty at this point. He'd slept in his boxers and she in her underwear and all was well. Or as well as circumstances would allow.

Pulling her pants down from the hook on the back of the door, she reached into her pocket for her cellphone. There were eight text messages. At the sight she remembered her phone had chimed just as she'd gotten out of the car to see Ben on her steps yesterday. Two from Grace and six from an unknown number. Victoria read Grace's messages first. No baby, just wondering where she was. Right. Regardless of what Devlin and Trent thought, she was definitely going to call Grace when it wasn't nearing six in the morning.

She read the first of the unknown messages and her heart raced.

Need to talk to you. In person. Soon. AJ

Victoria didn't know anyone named AJ and she didn't recognize the number.

**Really need to talk to you. Can't trust anyone else.
He's going to kill me!**

That was the last message, the one received just three minutes ago, the one that this time was signed: *Alayna.*

Alayna Jonas was trying to contact her. Victoria couldn't believe it. Her heart beat so loud she could hear it roaring in her ears. She needed to call her back.

No. What if her phone was being taped?

Maybe she could text her.

No. If this was a setup they could trace her number and find out where she was.

But she needed to talk to Alayna. Or rather she definitely needed Alayna to testify at trial next week. If the girl knew enough to contact her, she must know everything that was going on. For the next few minutes, Victoria paced the bathroom, wondering what she should do.

If she woke Ben, he'd want to call Trent and Devlin and they'd set up some sort of sting that would go in with guns blazing to bring Alayna back. Victoria knew the tone of text messages could easily be misconstrued, just like that of email messages. But she couldn't help but feel the fear reverberating through each message she'd read. Wherever Alayna was and whoever she was with, she was definitely afraid for her life. And Victoria didn't like that at all.

When she'd walked until she was dizzy from moving around in the small bathroom, she put the lid down and sat on the commode.

"Think, Victoria. Think," she whispered to herself.

Seconds later she was switching on the phone, hitting one of her speed dial numbers and waiting for Grace to answer.

Grace was not a morning person, and being pregnant only seemed to make that worse. She answered the phone sounding like there were a couple of frogs in her throat.

"Grace!" Victoria whispered urgently. "It's me. I need you to listen to me carefully."

It took Victoria two explanations before Grace was awake enough to understand what she was saying. At that point, she shifted from groggy sleepyhead to panicked best friend. Then it took another round of explaining to calm her down enough so that she was eventually saying, "I'm on my way."

Now Victoria needed to figure out how she was going to get out of this hotel room without Ben or any of their guards finding out. *I should just tell Ben,* she thought as she finished dressing and picked up the tube of toothpaste left in the bathroom. Squirting it onto her finger, she tried not to gag as she scrapped that finger over her teeth and did a quick rinse and spit.

If she told him, he would want to come with her. Worse, he would want to bring Trent and Devlin with them. That might make Alayna run. After all, if the woman knew who Victoria was and how to get in touch with her, she was sure she knew who Ben was and still had made it a point to contact her instead. That meant she didn't want to talk to Ben. Which meant Victoria couldn't tell him.

Then again, she thought with her hand on the knob to the bathroom door, what if this was all a setup and Vega was using Alayna to get to her? No. If Vega were with Alayna, Alayna would be dead. There was no doubt in Victoria's mind about that.

She turned the knob as slowly as she could manage and pulled the door open while her own breath was held. Across the room she saw that Ben had rolled onto his side, his back facing her. Thank goodness. Silently she apologized over and over as her feet moved silently across the carpeted floor. The middle door in between the utility closet and the clothes closet was the adjoining bedroom door. It was a quick plan, one she prayed would work even though she had zero experience doing things like this.

If she could get into the other room, she could leave out that door. Rio was standing guard in front of their room door, not that one. She should be able to slip out without him seeing her. Then what?

She'd made it to the adjoining room, having closed both doors behind her. For one second she allowed herself a release of breath, and a sigh because she prayed she was doing the right thing. On her hip her cellphone vibrated and she looked hurriedly down at the screen.

ETA 10min

How the hell did Grace get here that fast? She had to be speeding, which was just like Grace and would almost certainly piss Clinton off. Having his pregnant wife stand before him for a speeding ticket was not going to be cute.

Okay, this was going to be harder than she originally thought. Rio stood with his right side leaning against the wall to the door. His back was facing the door where Victoria had just come out. That should have made it easier, but Victoria was positive this man was a trained soldier. She bet he would hear her the minute she stepped into the hallway. The exit door was about ten to fifteen feet to the left, in the opposite direction of where Rio stood.

Think. Think. Think.

She pulled her phone out once more and dialed one of the numbers Ben had given her last night. He'd wanted her to be able to reach any of them if she needed them, so he'd given her Rio's and Ace's cell numbers along with Devlin's and Trent's. Victoria scrolled down her contacts until she got to Rio's, then hit call. Peeping her head out the doorway, she didn't hear any ringing and figured he had it on vibrate. She watched as he reached into his pocket and pulled out his phone. He said hello a few times and then hung up the phone. He knocked on the door and called to Ben. In her head she counted, waiting, hoping he would do what she thought he would.

And he did.

He used his key card to open the door to the room she'd just left. The minute he slipped inside, she slipped out and ran as if her life depended on it to the exit door. She made it down two flights of stairs, then headed for the elevator on that floor. She remembered using the freight entrance last night and took that same way to get to the back door. There she waited, tapping a foot against the floor as her heart ran a rapid rhythm in her chest.

"Come on, Gracey, come on."

As if Grace had heard her words, Victoria heard a vehicle pull up right outside the door. With one last prayer that she was doing the right thing, she eased open the door, saw Grace's ruby red Camaro, and moved quickly to get inside.

"Pull off slow. If you peel out of this parking lot, Devlin's right around back. He might hear you and be on our tail in seconds," she told Grace as she put on her seatbelt. "But hurry up. I don't want this girl to run."

"Right. Go slow, go fast, come now, stay home," Grace said snidely as she pulled out of the parking lot.

Victoria half thought she'd look into the rearview mirror and see Devlin at any moment. But she didn't and for a second she wondered why. By the time Victoria had finally replied to Alayna's text, asking where she was and receiving a reply, she didn't think about Devlin again. And she refused to think about Ben, or about how pissed off he was going to be when he found out she was gone.

❧❧❧

"What the hell do you mean she's gone?" Devlin yelled the minute he ran into Ben's room.

"Dammit!" Ben cursed for the billionth time. Where was she? Why would she leave? Last night she'd been afraid, he'd seen it in her eyes. Then she'd toughened up, told him she wasn't scared of dying. He'd held her in his arms all night. He hadn't made love to her because they'd both needed another type of reassurance. He'd felt her with him all night, not just physically but mentally. She accepted they were in a relationship just as she accepted their present situation. And now she was gone. What the hell did that mean?

"How could she get out of here without you seeing her?" Devlin demanded.

"She called my phone then hung up. I thought something was wrong in here. I thought it was some type of code, so I came inside." Rio looked like he wanted to kick himself and probably would have if Devlin wasn't standing right in his face, intent on doing the job for him.

"I think she slipped out the adjoining room when I came in here," Rio admitted.

"You idiot!" Devlin yelled again. "Where'd she go, Ben?"

Ben was shaking his head. He stood near the window, staring through the slit in the curtains that he'd made the moment he realized she wasn't there. He could see part of the parking garage, could see the sun rising, daylight making its grand appearance for the next few hours. And he felt empty, totally and completely empty inside.

"She would go to her mother and to see Grace. She's worried about them," he said solemnly, his teeth clenching when he finished.

"That's if she left on her own," Rio followed.

"Vega would have killed us both. He wouldn't just take her and I doubt she would have gone with him willingly," Devlin said.

Ben shook his head. "She's not with Vega. At least she didn't leave with him. She left on her own."

"How can you be so sure?" Rio insisted.

Ben whirled around for a minute, wanting to shake the hell out of the man who was supposed to be watching them. Then he decided against it. He'd been laying in the same bed as Victoria and he hadn't realized she'd left either.

"She would have fought Vega. With everything she had in her, she would have fought against him taking her. I would have heard and you would have heard."

"I agree about her fighting. She seems like a fighter," Devlin said. "I don't agree about Rio not hearing squat! It's apparent he wasn't paying very much attention."

Rio didn't say a word, just turned away. Then when he got to the door he asked, "Did you see any cars leave the parking lot?"

Devlin was a captain. He told his team what to do and what not to do. He asked the questions, he knew all the answers. Not this time.

"I came as soon as you called," he said.

"So she could have driven off while you were heading up here," Ben said. "Look for a red 2010 Mustang. It's Grace Ramsey's car. Victoria wouldn't have left without having a way home."

Devlin nodded to Rio. "Get on that now!" he told him. Then he turned back to Ben. "We'll find her, man."

Ben nodded, every muscle in his body tensing until he felt like any movement would break him in half. "Yeah, I just hope it's in time."

CHAPTER 17

"What kind of *Law and Order* mess are you mixed up in?" Grace asked as she drove down the interstate, barely keeping within the posted speed limit.

Victoria could do nothing but sigh. "It's complicated. Look, I'll just drop you back off at your house and then I'll go meet with Alayna. I'll call you right after the meeting," she told her, hoping it would be enough to stop the questions she'd been barraged with since climbing into the car.

"If you think I'm just going to let you go off to meet some witness who's been considered dead for the past few months, you are crazier than I already thought you were."

"Well, if you think I'm going to let you waddle into the middle of this mess, you're not as smart as I always thought you were."

Grace honked her horn at a white truck that had narrowly missed hitting the front end of the car as it cut her off, trying to get into the exit lane.

"Okay, arguing is stupid and it's giving me a headache. Why don't we go to my place and ask Clinton what we should do," she suggested.

Victoria immediately began shaking her head. "No!" she exclaimed. "I mean, I don't want to involve either one of you. I wouldn't have even called if I didn't need a ride home."

"Listen here. We've been friends for way too long for you to start keeping secrets. Especially secrets that involve somebody throwing bombs through your window and having you followed."

Grace was so melodramatic. But she was also loyal and courageous and the best friend Victoria had ever had. At this very moment, the emotion of wondering if she'd ever see Grace or her baby again was waging a war with her confidence about going to see Alayna.

"I just need to go alone. She wants me to come and see her by myself. Now you know who I'm going to see and once I drop you off, I'll even text you the address Alayna gave me. If you don't hear from me within the hour, call the police," Victoria instructed just as Grace pulled into her driveway.

Grace didn't respond right away. She parked the car and killed the engine, letting her palms rest on the steering wheel and stared straight ahead for a few seconds.

"I don't want anything to happen to you, Vic," she said, the crack in her voice almost bringing Victoria to tears.

She reached for Grace's hand, pulling it into her own and holding tight. "Nothing's going to happen to me, Grace. We've been friends for too long for this great duo to be split up now." Tears blurred her eyes as she spoke but she dared not let them fall, dared not let them make an appearance because if they did Grace would cry as well and then they'd both be blubbering messes.

"I have to do this. If I can get Alayna to testify, Vega will be put away for life. As long as he's on the streets, there are so many people in danger. I can't let that happen without at least trying to do something. This is my career, Grace, and it's my life I'm fighting for."

Grace turned to face Victoria, big fat tears dripping instantly from her long lashes. "I'm afraid for you."

Victoria nodded, the lump in her throat too thick to speak instantly. She reached up and wiped the tears away from Grace's cheeks. "Fear makes you weak," she heard herself whisper the words her father had instilled in her. "You're the strongest person I know, Grace. You're the strongest and the smartest and I love you with all my heart. I'll be okay." Then because more words, more time sitting here with Grace would definitely tear her apart, Victoria pulled her friend close for a tight hug. Then she let her go quickly.

"Now get back in the house and wait for my text," she said, climbing out of the passenger seat and walking around to the driver's side.

Grace climbed out of the car and Victoria touched both palms to her stomach. "Go back inside and get some rest. My niece is not a morning person, remember." She smiled when she felt a swift kick just beneath her left palm. Never had Victoria felt anything as amazing as the movements of a baby in utero.

"You text me in five minutes with that address and then you've got another fifty-five minutes to call me and confirm you're alright. If you miss either of those deadlines, I'm telling Clifton and I'm calling every police officer in Las Vegas to come and find you. Do you hear me?"

Grace smoothed back unruly tendrils of Victoria's hair. The quick ponytail she'd made was hardly her best effort, but beauty wasn't exactly what she was going for today.

Victoria nodded. "I hear you."

They didn't embrace again. Neither of them thought they could take it if they did. So Victoria climbed into the driver's seat and buckled her seat belt while watching Grace move slowly into the house. When the front door had closed behind her, Victoria backed out of the driveway. At the corner of Grace's street, she picked up her cellphone and texted Grace Alayna's address. Then she set the GPS on her phone and listened as it guided her to what, Victoria had no idea.

This had to work. She was running out of options and probably out of time. He'd offered her money, put it in her bank account and waited for her to use it. At first she hadn't because it wasn't about the money. It was about love.

Alayna sighed, pressing her forehead against the grungy window at the motel where she'd been staying. It was only five blocks away from where she'd been living with her grandmother. She'd originally thought about going further, but couldn't bear not seeing her baby. The idea to drastically change her appearance so she wouldn't be recognized came in the middle of one of the loneliest nights of her life. The night she'd made the mess of her life ten times worse.

Three years ago she'd been young and innocent, working in the mailroom at city hall. Her aunt had gotten her the job two weeks after she'd graduated high school and Alayna had been supremely grateful. After her mother died when she was ten, she'd moved in with her grandmother and her Aunt Jaynie, who'd never been able to have children of her own. It wasn't a dream job, but she received a paycheck every two weeks and after working the entire summer she'd saved enough to buy herself a piece of crap used car that gave her a sense of independence and thirst to achieve.

Larry was like a superstar in her eyes. She remembered the first time she'd seen him in person. He'd been standing in the elevator, his security team draped around him like he was the president of the United States instead of Clark County mayor. She'd been too afraid to get onto the elevator, even though Larry had smiled at her and one of his men—she would later learn his name was Timothy Hall, a lying bastard—had beckoned her inside.

It had only taken a day or so for Timothy to walk into the mailroom and escort her out. Her heart had hammered wildly as she thought she was being reprimanded for doing something wrong, or possibly fired. Instead, he'd taken her straight to the mayor, and that's when it all began.

Alayna's cellphone chirped and she looked down at the screen. The phone had been in her hand all night long, just as she felt like she'd been standing in this window for the same endless hours. With desperation clawing at her throat, she read the message and felt the burn of tears at the words. She was coming. Victoria Lashley was coming to see her, to save her.

Her hopes of being saved having been dashed so many times before, Alayna had almost lost faith. But that would totally break her grandmother's heart. Nothing else she did could be worse than not having faith in the God Ethel Jonas had taught her to love and trust. And even though she knew she'd sinned, so bad in another time and place she would have surely been stoned to death, she could repent her sins and be forgiven. That was the small glimmer in her mind that kept her going, that sparkled right next to the memory of her daughter. Lia was her life and Alayna refused to spend more time away from her. No matter what she had to get back home. She had to start thinking about Lia and not the broken heart that would never be mended because the man she'd loved with all her being was gone. That was probably for the best. She'd had months to come to that conclusion. Months to realize that men would continue to be users and abusers if she let them.

Moving from the window, she finally headed into the bathroom and turned the rusty old faucet. She waited a few minutes, and then a few minutes more while the water warmed before she grabbed the moderately clean washcloth to cleanse her face. Her eyes were puffy from crying bouts throughout the night. And her lip was split from the fight that had pushed her over the edge.

There was a soft knock at the door. It seemed much louder as it jolted her out of her deep thoughts. Alayna sucked in a breath and said a prayer. This was it.

⌒⌒⌒⌒⌒

"She's going to call me within the hour," Grace told Ben as they stood in her living room.

Judge Ramsey was standing right beside his wife, an arm around her shoulder, his pensive dark eyes glaring at Ben. He hadn't been too pleased to open his door at seven in the morning and find Ben with Trent and Devlin standing behind him like henchmen on his doorstep. But Ben was respectful, or as respectful as he could be under these circumstances. He'd explained why he was there without going into too much detail and asked to see Grace. When Grace had come into the living room, she looked like she'd been crying and had been expecting him.

"Where did she go?" Devlin asked impatiently.

To that Grace responded with an elegant eye roll and a squaring of her shoulders. On another day, in any other circumstance, Ben would have found the complete brush off funny and would have joked with Devlin about it for days to come. But not today, not now.

"She's in a lot of danger," Ben said, the words sticking in his throat with razor-edged sharpness.

"I know everything that's going on," Grace informed him. "You should have told her that when she first got this case dumped in her lap. Then maybe she could have gotten out before it was too late."

Grace's words were cool, not filled with vehemence so much as fear. Ben respected her, and he respected her relationship with Victoria. So he only nodded, taking her words and the accusation that went with them.

"I did what I thought was right at the time. Yes, I could have done things differently but I don't really know if we would be at a different point than we are now if I had," he admitted honestly. "But I'm not about to let him hurt her. That's why I need you to tell me where she went. Now."

He hadn't raised his voice. Judge Ramsey was not going to take that well if he did. And the last thing Ben wanted was an altercation between the Judge and Devlin. That wasn't going to work out well for any of them.

"I think we should contact the police," Judge Ramsey interjected.

Ben nodded. "Detective Noah Hannity is already aware of the circumstances, Your Honor."

"And why isn't he here? If this situation is as dire as you say, and I believe it is since my wife is trying valiantly not to shake and cry in front of you, why aren't the police already out looking for Victoria?"

"Because we have information that leads us to believe there's a leak in the police department," Trent offered. "I've been looking into the disappearance of Alayna Jonas for the past couple of months and the conclusion I've come to is that someone on the inside must have tipped Vega's men off about her whereabouts. Or, in the alternative, someone on the inside is one of Vega's men."

Judge Ramsey's frown was immediate. "That's a serious allegation," he told Trent.

"One I can back up," was Trent's response.

"Then you know who the leak is?" the Judge persisted.

Trent stood with his feet spread apart, hands clasped in front of him, shoulders squared. He looked directly into Judge Ramsey's eyes when he said, "I've got a couple of leads. But Victoria's safety supersedes that. Look judge, I've been on the battlefield, I've been in covert operations and for the past few years working all sorts of cases on the streets of Las Vegas and in other states. I've seen guys like Vega in my travels. He's a walking deadly weapon and if we don't stop him soon, the death toll is just going to keep rising."

"Unless we can take him down now," Devlin added in his dour tone.

Grace's eyes had bulged as fear really gripped her. She touched a hand to her stomach and gasped. The judge immediately directed her to a seat.

"It's alright, baby. Just take a deep breath. It's going to be fine…"

From a distance, Ben just watched. There was a connection here, an intimacy that was unlike anything he'd ever seen. This was a family, or they were about to be a family, and the love between them would be apparent. This is what Ben wanted in his future. It's what he wanted with Victoria.

Crossing over to the chair where Grace was seated, practicing what he thought were most likely Lamaze breathing methods, he knelt down and took her free hand in his.

"Grace, you know me. You know how long I've been in love with Victoria. I can't let anything happen to her. Not now when we've just found each other. Please tell me where she is," he implored.

Grace blinked, one tear rolling down her cheek. She took in a deep breath and stared back at him with blurry eyes. "The address is in my phone. She got a text from Alayna Jonas and she went to meet with her."

"Goddammit!" Devlin cursed.

"Not in front of my wife," the judge bellowed.

Devlin's lips closed tightly right after he apologized.

"Where's your cellphone, darling?" Judge Ramsey asked Grace.

She pointed to her purse on the table across the room. He retrieved it and pressed a few buttons to arrive at the message. With his face tight with consternation, he walked over to Trent and showed him the screen. Trent transferred the information to his phone.

"Thank you," he said to Grace and the judge. "Let's go," was directed at Devlin.

"You bring her back," Grace said to Ben. She'd pulled her hand from his grasp and grabbed hold of his arm. "You bring her back alive."

Ben nodded. "I will."

CHAPTER 18

"He said I was going to be safe, that he was moving me because that's what Larry asked him to do. I believed him." Alayna Jonas spoke in a quiet tone, tears streaming down her cheeks.

Victoria listened. She sat on a grungy couch in a motel room that smelled like mold. Dirty curtains were drawn tightly closed over the only window, all the chains and bolts applied to the door. There were huge stains on the worn carpet and she didn't even want to contemplate their origin. Across from her, on the edge of the only bed in the room, its awful floral print comforter rumpled from where she'd probably lain the night before, sat the young woman everyone had been looking for.

A year ago she was probably considered to be a gorgeous young lady with big brown eyes and long, dark brown hair. Her skin was sun kissed, her body curvy in all the right places, trim in the others. But her shoulders slumped and her eyes were puffy. This was a look Victoria figured the girl had been sporting for a while.

"So he brought you here after leaving the witness protection location?" she asked trying to keep her mind on the current situation, which by the cut on Alayna's lip and the bruises on her arm looked a lot worse than any of them could have imagined. No, that's not true. They'd all thought Alayna was dead.

Alayna nodded, hair falling to shield her face. With a shaky hand she pushed thick tresses back behind her left ear. She didn't look at Victoria, just kept her gaze down at her hands sitting in her lap.

"When I didn't hear from Larry after a few days, I figured something was wrong."

"Did you see any police officers after you were moved?" Victoria continued. She wished she had a notepad and pen to write down everything Alayna was telling her, but she'd been in such a rush to get to her she hadn't even thought of stopping by her place to get her briefcase.

"He would lock me in the room whenever he needed to leave. And he'd be gone for hours and hours, working I guess. But when he came back—" her words trailed off and she used the back of her hand to wipe at tears that flowed much faster. "He raped me over and over, said it was what I deserved for being such a slut and ruining everything. After a while, I just stopped fighting because what was the use? I thought he was going to kill me. And that made me mad. I don't want my daughter to grow up without a mother. That's why I called you Ms. Lashley. I need your help so I can be with my daughter." She'd looked up by then, staring right at Victoria.

It was an imploring and desperate stare that seared straight through Victoria, touching everything within that was female and prosecutor and protector all at the same time. She didn't give it a second thought, but rose from the sofa and went to the bed to sit beside Alayna. She took the girl's hands in hers and vowed, "I will get you out of this. You will be with your daughter again," she told her and meant every word.

"I just need to make a call to get someone to come and pick you up," Victoria continued, reaching into her pocket for her cellphone.

"Not the cops!" Alayna yelled. "Don't call the cops!"

Victoria's hand froze on the phone. She was about to ask Alayna why she didn't want the police called when she heard a sickeningly familiar sound. Glass shattered, falling like confetti over the dirty couch Victoria had just vacated. She held her breath as she pushed Alayna to the floor, clearly expecting tear gas to come flying through to choke them out. But that didn't happen. What came through the window this time could be considered worse, depending on who you asked.

"Noah's not answering his phone." Ben cursed at the realization and stopped trying to contact his friend, the only police officer in this city that he trusted right now.

He was in the passenger seat of Devlin's SUV as they sped down the highway, heading towards the exit that would take them to the Morningshade Motel where Alayna Jonas was staying.

"She's only been there a couple of days," Trent spoke from the back seat.

Ace and Rio were in the second SUV, which had taken the scenic route to the hotel just in case one of them was being followed.

"She's been missing for almost a year. Where was she before now?" Ben asked.

"The clerk at the hotel has an Ethel Mae Jonas registered at Morningshade since day before yesterday. I'm doing a scan of all the hotels in the surrounding area using this name," Trent said. He had his laptop and was pecking away, trying to find as much information as they could on Alayna Jonas. He'd already been working on this and didn't have much to go on except that up until the week before her disappearance, regular bi-weekly deposits both from the Clark County government and an account named TH Services Inc. had come in for almost two and a half years. The amounts from TH Services had sparked a red flag for Trent and he'd run a report to find out more about the company, but so far had come up with nothing.

"Nothing," he said after a few minutes.

"We're about three minutes away," Dev announced, taking the exit and coming to a slow, almost stop at the corner before turning down a side street. "Should be around this next corner," he said and made the left turn.

Ben's fingers clenched and unclenched. His gun pressed heavily against his back. He was licensed to carry a concealed weapon and had a year's worth of training at the shooting range. Every now and then he and a couple of his cousins, including Trent, went out to the range just for practice, then made a day of it by having lunch and playing ball afterwards. The Donovan men were big on protection, just as big as they were on following the law.

Only this time Ben wasn't sure he would be able to abide completely. He just didn't know that he wouldn't kill Vega if given the chance.

The first thing he noticed when they pulled into the parking lot of the motel was a parked police car. It was in front of room 608, Alayna's room.

"He's in there," he said, hurriedly opening the door and stepping out of the truck.

"Who?" Dev asked, moving around the front of the vehicle to join up with Ben.

"The leak," Trent answered. "The dirty cop is in there with Alayna."

"He's in there with Victoria," was the last thing Ben said before he started running across the parking lot towards the rooms.

CHAPTER 19

"Get up you, stupid slut!" he yelled.

Victoria still held Alayna's hand from when she'd pulled her down to the floor. No tear gas had come in, but something worse had entered. She could see his hand grabbing a chunk of Alayna's hair and pulling her up from the floor. Victoria wouldn't let her hand go, and she was jerked to her knees as well.

"Who the hell are you?" he asked, looking at her.

Before she could answer Victoria felt a wave of something. She narrowed her eyes and stared closer. She knew him. And the moment he took a second look, she could tell he knew her too.

"Goddammit! You better not have been running your mouth!" he shouted at Alayna, then used his grip on her hair to toss her over the bed. "As for you Miss Prosecutor, you're about to lose this case bigtime!"

He raised his hand to slap her and Victoria acted solely on instinct. After her father's death, she and her mother had taken every self-defense class they could find. Naomi actually held several belts in the art of Taekwondo while Victoria had leveled out at the blue belt because she'd entered college and became too busy to attend the classes.

But she could handle herself very well. The arm that blocked Officer Hall's ensuing assault and the follow up jab to his nose with a palm heel strike proved her point. Blood immediately spewed from his face and Victoria took the seconds that he stood there stunned and calling her all kinds of names to run and help Alayna up from the floor.

"Stay behind me," she instructed.

"He'll kill us both," Alayna whimpered, pulling on the sleeve of Victoria's shirt. "Let's just go. There's a window in the bathroom. We can get out while he's bleeding," she pleaded.

But Victoria knew that wasn't going to work. Hall wasn't going to be out of commission much longer. She looked around quickly, trying to find anything she could use as a weapon because he was definitely going to come for her first.

She knew who he was. Sure, Alayna did too, but he had her so afraid she hadn't even told Victoria his name and probably would have had to be thoroughly coerced to divulge that information. But he was greedy. He'd come for her and now Victoria knew exactly who he was. And it hadn't taken her long to figure out what he'd done. He was the one who'd taken Alayna. He could because he was a cop. He would have known where the other officers were holding her and it would have been easy for him to walk right in and grab her. Her question was why. But that would surely have to wait as, just as she'd expected, he swiped his hand over his blood soaked face and turned immediately to her.

"They should have killed you when they had the chance. I told them scaring you wasn't enough. But that's okay, I'll take care of it."

He reached into the front of his pants and pulled out a gun, big and black was all she really saw before the front door was kicked off its hinges.

Hall whirled around to see who'd decided to join his little party. Victoria gasped to see the gun was now pointed directly at Ben.

"Sonofabitch!" Ben yelled.

"Drop it!" Dev and Trent yelled simultaneously from behind him.

Ben saw Officer Hall, the smart-ass from the crime scene the night Victoria's house had been attacked. A quick glance over the man's shoulder and he saw Victoria with a frantically screaming woman right behind her.

"I'm not dropping anything. You're the intruders. I'm the goddamned law. You drop it!" Hall yelled with clear distaste.

"You're a crocked cop who's going down," Ben told him, still holding his ground.

He hadn't pulled out his own weapon and now wished like hell he had. If the gun were in his hand he'd shoot and damn the consequences.

"Just like before you don't have any evidence, Donovan. You can't prove anything."

Trent pushed past Ben. "I can prove you were the one who went into the safe house and set off tear gas so you could take the witness out the back door. You've had her all this time, while steady deposits have been dumped into your account from Sal's Pizzeria for some equipment I know damned well you never delivered. You're caught, jackass!"

He moved fast like lightening as he streaked across the room, yelling some sort of battle cry before tackling Victoria to the ground and rolling over with his arm tight around her neck, the nose of his gun pointing squarely at her temple.

Ben didn't think, only reacted.

His gun was in his back waistband. He reached for it and had it aimed straight between Hall's eyes before the man could pull Victoria to a standing position.

"Let...her...go," he stated slowly, his finger poised on the trigger of his 9mm.

"I got him Ben. You don't do anything stupid," Dev said from behind.

Ben shook his head. "He's the stupid one," he said, taking a step closer.

"Ben, no!" Victoria tried to scream, but the bastard tightened his grip around her neck.

"Shut the hell up! All of you just drop your weapons or I swear I'll shoot this bitch attorney. Then I'm going to kill that whiny whore who thought she was smarter than me, taking my money, then trying to run away!"

Ben's gut clenched, the sight of that gun touching Victoria's temple making him want to wretch or leap forward and kill, probably both. Rage simmered inside, building to an intense heat as sweat prickled his brow. She couldn't die. He just wouldn't let her.

"You're not going to kill her," Ben told him, taking a step closer.

He could sense Dev moving behind him, ready to shoot the second Hall's finger pulled the trigger. Well, Ben wasn't going to let it go that far. He was ready to shoot now.

"I'm going to splatter her brains all over this cheap ass motel wall and there's nothing you can do to stop me, rich boy!" Hall spat.

His gun hand shook. Ben saw it as they stood. He blinked rapidly, the pain from his broken nose probably kicking in. A millisecond later the lamp that had been sitting on the nightstand was smacked against the back of Hall's head. Victoria lurched forward just as he kept hold of his footing and aimed at her. Ben fired.

Dev fired.

Trent fired.

Officer Timothy Hall hit the floor with a sickening thud, his gun sliding a few feet away. Behind him Alayna stood shaking from head to toe, the lamp still in her hand. Ben took a step toward Victoria and, while she'd been watching him, her eyes wide with fear, chest heaving, fingers clenching at her sides, she turned away from him and went to hug Alayna instead.

A clap to his back stopped Ben's movement and he stood still, his gaze falling to the lifeless body of Officer Hall.

"You okay, man?" Trent asked, coming to stand beside him.

Ben had lowered the hand holding his gun, still a bit stunned that he'd actually fired on a human being.

"You didn't have to shoot him," Ben began. "You nor Dev," he said quietly.

"You're a suit-wearing justice man," Dev said after he'd knelt beside Hall to check for a pulse. "No need in you carrying a death on your shoulders."

"My bullet made contact," Ben said moreso to confirm with himself than anything else.

Trent nodded. "And so did at least three others. We'll never know which one killed him." Trent still had his hand on Ben's shoulder and he squeezed firmly. "You'll never know if it was yours or not."

Ben looked at his cousin seriously, gratefully. "So I'll never carry the guilt of being a killer."

Trent nodded once more, then tilted his head in the direction where Victoria was standing. "But you wear that hero thing pretty good. She looks a little shaken up."

She did and Ben wanted nothing else but to go to her, but she looked like she had other things going on, namely an almost hysterical Alayna Jonas.

Ben obviously had a conflict of interest, but that hadn't stopped him from trying to help Alayna Jonas.

"She should have an attorney before she goes into any type of interrogation," he said when Noah and Victoria were preparing to enter the room where Alayna had been placed after they arrived at the police station.

Timothy Hall's body had been picked up by the morgue and pronounced DOA. Good cops had swarmed the motel, shutting down the parking lot and the whole string of rooms under the number 608. Homicide detectives had been chomping at the bit to question Trent, Dev and Ben, but when Noah arrived he took over. He'd taken all their statements unofficially on the way to the precinct and officially when he was in his office. Now, it was time to see what Alayna Jonas knew for sure.

Ben suspected she knew a lot of things that could possibly incriminate herself. Hence the reason she needed legal protection.

"Come on Donovan, she's a witness in protective custody," Noah said with a slight frown.

"Then there's no need for you to talk to her about anything other than her testimony," he fired back.

"I can ask about her abduction by Hall and where she's been all this time," Noah countered.

Ben nodded. "And nothing else."

He held Noah's gaze for endless seconds, wanting to make sure his friend knew what he was trying to implicate without getting himself in anymore ethical hot water.

"He's right," Victoria intervened. "She should at the very least be advised that she can have an attorney present. But *not* you," she said pointing to Ben.

Ben agreed. "I have a colleague who can be here in fifteen minutes," he said, holding up his cellphone.

Noah cursed under his breath but Ben knew he understood they were all trying to protect both the witness and the successful prosecution of Ramone Vega.

"I'll go advise her of her rights," he said, heading into the room.

As if he'd actually spoken the words to her, Victoria nodded. "I'll go make sure her answer is duly recorded."

An hour later Victoria sat at one end of the long steel table, a legal pad and pen in front of her. To her left Alayna Jonas sat wringing her hands but squaring her shoulders, so determined she was to do the right thing. Ridge Langley, a defense attorney who Victoria had the honor of trying a few cases with and who had also gone to law school with her and Ben, sat right beside Alayna, his own legal pad and pen on the table as well.

Detective Noah Hannity, whom she'd learned was a good friend of Ben's and a trustworthy detective with the saddest dusky blue eyes she'd ever seen, sat at the other end of the table. He pulled a small tape recorder from his shirt pocket and pushed it so that it was now closer to Alayna. With an affirmative nod from Ridge, he pressed the record button and asked Alayna to state her name and current address.

"Tell me what you know about the night Congressman McGill and his wife were killed," he said to her.

Victoria had warned him he needed to get a completely new statement from her, that the previous one had been missing information. She couldn't present anything Alayna had told her at the motel; that conversation had been off the record. But Alayna could and promised that she would speak honestly.

"Teddy said my daughter wasn't his," Alayna started, her voice soft. "She wasn't. I knew that. But I thought if that witch Myrna thought I had his child, she would finally let him leave and then we could be together." She took a deep breath then let it out. "I know it was stupid, everything I've ever done has been stupid. That's why I'm trying to make it right now. I'm trying to do what's right for my daughter. Lia's all that matters to me now."

Noah tried to look like he wasn't effected by the words of this young girl, but the slight slump in his shoulders said he was. Victoria knew what he was going through because she felt it too. Alayna was too young and too immature to have to deal with two cagey politicians and one dirty cop. It was such a shame.

"What time did you leave the congressman's house?" Noah asked.

"Almost ten," she said. "I drove to the café at the corner and waited there for about half an hour. Sometimes we would meet there, so I just thought that maybe if he and his wife got into an argument about the baby he would come looking for me." She shrugged. "He didn't."

"Did you see Ramone Vega at Congressman McGlinn's house?"

"I was leaving the café. I stepped out onto the corner and a car stopped at the red light. It was a gray car, I could tell because the lights from the café were really bright. There were two people in the front seat and one in the back because none of the windows were tinted. Plus it was kind of cool so I guess they didn't need to run the air conditioning. The back window was rolled down. Mr. Vega was in the backseat."

Noah nodded and proceeded with the questioning. An hour and a half went by while Alayna poured out all the information she had. Victoria's pen moved viciously across the paper, using up more than half the legal pad for notes. With Alayna on the stand, her case against Vega was ironclad. He wouldn't get off this time.

As for Alayna, who had thought she was safe in protective custody only to be kidnapped by Timothy Hall, then continuously raped and beaten for the ensuing months, Victoria could only pray that the young girl found some peace in her life. She prayed she would be a good mother to her daughter and not fall prey to cruel men again.

Speaking of which, even though she would never classify Ben as being cruel, Victoria wondered what their first encounter after all today's events would be like. He'd looked so intense at the motel, so dangerously serene after he'd shot Timothy Hall, that she admitted—if only to herself—she was a little nervous. This thing with her and Ben had started so quickly, so dramatically, she couldn't help but remember that action movie where the hero warned the heroine that relationships started under extreme circumstances didn't end well. In the movie the heroine hadn't cared and they'd ended the movie on a long, passionate kiss, amidst the wreckage of a crashed subway train that at a madman's whim had been traveling at a high rate of speed.

Neither Vega nor Hall had instigated any speeding vehicles to cause massive damage, but they'd been deadly just the same. Not only was Hall on Peña's payroll, he was also the TH Services that sent regular payments to Alayna. The money was from Mayor Radcliffe. He'd been crocked for years and had just gotten a little greedier where Alayna was concerned because after a search of his apartment, officers had found proof that he was trying to blackmail the mayor about Alayna's existence. It was a good thing Ben and the others had gotten to him first. Hall was definitely on Vega's hit list.

Everything was falling into place, and the first thing she had to do was go into court next week and win this case.

No, that wasn't the first thing she had to do. She had to deal with Ben. There was no doubt in her mind he'd be waiting right outside that door and he'd be rightfully pissed at her for leaving him in that hotel room and not mentioning that Alayna had contacted her. As reserved as she was about their confrontation, Victoria had never been one to run from her problems. She left the interview room with her note pad firmly beneath her arm and her head held high. She could handle Ben Donovan and whatever he dished out. She was almost positive of that fact.

Just as she'd expected, Ben had been sitting at another officer's desk, just outside the interrogation room. The minute he heard the door open, he turned to see her coming out. She tried for a small smile but it died the moment his gaze met hers. He was not happy, not at all. Well, okay, she knew she'd been wrong by keeping him out of the loop, but really, hadn't he done the same thing by taking so long to tell her everything that was going on? That made them even, she thought as she made purposeful strides towards him. She was an arm's length away when her cellphone rang. She'd taken it off vibrator after she'd called her mother and Grace to let them know she was alright. Now it echoed throughout the room like a siren. Good thing it was a normal ringtone and not some inappropriate song that normally blared through their office.

Stopping she pulled the phone from her pocket and glanced at the screen. With a small curse she answered. "Hey Grace. I told you I'm fine. I'm just about to leave the police station and I'll call you when I get home," she said without waiting for a greeting. Then had to pause. "What? Okay, I'm on my way!"

She'd barely switched the phone off when she felt his hand on her elbow.

"Grace is having the baby?" he asked.

She nodded.

"Let's go," he said without hesitation before leading her across the room.

CHAPTER 20

Ben and Victoria rushed to the hospital. Their confrontation or conversation about today's events had to wait. Victoria was more than exhausted, but adrenaline had run through her veins the moment she clicked off her cell. To his credit, Ben, who she sensed was still a little on edge, had simply grabbed her by the arm and led her to the elevator at the police station. He took one of the SUVs from Trent and Devlin and began driving, not saying one word to her.

She supposed she could have talked to him during the ride, but she didn't bother. Instead she stared out the window, wondering if it were going to be a boy or girl. That seemed to be the easier train of thought, the more realistic one indeed.

The moment he pulled up in front of the hospital, she grabbed the door handle. "Thanks for the ride," she tossed over her shoulder as she moved to get out.

His hand on her elbow was unexpected, as well as his words.

"I'm going to park and we can go in together."

"But that's not necessary."

"It's what I'm going to do," was all he said in response.

Victoria didn't argue, mainly because he'd kept right on driving, quickly dispelling her notion of getting out of the truck. After he parked he once again took her by the hand, walking with fast strides to the parking garage elevators where they boarded one and took it to the main floor.

"Grace Ramsey?" she asked when they'd made it to the information desk.

"Labor and Delivery, fifth floor. Go right down this hall, make a left at the circle, take the elevators to the right," the sour faced nurse informed her without once looking up from her computer.

On any other day Victoria might have called her on her rudeness, but today just didn't seem like the day. Instead she turned, reciting the directions in a whisper and walked away. On the elevator she sighed and decided it was time for the inevitable.

"Look Ben, I know you're pretty upset with me right now and I can't really say I blame you. But this is not the time. My best friend is having a baby and there's nothing else I want in this world but to stand by her side at this glorious moment. I appreciate you bringing me down here but it's fine if you leave now. I'll call you in the morning."

"Are you finished?" he asked, releasing her arm finally.

Victoria took advantage of the moment and took a step away from him.

"I'm just trying to be honest."

"Oh, now you want to be honest." Ben chuckled, but it wasn't filled with any sort of humor or animation. "Look Victoria," he began mimicking her. "You are on point with the fact that I'm upset with you right now. But I've been to a few childbirths in my lifetime and I know that they are a time of joy and love. So I'm not going to go over how foolish and immature your actions were. I'm not going to say that you harassed me about being up front and honest with you, only to turn and do something dangerously stupid behind my back. No," he said holding up a hand when she would have begun speaking again. "I'm not going to say any of that, right now. For the moment I'm going to go to the fifth floor and sit in the waiting room while Grace, an old college friend of mine, has her first child. I'm going to smile and rejoice with her and her husband for this miracle they've brought into the world. Then I'm going to take you home."

The doors to the elevator opened and so did Victoria's mouth, only to snap shut quickly because she didn't know what to say. So she simply walked off the elevator, approached another nurse—this one moderately nicer than the other—and headed to Grace's room. She was happy to see Ben hadn't followed her, but smart enough to know their real confrontation had only been postponed. If there was one thing she'd learned about Ben Donovan in these last couple of weeks, it was that he was a man of his word. If he said he was going to be waiting right there for her after Grace had the baby, that's exactly what he meant. She didn't know how things with the two of them would end or begin again, or whatever, and when she walked into the room to hear Grace's high-pitched scream, she figured she didn't really have time to consider it any longer.

After three hours of sitting in the waiting room, nodding off, going for coffee, playing Words With Friends on his cellphone, and trying desperately not to think about the gun that had been pointed at Victoria's temple, Ben was more than ready to call it a day. It had been a very trying twenty-four hours for him and to tell the truth he wasn't sure he could take much more.

But when he heard a rumbling that sounded strangely like wheels, he looked up. Every muscle in his body seemed to tense and retract in the span of ten seconds as he stood and watched while a nurse pushed a baby bassinet and Victoria looked at him with a million-watt smile. He walked to where they stood and was scarcely able to pull his gaze from her but for the tiny sound coming from the bassinet. He looked down and everything about today, every second of worry and doubt, of fear and helplessness, of adrenaline and impulsive action, was washed away.

"It's a girl," he heard Victoria whisper. "Melody Grace Ramsey."

"Melody," Ben whispered. "Hello, little Melody."

As if she'd heard him, the baby's glassy eyes stared immediately in his direction. "Pretty little Melody," he continued, warmth rising in his body like flood.

"We'll be going to the nursery now," the nurse said and Ben stepped back from the bassinet, his fingers tingling with the urge to pick Melody up and cradle her in his arms.

"She's beautiful, isn't she?" Victoria asked from behind him.

"She is," was Ben's reply. Then he turned to face her. "And so are you."

He reached out, touching his fingertips to the spot where Hall's gun had touched. At that moment he'd wanted to yell with fury, to squeeze the trigger of his own gun, killing the bastard where he stood. But that moment had passed. Then he'd wanted to yell at her, to vent his frustration at her leaving him at the hotel, for not trusting him enough to tell him what she was doing. Now, as she turned into his touch, closing her eyes slowly, Ben wanted something else.

Ben wanted to hold onto her for as long as he possible could. Stepping closer to her, he let his other hand slip around her waist, pulling her body up against his.

"I love you, Victoria. I've waited too damned long to tell you that," he whispered, his lips brushing lightly over her forehead. "And I apologize for being such an idiot when it came to you. My mother always said I was impulsive and stubborn as hell. I guess I didn't learn from my mistakes ten years ago. But I want you to know that I respect you as an accomplished and independent woman. If I've ever come on too strong with you it's because I've always had a sense that you were something special. And I was right. You're too special for me to even consider letting you walk out of my life again."

He felt her fingers tangling in his shirt as she sighed, her body leaning into his.

"You are exactly the arrogant and self-important man I thought you were, Ben Donovan."

Ben would have been alarmed by those words but she was still touching him, still staring up into his eyes as if whatever she was going to say next was the most important thing he'd ever hear.

"But you're also a very loyal and caring man, one I respect as an excellent attorney and admire as a friend. We've both waited too long to admit how we've really felt. Today just proves how short life can be. We should really stop wasting time," she told him.

"I'm so glad to hear you say that," Ben told her, releasing his own heavy sigh. Then he used a finger to slip beneath her chin, tilting her face up to his. "There's something else I'll be glad to hear you say."

She smiled, slow and intoxicating, fresh and gorgeous.

"I love you, Ben Donovan."

Hours later Ben and Victoria were in the shower, letting the hot water trickle off their skin while both soliciting moans of gratification.

She stood in front of him, her bottom pressed into his groin, his erection growing persistently. He'd been holding her around the waist, but one of his hands slowly moved upward to grasp a plump breast. The other made a southerly descent, cupping the close-cut curls of her center. A finger slipped between her damp folds and she moaned. He loved the feel of her, so soft and slippery, ready and waiting. For endless moments he simply caressed her there, letting her desire trickle over his fingers the same way the water sluiced over their skin. In his other hand, her plump breast filled his palm inciting a jolt of pleasure from his hardened shaft.

"I love your touch," she murmured.

That was just grand because Ben didn't think there was anything more he loved than touching her. His response came with action instead of words as he pressed her up against the tiles, dipping his body with hers so that his erection could slip right through her wetness to thrust into her center.

"Ben!" She gasped his name.

"Yes, Victoria," he sighed, his lips flush against her ear, his hips moving in a sensual motion.

The water had gone cold by the time they stepped out to dry off. Ben carried her to his bed and they slipped between the soft sheets with the intent to sleep the actions of the day away. Instead, they made love throughout the night, whispering their newly found devotion to one another, planning for a future they prayed would come.

Two weeks later Victoria was walking out of the courthouse, briefcase, purse and a small box of trial paraphernalia in hand. She'd parked in the garage across the street, as she'd hoped today would be the last day of trial. She'd been correct. After only a day and a half of deliberation this time, the group of twelve men and women of various races had unanimously found Ramone Vega guilty of capital murder.

Mayor Larry Radcliffe still hadn't come forward to say that Alayna's baby was his, but on her grandmother's urging Alayna had filed a child support claim. Whether Radcliffe wanted it to be or not, the news would be very public, very soon. As for Sal Peña, he had a business to run and so Victoria figured someone within the ranks would be promoted as Vega headed off to prison to await his sentencing, which some were hoping would be the death penalty.

It was all behind her now, she thought as she walked down the front steps of the Justice Center. The trial was over. She could put these last few stress-filled months behind her. As she walked, she tried not to think of how hurt she was that Ben hadn't been there to hear the verdict. She'd texted him herself to tell him the jury was back, but he hadn't shown up in the courtroom. Disappointment weighed heavily on her shoulders as she walked. They'd become so close in such a short time, she already felt like he was a huge part of her life. Maybe she'd jumped too fast, maybe...

A white limousine pulled up to the curb just as she stepped off the last step onto the sidewalk. It was pristinely shined and as long as two regular sized vehicles put together. She was just about to keep walking in the opposite direction when the back door opened and Ben stepped out. In his hand was once again a bouquet of balloons, this time all white. On his face was a grin so wide she thought for sure he'd strain some facial muscles.

Victoria couldn't help it. She smiled as she walked towards him. "I'm beginning to think you just have a fetish for balloons," she told him.

He shook his head, leaning forward to place a loud, quick kiss on her lips. "Nope. Just remembered you really didn't get a chance to enjoy the other ones I bought. And with your big victory, I decided we'd celebrate."

The driver had come from out of nowhere, since she hadn't seen him get out of the car, but now he was at her side taking the box and briefcase out of her hands. He moved to put them in the trunk as Ben motioned for her to get into the backseat of the limo.

"I hope this celebration includes dinner reservations. I'm starving," she said as she slid across the leather seats.

Ben stuffed the balloons in first, causing her to giggle when she had to push them out of her face.

"No dinner reservations."

"What? Are you planning on starving me?"

Ben leaned forward as she spoke grabbing a bottle of champagne from the ice bucket on the console between them.

"I cannot drink on an empty stomach," she continued. "I'll be dizzy and sick and…"

He'd already poured each of them a glass as she'd been talking. He put one right up to her lips and leaned in until his face was scant inches away from hers.

"I made plane reservations instead," he told her.

"What? Plane? Are you going somewhere?" she asked, not totally sure what he was leading too, and almost afraid to wish.

"I'm going to Sansonique for the Donovan family reunion and you're coming with me."

"Where?"

"It's a private island that my family owns. We're having our annual reunion there next week. And you're going to join us."

"But I haven't met anyone from your family but Trent."

"I know. That's why I figured this would be the perfect time for you to meet them all. I mean, everyone won't be there, conflicts in work schedules and all that. But the majority of us will be and you'll have a great time. They're going to adore you, half as much as I do I think."

She didn't know what to say, didn't know what to think. It was like a fairy tale, those things Victoria swore she didn't believe in. But just like a handsome prince Ben had come in and wowed her with the simplest things. Not that a private island was simple, but the balloons, the lasagna late one night in her kitchen, the lunch in the diner had all been memorable times that she loved, almost as much as she realized she loved this man.

HEART
OF A
DONOVAN

Attendees of
The Donovan Family Reunion

The Seniors are listed in order by birth along with their wives. Their children (also in order by birth) and children's families are listed below them.

Senior — Albert Donovan
Brock & Noelle {Book 4 FULL HOUSE SEDUCTION}
Brandon
Bailey

Senior – Henry & Beverly Donovan
Linc & Jade and their twin girls Torian & Tamala {Book 1 LOVE ME LIKE NO OTHER}
Trent & Tia and their son Trevor {Book 3 DEFYING DESIRE}
Adam & Camille and their son Josiah {Book 2 A CINDERELLA AFFAIR}

Senior – Bernard & Jocelyn Donovan
(Keysa & Ian are in the Dominican Republic visiting Ian's family) {Book 6 HOLIDAY HEARTS}
Brynne

Senior – Everette & Alma Donovan
Max & Deena and daughter Sophia {Book 5 TOUCH OF FATE}
Ben & Victoria (still just dating) {Book 9 PLEASURED BY A DONOVAN}

Senior – Reginald & Carolyn Donovan
(Parker is on a business trip)
Savian
Regan {Book 10 HEART OF A DONOVAN}

Senior – Bruce & Janean Donovan
Dion & Lyra Donovan {Book 7 DESIRE A DONOVAN}
Sean & Tate (engaged) and Tate's daughter Briana {Book 8 SURRENDER TO A DONOVAN}

Non-Family Members in Attendance
Sam Desdune & Karena Lakefield Desdune {SUMMER HEAT}
Gavin Lucas
Devlin Bonner

PROLOGUE

Six Months Ago
Miami, Florida

Regan knew this dance very well.

He kissed her like a dying man, or rather, a starving man, and she was the sustenance that would save his life. His fingers moved through her hair, blunt tipped fingers scraping along her scalp sending rivulets of pleasure down to the base of her spine. She wrapped her arms around his neck, tilting her head slightly as his lips moved from hers to trace a heated line along her jaw and down the column of her neck.

"I can't stop wanting you," he whispered, his breath warm over her skin.

"I know," she panted. "It's like a drug. I want to quit but I can't."

He chuckled, his hands moving over her naked body.

"This is a good drug, baby. The best," was his reply as he lifted her into his arms.

She wrapped her legs around his waist. He thrust deep inside her, filling her until the next words died in her throat. He'd been standing against the closed door of the hotel room he'd secured for them. She hadn't gotten any further than that point when she arrived about ten minutes ago.

It started with a text.

4Seasons @8

It could be said that the Four Seasons was their spot. Of course it was also the location of the last charity function her family had hosted, but tonight it belonged to them. As it had on so many other occasions.

A few minutes before the text had come through, she'd been sitting at her desk battling one hell of a headache. Between her shoulder blades, it felt as if a lead weight had been sitting there for days. She'd wanted nothing else but to go home and sink into a hot bath when work was over. But when she'd finished work at *Infinity*, instead of driving straight to her apartment, she'd gone in the opposite direction towards South Beach. She'd gone to the Four Seasons.

The moment she'd entered the room, his hands were on her. No other greeting was necessary. Now here they were, him thrusting deeply, and her stroking with a matching rhythm. Her nails grazed his bare back as he bit lightly along her collarbone.

"More," he whispered. "I want more."

She pressed closer to him, rotating her hips as his hands gripped her bottom.

"I need more, Regan," he groaned, taking steps until they were near the couch.

He pulled out of her slowly, then lowered her until her feet touched the floor.

"I need more," she echoed in reply.

"Then let me give it to you," he told her, leaning forward to take her mouth in another hungry kiss.

With quick hands he turned her around after the kiss, pushing her so that she bent over the couch, her palms flattening on the firm pillows. He used his knee to push her legs apart, his hands to rub down her back, past the slit of her rear to the dampened folds of her center.

"I'll give you everything you want," he told her. "Everything and so much more."

"Yes," she moaned when everything became his throbbing length pushing into her core once more. "Yes."

The word slipped again and again from her mouth while something deep inside her screamed, "No! No!"

CHAPTER 1

Present Day
Sansonique Island
Western Caribbean

Ben kissed Victoria like his life depended on her participation. His hands cupped her face as he pulled her closer to him, tilting his head to take the kiss even deeper. Victoria grabbed him at the waist, her fingers clutching the material of the polo shirt he wore. Her hair blew in the slight breeze, just like the ankle length sundress she wore.

They were standing on one of the cliffs that hung precariously over the crystalline blue waters of the Caribbean Sea. Just down the incline, about ten or fifteen feet away from the couple that looked as if they were going to rip each other's clothes off at any moment, stood Regan. Looking, studying, acting like a damned perverted stalker watching her cousin with the new love of his life get busy in the fading afternoon sun.

Pathetic.

Nasty and pathetic, she corrected as she did an abrupt about face and stomped the rest of the way down the incline, heading towards the main house.

The whole family was here…well, at least a good portion of the Donovans had traveled to Sansonique for their annual family reunion. Sansonique was the private isle—part of a small strand of land masses nestled between the Cayman Islands and Jamaica called the Heart Islands—owned by the Donovan Corporation and each of the six Donovan brothers equally. Located in the Western Caribbean, Sansonique encompassed a little more than twelve acres of land which was divided by lush tropical hillside down its center and bordered by white sandy beaches. To the west was the Donovan complex, a small villa with the main house at its center. On the eastern side of the island was another series of buildings that had been abandoned before their purchase. Recently, however, as the Donovans were known for their keen business sense, they'd reconstructed these buildings to create a ten suite resort. After a family vote that took place via email, the resort had been named Camelot.

Each year, the Donovans met on the island for their annual family reunion. So far, in addition to Regan and her family, Ben and Max were here with their parents and their significant others and Max's absolutely adorable little girl, Sophia. Uncle Henry and Aunt Beverly were here with Trent, Linc and Adam and their families. Uncle Bernard, his wife and daughter Brynne were arriving on Wednesday. Bailey and Brandon, Uncle Albert's twins, had arrived with their father early yesterday morning.

She figured they'd all showed up since this week the family would also share in the wedding of the twin's older brother Brock Remington, who Uncle Albert and his wife adopted after Brock's father was brutally murdered and his mother was confined to a mental institution. Brock was marrying Noelle Vincent, sister of Linc's wife Jade. The two had been living together in St. Michaels, Maryland for a couple of years now and had finally decided to tie the knot.

People did that...got married, she meant. More often than not in fact, but Regan didn't see what all the hoopla was about. Marriage was for the clinically insane, she thought with a huff as she continued to walk back to the house. Why would any woman want to voluntarily give up her freedom, sacrifice everything she'd always worked for, fought for, to become some man's arm candy? With a shake of her head she tried to rid of herself of the thought.

Once upon a time Regan had thought differently. In fact, there had been years of her life when she'd done nothing but dream of her wedding day, her gown, her bridesmaids, the cakes...and, of course, the groom. Now at twenty-seven, and after having some experience with men under her belt, she was beginning to give up on that particular fairy tale. Her life was certainly different from what she'd planned, but she wasn't complaining. She had everything she wanted: a dream job that granted access to the brightest and best in the fashion industry and a loving family. Nothing else mattered—especially not those things that were out of her control.

"Hello, Regan."

All thoughts of control fled her mind as she heard the male voice. The material of her dress danced around her legs as the breeze picked up and her heart rate instantly increased. She swallowed, licked her lips and squared her shoulders convincing herself that what she thought she heard was wrong. Who she thought this was could not possibly be here on this island. Not now, not when she'd planned a week of rest and relaxation, a time to share with her family, to let down her guard and just exist. He was not here destroying all that, he couldn't be.

And yet the moment she turned around and looked up into those deep dark brown eyes, she wanted to curse. Instead her fists clenched at her sides and she resolutely smiled at him.

"Hello, Gavin."

Stunning. That was the word Gavin decided most accurately described Regan Donovan. There was everything traditionally pretty about her—the golden honey complexion, eyes an intense amber shade, hair always perfectly styled. Today it was pulled back from her face to cascade down her back in tiny braids that blended her natural dark brown hair color with a striking blonde. Growing up with four sisters had given him the acute ability to really scrutinize a woman and to also appreciate every perfect nuance she possessed.

However, Regan Donovan was far from perfect. That might actually be the most intriguing fact about her, at least in Gavin's mind. For as good as she looked to the eye, it was her personality that could be more than off-putting. In business she was confident and assertive, a definite authority on the African-American influence in the fashion arena. On a personal level, she was independent, exacting, candid and, lately, just a pinch shy of rude when he'd been lucky enough to be in her presence. When they were younger, he admitted to doing a lot of baiting when he was around Regan. He just couldn't help himself. She was like that beautiful shinning star atop a Christmas tree, the one he often looked up to as a young boy, longing to touch it, to experience its magic firsthand. But his mother had told him to wait, that one day he would be tall enough to not only reach the top of the tree to touch the star, but to put the star atop himself. That day had finally come the year he turned thirteen. Thanks to a growth spurt that summer he'd grown to stand at just about five feet tall. Of course, many years and a few more growth spurts had passed so that now he was six feet, four inches tall with long arms and legs that could have supported an NBA career.

Yet, no matter his height, here he was, still reaching for that seemingly unobtainable star.

"Lyra told me you were out here," he said, deeply inhaling her deliciously feminine scent as another breeze sifted past them.

"What's that they say about snitches?" she quipped, drawing her arms up to fold slowly over her chest.

He chuckled at what he knew to expect from her.

"What are you doing here?" was her follow up question.

"I'm on vacation," was his response.

"This is a private island that nobody but this family knows about. You are not family," she told him in a cool, curt manner.

Gavin recognized this for what it truly was, Regan's only defense mechanism. She didn't hate all men; he knew that from the many dates she went on when they were back home in Miami. He also knew how seeing her on those dates or hearing about them later made him feel. She would love for him to believe that she hated him, but Gavin knew better. They both knew better.

"I'd like to consider myself a family friend," he told her. "At least that's how Parker describes our relationship."

She raised one elegantly arched eyebrow. His groin tightened.

"Parker's a jerk the majority of the time, so I wouldn't place a lot of stock in what he says."

"Okay. Well, even if I ignore the comments about being a family friend, I couldn't actually ignore the business aspect of this trip."

Her lips tilted at the ends, a sure sign she was becoming annoyed. Only that action just made the blood pound more fiercely in Gavin's ears as lust threatened to end this otherwise cordial conversation. There was never a time that he was near Regan that he didn't want to grab her to him and kiss her into compliance. Flashes of how that kiss would ultimately play out sifted through his mind. Those thoughts signified his real reason for making this trip—he was tired of waiting for Regan Donovan.

"I thought you said you were on vacation."

Gavin shrugged, trying to appear nonchalant about this confrontation. "It's a mixture. A week on a beautiful Caribbean island has all the markings of seven days of rest and relaxation. But Parker asked me to take a look at your new resort."

"You own restaurants and Parker's work is primarily with the television station, so your story doesn't add up. Besides, Parker couldn't even make this trip, so again your reasons don't make sense?" She'd raised her voice and had quickly closed the space between them so that now when she poked her finger it landed center mass in Gavin's chest.

On the one hand he was grateful for the contact. On the other, he was grateful it was just her finger and not a bullet, with which she had threatened him before.

He looked down at her, eyes alight with the anger she'd allowed to take charge, lips almost trembling with the urge to unleash a little more verbal fire at him.

"You're a business woman, Regan. I'm a businessman, just like the majority of your family. There might be a chance that we'll be joining forces in the near future. I'm simply here to check out the possibilities."

He touched her lightly, taking her wrist and moving her hand away from his chest. She was about to say something when he used his other hand to cup the side of her face, tilting her upward as he bent forward.

"Don't talk, Regan. Just kiss me."

For the barest second, Gavin actually considered the possibility of her kneeing him in the groin, then leaving him howling in pain lying at the foot of the hill. But the moment his lips brushed against hers and he heard the familiar sigh that meant she'd momentarily given in, he felt safe. And the second their tongues collided, he felt as if he were on fire.

CHAPTER 2

It had been this way each and every time. That was the first thing she absolutely hated about Gavin Lucas. He was so damned attractive with his school boy charm and purely grown up sexual allure. Whenever he walked into a room, his slim but muscular frame and smooth as butter personality mesmerized everyone within his path.

Regan had known Gavin since their days running around Meadowland Academy, the private elementary and middle school they'd attended together. Gavin was three years older than her, but it seemed like he was always around when she was in school, from the day she'd been pushed by Blake Rothchild when she was in kindergarten. Blake was a spoiled, over-privileged first grader who thought just because Regan was a girl and a little shorter than the other girls in her class that he could take advantage of her. He'd soon learned his lesson when she'd kicked him in the groin and watched him stumble back in pain. That was the first time Gavin had appeared out of nowhere. The confident, well-dressed third grader took the blame for Blake's accident and served a day of detention as well as enduring endless hours of reprimand from the school's dean and his parents. She hadn't been happy about him taking the blame for her but she'd remained quiet.

Years later, when Gavin was about to graduate and move on to the high school of his choice, Regan had been a sixth grader. She'd watched the girls making fools out of themselves over him. It seemed strange to her because she hadn't thought he was all that. Obviously she'd been wrong.

Thankfully, she'd attended a different high school than Gavin, but she'd seen him as she attended a couple of cotillions where he'd chaperoned his sisters. Then he went away to college and so did she. The next time she saw him, she was twenty-two and he was twenty-five. They were in L.A., both young and attractive people far away from their homes and families. Regan was attending the Fashion Institute for Design and Merchandising and Gavin was just finishing his internship with a famous west coast chef whose name she couldn't remember.

Being in L.A. and seeing the adult Gavin had become made him seem different to Regan. It had been sort of revitalizing to talk to someone she knew and could share stories with while wondering about this person who looked so much better than she'd remembered. And she'd been twenty-two, she reminded herself. It was no wonder they'd ended up in bed together.

The remaining times she'd found herself in the throes of passion with this man were no less intense, but unfortunately more regrettable.

Now he was kissing her. And she was kissing him. Damn, was she kissing him. With every lap of his tongue she tried to devour him. His taste was intoxicating. Coupled with the scent of the ocean and the soft breeze against her skin, she thought she might actually be in heaven. His hands had traveled down her back to grip her bottom with the strength and fervor that always made her tremble. Her breasts swelled instantly, pressing against his muscled chest as she wrapped her arms around his neck, pulling him closer. This was where they always ended up, like magnets forever drawn to each other. In his arms, she was everything feminine and desirable, right where she wanted to be.

But she wasn't, not really. She was on her family's private island about to celebrate their family reunion and her cousin's marriage. This was definitely not the time nor place. Not to mention the fact that the last time she'd ended up in Gavin's arms, she'd sworn it would be her last.

With that thought, she pushed away from him. The push was so hard both of them stumbled. Of course, he held tight to her arms probably thinking she was going to fall. When she felt steady, she pulled out of his grasp.

"We're not going there again, Gavin. Ever," she said and hated that it sounded just like what she'd said a little less than a year ago.

"This is not like before, Regan. I think you know that," he told her in a smug, self-assured tone.

She hated that tone, hated how he thought he knew everything there was to know about her all the time. Gavin Lucas knew nothing about her. All he knew was what he saw—the face, the clothes, the name. That was all.

"Look, we're both logical adults. We adopted the 'friends with benefits' motto with success for longer than most could claim. But I'm over that now. Sleeping together whenever the itch arises is not enough for me anymore."

He took a step towards her and she took a step back. "It's not enough for me either."

"Good. We agree that ship has sailed and we move on. That means no more touching or kissing or…"

"No more wanting or needing. Can you really stand here and tell me you don't want me anymore? That what we've shared has simply run its course."

Regan knew what Gavin expected to hear. She knew what any other woman would say to his questions, to what he was proposing. But she wasn't any other woman and she hadn't come this far in her life to lay everything she had on the line for a man like Gavin.

"I'm over it, Gavin."

He shook his head. "That kiss said something different."

"Lust is basic. If you head to your local high school, you'll find it oozing out of every classroom. It means nothing," she said with the aloofness she'd adopted in her everyday life.

"You're lying," was his simple reply. "And just so we're both clear about my intentions, the other reason I'm here on this beautiful island is to prove to you that I'm also over the friends with benefits status of our relationship. I'm ready for more and I'm not leaving you alone until you seriously consider what we could be together."

She opened her mouth to speak but he was closer now, putting his fingers lightly to her lips. As irritated as she was, Reagan didn't swipe his hand away. The slight touch had incited more heat that swirled in the pit of her stomach threatening to push her forward to once again end up in his arms. It took all her strength to fight that sensation.

"I'll see you around," were Gavin's parting words.

He dropped his hand from her mouth and turned to walk away. For what seemed like endless moments, Regan watched until he'd vanished around the east wall of the main house.

"This is not good," she murmured with lips still tingling from his kiss. "Not good at all."

The table in the dining room was huge. It had to be to look remotely normal in the room that could easily fit her loft apartment inside. All of the rooms on the first floor of the main house were large and meticulously decorated in a contemporary style that reflected the chic, yet homely style of the senior Donovans. Each of the senior brothers' wives had some input in the décor—all except Aunt Darla, who had passed away leaving Uncle Albert, the twins and Brock alone more than ten years ago.

Two custom made twelve foot oak tables were lined together, high backed ornately designed chairs inserted all around. At exactly 6:30 in the evening, every Donovan that had arrived on the island were seated as Uncle Henry said the blessing.

"Ben's girlfriend is really pretty," Lyra whispered to Regan once they'd all begun passing bowls and fixing their own plates.

On the menu tonight was rotisserie chicken, mashed potatoes, steamed green beans, sweet corn and hot buttered rolls. Instead of hiring a cook for the week, the Donovans chose a more diplomatic solution. The women would prepare breakfast, thus freeing up the rest of their days for wedding preparations and activities. The men whose wedding preparations consisted mostly of playing golf and swimming, would handle dinner. This was something Regan was interested in seeing because her father was not a fan of cooking.

Regan agreed. "Yes, she is. Have you talked to her?"

"Just a little when they first arrived. She's an attorney as well. A prosecutor, which is kind of strange since Ben's a defense attorney. They haven't been dating long, but she's known him since law school," Lyra reported.

"Hmmm...the friends to lovers theme seems to be running rampant in this family," she snipped.

Lyra, probably because she'd known Regan for years, didn't look offended at all. Especially since it was only about nine months ago that Lyra—who had been taken in by Aunt Janean and Uncle Bruce when she was ten years old—had come back to Miami and realized she was in love with Regan's cousin Dion. They'd been married for six months now and still wore that undeniable newlywed glow.

"Nothing wrong with friends turning to lovers," Lyra added as she scooped a forkful of potatoes into her mouth.

"I second that," Dion chimed in.

Regan watched with only mild annoyance as Dion leaned forward to accept the kiss his wife offered—undeniable newlywed glow to the fifth power!

Sean, Dion's younger brother, groaned from across the table where he sat beside his fiancée Tate. "Please don't get these two started," Sean said.

Sean and Tate were a new couple as well, having gone through a pretty scary situation when Tate's ex had returned and kidnapped their two-year-old daughter, Briana. Sean had been shot as he, Dion and their family friend Devlin Bonner had faced Sabine Ravenell, the woman who used to be their top rival in the magazine business and who happened to be Tate's ex-husband's sister.

It was good to see Sean, Tate and Briana so happy after all they'd been through. But the engaged couple had a glow as well. That whole relationship thing seemed to be spreading through the family like some deadly disease.

"I don't want any of you cuddly couples to get started," Regan quipped.

"Aww, feeling like a third wheel, sis?" Savian, one of Regan's older brothers, said in his dry tone.

"Not as long as you're around," was her quick response. It was no secret that Savian was anti-relationship, and considering the last time any of the family had seen him with a woman, he was obviously anti-dating as well. While nobody really knew his reason for driving in the solo lane, they could all agree that his lack of companionship was making him an irritating grouch to be around. For that, Regan felt a certain amount of relief. As long as Savian was the hard-up irritable one, her single status wasn't an issue. Not to anyone except Gavin, who sat next to Savian but was currently engaged in a conversation with her father and Uncle Bruce.

"The difference with me is that I like my status," Savian told them all after taking a sip from his glass. "See, all of you are looking for that perfect someone, the ying to your yang. And it's only when you find that perfect partner that you believe you've entered into this euphoric state of being. I, on the other hand, reject the idea of anything so story-book predictable."

"Spoken like a man who's not getting any," Dion added, and everyone chuckled.

"What about you, Gavin?" Lyra asked, ignoring the loud clanking of Regan's fork as it fell to her plate. "Are you looking for love or do you share Savian's grim view of relationships?"

Regan tried like hell not to look at him, but she knew he was looking at her. She could feel the intensity of his gaze from across the room. Sitting only across the table from him made that intensity feel like an inferno. But she wouldn't be bullied, especially not at her familial home.

Gavin was staring at her. The minute she caught his gaze, the corner of his mouth lifted in a half smile that had actually made lesser women swoon.

"Yes, Gavin," she stated, offering an amazing smile of her own. "Please share your views on love and committed relationships."

He used a napkin to wipe his hands as he sat back in his seat. An answer was coming, Regan knew as surely as she knew her own name. He would respond and it would be something smooth and impressive, just as everything he ever said or did was. But would it be the truth? That's the one thing Gavin Lucas had never been capable of. In the years they'd been involved, he'd lied to her more than any man she'd ever known—more than she ever planned to tolerate again.

"I believe in true love," he started in a low, deep voice. "I also believe in one perfect partner. Two people who will compliment and complete one another. Not Savian's the ying to my yang, but the day to my night, the up to my down."

Regan wanted to make a puking sound. She wanted to roll her eyes and leave the table...his words were so nauseating. "You mean the Juliet to your Romeo?" she asked sweetly instead.

He smiled. "Exactly."

"They died you know," she snapped back. "So much for true love."

Silence ensued around her, or at least at their end of the table. She retrieved her fork, jabbing it into a piece of chicken. Just as she was about to lift it to her mouth she noticed them all staring at her, Lyra especially. With an unmitigated anger towards Gavin for showing up and potentially ruining her vacation, she slipped the fork into her mouth and chewed slowly. They could stare all they wanted. She didn't give a damn. Every one of them had their own opinions about love and relationships. She didn't have to agree with any of them and, in fact, didn't agree with any of them.

The one man she'd thought she loved had betrayed her and attempted to make a fool out of her.

Luckily, she'd come to her senses in time. She'd walked away as unscathed as possible and wasn't about to turn back. No matter how sexy he looked sitting across the table from her.

CHAPTER 3

Las Vegas

On a crisp sunny morning, an old renovated school bus that had been painted black—the windows covered with two-ply wire mesh, the front glove compartment re-configured to house three automatic rifles and locked for security purposes—drove at the speed limit down the Las Vegas Freeway.

Cars whizzed by as shirt and tie dressed drivers were late for work. A minivan pulled along the side of the bus. A baby was snapped into a child seat behind the driver and a little boy maybe four or five fastened tightly in a seatbelt behind the passenger seat. The boy pressed his face to the window, crocked his neck in an attempt to look up at the passengers on the bus. On instinct, a man made one of his meanest faces and watched with minor enjoyment as the toddler winced in fear and hurriedly sat back in his seat, eyes forward.

A wry chuckle escaped as he too looked forward.

"Ain't nothing to be laughing at, Vega. Where you're going there's nothing funny happening and nothing to make you happy."

He looked at the guard who'd just spoken—the other inmates called him a pig. Vega didn't only because he thought it was cliché. Unfortunately, the cop actually looked like a pig, with his wide flat nose pressed into the center of his face like a road block. His uniform, the official issue from the Nevada State Correctional Institution, was starched perfectly and smoothed tightly over his bulging girth. At his right side, keys jingled. On his left, a gun was holstered.

Vega continued to smile.

"Stupid ass," the guard said in response. He wasn't happy that Vega wouldn't go word-for-word with him, and so he walked up the aisle once more, egging on another, weaker-minded inmate who sat close to the front of the bus.

Vega kept his gaze forward for another couple of miles, then he looked at the digital clock at the front of the bus. It was the clock that served as a countdown to the last hours of their interaction with the outside world. He looked to his left exactly two minutes later and smiled genuinely when he saw the black Navigator pull up beside the bus.

He leaned forward and spit out the pin he'd been holding on the inner side of his jaw for the last four hours. That cute big breasted guard back at the central booking unit had passed it to him after he'd sucked her tits so long that she came hard and loud in the handicapped stall of the female restroom. The pin fell onto his thigh and he maneuvered his arms around from his back until his thumb and forefinger could grasp it, ever thankful for being double-jointed. Exactly three minutes later, he'd unlatched the lock of the handcuffs, a technique he'd learned from Big Sal on his sixteenth birthday. It took less than fifteen seconds to free the shackles at his feet.

On his way back up to a seated position, he began to cough. The sound was loud, hard and almost to the point of being gross, until the asshole guard turned back around to frown at him.

"You getting a case of the nerves now, Vega? Scared of what's waiting up ahead for you in the pen?" the guard asked, taking slow steps back up the aisle, closer to Vega's seat.

Vega continued to cough, his eyes watering with the effort.

"Better not puke on this floor or you're cleaning it with a toothbrush before you get off," he taunted.

Vega hunched his shoulders, his vision only slightly blurry as he readied for movement. On the same side as his keys was a baton that the guard had slipped from his utility belt while he walked. By the time he was standing next to the row where Vega sat, he'd had the baton extended and used it to poke Vega's right shoulder. In the next instant, Vega grabbed the baton pulling so hard that the officer fell forward. He reached to the guard's left a split second before the guard could get his own hand there, and flipped the latch on his holster to free the gun.

The first shot came exactly three minutes after Vega had initially spied the black truck. When the pig guard fell back, Vega stood and shot him again, right in his wide flat nose. Another guard stood near the front door, heading for the glove compartment. He took a bullet to the back of his skull. The driver swerved and radioed for help. In three long strides, Vega was next to him, gun pointed to his head.

"Pull the goddamned bus over now!" he told him.

"You're never going to get away with this," the guard warned him as he did as Vega instructed.

When the bus came to a stop, Vega looked ahead. The black SUV pulled off the road in front of them. "You won't live to find out," he quipped before pulling the trigger.

He yanked the keys from the guard's belt as the body slumped to the side and tossed them to the first inmate seated in the third row. "Make yourself useful," he told him, then kicked through the doors and walked off the bus like the free man he now was.

⁓

"You have a great family. Grace told me they were very down to earth and genuinely nice people. I'm sorry that I didn't believe her," Victoria Lashley said as she towel-dried her hair and stepped out of the private bathroom adjacent to the room she and Ben had been assigned.

It was a fantastic room—not as big as a hotel suite, but still roomy enough for a king-sized bed, two dressers, a small table with two chairs, two bookshelves and a recliner. What she enjoyed most about this room was the patio door that led to a small balcony where she'd stood earlier in the day looking out to the crystal blue water of the sea and inhaling the intoxicating tropical air.

"I always knew Grace was an intelligent woman," Ben told her.

He was sitting on the bed, his back propped up by a couple of pillows, his chest bare. For a second, Victoria let herself be distracted by the sight of Ben Donovan's expertly cut chest and abs. Of course her mouth watered in that second, her breasts swelled and her juncture ached. The quick and potent reaction to seeing him even partially naked was something she was still getting used to.

"I'm just not used to big families," she continued, tossing the towel into the wicker basket near the window. Thankful for the even shorter cut of her hair courtesy of her scissor-happy stylist, Victoria retrieved the bottle of spray conditioner from the dresser she would be using for the week. As she spritzed her locks, she saw Ben watching her through the mirror. A few months ago she would have never pictured herself doing something as domestic as preparing her hair and herself for bed in front of a man. After being hunted by a killer and threatened by a cop, she supposed anything was possible.

"My family likes you," Ben whispered from behind her.

He'd gotten up off the bed and now stood right behind her, his fingers touching strands of her hair.

"They're probably nice to all the women you bring home for the first time," she quipped, trying to pretend his touch wasn't so intimate that it made her nervous.

His hands stilled, then fell to brush along her neck. He reached around to tilt her chin upward so that she stared at him through the mirror once more.

"You are the first woman I've ever brought to our family reunion, to this island or to meet my family. Is that clear enough for you?"

"I wasn't trying to fish for information," she admitted nervously. "It's just that—"

Ben turned her so that she was now facing him, her back against the dresser. He removed the brush she'd been holding from her hand and wrapped her arms around his neck.

"It's just that this is as new to you as it is to me. We're both trying to figure this out. And for two tenacious attorneys, not having all the answers is a different experience," he told her when his arms were wrapped solidly around her waist.

"That's not what I was going to say," she sighed.

He smiled. "But it was close."

She could only smile in return, because he was right.

"Everything is going to be fine, Victoria. We have our whole lives ahead of us now that the trial and all that drama is behind us."

He was right again, she thought as she tilted her head for his kiss. The biggest murder trial of her life was behind her. Ramone Vega was in jail, Timothy Hall was dead, Mayor Radcliffe had resigned from office (which had her former supervisor shifting gears and preparing for a run for mayor instead of district attorney) and Alayna Jonas had been reunited with her family. Not to mention the fact that Victoria herself was vacationing on a gorgeous private island with a very attractive man that she'd never imagined would want her. All was definitely well. She just needed to relax enough to enjoy it.

They'd been dating for just over two months now and a few times had forgotten to use protection, Ben made a point of always being prepared now. As he kept her backed against the dresser, he'd reached around her to where he'd placed his wallet. In seconds, he'd retrieved a condom and slipped it in place. The moment Ben lifted her from the floor, Victoria eagerly wrapped her legs around him. "You're always prepared, aren't you?" she asked coyly, her center throbbing with anticipation.

He grinned, leaning forward to lick along her lower lip. "Only when you're near," he whispered in response.

Ben's desire for her was insatiable, and hers for him was much the same. He'd probably known she was naked beneath the short nightgown she'd slipped on after her shower, and now that he was sheathed, his entrance into her waiting core was swift and pleasurable. On a long, slow moan as he began to thrust deeply inside her, she whispered, "You're right, everything is fine. So…damned…fine."

CHAPTER 4

Breakfast had been a task since Regan, apparently taking after her dad, wasn't the world's best cook. Still, she'd been determined to put forth as much (if not more) effort than the rest of the family simply because that's the way she'd always functioned. Growing up in a house with two older brothers who wore the Donovan name like a badge of honor made her fiercely competitive and determined to please. Of course, determination often took a second seat to her stubborn independency so the likelihood of her succumbing to things she deemed weak or inconsequential was slim to none. Instead these traits had molded and shaped her into the successful woman she now was.

"If you burn that toast, you're never going to live it down," Lyra came up behind her to whisper.

Regan hadn't been startled but instead moved slowly, deliberately, to manually eject the four slices of bread from the toaster, all the while cursing her wayward thoughts for distracting her from the task at hand. "I'm not going to burn the toast," she stated firmly, praying she hadn't already done exactly that.

The slices she removed were of a darker shade of brown than she normally liked her toast but no parts had turned black yet, so she figured she was safe. Placing those slices on the silver platter her mother, Carolyn, had given her, she dutifully pulled more bread from the package and dropped them into the toaster. This was probably the safest assignment besides pouring juice into the decanters, which had been Carolyn's first assignment for her daughter when she entered the kitchen.

"You're distracted," Lyra said, situating her cutting board so she could stand close to Regan while she sliced thick pieces of country smoked ham.

"I'm tired," was Regan's reply. Tired and distracted had different implications. She didn't like what distracted implied.

"When are you going to just give in and sleep with Gavin Lucas?" Lyra asked in the quiet but serious way she at times possessed.

The words "I'm not" were on the tip of Regan's tongue, but they would be a lie. Nobody knew about the relationship she'd shared with Gavin all these years because it was the one thing she'd done as an adult that Regan wasn't proud of. She'd allowed herself to be a man's side piece. They'd always called each other friends and offered nothing but respect whenever they were in mixed company. But basically, that's what she'd been. Their secret had been safe for five years. And now, he was here, on her home turf. For once in her life, Regan wasn't sure how to handle a situation.

"I'm not distracted by Gavin Lucas, or by sex, Lyra. Just because you're getting some on a regular basis now doesn't mean you have to rub it in." She chuckled after that statement because she wanted to take Lyra's mind off her sex life and revert it back to the one her friend now shared with Dion.

Lyra had been her best friend since she'd come to live with Aunt Janean and Uncle Bruce. After years of playing with only her brothers and Dion and Sean, Regan had been elated to finally have a girl in the family close by. Bailey had lived in Dallas with her family and Uncle Bernard didn't have custody of Keysa when she was young, so she'd rarely seen her.

"I'm not trying to rub it in. I'm trying to share the wealth, so to speak," Lyra had told her. "Look, we're on vacation. He's here and you're here. Why not just get it over with? Once we get back to Miami, it'll be over and done, and you two can go back to hating each other. Besides, it's going to be a long week with you two snapping at each other every five minutes."

"Who's snapping at whom? And why? We're supposed to be getting ready for the wedding on Saturday. We don't have time for any snapping."

That was Jade, Linc's wife, who had been on the other side of the kitchen getting down all the dishes and silverware to set the table. Jade was normally very calm and kind of reserved. But since the wedding she was speaking of was her baby sister Noelle's, she was allowed to be just a little high strung.

"Nobody's snapping at anybody," Regan immediately replied. "However, we are still waiting to find out what our bridesmaids dresses look like."

An excellent shift of subject, Regan thought with an inward smile, even though Lyra had still given her knowing looks throughout the rest of the morning. It was just after noon now and Regan had another hour before she was to join all the women in Noelle's room. That's where Camille had taken their gowns to keep them from being seen.

Camille Davis Donovan, the owner and head designer of CK Davis Designs, had married Adam Donovan three years ago. Since then, she'd designed the wedding ensemble for Tia St. Claire, the supermodel who married Trent Donovan, and the majority of the evening gowns for the senior Donovans—Aunt Beverly, Aunt Janean and Regan's mother Carolyn—whenever they had a charity function or black-tie gala to attend. That didn't even include all the couture outfits Regan herself owned courtesy of Camille's ingenious design skills. To say Regan was über excited about seeing her dress was an understatement.

With that in mind, she'd decided to steal a few moments alone because once the caterers, decorators and musicians arrived tomorrow morning, the island would be total chaos. The plan was for all the vendors to stay at Camelot. This would give them an opportunity to test everything out before the paying guests arrived.

Sansonique was a picturesque island surrounded by the clear and refreshing Caribbean waters. On land, the parts that weren't covered with trees and tropical foliage, gorgeous one of a kind plants and flowers, were occupied by two stately dwellings which might resemble contemporary castles for modern royalty—the Donovan complex to one side and Camelot to the other.

She'd walked for a while, letting the warm breeze toss her braided hair lightly and ruffle through the knee length dress she wore today. Its tight fitting bodice flared out so that she had to hold onto the material to keep it from flying upward and exposing herself completely. That had made her laugh, just as the feel of the soft warm sand filtering through her toes had calmed her raging thoughts. She'd traipsed slowly through the forest from its entrance just beyond the border of the main house. The path was familiar to her as she moved away from the house.

This was deeper than she thought anyone in the family had ever gone. All of them were more enamored with the water and the beaches close to the house than what was beyond the dark depths of the forest. But not Regan. Ever the explorer. That's what her father had always said when she was little and would go off following behind the boys. Once Lyra had moved in, Regan had tried to stay close to the house more and she'd tried to do the things that little girls were expected to do. But inside, she'd always wanted to go off and do more.

At what she considered the base of the forest, the trees opened up. Hibiscus weaved a sort of path into the open where sunlight poured over more flowers and more greenery. In the distance she could hear the rush of a waterfall; it fell from the mountain into a creek that led out to the ocean in a crystalline flourish. But that wasn't where Regan was heading. No, her spot, the best place on the entire island where she could sit and look out to the water and get lost in the simplicity of it all, was just to the left.

About twenty feet away was a cliff that fell about thirty or forty feet to beach. She stood at that spot, looking out to what was possibly one of nature's greatest achievements.

"You shouldn't be all the way out here alone."

The deep voice startled her and she turned so fast she almost tripped over her own feet. Cursing, she looked up at him, clasping her sandals in her left hand just a little tighter.

"Don't you have some work to do?" she asked Gavin, who once again was smiling down at her as if they shared their own special joke.

She hated when he looked at her like that. Actually, the look made her tingle all over. He had dark brown eyes, cool like root beer, and when he smiled they warmed. His complexion was almost the same shade as his eyes and the close, neat cut of his hair and the beard he'd been wearing for the last year was always precise, adding smoothness to his already alluring swagger.

Dammit! She hated him and wanted him desperately at the same time. She was so screwed.

"I'm waiting for my supplies to come in," he said. "They should be here tomorrow."

When she didn't speak, he continued.

"I've been walking around the island since after breakfast. Camelot is in a good location. Only about a mile from the beach on one side, with plenty of scenic interior views on the other. The rooms are spacious, functional and classy. The restaurant is going to be key," he continued, moving closer inland as if he just expected her to follow.

"I still want to talk to Parker about the access onto the island. We can work out a contract with an existing charter company. But if we want to maximize the experience for guests, an entrance and exit is required. The current access works well and I found another spot closer to the resort. I know that's not my area of expertise, but he wanted my opinion on the entire resort, so I plan to give it to him."

It had been hard to ignore his words and even harder for her business mind not to kick in and start thinking about what he was saying. She ended up following him because she had something to contribute to his observations.

"But won't it seem awkward that a guest checks in at one place and check out at another?" she asked, stepping through a small patch of branches that hadn't been cleared from the path.

"It depends how far check-in and check-out are from the resort," he replied, not even looking back at her.

"Check-in and check-out should be on the eastern side. Preferably not too far apart. Maybe a deck just north of the resort. Check-out could be further that way." She pointed just south of where she could see the edge of Camelot.

His silence caught her attention and she turned to find him standing directly behind her, looking down at her as if seeing her for the first time.

"I knew there was more inside your head than just dresses and shoes," he said, lifting one long braid and twirling it between his fingers.

"Of course there is. I did go to college," she said, but couldn't muster enough energy for it to sound sarcastic.

"I know you went to college. I know the apartment you lived in while in college and the classes you took. I also know the date you graduated and returned to Miami with your family. And, this is the most important thing...I know about your college years, Regan. I know every man you dated while you were living in L.A.," he told her seriously.

She couldn't stop looking at him, no matter how much her brain was screaming to turn away. And he was staring down at her intently, like whatever she said next was sure to be the most important words he'd ever hear. Then his words sank in and she bristled.

"You spied on me while I was in college?"

He shook his head. "I wouldn't call it spying. I was very aware of who you surrounded yourself with."

"But you went to school in New York. That's where you studied and began your career in the culinary industry. You weren't in L.A. until my senior year," she said slowly. Her senior year was the year they'd first slept together.

"My oldest sister is a cop in L.A. I stayed with her while I studied under Chef Goutier."

"But why?" she asked still trying to wrap her mind around the fact that he'd watched her all those years, or had her watched she should say.

Regan was no stranger to private investigators and having secrets revealed. Her cousin Trent was a former Navy SEAL who now ran a PI firm with locations in Las Vegas and in Connecticut. Trent had also done some freelance work for the government, so he was more than versed in uncovering dirt on people, organizations and sometimes countries. He'd done just that during the potential hostile takeover faced by *Infinity*, the magazine where Regan worked which was owned by DNT, the media company run by her father and Uncle Bruce.

But Gavin was a chef. He owned two restaurants, Cora's Café in New York, which boasted rich southern cuisine, and

Spaga in Miami, which had a trendy American and Mediterranean feel. This was common knowledge, not because she'd kept any type of tabs on him. All this lead to her next question.

"Why are you here looking around and thinking about resorts? You already have two restaurants that are doing well? I don't get the connection with you and my brother," she said suspiciously.

Gavin picked up on the change of her tone instantly. He'd known the day would come where he'd be forced to answer these questions for her because Regan wasn't like any of the other women he'd known. She wouldn't settle for anything except the absolute truth. Lies and partial answers weren't going to work for her. She was too damned smart for her own good is what her brother Parker had told him once. Now, Gavin was seeing that for himself. And yet, none of them had told her why their families remained so close. Gavin wasn't about to be the one to get into that with her, not now anyway.

"You know that Parker and I went to school together," he began.

"And?" she asked, lifting a brow.

She wore little or no make-up today so her face looked fresh, her eyes big and expressive, lips lightly glossed and definitely kissable.

"And he and my sister had a thing before she met her husband and moved to L.A. When you decided what college you wanted to attend, Parker gave me a call."

For a split second, he felt bad, considering he knew how she felt about lies. But what he'd said was not a lie. It wasn't everything, but it was still the truth.

Her eyes had narrowed a bit as he talked and he wanted to laugh at her growing irritation. Not that irritating Regan was his goal, but he found it amusing and eye-opening how well he knew her though they'd never been involved in a real relationship.

"So Parker told you to have your sister keep tabs on me? Did he tell you to keep a list of my boyfriends as well, because that doesn't sound like Parker?"

"He told me to have Lydia look out for you. I told Lydia I wanted to know everyone you knew. And she provided that information." After she'd warned him and Parker that spying on Regan was a very bad idea.

"You idiot!" she said, pushing Gavin in the chest so hard he stumbled back.

"How dare you watch me like I was some infant on a playground!" Regan continued, her voice growing louder as she poked a finger into his chest.

Gavin felt like they'd played this scene out yesterday on another part of the island while discussing a different, albeit still touchy subject. This time he decided to let her argument play itself out since this was most likely a long time coming and a portion of the grownup inside him figured she was well within her rights to be angry. He shouldn't have had her spied on, but he'd wanted to know the moment she became serious with another man because that would be the moment he dropped everything in New York and headed across country to claim what he'd always felt was his.

"You had no right to spy on me, especially when you were probably in New York doing any and everything in a skirt that walked past you!" she continued.

Her finger poked him until all of a sudden her words abruptly stopped and her arms flailed out, grasping the material of his shirt for leverage. This action caught Gavin off guard since he'd already been backing up with her steady assault, and they both tumbled to the sandy ground with a thump.

She fell on top of him and Gavin kept his arms tight around her waist. Her hair curtained her face, tickling his nose as he tried to catch his breath.

"Get off me!" she yelled, squirming around in an effort to get away.

"Just wait a minute. Keep still," Gavin told her, trying to keep her in one place while kicking his feet to rid them of whatever they'd been tangled in.

"You're a jerk! And a liar! And I'm not going to play your games any longer," she was telling him.

But Gavin was only half listening. He'd seen something as they fell, a flash of light he thought, but couldn't be sure because the moment he saw it his arms were filled with a falling woman.

When her angry voice finally penetrated his thoughts, Gavin cupped the back of her head, crushing his mouth over hers. The kiss was, as usual, filled with passion and desire and laced with just a hint of the hunger they had for each other. But for Gavin, it kept her quiet and made her go still in his arms.

"I hate you," she whispered when he finally allowed her to pull away.

"You're a crappy liar, Regan," he told her as he let her shift to the side, sliding off him. He sat up and looked down at his feet. He reached for what had tripped them. Clothes.

"You throwing your clothes out on the beach now? Who were you out here with, one of the florists?" she asked sarcastically.

"Florists?" he questioned.

She flipped her braids back and glared at him. "The only other people on the island besides family, and you, of course, are the florists for the wedding. Tall, straight black hair to her waist—I think her name's Vivi and her four assistants. They had so much to bring out here, they came last night while the other vendors are coming in the morning. So did you get horny and decide to sleep with one of Vivi's young helpers?"

"Firstly," he said, looking down at the clothes then quickly back to her, "I don't make a habit of sleeping with women outside. And second, there's no other woman on this island, now or ever, that I'd come looking for when I was horny but you."

"Well, I'm not available anymore," she told him, then moved until she was standing over him.

Gavin stood as well, still holding the clothing items in his hands. He shook it out, sand flying everywhere. She stepped back so it wouldn't get on her dress, which was futile since she had sand everywhere else from their fall.

"It's a jumpsuit," he said. "A man's jumpsuit."

Regan looked at him, one eyebrow raised. "You into men now?"

"Not funny," he told her, looking towards the thick copse of palm trees he was sure he'd seen the flash of light come from.

CHAPTER 5

"Tell me again how you got sand in your underwear if you
and Gavin weren't getting busy on the beach?"

Days like today were the times Regan wondered what the
real purpose in a best friend was.

"From the look she's giving you, Lyra, I'm guessing she
doesn't want to talk about how the sand got there...or
anywhere else it might be," Tate Dennison said with a chuckle.

Tate was Sean's fiancée. They'd become engaged about ten
minutes after Sean had saved Tate's daughter Briana's life and
the doctor's said he would recover from the gunshot wound
he'd incurred while doing so. That and the fact that she was a
pretty insightful columnist at their magazine had instantly
made her a part of the Donovan family.

"Wait, you're sleeping with the chef guy?" This came from
Tia, who had been lounging in an ivory colored chaise that
perfectly matched the stiletto heels she wore, heels that
complimented the sage green jumpsuit that clung to her lithe
model's body.

Tia was gorgeous. There was no other way to put it. Her
face had graced magazines, billboards, runways and recently
the pilot for the fashion and entertainment show Regan had
been working with Savian to develop. She also made whatever
Camille designed look ten times better, which did a hell of a lot
to boost sales for CK Davis Designs. Tia's looks also went a
long way to driving Trent insane whenever she traveled away
from him for work, which happened far less frequently now
that he'd married her and they'd had a son. Trent was the
personification of overprotective, and where Tia and Trevor

were concerned, he was in Regan's estimation officially renamed Borderline-Crazy-Stalker Donovan.

"We fell," Regan reiterated for about the third time. "We were talking and he was backing up and he tripped."

"And you fell on top of him, right?" Lyra asked, absolutely unable to contain her grin.

"You were on top and you still got sand in your panties?" added Camille, who had been pushing a dress rack into the room from, of all places, the bathroom. "That's really uncomfortable. I hope you showered or you're not trying on this dress."

"Yes, I showered," Regan told them with more exasperation than she ever thought she could feel.

"Maybe you two should keep the sex to the bedroom," Jade said, jumping off from the bed where she and Noelle had been sitting to stand by the dress rack with Camille.

"I did not have sex with Gavin on the beach," she said through clenched teeth.

"Oooh, grouchy," Noelle added when she finally looked over to Regan. "Maybe you *should* have sex with him on the beach. The first time Brock and I had sex was in his pool, and let me tell you…whew! It was freakin' fantastic!"

Jade put her fingers into her ears and instantly started shaking it back and forth. "TMI, TMI, TMI," she chanted.

The other women laughed, except for Regan.

"Really? Can we just get this dress unveiling over with," she said. "Before Noelle gives us anymore details about her and my cousin getting it on in the pool that I know I've been in since they met."

"Oh, and the poker table! My goodness! That was a-may-zing!" Noelle said with a smile that gave even more appreciation to whatever she and Brock had done on that poker table.

"Okay, okay, we'll have to save the sex talk for Friday night's bridal shower. Right now I want you all have to a seat somewhere and get ready to be dazzled," Camille said with a bright smile.

Camille wasn't as tall and svelte as the other women in the room but her voice commanded their attention just as swiftly as if she were. Today she wore white linen pants and a pink tunic that almost hinted at another pregnancy, but Regan wasn't about to make that assumption. Josiah, Camille and Adam's son, was just a little over a year old. Surely they weren't expecting again so soon. Regan knew she never wanted to have children back to back that way.

The women quieted, to Regan's elation, and all took a seat either on the bed with Noelle or in one of the chairs. Regan stood leaning against the small window seat directly across from where the dress rack had been placed. Not all of Noelle's bridal party was present. Her best friend Karena Lakefield Desdune was a matron of honor, along with Jade. Karena and her husband Sam, who was also Trent's partner in D&D Investigations, lived in Connecticut. Karena was an art buyer and traveled a lot, so she was currently in Europe but would arrive on the island on Thursday, just in time for the big event.

"So we're all here to celebrate Noelle's big day," Camille began.

"It's about damned time," Jade said, moving to the nightstand to grab a glass of champagne from the tray Aunt Beverly had brought in. The seniors didn't stay for the unveiling, as Aunt Alma had said, "This is girls' time. Noelle should be with her bridal party at this moment."

Regan agreed with her and was even more grateful since the conversation had gotten off to a really bad start. The last thing she wanted her mother to hear was how she'd been rolling around in the sand with Gavin.

Camille cleared her throat at the chuckling that had ensued. "With that being said, and with Noelle's permission, it is my pleasure to unveil the gowns that have been designed for you."

Regan tried to remain focused. She tried valiantly not to think about Gavin, about his hands on her or his mouth ravishing hers. She'd told him she wasn't available to him anymore, but he hadn't looked like he believed her. It was imperative that she stay away from him, that much was obvious.

"Don't you like your dress?" Camille asked.

After the oohing and ahhing of the dress reveal, Regan had gotten lost in her thoughts again. As she looked up at Camille, the others had already grabbed their dresses, hurrying to try them on.

"I thought about the first episode of the reality show and my fall line as I designed these dresses, even though it's a summer wedding," Camille said.

She'd touched Regan's shoulders, slowly guiding her until she stood and walked her over to the wrack with the one remaining dress.

"For episode one, I was thinking we could open with a a small glimpse into my L.A. factory. We could use some of the sketches. I brought them along with me so you can take them back to Miami. I know Parker and Savian will want a visual of where we plan on going with the show."

Camille was still talking as Regan reached out to touch the dress. "It's beautiful," she said slowly.

"You really like it?" Camille asked. "I know it's not your usual style. It's not Noelle's usual style either. But I decided to go with quiet elegance instead of fashionable sexiness for the bride.

Regan let her hands slide along the length of the dress. The color was navy blue, not the usual summer wedding color, which for starters was a shock. It was strapless and straight all the way down to the flair of the mermaid bottom. At the waist was a turquoise sash, thin in front, falling in a neat twist at the back.

"Quiet elegance," she said, repeating Camille's words. "It's still sexy, but in a more subtle way."

"Right," Camille said with a nod, then lifted the hanger from the wrack. "Go try it on. It'll take your mind off Gavin," she added when Regan hesitated to take the hangar from her.

The words made Regan quickly reach for the dress. "Why would you say I'm thinking about Gavin, of all people?"

Camille tilted her head and smiled. "Regan, I've known you for a couple of years now. In the last few months I've gotten to know you even better and I've heard you talk of only one man. That look on your face is male inspired. Process of elimination leaves Gavin Lucas as the culprit."

Regan frowned. Since when had she become so transparent? She figured it was best to just leave this conversation just as she had the last one, and turned to walk towards the bathroom to change. Camille touched Regan's shoulder and she turned.

"Plus, Lyra warned us all before you came in that you were sulking because Gavin was here," she said with a chuckle.

"I should have known," Regan dryly replied.

The bathroom was full, so she found a corner of the room that was empty and stepped slowly out of her own clothes, then into the dress. Without asking anyone to zip her up, she moved to the floor length mirror and looked at herself.

Camille had been spot on with this design. It was quiet elegance and couture design all bundled into one. Regan wondered if Gavin would like the dress, if he would think she was sexy in it? She wondered if seeing her walk down the aisle in someone else's wedding would ignite any ideas in his mind.

"How could Gavin not be anything but in love with you, Regan? You're lovely in that dress. He won't be able to resist you," Lyra said, coming up behind her to zip her up.

Lyra wasn't a bridesmaid, but she'd vowed to help out with the wedding as much as possible.

If only Lyra knew. The last thing Gavin Lucas was thinking about was falling in love with Regan.

⤷⟡⤶⟡⤶⟡⤶

Nine pairs of eyes watched in silence as Gavin dropped the overalls he'd found earlier on the beach in the center of the pool table. After parting ways with Regan, he had needed some space and a little time to think about what his next move would be where she was concerned. She'd told him that she was no longer available for him. This wasn't the first time he'd heard that or something similar coming from her. He refused to believe it. Or rather he wasn't ready to accept the totality of her decision. Regan Donovan deserved more than what they'd had in the past years. He knew that now and was ready to make that happen if she'd ever stop arguing with him long enough to hear him out. Maybe, he'd thought, it might be time to do more showing than telling, since Regan wasn't the best listener.

But first, his gut was telling him there was something wrong with the overalls he'd found and the light he'd seen earlier. Regan had reminded him about the other guests that would be on the island for the upcoming wedding and that could be an explanation, but still, something just didn't feel right about it. Gavin always followed his instincts. It was something his father, who had been a police officer, had taught him.

"Good or bad, go with your gut," Anthony Lucas had said to his son one balmy Miami the spring of Gavin's high school year. Two weeks after his graduation, Anthony Lucas had been murdered.

"If that's what you're wearing to my wedding, I'm going to have to ask you not to come," Brock Remington said.

Brock was tall with a muscular build. He was a businessman like the other Donovan men, but there was a rustic demeanor to him that Gavin could appreciate since he hadn't been born into a wealthy family either. From what Parker had told him, Brock had been adopted into the Donovan clan and loved by them as if they had the same blood. Another thing he could appreciate about the man—he had a family to stand behind him no matter what.

When Gavin had first entered the room, the men had been scattered about. To the left, where floor to ceiling windows brought in the sunlight and scenic view of the island, Trent and Max were playing pool. Brock and Linc were at the bar, most likely talking business since Brock's fiancée and Linc's sister-in-law managed one of Linc's casinos in St. Michaels, Maryland, where they lived. The right side of the room boasted a twenty-seat home theatre that faced a seventy-five-inch Samsung Smart TV on which they were watching a rerun of the latest Super Bowl game. This is where Adam, Dion, Ben and Savian where sitting until Gavin had announced he had something he wanted them all to see.

"It's not mine. Regan and I tripped over this on the beach this morning. And a couple seconds before we fell over it, there was a light, like maybe a flashlight or something in the trees a couple feet away." Saying it aloud increased the clenching in his gut.

"And you're just a chef, right?" Trent asked, giving Gavin a serious look.

This wasn't the first time Gavin had met the Donovan family, which was the main reason Parker felt it would be alright for him to visit the island during their family reunion. Bruce and Reginald Donovan had been avid contributors to the Fraternal Order of Police in Miami, a fact Gavin hadn't learned until they'd showed up at his father's funeral. The connection between the Donovan men and his father hadn't totally been revealed to Gavin, but he'd always wondered how he and his sisters had been afforded the luxury of attending private schools on their parents' nursing and cop salaries.

"He's a chef by trade, but his dad was a cop. Maybe he's figured out a way to combine the two careers somehow." Savian added a wry chuckle in the hopes of lightening the mood, but coming from him, it sounded stilted.

"Regan interviewed him for the magazine a few months ago. Parker and I thought we might try to develop a reality cooking show with Gavin as the star. Then we got word that Camelot was ready to open and my dad suggested Parker contact Gavin about expanding one of his restaurants down here," Savian finished, sounding like he'd just given a work presentation.

"But instead of being at Camelot, he's finding clothes lying around on the island?" Trent asked, his voice, as usual full of skepticism.

Savian shrugged. "My parents have known his family for a long time. He can be trusted. And like I said, his father was a highly decorated detective in Miami. If Gavin has a hunch or thinks something's off, we should listen." He gave Trent a serious look.

Gavin nodded his appreciation at Regan's older and more somber brother. The rest of the family had been distrustful of him. He didn't blame them, considering he was technically the outcast. After Savian's words however, everyone but Trent looked a little more comfortable with him.

"Don't you think it's weird that overalls would be found on a beach of a private island?" he asked Savian.

The man's intense green eyes held Gavin's gaze for a few more seconds before he nodded.

"Twice a month a cleaning company comes to the island to maintain the houses. Landscapers visit a little more frequently, sometimes four times a month," Linc offered. "In the past year construction crews have been here day and night. My parents keep a detailed record of anyone stepping foot on this island and when they were here. But construction workers don't wear overalls, especially on a tropical island work site."

Brock rubbed a hand down the back of his neck and sighed. "About a month ago, Noelle and I flew out with our event planner. She had a few assistants with her, but none of them wore uniforms or overalls for that matter. The vendors we hired were given pictures of select spots on the island in order to properly plan the wedding and reception."

"You obviously need the vendors here for the wedding. When are they expected to arrive?" Ben asked Brock.

Ben was a defense attorney known for his unsavory clients, so Gavin paid special attention to his reaction.

Brock nodded. "The florists came in last night. Tomorrow morning musicians, caterers, decorators, all screened and approved by Uncle Henry and Aunt Beverly mind you, will arrive on chartered ferries."

It was Trent who finally picked the overalls up from the pool table, surveying them before looking to Ben with a grim expression.

"These are government issued," he said, then turned them over again. "See right here, that's a number," he told them.

Around them everyone was silent for a few seconds, either not sure what Trent was trying to say, or hoping they hadn't heard his words all together. Finally, a few of them moved forward to see what Trent was referring to. Gavin joined them.

"It's an inmate number," Trent continued slowly.

It seemed as if he didn't want to tell them this anymore than they wanted to hear it.

"No," Ben immediately whispered, shaking his head. "The trial was over last Thursday. He was scheduled to be transported on Monday."

Trent frowned, his fingers clenching on the overalls. He looked at Ben intently. "Call your office. Find out if they've heard anything, or if anybody suspicious has been there. I'm going to call Dev and have him check the prison."

"You two want to fill us in on what's going on?" Linc asked, his brow furrowed.

"It's just a hunch," Trent told them.

"A good man once told me to always follow your gut. That's why I brought the overalls to everyone's attention in the first place," Gavin replied.

Trent nodded. "That good man was very smart."

"Why don't we all just chill for the moment. Let Trent and I make some calls and then we'll meet up again later this evening with some answers," Ben offered.

The man was frowning so deep, Gavin thought his face might actually freeze that way. Whatever he wanted to find answers to wasn't going to be good.

"In the meantime, I'd appreciate it if nobody would tell Noelle about this," Brock added. "She's been so calm about the wedding so far. I've been just waiting for her to crack. This might be the thing that pushes her over the edge."

Linc shook his head. "No. We're not saying anything to anybody that's not already in this room until we know for sure what's going on? Agreed?"

"Sean's not here," Dion spoke up. "Since Tate went with the bridal party and our moms are starting dinner, he volunteered to help Victoria with the kids. But if something's going on, I want him to be prepared to protect his family."

Trent nodded. "You're right, Dion. I'm also going to have Devlin check on our Miami enemies just to be absolutely sure. It seems the Donovans have been drawing them like fleas lately. Have Sean meet with us tonight. Is 10 good for everybody? We can come back here," Trent asked them.

There was a variety of nods and replies, but they all agreed.

"Gavin, can I see you outside for a sec?" Savian asked.

With a nod, Gavin agreed, and they left the room.

"So you just threw Victoria right into the kids' fest we've got going on here?" Max asked his younger brother.

Ben shrugged. "She didn't want to intrude on the women. Said something about being the outsider to the bridal party. I didn't want to argue, even though I think the ladies have been pretty nice to her."

"Deena's not in the bridal party, but she went to whatever type of pow-wow they were having. But you know Deena's used to being the outcast," Max said of his wife.

"I hope this isn't who I think it is," Ben murmured quietly, having not heard most of what Max had said.

Max clapped his brother's shoulder. "He's in jail, man. That case is over and done with. Christ, Trent and Devlin killed the other guy that was involved. It's over."

Ben shook his head, hoping the words his brother spoke were true.

CHAPTER 6

"You wanna tell me the rest of that story," Savian asked the moment he and Gavin were alone.

Gavin gave him a nod and started walking down the hallway that lead to the living room and out onto the large veranda. Once they were both outside, he turned to Savian, slipping his hands into his pockets as he looked the other man in the eye.

"Always look a man in the eye," his father had told him. "Especially if you want his respect."

"Regan and I were walking and talking about the resort and some ideas I wanted to speak to Parker about. We tripped over the overalls," he said, then waited for Savian's response.

If it had been Parker, Gavin would expect an immediate smile, then possibly some crude comment about him and his sister. Parker thought the tension between him and Regan was entertaining. Gavin suspected the man was quietly rooting for him and Regan's relationship to succeed. Something about Parker's failed marriage had made him a little softer when it came to love connections. Gavin had watched that change for the past couple of years and wondered when Parker would once again dip his foot into the relationship pool.

But Savian was different. He didn't do relationships and didn't make any secret of it. And he damn sure didn't want to hear about his sister in a relationship, of that Gavin was almost positive.

The grim look Savian was now giving him proved that point.

"You and Regan," he said with a sigh. "You two are like oil and water. You don't mix and yet you keep inflicting this crazy torture onto each other."

Gavin nodded. "That's a pretty good description of what Regan and I do. But this time we were only having a conversation and we tripped over the overalls. I saw the flash of light as we tumbled to the ground."

Savian sighed. "I know I don't have to tell you how protective this family is."

"No, you don't. I have sisters, remember? If there was a guy taunting them, I'd get in his face too."

"And Parker sent you here anyway," Savian said with a hint of a question.

"Parker's a businessman, Savian. Just like the rest of us. What's between Regan and me is personal. I know how to separate the two."

"And you think I don't?"

"I think you're trying to figure this all out so you can explain it to your cousins. I appreciate the backup in there, and have only the utmost respect for your cousins. At the same time I know what I saw and I don't think it's a coincidence or a normal occurrence that those overalls were out there. Like it or not, there's something going on."

Savian sighed. "That's what I'm afraid of. That there's something going on out there, and between you and Regan."

Gavin remained silent for a minute, giving each of them time to get a hold of their baser male egos and attitudes. Then he pulled a hand from his pocket and rubbed his chin.

"I care about your sister, Savian. I'm not out to hurt her in any way, I can promise you that."

The corners of Savian's mouth lifted into a smirk. "I'm a little more worried about her physically hurting you, Gavin."

The two of them parted ways soon after, with Savian hopefully a little more comfortable with Gavin's presence and Gavin more certain than ever before to keep a close eye on Regan. Because if his hunch was right, the Donovans were about to receive some uninvited wedding guests.

❧❧❧

Regan was tired. The beginnings of a headache had started to stir as she'd sat through another spirited dinner with her family. Of course she relished the time together and felt blessed to be with them all. She was well aware that most people weren't afforded this opportunity to spend time with a good majority of their family. And it was a reunion after all, so instead of staying in her room lounging or going to the beach and lounging, she knew she had to fellowship. But it would help if her body could get with the social program.

"Stress is a killer, Regan. Taking care of yourself must become a priority."

Those were the words of Dr. Sheridan, her primary care physician who was a step away from administering high blood pressure medication to Regan at her last visit over a month ago. Since that time, Regan had sworn she would get herself and her life together. She would take some time off from work and cut down her eighteen-hour days as much as possible. With taping for Camille's reality show beginning at the end of the summer, she needed to be on point and healthy. This trip was supposed to help with that.

Then Gavin had appeared and memories that, only added to her stressful lifestyle resurfaced. Not that she'd completely forgotten them in the first place.

Once alone in her room, Regan had showered, letting the warm water sluice over her tense muscles slightly relax. After her shower, she opened the doors to her balcony. Each room that faced the back of the house had a balcony and she always selected this specific room when she was on Sansonique. The view of the water and the treetops was majestic. It was just after 9 and the sky was already dark, the air still humid but not stifling.

Outside of being on the beach—which she'd been unable to visit this morning since she'd overslept and then had to rush down to the kitchen to help prepare breakfast—the balcony was the best place to practice. Three weeks ago, Regan had begun taking yoga classes to help relieve stress and to find some sort of balance in her life. Dressed in yoga pants and a sports bra, she lay her mat onto the tiled floor and sat crossed legged. She began with deep cleansing breaths, one hand to her heart, the other to her lower belly. In for four counts, then out for four. This worked tremendously to calm the slight thumping in her temples. After six deep breaths, she lifted her arms skyward, letting her fingertips touch. Slowly she lowered her arms down to her chest, keeping her hands together as if in a praying position. Then she bowed and was about to set her intention for this practice.

A soft knock at her door interrupted her.

Not getting up to answer it wasn't an option. If she'd been back at her apartment in Miami, she would have considered ignoring the intruder, especially at this time of night. Unannounced visitors were not her high on her list of likes. But in this house full of people, with her cousins and aunts and uncles all roaming about with anxiousness over the wedding and wanting to catch up on everyone's lives, she knew not answering wasn't going to work.

But when she opened the door, the person standing on the other side was the last person she wanted to see.

"You skipped dessert," Gavin said, holding a tray with a huge hot fudge sundae in its center.

"Gavin, please," she begged. Regan didn't know how much clearer she needed to be about their relationship, or lack thereof. Of course, the fact that she melted in his arms each time he touched her didn't go a long way to reinforcing her point. But she'd vowed to stop that nonsense as well.

He held up a hand to stop her protest.

"It's just dessert, Regan. I know this is your favorite part of a meal. We'll just eat it and watch television or talk. That's all, I promise," he said.

"I was about to go to bed," she insisted.

"I can't sleep," he told her. "Not when I know you're this close and I can't reach out and touch you."

His voice had lowered, but he hadn't made any move to come into her room without her permission. He'd changed from the slacks and polo shirt he'd worn earlier to boat shoes and linen shorts with a matching shirt. He looked young and handsome, like he could one minute pose for *GQ* and the next for *Playgirl*. His dark skin peeked from beneath the short sleeves of his wheat colored shirt, roped veins snaking upward to what she knew were muscled biceps. His goatee was soft she remembered, as she loved to rub her palm along the line of his jaw after they'd made love...had sex, she corrected herself. All that was between them was sex.

And a delicious looking hot fudge sundae.

She took a step back and moved to the side. With a wave of her arm, she signaled for him to come in. "Don't think I missed the fact that you said 'we' can have dessert," she quipped, trying for a lighter mood.

"You know I always share with you, Regan."

Gavin set the tray on the dresser and turned to her. "Am I interrupting your workout?" he asked, looking from Regan to the balcony, then back to her again.

"Yoga," she told him, and moved to close the balcony door. "And yes, you interrupted."

"Don't," he said while touching the arm she'd reached out to the door. "Let's sit out there and have dessert."

"There are no chairs," she told him. "I moved them over there."

She'd nodded to the far corner of the room where the two lounge chairs were stacked together, but Gavin ignored them.

"Let's sit on the mat," he said.

He removed the sundae from the tray, took the two spoons, then nodded towards the balcony door. "After you, baby."

Regan sighed.

He smiled. "After you, Regan."

She stepped back onto the balcony and wished like hell she were alone—with the sundae of course, but still alone. A little wave of shock rippled through her when she watched him squat, sit on one end of her yoga mat and then hold his hand up for her. She didn't take his hand, but she did sit at the other end of the mat facing him. He picked up a spoon and she followed suit.

"Perfect," she said after her first spoonful. "I love hot fudge sundaes."

He grinned. "Heavy on the fudge and whipped cream, no chopped nuts and double cherries. I know what you like."

Why did that not sit well with her?

"You like ice cream too," she accused.

"I like eating ice cream with you. Remember the first time we shared a sundae?"

"I remember you ate half the sundae and left me the creamy mush in the bottom of the bowl." They'd been in L.A. during the fall of her senior year.

"Well, it wasn't my fault you didn't like the chopped nuts and the waitress had practically covered the sundae with them. I was just trying to help you out," he said, scooping another big chunk of ice cream into his mouth.

"Whatever you say, Mr. Lucas," she replied.

"What I say, Ms. Donovan, is that you're a beautiful woman."

His words were soft, smooth, like Gavin was the majority of the time. "Gavin, let's not do this. We've had this talk already," she insisted.

He shook his head. "No. You had the talk. I listened, then you left. And every time I've seen you since then, you've done everything in your power to get away from me. I wouldn't actually call that having a talk."

She twirled the spoon between her fingers, staring down at the ice cream before bringing her gaze up to meet his.

"You're right. Say what you want to say," she told him with resignation. She wanted to simply hear him out, then tell him goodnight.

He laughed, and Regan didn't know if she should be offended or not. She was giving him the opportunity to give her his thoughts on ending their involvement, but he wasn't taking it.

"You remind me a lot of my sister Suzanna. She's three years older than me. Suzanna loves to be in control all the time. When she was in high school, she never freaked out over an exam because she studied until her eyes went crossed the night before. Now, my oldest sister Lydia, as well as my two younger sisters, they all frantically ran through the house every morning trying to find something to wear." He paused, smiled, and shook his head. "Suzanna picked out her clothes for the entire week and ironed them all on Sunday night. And when she started dating, unlike the others who at one point or another had their hearts broken by some idiot boy, Suzanna never had that problem. Do you want to know why?"

He'd never talked about his family before, so Regan had been a little taken aback with his question. Sure, she'd known Gavin since they were in school and she knew that her father and uncle knew his parents, but their families had never gotten together for cook-outs or anything like that. And whenever the two of them had been together—well, it wasn't to talk about his sisters or her brothers, that was for sure.

"Because she was always in control," she answered finally.

He shook his head. "Because she ended it first. That way her heart was always protected."

Regan sighed. "That's not what I did, Gavin." She dropped her spoon into the bowl and let her hands fall into her lap.

"What did you do?"

"We didn't have a relationship. It was like some high class booty call with us. You text me, I show up. I text you, you show up. All that was missing was the money left on the night stand in the morning." As horrible as that sounded to her, pain from how true it was rippled through her chest.

The last was said with a definite snap and Gavin looked as if she'd reached out and slapped him instead.

"I mean, that was fine. It's not like I did anything against my will," she continued, trying to soften the blow a little even though she didn't know why. She was sure Gavin didn't care. His actions had proven that point.

He set the bowl down and clasped his hands calmly. The flickering in his eyes, however, wasn't calm. They'd darkened, a muscle in his jaw ticking as he sat quietly.

"Our relationship wasn't a usual setup, I can admit that. But it worked for us. You're a very busy woman, Regan. And I have my work, my goals. I figured it was a compromise for two ambitious people."

She nodded, recognizing the composition of what they'd had together. "You're right. Neither one of us had time for formal dates, weekends away, phone calls and whatever else comes with a real relationship."

"You make it seem like our time together wasn't enjoyable."

Regan shook her head. "No. That's not what I'm saying. I think we both know there was a level of enjoyment between us that was, well, that was unsurpassable." Because she didn't know what else to do, Regan stood. She moved to the railing and stared out into the dark night. "It just wasn't enough," she said quietly.

And there, they finally agreed.

Gavin wanted more from Regan, he wanted more between them. He wondered if the stubborn and tenacious female standing before him would welcome that. This time last year he'd started to believe she just might be on the same page as him, that this casual relationship they'd initiated may have actually changed to something more serious.

Then again, the rigid set of her shoulders and the way she'd been pushing him away for the past couple weeks said something else entirely. Also concerning to Gavin were the pill bottles he'd spotted on her dresser.

He stood, moved to stand right behind Regan, but didn't touch her.

"I'd like to take you out on a date, Regan. A real date. Maybe dinner and a movie," he suggested.

The tropical scent of the air mixed with her softer scent. Whatever product she used in her hair drove him crazy any time he was close to her, as did the beautifully toned skin that showed beneath the skimpy workout clothes she wore. The complete package of Regan Donovan wreaked havoc on everything that was sane in Gavin's world. And that's precisely how he knew he had to have this woman completely.

She shook her head. "That's not the kind of man you are, Gavin. You just said how busy you are trying to reach your goals. I know you want to open more restaurants, that you want Spaga to expand. Hell, you're even here now talking about going into some joint venture with my brother. You're going to have restaurants all over the world in the future. A relationship is the last thing you have time for."

"Priorities, Regan. That's what we both need in our lives. For so long it's been work, work and more work. We've both set goals and for different reasons feel like we have to reach them no matter what. That's what we have in common, that's what initially drew us to each other."

She turned then, and they were so close Gavin had to step back a little to allow her some space.

"Sex drew us together, Gavin. It's been the unbreakable bond between us for the past five years. Let's not kid ourselves in that regard."

Her eyes sparkled in the moonlight. He was taller than her, probably by about six inches. The top of her head would touch his chin when she wasn't looking up at him as defiantly as she was right now.

"I couldn't deny the physical bond if I wanted to," he admitted, then finally gave in to impulse and traced a fingertip along the line of her jaw. "But there's something else now, Regan. I feel like there's something else between us."

"You're wrong," she said in a low whisper. "There's just the sex and that's not enough for me anymore."

It was Gavin's turn to nod. "I've been thinking a lot lately about my goals and what I really want out of life. You're right, I would like to open more restaurants. When your brother called me about the resort partnership, I was a little skeptical at first, but who wouldn't jump at an opportunity to work alongside the Donovans. Then it hit me. The real reason I agreed without too much thought to what Parker was proposing was you."

"I don't understand," she admitted, an act Gavin knew had to be hard for her.

"I'm going to ask you to do something for me, Regan. And I want you to think about it overnight and give me your answer in the morning.

"Gavin, I don't want to play games. We're both too busy for that."

He touched her shoulders then, feeling the pulse of heat at their contact move slowly through his body. His hands inched down the length of her arms until he entwined his fingers with hers.

"Give me the chance to prove that we can be more than an upscale booty call, as you referred to our previous involvement. Let me show you what we could be like together, in a real relationship."

She opened her mouth to speak and Gavin shook his head. "All I want you to do tonight is think about it." He leaned in and kissed her lips quickly because there was no way he could leave this room without tasting her, even if the taste was a bit chaste for his pleasure. "Just think about it and we'll talk in the morning.

He knew she wanted to protest, to tell him again it was over, but Gavin didn't give her the chance. He released her hands and quickly bent to pick up the bowl. Moving into her room, he grabbed the tray and made a hasty exit. Once the bedroom door was closed behind him, he breathed the breath he'd been holding since he'd touched her for the first time on that balcony. Telling her exactly what he wanted hadn't been his plan. He'd decided to go with the showing element. The plan had shifted a bit and he wasn't totally sure why. It was in his nature to get what he wanted, to reach out and take what would make him happy. But Regan Donovan wasn't going to be taken, not easily anyway.

Gavin moved through the spacious house thinking about Regan and what their talk tomorrow would possibly bring. He wanted her more than he'd ever wanted anything else in his life. If she turned him down, if she said she didn't want a relationship with him, what was he going to do? He shook his head as he looked down at his watch. She wasn't going to say no. There was more between them than sex. He knew it and he was positive she knew it as well. It was just a matter of time before they both got what they wanted.

It was twenty minutes until ten. He wanted to make a call back home before his meeting with the guys, so he headed out the back kitchen door. Camelot was a fifteen minute walk from the Donovan complex, less if he jogged as he had this morning for breakfast. Originally, he'd agreed to stay in the guest house, but figured he'd get a much better feel for the resort if he spent some time there.

Travelling all the way back to his room wasn't an option, but Gavin didn't want to chance anyone overhearing his call, so he left through the back door, walking towards the guest house. He'd pulled out his phone when he heard a sound behind him. He turned and was greeted by white hot pain.

CHAPTER 7

"Gavin's a good guy," Savian reiterated when the men had once again assembled in the game room. "He and Parker are tossing around ideas that might put another feather in the Donovan Corporation cap."

"So Parker sends him to our private island the week of my brother's wedding?"

Brandon Donovan, who was not used to being in family meetings, spoke up. He was an investment broker who had, up until six months ago, worked at TJB Investments in Houston. After leaving the corporation that Tyson Braddock had built, Brandon had moved to Atlanta to head up the compliance division of a huge firm there. He and his twin, Bailey, who were younger than Brock, both wholeheartedly supported their brother and his marriage to Noelle.

"There's another reason that Gavin's here, now," Savian said slowly, lifting his glass to take a slow drink first. None of the men in this room were going to be happy with what he was getting ready to say. Hell, Savian hadn't been happy himself when he'd talked to Parker a couple of hours ago. It was true that Parker was the oldest of Carolyn and Reginald's children, but he was also the most laidback of the three, the carefree and fun-loving one. So it was no wonder he'd decided that he would have a little fun by putting Gavin and Regan in close proximity. Savian, who prided himself on being mature and focused (and preferring not to get on Regan's bad side if he could help it), would have never done something so foolish.

"Well, don't keep us in suspense," Linc said impatiently. "We need all pertinent information on the table right now, especially if we're going to be following this guy's hunches."

Savian looked around the room once again at all the Donovan men who had assembled. There was no telling what the exact reaction was going to be, but he knew it wasn't going to be good. "Parker thought it would be cute to have Gavin and Regan stuck on this island together for a week," he said quickly, then clapped his lips shut to wait for the explosion.

It came first by a burst of laughter from Dion. "She's going to kick Parker's ass the moment we get back to Miami."

Sean, who knew firsthand what Regan's wrath was like, shook his head. "That's for damned sure."

"Wait a minute," Adam said while he held up a hand. "You're saying that Parker was trying to be a matchmaker, so he sent this guy to our private island?"

"The business aspect is true. If Gavin partners with us and opens a Spaga at Camelot, rentals will definitely increase. Before we left, I gave my dad and Uncle Bruce a proposal for a cooking show centered around Gavin and his recipes. Both endeavors could be a win/win for the family as well as for Gavin," Savian told them.

The DNT Network was a cable television network with expansions into multimedia through their magazine and entertainment management company. Reginald and Bruce ran DNT. Henry, Everette and Albert still had their hand in the day-to-day operations of the oil companies, while Bernard worked primarily in foreign and domestic investments domestic from his home office in Seattle. For the most part, the family always kept each other abreast of their business status. The fact that the senior brothers equally owned Sansonique meant that any decision on whether or not Gavin would open a restaurant at Camelot would be decided by all of them.

"My dad sent me a copy of the proposal," Dion chimed in. "And Savian's right. The partnership would be a win/win all around with Gavin's rapidly growing success in Miami."

Max nodded his agreement. "Deena's sister is married into the Desdune family. They have a Creole restaurant in New York and were thinking of expanding down into Miami. Sam Desdune has mentioned Lucas and the buzz he's generated down there. It definitely has his parents thinking twice about coming further south, even though their family is pretty confident they still have a viable market since Spaga is primarily American cuisine."

"In the tradition of full disclosure, I think we should also acknowledge the tension between Gavin and Regan," Sean added in his relaxed tone.

"Tension that Parker ignored by trying to push the two of them together? That doesn't sound like a smart plan," Linc commented with a raised brow.

"But it does sound likes Parker's demented sense of humor," Adam added while lifting a bottle of beer to his lips for a drink.

Sean, who was generally the peacekeeper among the Miami Donovans, spoke up again. "Just a few months ago Dion ordered Regan to personally interview Gavin and his new restaurant as our special feature on black entrepreneurs in the Miami area. We actually took bets on whether or not she'd kill him before the interview could make it to press," he finished with a grin.

"But Gavin's a good sport," Dion concluded. "He's still interested in doing business with us, despite Regan's stony reception of him. And the article was fantastic. Distribution increased five percent with that month's edition."

"And now the guy is here and he's seeing lights, picking up clothes on the beach—the beach that he was walking on alone with my cousin. I gotta say I'm not amused guys," Ben added in a grim tone.

"All the personal hot and cold running between them aside," Savian began after setting his glass down on the table, "the fact still remains that Gavin's father was a decorated member of the police force for more than thirty years before he was killed in the line of duty. Gavin was his only son. The four daughters and his mother are still living. And while Gavin studied culinary arts and is making his mark in the restaurant business, he's a lot like his dad. I'd follow his instincts any day."

And for Savian that was saying a lot. The serious looks on the faces around the room took note of that fact too.

"So Ben, did you find out anything on your end?" Linc asked.

Ben hadn't sat down. He and Trent were the only two still standing in the big room, and they both looked to each other before Ben finally answered.

"Ramone Vega escaped from a prison transport yesterday afternoon," Ben solemnly reported.

Trent spoke up next. "Devlin had already heard and was on his way back to Las Vegas from Seattle when I called him. He was scheduled to board the jet two hours ago. He'll be here before the night is over."

"Wait a minute," Brock said, coming to his feet and dragging a hand down the back of his head. "Who the hell is Ramone Vega? And why is Devlin 'Death' Bonner coming to my wedding?" he asked, irritation clear in his voice.

"Vega is a contract killer I previously represented. Last week Victoria prosecuted him and won. He was given two life sentences, to be served consecutively, in Ely State Prison. He escaped from the bus that was transporting him there. Killed two guards and left the keys for the other inmates to release themselves," Ben said as if he were giving a statement of facts.

"Wait a minute," Brandon started, sitting forward in his chair, resting his elbows on his knees. "You were defending a killer and your girlfriend was prosecuting him? I know I'm not a lawyer but isn't that a definite conflict?"

Ben sighed heavily and looked more than a little weary about the situation. Savian figured it wasn't an easy explanation. Relationships and all those commitment trappings usually weren't, and that's precisely why he steered clear of all that bullshit.

"I represented him in a case that ended with a mistrial. I declined to represent him for the second trial. Victoria didn't prosecute the first case, she did the second. I had evidence that he was guilty and I shared it with Victoria. To say Vega wasn't pleased with the turn of events is an understatement," Ben told them.

"You can say that shit again!" Brock yelled. "Christ, Ben, that guy's gunning for blood now. And probably not just yours. He's certainly going to come after Victoria. And what about the rest of the women here? Now we have to defend all of them against a hitman!"

Brock was absolutely right. This wasn't just about Ben and his girlfriend any more. It was about all of them on this island with no law enforcement and no training against a killer.

"And that's why Devlin is on his way," Trent intervened.

"But he's only one man," Brock interjected. "If there is actually a killer walking around free on this island, don't you think we need a little more protection than that?"

"Devlin's not just a man, Brock. He's a soldier, a trained killer himself. I'd trust him with my life. Hell, I have trusted him with my life on more than one occasion," Trent told him.

"I see where you're going with this," Max said to Brock. "I used to think of Devlin as just one man as well, especially when he was the only man protecting vowing to protect Ben from this lunatic in the first place. But he's good at what he does. He has a small team and along with Trent they get the job done."

"Except this killer is not in jail, he's on this island with us," Brock added, rubbing a hand down the back of his head.

"For now we'll keep this operation small," Trent told Brock. "The moment I start to feel like Dev and I can't handle this, we'll call in reinforcements. How does that sound to you?"

A muscle in Brock's jaw clenched. "I'm just thinking of the family, the females, Noelle." He sighed. "I trust your judgment, Trent, you know that. If you think this man can help then bring him in, now!"

"Bring in the man who travels with the shadow of death on his shoulders," Brandon said quietly.

"The man who saved my little girl," Sean added.

"And my wife," Trent added. "Devlin is a good guy and he's bringing my best security equipment with him. If there's someone on this island that we don't want here, Dev and I will find him and we'll handle him."

"I'll handle him," Ben said through gritted teeth. "Once and for all."

"Wait a minute," Savian said, finally coming to his feet. "Has anybody seen Gavin?"

Regan hadn't been asleep long. Still, it felt like she was trying to fight her way through a thick heavy fog as Lyra shook her furiously and Bailey called her name a million times.

"I'm up, I'm up," Regan finally said through a sleep-hazed yawn. "You'd better be telling me I don't have to report for breakfast duty," she whined.

"No. This is not good," Lyra said seriously.

Her tone had Regan's eyes opening wide, her body instantly alert as she struggled to sit upright in the bed. It was a little difficult with Lyra planted right next to her on one side and Bailey on the other. A quick look also revealed Camille and Tia giving her very serious and very dower looks.

"What's going on?"

"It's Gavin. He's been hurt," Bailey told her after she'd taken her hand.

Bailey and Brandon were twins but looked as different as siblings born on different dates. The one thing they shared was the burnt orange complexion inherited from their mother, who had been a direct descendent of Shawnee Native Americans that migrated from the east. The auburn highlights Bailey always wore in her hair added to her already exotic looks. That coupled with her very curvy body had garnered Bailey eye candy status as early as her sophomore year in high school. And that's precisely where Bailey Donovan's girly tendencies ended. After high school, she'd wanted to join the Marines. Brock and Trent had put a quick stop to that notion. Not to be defeated Bailey, secretly entered the police academy in Dallas. But fighting crimes, even in a city like Dallas, wasn't really quenching her adrenaline-thirst, so she'd taken criminal justice courses and obtained her private investigator's license in the hopes of possibly working for the FBI. When Trent (who seemed to always know everything about everybody) found out, he quickly came up with a solution that would keep his cousin safely in his and the rest of the male Donovan population's sights—he gave her a job at D&D Investigations.

Ever defiant—but secretly excited about the opportunity— Bailey only agreed to accept the position if she didn't have to work directly with Trent. So she moved to Connecticut to work at the D&D branch there, which was run by Sam Desdune, also an ex-cop.

"What do you mean he's been hurt?" Regan asked after she'd finally been able to wrap her head around Bailey's words.

"Trent's friend found him outside, unconscious," Tia said while stepping to the end of Regan's bed.

"Trent's friend? Unconscious? What—"

Bailey had her by the shoulders once more. "Why don't you get dressed and we'll go down to see if he's awake? They have him in the game room, so they wouldn't have to wake the seniors."

"Good plan," Lyra said as she pulled back the comforter and waited for Regan to climb out of bed. "Aunt Janean would have the entire emergency room staff from the closest mainland hospital here the moment she found out."

Bailey had scooted across the bed and was already helping Regan put her arm into the robe she held out. Lyra pushed her other arm in just as Camille offered, "I'm sure he's going to be fine. Maybe he fell and hit his head? It's really humid out here he could have gotten a touch of heat stroke."

"He didn't have heat stroke when he was in here hogging up the entire hot fudge sundae," Regan snapped, moving towards the door.

She'd already pulled it open when she realized her error. There was silence behind her and when she turned back, it was to four sets of eyes staring questioningly at her.

"Gavin was in your room?" Camille asked.

"Tonight?" Tia chimed in.

"Sharing ice cream with you," Lyra said with a knowing look.

She could try to brush them off, but that was going to take too long, and she really wanted to see Gavin. "Yes, he was here a while ago. We shared a sundae and he left. That's all that happened," she said before leaving the room.

"Damn. I'll be glad when more than eating ice cream happens between those two," Lyra said, heading for the door.

"Well, he's gotta wake up first," Tia quipped.

"Not necessarily," Bailey said with a little giggle as she led the way out into the hall.

～～～～

"You weren't supposed to hit him!"

He was yelling again. It seemed like all he ever did was yell and he was supposed to be the professional.

"He wasn't supposed to come out here," was the bland response. "And I didn't kill him."

"Right," Vega mumbled grumpily, "and that's a plus."

"Look, I'm here aren't I? I did everything I said I would and I'm ready for the next step. You wanna stop all your bitching and get this shit done so we can get our money and be gone!"

He was fast, his fingers tightening quickly around the throat that had just spoken. "Don't get cocky. Remember this is my show. Everything that happens from this moment on is because I allow it. You got that?"

Nodding was difficult, swallowing was impossible, holding onto the bladder that threatened to break any minute was the truest test. But fear had never been a strong opponent, so a quick blink of the eye gave a sufficient answer.

"Good. Now get the rest of my gear set up. They'll find him and they'll know somebody is on their precious island. Things are gonna go down quick, but on my terms," Vega said, moving to the window using binoculars to look up to the main house once more. Ben Donovan, his stuck-up prosecutor girlfriend and the rest of their privileged and greedy family were going to pay, according to his terms.

～～～～

Devlin Bonner stood in the farthest corner of the room, away from the many people hovering over the couch where the man he'd found outside lay. Once he'd gotten him into the house, Trent had told him it was Gavin Lucas, a friend of the family and soon-to-be-business associate. His wound was superficial, but Devlin would feel a lot better if he'd wake completely up sooner rather than later.

"Tate was coming down to get Briana some juice. She saw us coming in," Trent told Sean when he'd come back into the game room after meeting Devlin at the door with Gavin.

"And that means every woman in this house is going to know about this in about five minutes," Dion said grimly.

"I'll go talk to her," Sean told them, standing to leave the room.

"Hopefully he'll wake up before any of them find out," Trent said, looking around the room to see where Devlin had gone.

He and Trent had a connection. It had only taken him about ten years to admit that to himself and not run like hell away from it. Connections weren't really Devlin's thing, never had been. But in Trent Donovan, he'd found the brother that nature never saw fit to give him. And Trent's family—well, his brothers and their wives—had sort of filled the family gap for him, as much as Devlin would allow them to. Growing up alone sort of gave the impression that solitude was best. Devlin had managed to live thirty-six years in that blissful state and had no complaints. That's why it was so easy for him to slip to the side when all the Donovans were around like this. Too many people led to too many questions and he'd always been a prime target for questions.

After locking gazes, Trent returned his attention back to the guy on the couch.

"Gavin," he called to him. "Gavin, come on, wake up, man."

The patient groaned just as there was a slight commotion at the door. Then Tia Donovan pushed her way inside the room.

"What happened?" she asked Trent instantly. "And don't bother telling me nothing. Devlin's here, so I know something's going on."

Devlin had almost smiled at Tia's strange greeting. Then again, he'd become accustomed to the leery gazes from the women in this family, as each time he showed up their men were usually about to get involved with something that could get them all killed or at the very least pretty badly hurt. Case in point—Gavin moaned from the couch.

"He fell," Trent offered, moving quickly to stand between his wife and Gavin's unconscious form.

"How did he fall?" she asked.

Adam interrupted. "It's raining outside."

"It wasn't raining before dinner," Tia added over her shoulder to her brother-in-law.

"There was a light drizzle when Lyra and I had drinks on the back deck," Dion added.

Tia looked skeptical and Devlin smiled inwardly, remaining out of the line of fire. She was undoubtedly one of the most attractive women he'd ever seen, and she was dangerously smart, which Devlin suspected was the main reason Trent had fallen for her.

"I should tell Ms. Beverly. She'll have a fit if something happens to someone on this trip," Tia began.

"No!" Trent said adamantly, causing Tia's eyebrows to raise. "I mean, she's probably asleep. Don't bother her."

"Well, maybe you're right. But I should tell Regan. I get the impression the two of them are close."

Trent's relief was apparent. There was something about this Gavin person and his cousin Regan that Trent knew and wasn't about to share with his wife. Unfortunately, Devlin got the feeling Trent's relief was going to be short-lived.

"Just Regan," Trent told her. "Nobody else needs to know now."

Tia looked as if she might argue, but turned and left the room without another word.

"Did you check the perimeter?" Trent asked the moment Tia was gone.

Because this was more his forte, definitely more so than the familial drama that was playing out in front of him, Devlin spoke up readily. "Partial footprints were leading away from where I found him. Rain's coming down a little harder now, so it's pointless to try and follow them. The ground's pretty mushy right about now."

"No word on Vega?" Ben asked in a cool, clipped tone.

Ben Donovan had been a surprise, standing and shooting a crocked cop down as if he were a trained killer. That wasn't an easy task, Devlin thought with a sigh. He did it and could probably do it in his sleep, but that's because that was all he'd ever done. Ben, on the other hand, came from a good family, with good morals and careers and so much to live for. Then again, it was either kill the cop or stand by while he killed

Victoria. Devlin had a feeling that wasn't really an option for Ben.

Devlin only shook his head. "If he's here, we'll find him."

"This isn't a small island, and a big portion of the land is forest, which lends to a perfect hiding place," Brock announced.

"But what Vega wants is in this house," Devlin said calmly. "He's gotta come here to get it."

Brock dragged a hand down his face. "There are events planned for every day beginning tomorrow afternoon. There's no way we can keep the women in this house. Noelle's going to flip when she finds out there's an extra guest as it is."

Brandon moved to stand next to his brother, clapping a hand on his shoulder. "It's going to be fine, Brock. I really don't think this guy would come all this way to take a shot at Ben or his girlfriend."

"He did," Ben said slowly. "I should have known he wouldn't stop."

"A jail sentence should have stopped him," Trent said. "Don't beat yourself up about this."

"Look, for tonight we'll tell the women Gavin slipped and fell. If it's still raining in the morning, the outside events will be moved inside, so they'll be fine. If we have to go outside, we'll just make sure that they're not alone. A couple of us will make sure we stay near," Linc instructed.

"Shit! What about the kids?" Adam asked.

"We'll keep them close. Adam, you were already on babysitting duty earlier. You and I will just make sure we're always with them as well," Max offered. Adam nodded his agreement.

"I've got Ace and Rio with me," Devlin said, referring to his associates "They're the only ones I could find on short notice. Rio can stay with you and the kids." Devlin nodded to where Max stood near the window. "Ace will try to help with the women. I'm going to check out the island."

"I'm going with you at first dawn," Trent told him.

Devlin was already shaking his head. "Your family's here. You should stay and protect them."

"Protect us from what?" Tia asked the moment she walked into the game room once more.

This time a line of women followed, and one person quickly broke away to immediately head towards the couch.

"Why is he still unconscious?" Regan asked. "Has anyone called for a paramedic?" She touched his forehead and Gavin moaned, moving his head slightly to the side. "Can you hear me?" she asked.

"Devlin's certified in first aid," Trent told her, looking from Regan to his wife in exasperation. "Didn't I tell you he just fell?"

"Well, then he needs medical attention," Tia retorted.

Trent looked gruffly at Camille and Lyra, who had gravitated to their significant others after disbursing from the line. "None of you look like doctors or nurses for that matter," he snapped.

"Lyra said Regan would want to know, so we had to bring her down to see him," Camille said.

The men looked to Savian, no doubt remembering what he'd said about Parker playing matchmaker between Regan and Gavin.

"Gavin, can you hear me?" Regan continued. She'd squeezed herself onto the small space between Gavin's muscled body and the edge of the couch, lifting his hand in hers.

He moaned again and his eyes fluttered.

"Get him something to drink," Trent said over his shoulder to no one in particular.

Camille took the assignment and went to the bar to grab a bottle of water. Trent knelt, reached inside the suitcase once more and then moved to the couch.

"Gavin, man, can you open your eyes?" he asked, standing behind where Regan sat.

Gavin's eyes trembled once more, and then cracked open slowly.

"What the hell happened?" he asked groggily. "I feel like I was hit by a Mack truck."

"Just a little accident," Trent hurried to say. "Can you tell me how many fingers I'm holding up?"

Gavin answered correctly and Regan seemed to relax a bit.

"Follow my finger," Trent continued and Gavin's eyes moved back and forth.

Regan watched, barely realizing she was holding her breath as Trent asked each question and Gavin performed the task. Her heart had been hammering in her chest since Bailey had told her he was unconscious.

"You slipped and fell outside..." Trent started talking in a voice that was oddly slow, but Regan figured he wanted to make sure Gavin's head injury wasn't too bad. But he hadn't been talking that slowly before.

"It started to rain after dinner, so the grass is really slick. You probably lost your footing or something. Devlin found you outside. You remember I told you about my friend Devlin earlier?"

Gavin blinked, then opened his eyes once more. "Yeah. Glad he made it here in time."

"In time for what?" Regan asked. She turned back to look at Trent, who looked down at Gavin. Then she looked at Gavin, and he looked at her.

"In time to pick my ass up off the ground," he said, then lifted his lips in a crooked smile. "But now that I have a pretty lady here to take care of me, I think I'll be alright."

"That's what I thought. Take a couple of these for the pain," Trent said while handing Gavin the pills he'd retrieved from the first-aid suitcase. "And we'll get out of your way."

It took a few minutes for everyone to file out, and while they did, Regan made sure Gavin put the pills into his mouth. Camille had passed the bottle of water to Regan before leaving the room. She now gave it to Gavin.

After everyone had left, without further preamble she said, "Okay, now you can tell me what really happened."

He'd laced his fingers through hers and shifted on the chair. Then he grimaced and she felt a slither of panic.

"You're in pain. Maybe I should get Trent to call the mainland for a medic transport."

"No," he said, his voice a little raspy. "I just took the pills. Let's give them time to work. I want you to stay right here."

"Right," she said with a sigh. He would want her to stay on this chair sitting right next to him because he probably knew just how hard it was for her to do so. "I'll just move over here," she added, attempting to get up.

He reached for her arm. "No, I need you to stay right here, Regan.

She didn't move again, even though he was looking at her in a way that made her just a little uncomfortable. Not in the sense that he might do something to her, but in the sense that she was imagining him lying out in the rain on the ground unconscious. What if Trent's friend hadn't arrived when he did? What if she'd slept through the entire night with Gavin outside? Could he have died? And could she have survived the guilt if he did?

"Wait a minute," she said suddenly. "We sat on the balcony eating that ice cream and it wasn't raining."

Gavin lifted a hand to squeeze the bridge of his nose. "Then it must have started between the time I left your room and went to the kitchen to wash out the dishes. I don't know."

"Do you normally have balance issues?" she continued.

"Regan, I've just been whacked over the head, and while I'm not seeing double, I'm feeling like the world is orbiting around me. Your hand in mine is the first real comfort I've had since opening my eyes."

"In other words, shut up?" she asked raising a brow.

He looked up at her. "You said it, not me," he replied with a smile.

CHAPTER 8

Sometime during the night, Regan had stretched out on the sofa beside Gavin, her back pressed tightly against his front as he held her close. And sometime after that he'd become very aware of the softness of her backside pressed against his front and his body dutifully responded.

He buried his face in her hair, felt the tickle of the braids against his skin. His arms closed tighter around her and she made a sound— a sweet little sigh that made his pulse quicken. Gavin's eyes remained closed, the pain in his head still very real and dulled only by the two painkillers he'd taken and the soft lady in his arms. He thrust his hips forward slightly, his thickening arousal pressing against the delectable curve of her bottom.

As if she were on the same train of thought as he, Regan pressed backward, rubbing herself over his erection. He swallowed deeply, his hand moving from where it rested over hers upward to the swell of her breast. His fingers spread cupping the soft mound. "Regan," he whispered, unable to remain quiet a moment longer.

She didn't verbally respond, but moved her hand until it covered his. She wore pajama bottoms and a tank top. When he'd first seen her, she'd also had on a silky cream colored robe. She'd taken that off as she sat on the couch with him, saying it was too warm in the room for it. At the time he hadn't paid the comment much attention, but now, as he kissed the bare skin of the back of her shoulder, he was eternally grateful for the tropical climate they were in.

Her skin was soft and tasted like honey, a fact that had stuck with him since the first time his lips had touched hers. She moved again, sighing as his trail of kisses moved upward toward her neck and then her ear. He licked her lobe, bit it softly, licked once more and then heard his name whispered through the silence of the room. He loved that sound, his name on her lips, no matter how many times he heard it.

"I want you," was his reply.

"Yes," was her response.

His hand moved, going beneath her tank top until he held her bare breast in his hand.

"I always seem to want you, no matter what," he told her honestly.

She responded this time by reaching her hand back between them and cupping his length. Her fingers gripped him, stroked him, the heat of the connection seeping easily through the thin linen shorts he wore. In the morning, he would ask himself how she'd moved so deftly, releasing the button of his shorts, slipping the zipper down and fishing her hand inside until they were finally skin-to-skin.

He moaned, couldn't do anything else, and closed his eyes as her fingers closed around his length, stroking from the base to the tip. Earlier this evening Gavin, had asked for the opportunity to show her that there was more to them than just sex. He wanted the opportunity to properly date Regan, to hopefully make her fall in love with him. She hadn't replied. And now...

"Wait, wait," he whispered, pulling his body back so as to break the contact. "I know I said I wanted this, but—"

His words were cut short as Regan stood from the couch and looked down at him.

"You're talking way too much, Gavin," she said in a low voice a second or so before she grabbed the hem of her tank top and pulled it over her head. She'd stepped out of her pajama pants before he could gather a coherent sentence.

"Regan," he'd barely managed to say before she'd pushed his shorts and boxers down his legs and straddled him.

"No. More. Talking." Her voice was low but demanding, her eyes dark with desire.

Gavin lifted himself up slightly fighting against the wave of dizziness and the slight pounding at the base of his skull. He reached up, cupped her face and pulled her lips down to his. The kiss was slow, yet fevered, his tongue brushing over her with long, languid strokes.

She pulled away, pushing him back down gently. Regan straddled him, not hesitating as she lowered her hips, settling herself onto his length. Gavin hissed, clenched his teeth at the familiar warmth that gripped him. She retracted slightly, only to suck him in—deeper this time—with one torturously slow movement. He closed his eyes, let the passion of this moment soothe the pain of the last few hours, let Regan Donovan take him to a place he'd only ever ventured with her.

Hours ago, she'd told him this wouldn't happen again. He'd asked her for more, but she didn't believe there could be more between her and Gavin. And she had a very good reason for that thought, one that started with a night they'd gotten their signals crossed. That day would forever go down in history as one of the worst days of her life.

And yet, here she was, riding him like she'd missed him all her life. This urgency was deep and persistent, despite her brain's stern warnings. Her body was determined to have its way. She circled her hips, lifted slightly, and then sank back down until he was so deep inside her their bodies seemed conjoined. Her breath came in heavy pants as Gavin held her hips, letting her have complete control. Yes, she knew he was allowing her this. Gavin was a voracious lover. He could be slow and gentle or fast and furious. They'd had wild and wicked nights and sweet and sexy mornings. He knew her body almost better than she knew it herself. And she liked to believe she knew his. This—the physical connection—had been undeniable from the start. The rest...no, there was no rest. This was all that would ever be between them. And she thought she didn't want it anymore.

But she did.

Dammit, she did.

His fingers dug into the skin of her hips and then down to her bottom as she continued to move over him. She kept her eyes closed, but knew that he would be watching her. He loved to watch her. She loved how his intense gaze made her feel. Release ripped through her strongly and swiftly, almost completely wiping away all her doubts, replacing them with sensations she'd never felt before. Her chest heaved and she struggled for breath, falling forward to rest her head on his chest.

"They said you were unconscious," she whispered between breaths, and then stopped because she couldn't bring herself to admit what she'd felt when Bailey had said those words.

"I'm fully awake now," he replied as his hips thrust upward again.

He wrapped his arms around her, holding her tightly as he stroked deep inside her. Sliding his hands down to cup her buttocks, he continued to work her feverishly until his breathing was hitched, his release coming with quick jerks and muted moans.

Several moments passed before either of them spoke, and Regan tried to figure out what would be the most graceful exit. She was naked on top of the man she'd sworn to never be naked on top of again, and he'd just sustained a head injury. It was probably safe to say there was no graceful exit in sight. With that thought, she did what she always did in life—forged ahead no matter what.

She lifted herself from Gavin's chest, avoiding eye contact as their midsections dislodged and she could finally stand and turn her back to him. Modesty wasn't a trait she possessed, especially not with Gavin, so she didn't rush to pick up her clothes, even though she wanted to hurry up and get out of the room.

"Regan."

She'd just pulled on her top, her pants having been the first item of clothing she donned. It occurred to her that he was still injured, which meant she could probably hurry out of the room without him being able to chase after her. Not real happy with that thought and never having run from any obstacle in her life, she took a deep breath and released it slowly before turning to face him.

He'd pulled up his shorts and sat up on the couch, leaning forward slightly so that his elbows rested on his thighs.

"I heard what you said earlier, and my intention is still the same," he told her.

The room was dark but for the moonlight that streamed through windows towards the back of the room. The game room was one of the largest in the house since it was meant to accommodate a number of family members whenever they were here. Being a woman who had enough of her male siblings back in Miami, Regan preferred being on the beach when they were here.

"I heard what you said earlier," she began, and cleared her throat to continue, but couldn't. What would she say? How could she tell him that it was her own ego that was keeping them apart?

He continued to look at her. It actually felt like he was looking through her to all the things she felt but couldn't say.

"I'm glad you came down," he spoke slowly.

She smiled because he was too handsome not to. Even wounded, his strong jawline and muscled arms were attractive. His face, while cloaked in darkness, still had her catching her breath, wanting those eyes to only gaze into hers forevermore.

"Are you going to be okay down here alone?" she asked, really needing to get the hell away from him.

"No," was his reply. "I need you to stay."

❀❀❀

"What's going on, Ben?" Victoria asked the moment Ben closed the door to their room. "And don't you dare tell me nothing. You've been closed up in that room whispering for hours and Devlin and his partners are here."

The one downfall to being in love with a beautiful and intelligent attorney was that lying to her was never easy. Ben felt like it was a necessity in this case, but he and Victoria had gone through so much in the short time they'd been together as a couple he wasn't sure keeping the truth from her was worth the risk. Could it keep her safe? It might and it might not. They'd been down that road before. He'd tried to keep what he knew about Vega and the murder of Congressman McGlinn and his wife away from her, with the thought that the less she knew, the safer she would be. And he'd been wrong. Her house had been smoke bombed, and she'd been held at gunpoint by Timothy Hall, the corrupt police officer hired to keep the mayor's mistress—who also happened to be the late congressman's mistress—hidden.

She was sitting on the edge of the king-sized bed, her black silk robe pulled tightly over what he knew was a lacy black nightgown, one he'd purchased for her especially for this trip. The black brightened her butter-toned complexion and stormy gray eyes so that when he looked at her, he was even more in awe of her beauty and of the blessing that she brought to his life.

Ben had been struggling with his work as a defense attorney for quite some time. The revelation of Ramone Vega's guilt and his part in the man's first mistrial had him on the brink of walking away from the career he'd worked so hard for. It was Victoria, with her unwavering strength and belief in the justice system and the job she was doing, who had encouraged him to stay on his path, to believe there were still some innocent until proven guilty people out there. Tonight, he was struggling to hold onto Victoria's optimism.

"Vega escaped," he said solemnly, hurrying to say the words and hating them just the same.

She was instantly up off the bed. "What? How? When?"

Ben touched her shoulders. "Let's sit."

"I don't want to sit. I want answers."

As he knew she would. "I know, but it's after midnight and I'm exhausted. This is not at all what I anticipated when I invited you to join me at this reunion. I have some answers for you, and I'd just like to sit down and tell you about them." As if to really bring home his point, Ben sat on the bed, patting the spot beside him.

She sat, touching a hand to his cheek. "I'm sorry. Of course, you're tired. You were very distracted today. I ended up talking to your parents more than you did."

"My mother really likes you and my dad already considers you his daughter. I guess it's a good thing I'm already in love with you or I'd be in a tough spot." Ben tried to laugh, tried to make this situation a little lighter. The reality was it was serious, deadly serious, if what they were thinking was true.

"He had it planned. His getaway vehicle had to be riding alongside the transport bus the entire time. He killed the guards and walked off just like he was a passenger who had made it to his destination."

Victoria nodded as if this were an expected course of action. For a killer like Vega, maybe it was. "Do you have any idea where he is now or where he's heading?" she asked.

That was a question Ben really did not want to answer. But to adequately protect her, he felt Victoria needed the full story. The men had decided not to tell all the women and he'd agreed that everyone did not need to know. Victoria was different. She'd prosecuted Vega, sat in the courtroom across from him for a week and a half, endured his threat against her life and prevailed. She deserved to know.

He took her hands in his. "We think he might be on the island. Earlier today, Gavin found a jumpsuit on the beach and he thought he saw a light or something going into the woods. Just a few hours ago, Gavin was knocked out cold and left in the rain. Trent had already called Devlin and he was the one to find Gavin when he arrived."

"Oh my," she gasped, then quickly regained her composure. "Where is Gavin now? Is he alright?"

"He's gonna be okay. He lost consciousness for a little while but Trent and Devlin thing it was just a minor concussion. They gave him some pain pills and Regan was with him when I left, so nobody's going to get a chance to hit him again with her around." He chuckled at the thought. His cousin was as strong if not stronger than some of the men in the family, although none of the men would be quick to admit that, egos and all that abound. As kids they'd all spent time together during the summer, and Regan and Bailey together were a force to be reckoned with, despite what Trent and Max may have thought. Those girls were now women. They were good looking and smarter than most men—a deadly combination.

"You have a great family," Victoria said quietly. "I'm so sorry to have brought this on them."

"No. Don't do that. This isn't your fault. You did everything you were supposed to do. You got the conviction."

"The conviction that Vega ignored. He's out for blood this time, real blood. Yours and mine," she said seriously. "What are we going to do?"

"I'm not going to let him hurt you," he told her.

She smiled. "And I'm not going to let him hurt you. But that's not telling me what the plan is."

"Devlin and Trent are working on the plan. The primary priority is to keep everyone safe. Second is to keep this as quiet as possible because Brock might go ballistic if this week is ruined for Noelle." Ben watched her closely as he said his next words. "I don't really blame him. I would want our wedding to be extra special for you."

Victoria didn't respond to that. He hadn't thought she would. It had taken a while for Victoria to warm to the idea of the two of them together. Their past as law school students in the same school and her initial opinion of him being an arrogant rich guy was still a sore spot in their relationship. Even though Ben didn't want to admit it, it was still a minor block in their progression. He sensed that being around his family—his very well off and influential family—made her uncomfortable. She'd mentioned that him having money and her working a municipal job was one of her biggest issues with them being together. Of course, he'd dismissed it then, but since they'd been on the island he was thinking that maybe it was time to take her reservations a little more seriously.

"I agree. Noelle and Brock should have the perfect wedding just the way they planned it. There's an air of excitement here that can't be ignored. What if I go back? Maybe Vega will follow me?"

"And what if cows drop out of the sky right this minute?" he asked incredulously. "Are you crazy? No, you're not going back. If Vega wants you, he's going to have to go through me to get you."

She shook her head, a sheen of tears in her eyes. "He won't mind doing that."

"Listen to me, Victoria. If Vega wants a fight, he's walked into the right place. Nobody here is going to let him do the harm he most likely has planned. This is not going to end in Vega's favor, I can guarantee you that."

"But is it going to end?" she asked quietly. "Because I thought when he was convicted we were done with this asshole. I was wrong before."

"And so was I. But it won't happen again. Ramone Vega will leave this island in a body bag, end of story," he told her, adamantly believing every word he spoke and praying he'd be the one to put an end to the bastard's reign once and for all.

CHAPTER 9

"Security's gonna be a bitch," Devlin said, his face already fixed into a frown.

Trent could only nod the next day as they stood on the front lawn, watching as crates and boxes were carted into Camelot. People Max and Noelle had hired to help make their wedding celebration a joyous event streamed in and out. Two charters had been booked to bring them all over from the mainland. It was a good thing the resort was finished to the point where guests could at least stay in the rooms, or they would have a hell of a time hosting a wedding here.

"We're expecting about fifty additional guests who won't arrive until Friday afternoon," Trent said, taking a sip from the glass of lemonade he'd snagged from the kitchen at Camelot when Gavin's staff were busy unpacking.

Devlin sighed. "Only fifty. Isn't that a little small for a Donovan wedding?"

"Max isn't big on the social scene in his town and Noelle doesn't have a lot of family. The bulk of our family is already here. Mostly it's our parents close friends who they couldn't leave out for fear of causing a social uproar," he told him. "But you're right, security is going to be a bitch."

"I was out again this morning. Found more footprints."

Devlin stared out to the water. He'd make eye contact with every person that passed, but he wouldn't say a word to them. The black pants and black t-shirt he wore coupled with his black boots was more than out of place on a tropical island, but it was who he was. Trent had learned long ago not to question Devlin or his techniques. Still, nobody knew Devlin like Trent did, and that's why it was alright for him to say, "Man, you sure you don't have something else to wear? It's like eighty degrees out here now and it's barely noon. In another hour or so you're going to melt."

Devlin didn't even look at him when he replied. "I'm cool."

Trent laughed as he shook his head. "No you're not. Sweat's going to bead down your bald head in a minute."

"And I'll still be cool," he replied. "I need a map of the island. I want to know where everything is. If Vega's here, he's got to set up camp somewhere."

Trent nodded. "Yeah, I thought about that. Linc's going to have his assistant scan it and email it to him. I'll get it to you as soon as he gives it to me."

"Damn."

Something about his tone was different. It wasn't the usual dry and candid way Devlin had of speaking. It was almost as if...Trent's words trailed off as he looked up to follow his friend's line of sight and groaned.

"Before you even think about telling me that same pile of lies you told your wife, remember you trained me," a familiar voice declared. "You and Sam and Bree, so I know a thing or two about reading people and their body language. Right now, yours is saying 'oh shit, she's right'. And his..."—she hesitated as she looked at Devlin—"his is just saying 'bring it on', which I'm going to try and avoid for the time being. Now, I'm going to ask you this one time and I expect to get the truth. What the hell is going on?"

Trent took another long swallow of lemonade before he dared to speak. She'd walked up on them like a woman on a mission and, after being married and hanging around other married men, Trent knew there was nothing worse than a woman on a mission. Except maybe a woman scorned, but he didn't even want to think about that right now.

"Bailey Donovan, meet Devlin Bonner. Dev, meet my cousin, Bailey," he said by way of introduction. She was wearing something on her legs that looked like skin except it was the brightest pink color he'd ever seen. Her top was long, thank the heavens, but the flowing material was sheer and gauzy and the high heeled sandals she wore just made her look even more feminine. He wanted her to turn around and go back into the house to change, but he knew that would undoubtedly lead to another argument that would somehow engage all the women on this island. And really, for as tough as Trent knew he was, taking them on wasn't going to go well.

"Hello," she said with a snap as she looked at Dev then immediately back to Trent.

"Nothing's going on Bailey. Dev just came to help with keeping all these people under some type of control. It looks like this wedding is going to be a much bigger deal than Max thought."

Bailey shook her head, shoulder length hair moving as she did. "Don't try it, Trent. He only shows up when things are serious."

She hadn't looked at Dev this time, but jerked a thumb in his general direction. A glance in Dev's direction showed he'd stopped staring straight ahead and was no longer making eye contact with everyone who walked past him. He was looking at Bailey.

"Leave it alone, Bailey. Now is not the time," he warned.

"Now is not the time for what? To want to help protect my family from whatever might be going down? You do know that this is my brother's wedding right?" she asked.

Trent sighed. "I'm not going to let anything happen to any of them, Bailey. What I need for you to do is go back inside and tend to all the bridesmaid or female stuff that needs to be tended to."

The moment the words were out, Trent knew they were wrong. She was in his face instantly.

"Don't give me that 'me man, you woman bull,' Trent. I'm a trained investigator. Hell, I've even helped out the FBI, so don't treat me like I'm some helpless airhead that needs you to fight my battles."

"This isn't your battle, Bailey."

She didn't step back but her face did soften slightly. "No. But it's my family."

"I know," Trent replied. "Trust me, Bailey. I'll tell you whatever you need to know, when you need to know it."

"But you're not going to tell me right now?"

Trent shook his head and then sighed. "Just keep your eyes open. When you and the ladies go on that cruise this afternoon, just stay alert. Understand?"

The way she looked at him said she understood. The small and almost deflated sound of her voice when she replied simply, "okay," said she was disappointed, again. It seemed like Trent was always disappointing Bailey. But he was also protecting her.

"She's a handful," he said to Devlin when she'd stalked off.

A few seconds passed before his friend replied, "She's definitely something."

Regan stared on in awe as Brock commanded the yacht with genuine experience and expertise. It fit that he'd become a sailor since he lived on Maryland's Eastern Shore, but up until now she'd never connected the two. He wore white shorts and a white polo shirt and stood at the control board looking through the front windows like a man totally at home with his surroundings.

"Parker's idea to offer tour packages at the resort was ingenious. To think we all had him pegged as simply a media mogul," Brock said, giving Regan a tentative grin over his shoulder.

She smiled in return. "Yes, Parker's a man of many talents. I mean, I knew about the renovation of Camelot but I hadn't given it much thought beyond selecting the name. I wasn't aware of all the details." The main detail being that Gavin might be working in partnership with them.

"Parker and Linc met up with Adam and Max just before Thanksgiving I believe. They called me to talk about the construction costs and ideas. We flew down here before Christmas and everything moved pretty quickly since that time," Brock told her.

Since Adam and Max owned a company that specialized in rehabbing luxury homes and resorts, it was logical that they were in on the meeting.

"We don't normally do resorts," she said. "I mean, of course, Max and Adam do them, but the Donovans haven't been up to putting their name on one. I wonder what changed their minds."

"Economics," Brock said with a shrug. "We own all this land. It's a shame to let it go to waste."

"Yeah, you're right. I guess I'm just worried about how it'll effect the station and all that we have going on at home."

Brock turned from the control board, taking a seat in the captain's chair that looked more like a high-tech barber's seat. "Parker just spearheaded the effort. The plan is to hire experienced personnel to actually run the resort. That's why he tapped Gavin to manage the restaurant."

She folded her arms over her chest. "I definitely did not know about that ahead of time."

"So I heard. But Gavin's a good guy. I hear good things about both his restaurants," Brock told her evenly, while looking at her suspiciously.

She sighed heavily. "And now he's down here falling and knocking his head so hard he's rendered unconscious when he's only supposed to be looking at a restaurant site and coming up with a new menu."

Brock cleared his throat. "That was an accident."

Regan wanted to question Brock's response. She wanted to dig deeper into what happened last night. The memory of Gavin lying on that ground partially conscious stopped her. The important thing was that he was alright. At least she knew in her mind that should have been the most important thing.

"You know Trent's going to get to the bottom of it."

"Right." She gave a little chuckle. "Trent lives for this kind of stuff. Especially since Tia and Trevor have him pretty much grounded in Vegas, he has to get his adrenaline rush where he can."

"And from what I hear, he's been getting it a lot lately. Sean and Dion had some things going on, didn't they?"

Deciding she was tired of standing, Regan went to the seat beside Brock and sat. "I called it battle of the ex's," she told him with a dry chuckle. "Dion had some obsessed chick shooting at Lyra and Sean's fiancée was having baby daddy drama. I'm just glad Trent and Devlin could come out to help.

It was a mess. I thought Aunt Janean was going to trade in her Gucci bag for a holster and gun at one point."

Brock smiled at that. "Now that would have really been something. I bet those ex's would have gladly left Miami and never turned back if they had to deal with Aunt Janean."

"Right," Regan replied, looking out at the crisp blue water.

"You ready to ask me what you really want to know now?" Brock asked knowingly.

The cousins knew each other almost as well as their own siblings, even though most of them lived quite a distance apart. Whenever they were together, it was if they'd just seen each other the day before.

"I don't want him here," she admitted. "Especially not if he's going to get hurt in the process."

"He's just a guy that owns a restaurant, Regan. Why are you acting like it's something more?"

"I'm not!" was her quick retort. It was too quick, but she realized that too late. "I just don't like the idea of someone getting hurt on our property. He could sue, you know."

Brock shook his head. "Gavin Lucas is not going to sue us."

"He might," she continued. "Or he might decide not to partner with us. Do you know if Parker has someone else in mind?"

"I saw Gavin at breakfast this morning and he doesn't seem to be blaming any of us for last night's accident. I think you might be going overboard with the worry."

"I'm not. He needs to get off this island, sooner rather than later," she said.

"Is that an order?"

Regan spun around at the sound of Gavin's voice.

"I'll take that as my cue to leave," Brock said with a smirk. As he moved out of his seat, he leaned over to whisper in Regan's ear, "If this is personal, you need to deal with it before the business deal is done linking him permanently to the family."

Like I didn't already know that, she thought to herself.

"You doing okay out here?" Brock asked Gavin. "You took a pretty good hit on the head last night."

"I'm fine. Ms. Carolyn gave me motion sickness and pain pills before we left. And she told me to find a seat and sit down for the ride," he added with a chuckle.

Brock smiled. "Sounds just like Aunt Carolyn, always trying to take care of everyone. Don't know that the trait was handed down to her children, but Regan will probably make sure you're okay for the duration of the ride."

Regan did not return Brock's smile, and turned to face the front of the boat as she heard Gavin approach.

"So now you want me off the island?"

"I want you safe," she said quickly. Really, she needed to think before she spoke from now on.

He nodded as he slipped slowly into the captain's chair. "I'll take that as a good sign then."

"Really, Gavin. Maybe you should head back to the states to get your head looked at. Trent and Devlin are not doctors," Regan insisted.

"No, but they have a medical arsenal in that suitcase of theirs." She was about to say something else but he held up a hand to stop here. "I feel fine and I've already put a call into my primary care physician, at your mother's request. If he thinks I should come back for more medical attention, I will."

She sat back in her chair and continued to stare forward.

"About last night..." he began.

"I don't want to talk about that." She took a deep breath and released it. "I mean, it happened just like it's happened before."

"And you're fine with that?" he pushed, even though she was sure he knew she wouldn't want to talk about this.

"Sex has never been a problem for us Gavin," she admitted.

"Then what is the problem, Regan? Because I feel like there's something between us that I don't know about. I want to try and make this work, but there's something blocking that progress. It would be great if you could just tell me what that is."

Regan turned in her seat to get a better look at him. He wore a Yankees baseball cap that matched perfectly with his dark blue khaki shorts and light gray t-shirt. The bandage on the back of his head, close to his neck, was visible and had her stomach tightening at the sight. Dark eyes stared back at her as he waited patiently. Patience was a virtue Regan absolutely did not possess, no matter how long her mother had been praying for her. When she wanted something she reached for it and most often received it, but she hadn't allowed that knowledge to swell into some type of pre-ordained truth. Gavin Lucas was living proof that she didn't always get what she wanted.

"Look," she said finally, "he had a good run. For years, we've given each other what we needed physically. It might simply be time to move on from that."

He didn't respond instantly as she thought he would, but pinched the bridge of his nose instead.

"Are you in pain? Do you need me to get you some medication?" she asked, all too aware of the fact that he could have been dead right now.

Regan didn't like that thought, hadn't liked it the moment Bailey announced he'd been hurt. And after spending the night with him, she found the thought of his demise was even harder to swallow, all of which confirmed what she'd been desperately afraid of for the last few months. She was in love with Gavin Lucas.

"My head is fine," he said quietly.

He reached for her hand then, holding her fingers in his. "I know what we had, Regan. And like I told you last night, I want more than that now."

"You mean you want more than that today? This week, maybe because we're on this island for seven days together. But what happens after that Gavin? What happens when we return to Miami and you go back to your life? I'll go back to mine and we'll be on opposite sides of the spectrum once more. Doesn't it just make sense to make a clean break now?"

Before I become too emotionally invested, she thought dismally.

"What makes sense—"

His words broke off as a long curse sounded throughout the cabin.

"We're taking on water!" Brock shouted.

"What?" Regan asked.

Gavin was already slipping out of the captain's chair, moving to the side to look out the window.

"She's listing on the starboard side," he said solemnly.

Regan stood now, icy tendrils of fear moving along her spine. "What are you saying? Brock, what's going on?"

"There may be a puncture somewhere along the bottom of the boat. When I left you earlier I went down into the galley to get a drink and saw the floor's full of water. We've been taking on water the whole hour we've been out here," he said, frustration clear on his face as his brows wrinkled and his lips drew into a thin line. He leaned forward and punched some buttons on the control board before putting both hands on the wheel and turning slowly.

"How many do you have onboard?" Gavin asked.

"Noelle was a little frustrated this morning when so many of the ladies opted to stay ashore. There's only five who came onboard, with the three of us making eight," Brock told him.

Gavin nodded. He talked as he moved around where Brock was now standing at the wheel to stop beside Regan. "Life vests?" he asked.

"Along the base by the stern in the bottom compartments. Noelle knows where they are. She can help—"

Brock's words cut off and Regan went to him.

She put a hand to his arm. "Get your jacket on. We'll get Noelle. How long until we're back on land."

"About half hour if I push it," he answered.

"Then push it," Regan told him as she followed Gavin out of the small cabin.

❧❧❧

Gavin looked out to the water and felt a clenching in his gut. The island was just barely visible, like a bump of dark ridges along the skyline. He saw the ladies—Noelle sitting cross legged on a side bench, eyes covered by large framed sunglasses, streaked hair pulled back from her face; Jade, Tia, Bailey and Victoria sitting close to her, laughing and enjoying mimosa's and sunshine. Beside him Regan stood ready to take charge. She would ignore the fact that he was there and could help as well, if he let her.

"Ladies, I have to ask that each of you stand up and put on a life vest," he said before Regan could speak.

He didn't look to his side, but felt the instant she turned her fierce gaze on him. It was in her nature to take control, to do whatever task it was that needed to be done. He knew that's how she worked at the magazine and how she ran her personal life. Gavin was used to having a certain measure of control himself, which he readily admitted was probably the prime issue between him and Regan.

"What's going on?" Tia asked, immediately standing.

Regan stepped in front of him then. "Brock's turning around. We're going to head back to land."

"So soon?" Bailey asked skeptically. "Did something happen?"

This was the cousin that worked as a private investigator. Gavin could almost see the wheels of thought churning in her head as they spoke.

"Yes," he replied. There was no use in lying to this particular bunch of women, or trying to soften the blow.

He knew Regan too well for that, and had heard about the strength and independent streaks in Tia and Bailey. Even Ben's girlfriend looked like she knew something was amiss.

"So we're going to put on our life vests…" Regan began again. She'd taken a step towards the women as Noelle had already unlatched the compartment where the vests were stored and begun handing them out.

"Brock says we'll be back on land in about thirty minutes," Gavin told them.

Victoria snapped her vest on and approached him.

"Tell me what's happened," she whispered to him. "Does this have something to do with Vega?"

Trent and his friend Devlin had briefed Gavin this morning. About twenty minutes after he'd awakened on the couch alone, they'd come into the game room to check on the status of his wound and to ask who or what he saw outside the previous night. After he'd recounted his story, they'd told him about Ramone Vega's escape from prison.

"I felt the pain of the hit and fell to the ground. For the last seconds that I was conscious I could see someone running away, feet and legs mostly, and it was dark," he'd told them. "I must have surprised whoever it was because as I fell they cursed. It was a female voice."

Trent and Devlin had looked puzzled by that admission.

"I don't know who's responsible," Gavin told Victoria, feeling secure in the fact that for the most part that was definitely true.

"But there's trouble on the yacht?" she persisted.

Gavin nodded. "There is trouble on the yacht."

CHAPTER 10

"Did you get Brock's text?" Linc asked Trent the moment he joined him on the patio.

Today the men were slated to play golf. The resort offered an extensive course and the senior Donovans wanted to check it out. By the end of this vacation, they would all have firsthand experience of how Camelot would be run and what their future guests could look forward to.

The golf game had run from six in the morning to just about noon when the men broke for lunch. The midday meal had been catered by Gavin and the three members of his staff who had arrived this morning along with the wedding vendors. The plan was originally for Gavin to also oversee the serving of lunch and to answer any questions the seniors might have, but after last night's events, Trent and Devlin had decided it was safer for Gavin to take the yacht tour with Brock and the women.

At any rate, it didn't appear that Trent and Linc would get an opportunity to taste the lunch.

"I did. Devlin's heading down to the dock to wait for them to get in. He said he's about thirty minutes out," Trent said, his jaw clenching tightly the moment he stopped talking.

That was a sure sign that Trent's patience was being tested. Considering Trent barely possessed an ounce of patience, Linc was thinking he'd explode at any minute now. Adding that to the fact that Jade was also on the yacht, Linc could totally relate to what his brother was feeling at this moment.

"How much water onboard?"

Trent folded his arms over his chest, his feet a measured distance apart as he stood looking out to what they could see of the water from this distance. "Gavin just texted me. He went down to have a look and it's at least two feet in the galley."

"Dammit!" Linc cursed, rubbing a hand down the back of his head.

"I didn't say anything to anybody else and Brock only sent the text to you and me," Trent offered. "Now the question is how to keep everyone from freaking out."

"You think this ex-convict guy is roaming around the island...for what? What does he want?" Linc asked. "And why mess with the yacht? He has no way of knowing who would be on there and when?"

"Ben's last client was a hired killer. He tried to kill Ben and Victoria before getting sentenced to life in prison. It makes sense that since he escaped he would come for them again. As for the yacht, other than the scheduled ferries coming and going twice a day, it's our only transportation off the island without us calling for the Coast Guard." Trent stopped and looked seriously at his older brother. "Gavin said he heard a female voice just after he was hit."

"So it's not Ben's killer? There's some crazy woman running around hitting people in the head?" Linc was shaking his head as he spoke.

"I'm not sure. And all these additional people on the island are only going to make figuring that out more difficult."

"That's certainly true. Maybe I'll take one of the rooms over here just to keep an eye on things," Linc suggested.

"You sure Jade will want to be this far away from Noelle with the wedding coming up?"

Linc slipped his hands into his pockets and shrugged. "This will put her closer to the vendors, and since the reception is taking place in the resort ballroom, we'd all end up over here anyway."

Trent gave a wry chuckle. "That's a good scenario to present to her when you ask. It might keep her from immediately turning you down flat."

"You haven't been married long enough to know how the powers of persuasion can work in your favor, my little brother," Linc added with a genuine smile.

"Maybe so, but I know that even with your powerful charm, Jade still calls the shots," Trent countered.

"Just like Tia does in your household, I imagine."

Trent nodded. "That's precisely how I know how this will end."

It was good that the brothers could have a moment of shared contentment, good that they could all sit back and relax for the time being. Her hair blew in the wind as she stood in the distance behind a thick copse of palm trees, watching. Dark sunglasses covered her eyes and she rubbed her wrist that was still a little sore from the way she'd swung the crowbar she'd been carrying to her hideout when that idiot man had appeared out of nowhere. It hadn't been time for her to make her appearance known, that much was true, and she'd listened for longer than she'd cared to last night about that very fact. But truth be told, she didn't care. She'd come here for revenge, hooked up with him again for only this reason, and dammit, she intended to succeed this time!

They made it back to shore just as the yacht started to list to the right. Gavin was off first, guiding each of the women down the plank to where Trent, Linc and Devlin awaited them. Tia fell into Trent's arms while Linc immediately scooped Jade up so that her feet left the ground, spinning her in a slow circle.

It was odd, the immediate feeling of loneliness that swept through Regan like a summer storm. Wrapping her arms around herself, she stood perfectly still, willing the feeling to go away and attempting to dismiss it as the remnants of fear for the ordeal they'd narrowly escaped. The half-million dollar yacht the family owned was going to sink if they couldn't get that hole repaired immediately. And even if it was repaired, water damage to the yacht might cost them more than if they just lost the vessel entirely. But they were all safe, and that's all that really mattered.

"You okay?" Gavin asked, coming up behind her, placing a hand on her shoulder.

This was the first time they'd been alone since finding out the yacht was taking on water. She'd watched him calmly comfort each one of her cousins, keeping them organized as Brock focused on bringing the vessel back to land.

At first all she could do was nod. Words were forming in her mind, but dammit, they weren't coming as easily as she would have liked.

"It's alright," he continued, moving closer this time, wrapping his arms around her waist. "It's okay. You're safe now."

And that's exactly what she felt. Enclosed in his arms, her feet on solid ground, the sound of the ocean a short distance away instead of wobbling just beneath the rim of the yacht. They weren't sinking and she wasn't drowning. Her head lolled back onto his shoulder and Regan closed her eyes.

For all of three seconds.

Then it was business as usual.

Gavin was still the one man she feared most in this world. And whatever Regan feared, she pushed out of her life because there was no room for fear.

She pulled away from him, clearing her throat as she turned. Then brushing down the front of her shirt and her shorts—even though there was nothing on them—she finally looked up to meet his glare. "I'm fine," she said simply.

"It's okay, Regan. All of us were a little worried we wouldn't make it," Gavin continued.

He hadn't looked worried at all. Instead he'd looked way too sexy and sure of himself, even as he'd finally donned a life vest. He'd stood at the head of the deck giving orders in his low voice, looking everyone eye to eye so they'd know to trust him even though they'd only met him two days ago. He hadn't looked afraid.

"You can stop now. I don't need you to calm me down. I'm fine," she said, and then sighed because even to her own ears that sounded bitchy. That wasn't her intent. "Look, I'm cranky and I'll admit a little shook up from what just happened. I'm just going to go back to the house and maybe try to take a nap."

He nodded and opted to keep his hands to himself. She could see him exercising restraint, staying in the spot where he

stood instead of coming close to her again. A part of her
wanted to admire him for that ability. She was having one hell
of a time restraining her wants and desires where he was
concerned. But it was the safest route, of that she was sure.

"I've got to head back to Camelot anyway. My first dinner
for the senior Donovans is tonight. I want to make sure it's
memorable," he told her with a slight smile as he finished.

It was a memorable moment, with him standing haloed by
sunshine and crystalline blue waters, white sand beaches and
palm trees.

"Right. They're a hard bunch to please, but I'm sure you'll
do well."

Gavin never failed. He never looked overwhelmed and
probably never really worried about what his next career move
would be. He knew exactly what he wanted at all times and he
went after it.

Just as he'd gone after Raquel McClean that day when
Regan had thought she was supposed to meet him at The Ritz.

"Will I see you at dinner?" he asked.

"I don't know," she replied, already shaking her head. "I'm
not really feeling well."

"Should I have someone call for a doctor?" he asked,
instantly taking a step towards her.

"No," she answered quickly. "No, it's just a headache. I'll
probably feel much better after some lunch and a nap." And the
pain pills she'd been prescribed for her migraine headaches, the
ones that had precipitated the diagnosis of high blood pressure.

She started to walk away and knew with absolute certainty
he wouldn't let her go that simply.

He touched her elbow, lightly, so that if she really wanted to
get away from him, she could.

"Regan, about last night," he started, "that's not what I
meant to happen."

"I know, Gavin. You didn't mean to fall and hit your head
and I didn't mean to let my physical needs take control. It
won't happen again," she told him solemnly. "It can't."

With that, she was gone, moving quickly up the path leading
back to the main house. She didn't look back at her cousins
who still stood on the beach, discussing the yacht no doubt.

And she definitely didn't look back at the man who was slowly driving her insane.

CHAPTER 11

Regan walked slowly to the end of the bricked terrace and stared out towards the calm waters of the Caribbean Sea. The verandah was covered, so shade was abundant, but just beyond its borders, the sun shone brightly over the surrounding grass. Bursts of color by way of native island flowers stretched as far out as the end of the excavated property, where the line of forest began. Savian had no idea what the flowers were called, but their vibrant hues of pink, orange, yellow and purple coupled with their alluring scent was enough to make anyone feel happy to be here. So why was Regan standing there looking anything but?

He stood with the sliding glass doors behind him, watching his sister attempt to disappear into the scenery. She'd come out here to escape the house. Despite the earlier drama surrounding the yacht, the rest of the family were abuzz with festivities. Uncle Bernard, Aunt Jocelyn and Brynne had arrived, and since none of the family saw them often, it took about half an hour for that excitement to die down. There was a do or die game of chess being played by Uncle Bruce and Uncle Albert. The aunts, along with his mother, were huddled over cups of coffee when he was unfortunate enough to pass through.

"Savian, you are looking more handsome every time I see you," Aunt Beverly had said. "Just look at those gray eyes. You know your grandfather had those same eyes. They hop around throughout the family but only settle on the men."

"Yes, just like my Max. I wondered if Ben would have them too, but he got my eyes," Aunt Alma had replied, a smile ready on her face.

If there was one thing Savian could count on, other than the sun rising and setting each day, it would be that Aunt Alma would always have a smile and a pleasant word for someone. She always seemed to be happy, a trait she'd passed along to Ben. At least that was the way he'd known Ben before. Now, it seemed this last case had his cousin totally on edge.

"I was just heading outside for a walk," Savian had said by way of trying to get the hell out of that kitchen as quickly as possible.

But Aunt Janean had stood and touched a hand to his elbow. "Come on and have a cup with us, Savian. You're always rushing off somewhere."

"Somewhere alone," his mother had said with a tsk before taking a sip from her cup.

The next fifteen minutes consisted of each aunt asking about his love life, or lack thereof, and his mother sending him "I-told-you-so" looks. He'd been about to yell for mercy when Aunt Janean mentioned Regan.

"She's been up in her room since they came back from the boat. That's not like her," she'd said.

His mother had nodded. "I know. I tried going in to talk to her, but she said she had a headache and wanted a nap. She's been looking so tired lately."

Savian silently agreed. Regan had looked tired at work and he'd hardly seen her outside of the office. Back in Miami, Aunt Janean and his mother rotated having Sunday dinners at their homes, but Regan hadn't been present at any in the past four or so weeks.

"I'll go look for her," he'd offered.

"Be careful with her, Savian. You know how temperamental she can be when she thinks you're hovering," his mother had warned.

Regan did have a bit of a temper and a mile-long competitive streak. There was nothing he, Dion, Parker or Sean could do when they were growing up that Regan wasn't up for trying and usually surpassing them at. She'd climbed trees without batting an eye, swam until her eyes were red-rimmed and her chest was heaving, and drank soda until she burped for days in their famous soda drinking contests. There was nothing his little sister couldn't do, or didn't think she could do. That competitiveness had only increased as she grew older until now he got the feeling she was working so hard at *Infinity* to prove a point. But this was their family business. It wasn't a race and nobody was keeping score. Somehow, he didn't think Regan felt the same.

Now he'd found her, and his heart had quietly ached for her. She looked so sad as she stood about ten feet away from him. The distance wasn't very short, but he couldn't help but imagine how far apart he and his only sister truly were.

"Hiding out?" he asked when he'd finally grown tired of watching her.

He'd walked the short distance so that he now stood right next to her, staring out into the distance just as she was. She wrapped her arms even tighter around her body, if that were possible. Her hair was pulled back from her face, held in some type of band that must have been made of magical material to hold all those braids so securely.

"Just getting some air," was her response.

Savian nodded. "This is the best place to do that. I love coming down here."

She sighed. "I did too."

"You did? As in past tense?" he paused, not really expecting her to reply.

"Why did Parker really send Gavin down here? He could have come to visit Camelot at any time. It didn't have to be this week," she told him.

The words sounded similar to what he'd asked their brother himself in their conversation yesterday.

"You know Parker, Regan. No matter how old we get, he still gets a kick out of agitating you. And since you made no secret how much having to interview Gavin bothered you, Parker figured he'd keep the gag going."

"Well, you can tell him it's not funny," she snapped. "I won't be speaking to him for quite some time."

Savian didn't smile ,and he didn't like the sound of her voice. This wasn't the Regan he knew. The Regan he knew would have already called Parker to give him a good piece of her mind for sending Gavin down here. Then she would have made some awesomely painful threat that she would have definitely followed through on the moment they returned to Miami. This quiet retreat was not the norm for his sister.

"You want to tell me what's really going on between you and Gavin? And don't waste your time by saying you hate him, because if that was the case you would have simply hurt him by now."

Regan stepped away from him then, her sandaled feet hitting the grass as she moved from beneath the canopy. She didn't walk far before turning back to face him.

"Why are men such jackasses?"

That was definitely not what he'd expected to hear.

"Excuse me?"

Her hands moved to her hips, her stance confrontational in every sense of the word. If he were anyone other than her brother, Savian would be nervous. Actually, he was still a little leery of what she might do next.

"I played by the rules. I didn't ask for anything beyond what I was getting and even that wasn't enough. Jackasses!" she spat, then clamped her lips shut like she hadn't really meant to say any of that.

Savian was quiet for a minute as he gave his mind time to digest what she'd just said. Had Gavin Lucas actually hurt his sister in some way? Oh man, that wasn't going to be good if that were the case. But before he rushed to judgment, he decided it might be better to let Regan explain a little more.

"Are you and Gavin seriously involved?" he asked in what he considered his best calm voice, even though his insides were already preparing for an onslaught of anger depending on her response.

She shook her head. "I just should have known better, that's all. And now he's here acting like he wants us to do the dating thing to see how things go. How does he think they're going to go? Doesn't he know you can't go backwards?"

Okay, now Savian was afraid that his very intelligent and savvy sister was losing her mind. Babbling was not one of Regan's traits.

"What do you want from him, Regan?" he asked finally.

She stopped again, let her head fall back and looked toward the sky. "I don't know," she said almost so quietly he didn't hear her.

"Then I think he might be the better person to have this conversation with," he said, because, yeah, he didn't like talking relationships, or what he thought might have been her and Gavin's attempt at a relationship.

She sighed heavily, then looked back at him. "I think you might be right, Savian. For a change," she added with a smile.

Gavin looked perfectly at home in the large industrial style kitchen. Dressed in black slacks, a sky blue dress shirt, sleeves rolled up to his elbows and a concentrated look on his face, he moved like a man on a mission. The stove was filled with boiling pots and behind him at the nine-foot-long stainless steel table, four other people dressed in white and wearing chef's hats moved back and forth, cutting this or arranging that. In the next instant, he was at one of the huge sub-zero refrigerators, pulling open a door that looked double his size and leaning inside to come out with a tray of something she couldn't identify from where she stood. He gave instructions in an almost cordial tone that she figured was widely respected and quickly carried out by his staff.

She should leave, Regan thought fleetingly. She shouldn't have come when she knew he'd be working. This was an important dinner for him. She'd overheard her father and her uncles talking about it.

"He'll do fine," Reginald had told his brothers. "He's his father's son."

"His father was a cop, not a chef," Everette had interjected.

"A damned good cop," Henry added.

Everette frowned. "A cop that got himself killed."

Reginald shook his head quickly. "That wasn't his fault," he told them, his tone a little gruff.

"No. It wasn't," Bruce continued. "Anthony was a good man and he loved his family. Gavin slipped into his father's role seamlessly after his death."

"I'm surprised he didn't become a cop like his father. He'd already enrolled in the academy," Reginald told them.

"Then what happened? Why is he now a chef being considered as a partner in a Donovan family business?" asked Bernard, who had only just arrived on the island.

"His father was killed in the line of duty," Reginald said quietly.

Regan had walked away then, not caring to hear any more about the tragedy in Gavin's life. He was the only son and so had felt obligated to fill his father's shoes and take care of his mother and sisters. Now, his sisters were grown and taking care of themselves, as well as helping out with their mother. That much she'd already known about him. It was everything else that had her still questioning the man Gavin Lucas claimed to be—everything else and specifically Raquel McClean.

"You trying to sneak a taste before dinner?" Gavin asked, wiping his hands on a white towel he'd had draped over his right shoulder.

He was standing directly in front of her now. If she lifted a hand, she could touch the sharp line of the perfectly manicured goatee she secretly adored. For a minute, she considered stepping back, trying to find a safer place to stand. Then she reminded herself that she wasn't afraid of Gavin. Only of what his reaction might be to what she had to say. Even so, Regan stayed where she was and, after a deep breath, asked, "Do you have a minute? I need to talk to you about something."

There was a pause filled with about fifteen seconds of Gavin looking at her as if he were trying to read her mind.

"It would be a lot easier if you let me tell you instead of trying to figure out what I want on your own, don't you think?"

He smiled at her question, a slow smile that had the effect of two strong hands running along her naked body, with hot oil, slipping and sliding in all the right places and...hurriedly she looked over his shoulder. "There are a lot of people around, but I can say what I have to say right here then leave?"

"No. We'll go someplace a little quieter." He touched a hand to her elbow and led her towards swinging double doors.

There was another room with more people moving about carrying various wrapped trays and measuring ingredients.

"It looks like you're preparing for an army," she said as they moved by without stopping.

The kitchen was located on the lower floor of Camelot. From blue prints she'd seen in her father's home office, Regan knew there were two service elevators to transport the staff up to the main dining room where registered guests would be served. Gavin led her down a narrow hallway and through a door that he quickly closed behind them. She looked around to what appeared to be an office with its functional desk and chair and computer, and nothing else.

"Is this quiet enough?" he asked, leaning back against the desk to fold his arms over his chest.

"It's fine," she replied. "Is this your office?"

Before he could answer, she was shaking her head. "It doesn't matter. That's not what I'm here for."

"Okay," he said slowly. "What are you here for, Regan?"

She took a deep breath and recited the words, "do or die" in her mind. That's what Parker always said when she was doing something he'd dared her to do, or something she'd sworn she could do but wasn't absolutely certain about.

"I saw you and Raquel at the Ritz," she blurted out.

His shoulders squared and she figured it was best to continue without stopping.

"I thought we were supposed to meet that night and when I showed up you were leaving the bar with Raquel. I thought maybe you'd just run into her while you were waiting for me. We'd been so discreet with our meetings, I didn't want to interrupt. Besides, I figured she would be leaving soon. But she didn't. You left the bar with her and moved towards the elevators."

She could see that he was following her words, possibly remembering every second of that evening, just as she had on too many occasions.

Still, she continued.

"You kissed her in the hallway before the elevator arrived. It wasn't a friendly kiss."

Gavin lifted a hand to his face, smoothed it over his goatee, and kept his gaze focused on her.

"I know what was between us was supposed to be no strings attached. We'd agreed on that from the beginning. But—" her words trailed off, the momentum of her "do or die" speech having all but dissipated. The pounding of her heart was a more prominent issue at the moment.

"But what, Regan?" he asked softly. "Tell me how you felt when you saw me kissing Raquel."

Regan tilted her head, hearing his words as a dare. The idea of this conversation had made her anxious, while Gavin's blasé reaction was making her angry.

"I felt betrayed!" The words were like a flash of lightning in her mind because they were one hundred percent honest and this was the first time she'd actually admitted to the betrayal, even to herself. "I wasn't seeing anyone else, hadn't even been dating anyone in Miami and there you were not only with someone else, but with her at our place. So I felt like you were sending me a big 'screw you' message. I left and—"

"And you didn't return my calls or messages for the next two months," he said, standing from his lounging position.

It didn't take much for them to be face to face in the small space, and, again, backing away wasn't an option.

"I got your message loud and clear. There was no reason for further explanations."

"How could I explain what I didn't even know you'd witnessed? Why didn't you interrupt us? Say something? Stand your ground?" he continued, tossing the questions out like they were the most logical suggestions.

Hearing them made Regan even angrier, because he was right. Still, her temper flared. "And what, claim you as my man and tell Raquel to keep her hands off?" she snapped.

He didn't even look startled by the words. "Yes, exactly," he replied, then shook his head. "No, that's not totally right. What I mean is that both of us should've been a little more honest with ourselves about where this relationship was going. I should have never agreed to have drinks with Raquel when I knew I was feeling something stronger for you."

Regan opened her mouth, then clapped her lips closed. She wondered how she would have reacted if Gavin had told her months ago that he wanted a more committed relationship with her. Still, she inhaled and exhaled and spoke very slowly, "You were not my man. There were no strings attached. We agreed, remember?"

Gavin touched a hand to her cheek. "That, Regan, was the biggest mistake I've ever made in my life."

"It's done," she said, turning her head so that his hand slipped away. "I just thought you should know the reason I decided to walk away from our arrangement."

"I appreciate you finally telling me," he replied, refusing to move away from her even though he knew that's precisely what she wanted.

This was his office, or would be when and if they signed the partnership contracts. There wasn't much in here now and he wasn't sure how much personalization he'd actually end up doing since moving to this island hadn't exactly been his life's plan. But if he opened a Spaga at Camelot, he'd definitely have to dedicate some of his time to being on Sansonique. And away from Miami, where Regan and his family lived.

"You're right. I should have told you sooner. Then maybe you wouldn't have come here."

She'd looked at him and then quickly looked away as she said those words. Gavin felt a pang in his chest. It wasn't what she was saying that bothered him. The bigger issue was how Regan had been acting. It wasn't like her and he'd been very concerned. Whatever was really bothering her, he wanted to make better, and he most especially wanted that tired and defeated look she had in her eyes to disappear.

"I've wanted you for a very long time, Regan. For not so long a time I've known that I wanted more than our no strings attached agreement. I told you this the other night. So even if you'd said all this to me that night at the hotel, I would still be right where I am now. Because this is exactly where I want to be."

She began shaking her head and he cupped her face in his hands. "I'm not going to leave because you think it'll be easier that way. Nothing happened with Raquel and I that night. Yes, we kissed. Raquel wanted something I couldn't give her. That I did *not* give her. We never even made it onto the elevator."

"But you were supposed to go upstairs with her, instead of me?" she asked. "That was your plan all along."

He could lie. Another man might have done that precisely that in this circumstance. But Gavin wasn't another man and more importantly, Regan wasn't any other woman. She was *the* woman he knew he wanted to spend his life with.

"Raquel asked me to join her for drinks after work. I agreed. Although now I think I may have sent the agreement text to you instead of to her. I vaguely remember Raquel saying she almost didn't show up because she wasn't sure I was coming. I'd dismissed it as her playing coy at the time. At any rate, my plan, once I sat at that bar with her was to tell her that I was seeing someone."

"Then you changed your mind and figured you'd sleep with her first, then tell her? You know what, just forget it, Gavin. This is never going to work between us," she said, pulling away from him.

Her hand was on the door knob when Gavin reached around her, flattening his palm on the door so she couldn't pull it open.

"Just let me go," she said in a voice so small and so tired he almost exploded with fury and despair.

"No," he whispered instead, taking another step so that his front was flush against her back.

She moved and he moved with her until they were both pressed against the door.

"I made a mistake with Raquel. I told her what I had to say, she said some things and.." His words trailed off and he sighed. "Dammit, Regan, I'm not proud of what I did or what I almost did. I don't want Raquel and I never have. I only want you, Regan," Gavin sighed, his lips close to her ear. "Only you."

"I can't do this, Gavin. It's too hard and I just don't have the time or the energy," she said, continuing to shake her head.

"Then don't do anything, Regan." He touched his hands to her shoulders, turning her gently so that she now faced him. "Let me be there for you. Let me romance you. Let me show you how good we can be together."

When she opened her mouth to reply, Gavin didn't hesitate. He leaned forward, letting his lips take hers in a soft but urgent kiss. And as it always did whenever he kissed her his pulse soared, his body tightening. As for Regan, her response was quick and just as fiery as his as she wrapped her arms around his neck, tilting her head to accommodate the kiss. She pressed her body into his so hard, Gavin forgot where he was and had immediately began pulling her shirt from the hem of her shorts.

She stiffened, then pulled away. Her arms remained around his neck as she looked up at him through lust-hazed eyes.

"If we were dating I wouldn't let you have me in a make-shift office with my back against the door," she said in a breathy whisper.

"Regan, come on, we've been here before. Well, not exactly here, but certainly with your back against the door."

She smiled, and it was like a sucker punch to the gut. Gavin almost lost his breath.

"That was when there were no strings attached," she told him. "You offered to show me romance. I'm going to take you up on that offer."

In a quick move that he still wasn't sure how she'd pulled off, she'd moved away from the door, out of his reach, and was now pushing her shirt back into her pants.

"Have dinner with me tonight?" he asked impulsively, wanting to spend every moment he could romancing her now that it seemed she was on board with the plan.

She shook her head. "Nope, not tonight."

"Regan..." he started to say, but she held up a hand.

"You have to work tonight, remember? But I'll give you a heads up that I love walking on the beach just before bed. I think it would be more than romantic to have a certain guy walking with me."

Gavin stepped to her then, threaded a hand through her hair until he was cupping the back of her head. "I think a certain guy would love to walk along the beach with you."

He kissed her again, just as that smile began to spread over her lips and his chest tightened, filled with everything that was Regan Donovan.

CHAPTER 12

Like a mermaid—that's what her mother had always called her—Vivianna Chavis emerged from the warm water, using her hands to brush her hair back, water cascading down her body. She walked to the shore towards the spot where she'd left her towel and bag.

Sure she was in Sansonique for a job, but this was a gorgeous Caribbean island. And it was privately owned by her client's family. Of course she was going to take advantage of those facts. Besides, she'd already decorated the dining room for the special meal that would serve as the rehearsal dinner since both the bachelor and bridal parties were scheduled for Friday evening.

It had been more than a little stressful ordering flowers for the entire wedding—ceremony, bridal party, groomsmen and reception included, then having them all packed and shipped to an island that was beautiful but too humid for any plant or flower that wasn't tropical. Her mother had wanted to come, but Vivi put her foot down. It was time for the mermaid to swim away from the nest. She was from St. Michaels; to say her parents were overprotective was an understatement. But with Noelle on her side, they'd been able to convince her parents that everything would be fine, so Mr. and Mrs. Chavis could stay home and run the seafood market that was their livelihood. Vivi would forever be grateful to Noelle for giving her this chance.

While the entire town thought she was a bubblehead, too pretty for her own good and too naïve to know enough to get her anywhere, Noelle had always encouraged her, stopping by the little kiosk she had set up by the docks to purchase fresh flowers for her office or home just about every day. Handling the complete floral design for Noelle's big day was the biggest highlight of Vivi's life.

Well, that and swimming in water so crystal clear in some places she could see right down to the coral decorated sea base. She fell to her knees on the towel, still trying to catch her breath from the swim. The sun had just set, casting the beach in a romantic indigo tint that made her think of Robbie, her stubborn as ten mules boyfriend back in St. Michaels. She'd begged him to come on this trip with her, but he'd said no.

"If we're going to someday soon have our own big lavish wedding, I need to keep busting my butt to make us some money," he'd told her in that no-nonsense way of his. "Now you go and make me proud."

He hadn't even kissed her goodbye, which made his words seem more like a pat on the head instead of any type of encouragement. Vivi loved Robbie. She had since they were in the sixth grade and he put his hand up her skirt. Of course that little stunt had earned him a bloody nose, but he'd looked so cute that night his mother made him knock on Vivi's door to apologize that she'd offered him her fruit-punch juice box the next day at lunch. They'd been together every day since then.

Every day except today, which had been a lovely sun-filled day that she'd spent mostly indoors working on the centerpieces for the dining room tables. She'd taken some time to do a little sight seeing, bummed that her assistants hadn't wanted to join her, citing it was too hot as their excuse. Now, as the sun had already begun to set, she'd been taking a swim before heading back to her room for a warm shower and then bed.

Vivi had decided not to think about Robbie or floral arrangements or anything else for the next few minutes or so, she lay on her stomach and closed her eyes. She could hear the steady rise and fall of the waves and feel the warm breeze over her still damp skin. This was the perfect business and personal trip all rolled into one.

She never would have guessed it would be her first and her last.

This wasn't how Vega usually worked. In fact, it was far from how he normally chose to handle business. But this wasn't business. It was personal. Very personal, Vega thought with a deep inhale.

The scent of blood was nothing new to Vega and didn't make him nauseous or aroused or any of those other indicators that he might be a sexually sadistic killer. Because that's not what he was. And he wasn't a sociopath either. That's what those idiot social workers who'd come to talk to him in the jail had tried to prove. He hadn't strangled and mutilated cats when he was younger and didn't dream of different ways to end human life on a daily basis.

No, Ramone Vega was a businessman. He had a skill that he'd improved upon over the years and provided a service, just like any other career-minded individual walking this earth. Okay, so his service was considered illegal and highly immoral by most. Who gave a rat's ass? It was his job and it paid well. It paid extremely well.

And someone had tried to take all of that from him. Someone named Benjamin Donovan. Sure, it was the prosecutor, the pretty little piece Donovan was sleeping with that finally put a nail in Vega's career coffin, but Donovan had set the ball in motion.

Declining to represent him in the second case was a problem he'd foreseen, and that's why he'd tried to convince Donovan to reconsider. But the guy had been stubborn. And then he'd been stupid by not only telling the prosecutor what he knew, but in helping her to find the one person who could corroborate their story. Alayna Jonas was trash. She'd proven that by sleeping with the mayor and the congressman. But Vega didn't give a damn about her. He could care less who the father of her baby was. All he wanted was to do his job. And they'd all messed that up.

Well, now he planned to do a bit of messing up of his own.

He'd found her in the exact spot he'd been directed to, on a tiny stretch of beach just outside of the building he'd watched the Donovan family go into a little earlier. They were about ten miles from the back deck of the building, hidden partially by a copse of trees, so even if someone came out they wouldn't notice them, especially not as night thickened the sky.

She didn't squirm anymore, the cute little female he'd been led to. He'd asked for a pawn, someone he could use to get his first message to Donovan and make it loud and clear. Tears that had a few moments ago run fresh and wet down her cheeks had already begun to dry in the humid island air. Her mouth still hung slack, waiting for another groan or attempted wail for help. He pulled her arms up over her head, tying them with rope, then lacing the rope through the big hole he'd ripped in the center of the piece of paper he'd carried with him from the bus. With a nail he'd found in the old shack he was staying in on the island, he pressed the note into the ground and tied the rope around it. Then he looked down at her once more. He hadn't shot her, hadn't wanted the noise to alert anyone to what he was doing. This time he'd had to use his hands, wrapping them slowly, tightly around her neck. She'd fought him, kicked and tried to scream, swung her arms, catching him across the cheek with a swipe of her nails. For that he'd jerked her around a bit, until her head hit a rock he hadn't even known was there and split wide open.

He had blood on his fingers. Looking down at it, he wiped his hands along the towel that was twisted but still under her body for the most part. It was a nice looking body, one he might have enjoyed for a night or more if sex had been a priority in his mind. It wasn't, which had been a surprise to the dumbass female that'd been sent to help him with this little errand. She was attractive enough, but she talked too much and knew next to nothing. She was bossy and arrogant and thought she had just as much right to be here as he did. For the most part, Vega let her have her space, secure in the knowledge that before he left this island she'd be lying in the sand in a similar position as this pretty young chick.

Finally he stood looking down on her and thinking how perfect she looked. Perfectly dead and ready to deliver the perfect promise he was making to Ben Donovan and the rest of his family. Vega looked at the paper once more, at the red ink he'd used to write on it, and felt a smile spreading.

"I tried to warn you, Donovan," he said. "Now, it's too late."

The dining room, or what would be called Spaga if the partnership went through, was certainly large enough, with one wall that housed high-boy tables, another with cozy booths and the center tables with chairs. There was a bar, but Gavin knew he'd want that expanded. It was an island resort, and people would come here to relax and unwind, have a good time. Tropical drinks would enhance their experience, some specialties that could be constructed to match a few of his menu items. Thoughts ran quickly through his mind as he stood in the doorway, hands in the pockets of his dress slacks, waiting for the Donovans to arrive.

Dinner was at seven, a little later than the family had been having dinner since they'd been here, but he'd wanted them to get the full feel of the room and thought the evening dusk would be the best time. It wasn't quite dark outside, the sun having begun its descent almost thirty minutes ago, coloring the sky with an array of intense orange and purple hues that would eventually go into a deep indigo. Right now the tabletops were black with bamboo inspired candleholders in the center. It gave the room a warm glow as the windows along the back wall were opened so guests still had a view of the sea. His vision was for a more streamlined look, maybe a honey toned wood tabletop with black chairs. The same colored wood would flank the bar and cabinets over the bar with a patterned wallpaper on the side wall where the booths were.

"You look right at home," a male voice said from behind.

Gavin turned slightly to see Trent moving to join him. This was the bad boy Donovan, the one nobody wanted to mess with for fear the trained killer would shuck his millionaire status and actually slit their throats. For Gavin, as this trip was the first time he'd met the legendary man, he'd gotten a different feel from him.

Trent was a family man. It was perfectly clear in the way he looked adoringly at his wife and son, at his parents, his brothers and cousins. He was enjoying this trip, surrounded by even more family, laughing and reminiscing with his brothers. And in an instant that had changed. The night Gavin had been struck, Trent immediately went into soldier mode. Gavin had noted the intense look on the man's face, the furrow of his brow, the kill instinct immediately coming into play.

"I'm starting to get a feel for the place," he responded finally, giving Trent a nod.

Trent was dressed for dinner in dark slacks and a gray polo tucked in neatly. On the outside, he looked like a vacationer, but Gavin was willing to bet this entire deal the man was armed and ready should whoever hit Gavin show their face tonight.

"Do you think you could live here full time?" Trent asked him.

Gavin was shaking his head before he really knew what the answer would be. "Not full time. But I could definitely spend some time here. The first month or so of the restaurant's debut definitely. I take great care in hiring my staff, especially the managerial ones. I wouldn't leave until I knew Spaga was in the right hands."

Trent nodded. "You sound like Linc and his casinos."

Lincoln Donovan owned two casinos, Gramercy I and II. The first one was located in Las Vegas, where Linc, his parents, brothers and their families lived. The Gramercy II was located in St. Michaels and was run by Noelle, who was slated to marry Brock, the cousin, in two more days. The Donovan family tree had been imprinted in Gavin's mind since he'd poured over the folder with all their information in it on the flight down here.

"You own your business, too. I'm sure you felt like this when you opened your first firm," he told Trent.

Trent moved further into the room, walking down the center looking around as he moved. "We don't get nightly guests at D&D. Our clients mostly want to stay under the radar," he said before stopping at the bar, rubbing his hand along the gleaming black marble surface. "Appearances are not our focus."

Gavin had followed him and now stood at the bar across from Trent, watching as the man took a seat. When Trent nodded, Gavin took the seat next to him, knowing their cordial conversation was over.

"All the family will be in this room tonight," he began. "I'll have someone posted at the front entrance and I want someone downstairs at the kitchen entrance and near the elevators just in case. Just wanted to run all that by you in case you see some strange faces down there."

Gavin nodded. "I see. Thanks for giving me the head's up." Gavin knew he didn't have to. Trent was part owner of this resort; he could do what he damn well pleased without getting Gavin's approval. The fact that they were having this conversation meant Trent respected him and his position. Gavin felt good about that fact.

"We'll need to use both those elevators. I'll make sure nobody takes the stairs. All the staff are dressed in black pants and white shirts with Spaga in green on the left hand side."

Trent smiled and pointed to Gavin. "Like yours."

"Yeah," Gavin added with a chuckle. "Like mine. We'll begin serving at 7:15, give everybody a chance to arrive, say grace, etc."

"Good. How many courses?" Trent asked. "I skipped lunch. If I have to wait another hour to get to the real food, I'm going to be grouchy."

"You mean more so than you already are?"

Gavin's attention suddenly shifted. She'd entered the room quietly, but Gavin had known the second she'd crossed the threshold. His gut had clenched in anticipation, his mouth watering at the mere thought of how good he knew she would look. And when he slipped off the bar stool to greet her, the tightening in his chest only barely threatened to send him into cardiac arrest.

"I'm not grouchy," Trent was saying from behind him. "I'm intense, or so my wife likes to say."

To his chagrin, Regan moved past Gavin to lean in for Trent's kiss to her cheek. Then she turned back to him and before she could say a word, he'd moved in to kiss her as well, but on the lips instead of the cheek. She didn't shy away, but looked up at him with a small smile upon his retreat. Her eyes seemed to sparkle tonight, unlike earlier when they'd been clouded with exhaustion or fear or whatever he knew he'd seen in them. She wore a peach dress, one sparkly strap crossing her right shoulder, leaving the left one bare. The dress hugged every delectable inch of a body he knew all too well, stopping at her ankles so that her polished toenails were viewable through the open toe of her nude toned sandals. Her hair had been pulled into some kind of bundle that rested on the right side, diamonds sparkling at her ears and around her neck.

"It looks good in here," she said when the silence had stretched on too long.

Gavin swallowed, trying to let the complete sight of her coupled with her alluring scent settle in without embarrassing himself.

"Yeah, I think Gavin has some other plans brewing though," Trent chimed in.

"Really? So you're really interested in this deal?"

The way she looked when she asked told him she didn't know how she felt about that possibility. A year ago, Gavin wouldn't have cared what she thought. Hell, he probably wouldn't have noticed that she was having any reaction to this deal at all. Six months ago he would have wondered what her feelings might be about him going into business with her family. Tonight, right at this second, a shred of worry crept along the base of his spine. This deal was important to him. But Regan was more important. He wanted to know how she felt and realized that, in the end, her feelings just might be a deal breaker.

"Ideas are formulating, but nothing's etched in stone," was his tepid reply.

"So what's on the menu?" she asked, with the intent to shift the mildly uncomfortable subject, he suspected.

"You'll see," he said and reached for her elbow. "Let me show you to your seat."

"Wow, I get preferential service," Regan told Trent over her shoulder.

"I wonder why," Gavin heard Trent say good naturedly.

❧❧❧

They were just about to eat dessert, the room abuzz with conversations from the adults and toddlers. As Regan looked around, her heart swelled at the sight of so many of her family members in one room.

"You look well rested tonight. Did you sleep all afternoon?" her mother asked when she'd come over to the table where Regan, Dion, Lyra, Sean and Tate had been seated. Briana was in a booster seat at the end of the table near Sean and Tate. The little girl was adorable and was rarely far from her doting father's line of sight.

"I did get a nap," Regan replied, determined not to say too much or too little.

Carolyn Benson Donovan had a sharp mind, an eagle eye and a flair for fashion just like her daughter. She was the mother most girls dreamed of having—kind, understanding, always ready and eager to go shopping. Regan had loved all those things about her. And she was as intuitive as a psychic. Regan didn't like that so much.

"Come, let's look out at the sea. I know how much you like the water," Carolyn insisted.

After excusing herself from the table, Regan followed her mother to the far end of the room where windows and a pair of patio doors opened to the outside. They stepped onto the dark wood deck, feeling the warm breeze of the evening, smelling the rich tropical air. In the distance, there were night sounds, the many species of animals that inhabited the island going about their nightly routine.

"It's lovely here. I'm so glad we started coming here for the reunions," Carolyn began.

Yes, it was a beginning, because Regan was sure her mother did not bring her out here to discuss the family or Sansonique for that matter. But, again, she wasn't about to give more information than necessary.

"It's so pretty here. I think it might be a great location for a photo shoot for Camille's summer fashion show. Now that Camelot is up and running, we could tape the show and air it on the network as a pay-per-view special," Regan suggested.

"I hate to disturb this solitude with work, Regan. I much rather the idea of us coming here to wind down and now opening Camelot to others who need to do the same," Carolyn said, turning so that she now faced Regan.

And now the rest would come like a slow-brewing storm, starting with the slow drizzle, followed by thunder if the drizzle went ignored, and ending with fierce lightning when need be.

"It was just a thought," Regan replied lightly and looked off to the water, feeling her mother's gaze so intent on her it was almost a muted type of heat.

"I'd hoped I wouldn't have to ask, but I see now I have no choice."

"Ask what?" It was just easier to let her mother lead the way.

Carolyn tucked the one wayward strand of hair that had dared blow free of her neat chignon back behind her ear. She folded her hands in front of her and looked at Regan patiently.

"You're not well, Regan. I can see it in your eyes, in the way you walk. I hear it in your voice each time you tell me you're fine. Now, I could tell your father who would no doubt threaten people, namely your doctors, until he had the information he wanted. Or I can stand here with you, woman to woman, and ask you what's going on." Then Carolyn tilted her head. That was the sign that she would get off if she had to and that you'd better beware if she did.

Regan took a deep breath. She didn't break eye contact with her mother. That would be cowardly and she'd never been that in her life.

"It's high blood pressure," she said slowly.

Carolyn nodded. "It runs in the family."

"I know," Regan replied. "But it's early and I'm not on any medication. I'm going to get it under control and everything will be alright."

Again Carolyn nodded. "You're going to get it under control. It's going to be alright because you said so," she said in a flat tone.

"Mama..." Regan heard herself say. It bothered her that she sounded like the fifteen year old pleading her case to go to the cotillion without either of her brothers as a chaperone.

Carolyn lifted a hand to stop her daughter's protests.

"You are twenty-seven years old. You're a successful editor and now television producer. You're beautiful and well-bred and all things a million little girls in this world dream to one day be. But I swear Regan Lorae Donovan, you are not the smartest apple in the bushel."

Regan sighed. The thunder was rumbling.

"You are only one person and life is not a race. I've watched you soaring forward for so long I get dizzy if I don't take a break. Now, after learning this, that's exactly what I expect you to do."

"I'm on vacation now," Regan interjected.

"And you're walking around here with your forehead scrunched and your lips spread in a tight line like you're about to explode at any moment. I saw you come down to the kitchen late the other night to get something to drink. You looked like you were about to buckle in pain. I knew then it was bad."

"I just had a headache."

"A headache brought on by stress and over exhaustion. Now I want it to stop. I want you to use some of the brain I know you have and get yourself together. This is not about *Infinity* or competing with your brothers. It's not about DNT or making your father proud. It's not about anything but living life the way the good Lord intended you to, healthy and peacefully," Carolyn continued.

"Mama..." Regan tried again.

"I'm not going to tell you this again, Regan."

"I hear you."

"Then listen to me."

"I am."

But the next thing Regan heard was not her mother's voice. There was a scream that echoed through the night like it had come right through a bullhorn.

Both Regan and Carolyn jumped.

Instantly—way too fast for him to have been anywhere but right on the deck with them, an issue Regan would question later—Gavin was by her side.

"Are you two okay?" he asked.

"We're fine," they replied in unison.

"Everybody inside!" Trent yelled out onto the deck.

As they moved inside, there were shocked looks all around. Devlin had appeared again, moving to stand beside Trent.

Gavin stood close to Regan, but he kept watching Trent and Devlin. Ben, who had been sitting at the table with his parents and Victoria, had escorted Victoria to the table with Max, Noelle, Brock and Deena, and then went to stand with Trent and Devlin.

"I'll be right back," Gavin said to her finally. "Don't leave this room."

"What?" she asked, grabbing his arm as he started to walk away. "What's going on?"

"I don't know," he replied, but Regan wasn't sure she believed him.

"Just stay here," he reiterated, his voice a little more stern than it had been before.

"What's going on?" Bailey asked, coming up to stand next to Regan.

"I don't know," she replied.

"I'll bet she does," Bailey said, looking towards Victoria who had gotten up from her seat and walked right up to the conversation between Trent, Devlin, Ben and now Gavin.

Regan watched them closely. Devlin had frowned at Victoria's intrusion, but Devlin frowned at just about everything. Ben had looked flustered but didn't argue as she stood right beside him, crossing her arms over her chest.

"He looks like he's ready to kill," Bailey murmured.

Regan knew instantly who she was referring to. "Each time I've seen him, he's looked like that. Maybe he was born that way."

"Uh huh. I don't think so," Bailey continued. "But you've gotta admit it is kind of sexy."

Regan turned so fast her neck almost cracked. "Really?"

Bailey waived a hand at her cousin's shocked expression. "Don't even go there. He's a good-looking guy in a rough, tough, slightly scary kind of way. But now's definitely not the time to start drooling over a man."

Regan was about to say something to that, but Bailey had already grabbed her by the arm saying, "We're about to find out what the hell is going on around here."

They moved across the room, finally stopping right beside Victoria who had just been left alone by the men, one of whom Bailey thought was sexy and Regan thought was scary as hell.

"What's going on? Where did they go and who was doing all that screaming?" Bailey asked in quick succession.

Victoria's light eyes widened in surprise, and then she smoothed her hands down the front of the slate gray silk jumpsuit she'd been wearing. Regan had liked Victoria when she met her; the woman was professional and pretty and looked at Ben like her Prince Charming had just ridden right into her life. That was the standing criteria for the women that Regan watched enter her cousins and brothers lives. Parker's unfortunate first marriage had ended badly, and that, as she'd told her older brother on numerous occasions, was because he hadn't brought the woman to meet her first.

"I...I don't know," was Victoria's reply.

Bailey laughed. "You might be a great prosecutor but you suck at lying under pressure," she told her. "Now I know something is going on and I'm guessing it has to do with who whacked Gavin over the head the other night. Now where did those guys just hustle out of here to?"

"What? You don't think Gavin just had an accident?" Regan had suspicions about the story Trent and Gavin had fed her about his injury, but upon further thought there really wasn't any reason to doubt it. Until now.

"No," Bailey replied quickly. "And she doesn't either." She looked at Victoria once more.

"Ben's going to kill me," Victoria whispered.

Bailey switched sides, leaving Regan to lace her arm through Victoria's. "Honey, you aren't a part of the Donovan family until you piss off one of its men."

With a heavy sigh, Victoria said, "Come with me."

Foolishly, she knew, Regan thought about Gavin's insistence that she stay there. Then she looked around at all the worried faces of her family members and figured she needed to know if something was going on, especially if that something somehow effected them.

They were in the hallway just outside the dining room when Victoria turned to them.

"They think someone's on the island. An uninvited someone," she continued.

"I knew it!" Bailey said with a bit too much excitement in her voice for Regan's taste.

"Who is it?" Regan heard herself asking, her tone matching the conspiratorial whisper that Bailey and Victoria had.

"They don't want to cause mass hysteria. Brock's threatening to hurt anyone who spoils this wedding for Noelle," Victoria warned.

"Brock's been blustering for years. It's about time that time bomb exploded," Bailey added. "But really, none of us want Noelle's wedding ruined. It would make sense if we knew what was going on. It'll be easier to keep her protected from the truth if we know what we're dealing with. Noelle's never going to sit back and trust what those men tell her blindly."

"I'm afraid I have to agree with her," Regan said. "Noelle will suspect they're lying to her, especially after everyone heard that scream. If we know, maybe we can help deflect her thoughts a little better."

Victoria clearly looked undecided, but then she threw her hands up in the air and sighed. "Okay, I guess we have to stick together."

"I'm liking her more and more," Bailey added.

Regan was in no way expecting what Victoria had to tell them. A convicted killer was on the island hunting Ben and Victoria and probably Gavin now since they'd tried to kill him but failed. She was still trying to register her feelings about that when Ben came running down the hall.

"Where's Brock?" he asked.

"Inside," Bailey replied calmly.

Seconds later Brock came out with a fierce look on his face. That prompted more people to come from the dining room—namely, Noelle followed by Jade and Tia.

"Okay, what the hell is going on?" Noelle asked, her three-toned hair stacked high on her head in an array of curls. Tonight she'd looked lovely in a peach above the knee halter dress, a diamond choker at her neck and an even bigger diamond on her left finger. Now, however, her light brown eyes were laced with worry, her usually full lips thinned into a line that said she was definitely not happy.

At her side was of course her older sister, hand locked in Noelle's. Jade tried to look less worried, but it hadn't worked. Tia looked directly at Bailey.

"What do you know?" she asked.

Regan looked at Bailey, whom she knew was weighing whether or not to pull Noelle into this. Normally there wasn't any reason Bailey would bite her tongue for anyone. This time, though, there was so much at stake and Regan understood the hesitation. Noelle had been through so much after losing her grandmother and all the inheritance left for her and Jade and then the messy scandal with her ex, Luther. This wedding and Brock being in her life were the best things to ever happen to her, so she'd told them all a time or two.

"There's a situation..." Bailey began but was stopped as Gavin, Brock and Trent came back through the front doors.

The men stopped mid-stride to glare at the women who had assembled. The women, all but Noelle, did the same. Noelle moved through the circle the ladies had inadvertently formed around her and went straight to Brock. With her hands going to his biceps, she asked calmly, "What's going on? And don't even think about telling me nothing. All of you have been whispering and having secret meetings and now everybody's gathered out here. Somebody's screaming their lungs out on the island. I want to know what's going on and I want to know now."

Regan met Gavin's gaze, noted how worried he looked and gave her own imploring look, to which he simply shrugged.

Brock seemed to hesitate a second and then sighed, lifting his hands to rub up and down Noelle's arms. "It's Vivi," he began, then cleared his throat. "She's dead."

The gasps in the hallway could not have been better synchronized as every woman present was shocked by his words.

"What? How?" Noelle began, her voice cracking slightly.

Again, Jade hurried to her sister's side. "Where's Linc?" she asked, looking over to Trent.

"He's probably inside using his cell to call for the Coast Guard and the Royal Police," Trent said. He moved to the doors of the dining room, making sure they were securely closed. "Look, we're going to tell everyone, all the adults anyway, but we don't want mass hysteria starting. Now, the remainder of the vendors are being assembled in the ballroom. Adam and Brandon are taking care of that. We'll brief them separately. I'd like to get all the kids into one area and then talk to the family."

"I don't want my daughters somewhere alone if people are being killed on this island," Jade immediately protested. She'd turned to Trent and was heading to the dining room doors as she spoke.

He touched her shoulders. "I'm not going to let anything happen to my nieces. You know that, Jade. I plan to have an armed guard with all the kids at all times now. But you know if you're upset, they're upset. Is that what you want?"

Jade inhaled deeply. "No. But I want to go to them now. I can't believe this is happening."

Trent nodded, pulling his sister-in-law into his chest for a quick, tight hug. "I know. But we're going to get to the bottom of it. Why don't you go on inside. Get Camille and Lyra and Tate and round up all the children. I'll be there in a second."

Jade nodded to Trent and looked back at Noelle, who stood by Brock crying quietly.

"I'm staying with Brock," she informed her.

Jade nodded and then stepped back into the dining room.

"Okay. Vivianna Chavis was strangled, her body left just to the south of the building, along the path we would have taken to walk back to the main house. Her assistant found her. That's who screamed." Trent took a deep breath, exhaled slowly, a muscle in his jaw twitching.

"I cannot believe this." Noelle sighed, shaking her head. "Vivi was only twenty-five. This was her first wedding, *my* wedding. And I brought her here. It's my fault. I should have listened to her parents when they said she wasn't ready. I shouldn't have forced the issue. And now I have to explain to them what's happened." Her shoulders shook as tears poured down her face.

Brock pulled her to him, holding her close. "Don't do this to yourself, baby. You couldn't have known this would happen. None of us could and you couldn't have stopped it." he said, solemnly looking over Noelle's head to Trent.

So much had gone through Regan's head in the last few minutes. A woman was dead, on this island, just a day after Gavin was hit and knocked unconscious, on this island. Nothing and no one could have stopped her from crossing the hallway until she stood right beside Gavin. Grabbing him by his shirt sleeve, she leaned over to whisper into his ear.

"You owe me an explanation," she said. "A real one."

Gavin nodded. "Later. Right now we need to make sure your family knows what we're dealing with."

"It's bad isn't it?" she asked. "What we're dealing with is really bad. That's why Devlin and his men are here."

Gavin's lips thinned. His jaw clenched as he weighed how to answer that question.

"Don't lie to me again, Gavin," she said seriously. "I let the Raquel situation go and I'm just realizing you lied about getting hit. Third strike and you're out."

He looked down at her with a slow shake of his head. "No, Regan. I won't lie to you again. It's really bad."

⁂

Hours later, the senior brothers stood in the living room of the main house, their looks dour and filled with concern as they watched their children. The senior Donovan men were all tall and broad-shouldered with signature stern looks. As they'd aged, their body sizes had changed, but not to the point that any of them looked less distinguished or formidable.

"This nutcase is after you, Ben?" Everette asked his youngest son.

Ben stood, folding his arms over his chest, clearly prepared to take the heat. "Yes, sir. We thought he was on his way to prison. The message he left on the body was clear. He's here for me."

The message had been a copy of Vega's commitment papers, the order the judge had signed that would bind him to the penitentiary for the remainder of his natural life. He'd pulled Ms. Smith's hands up over her head, tying her wrists to show her submission to his power. According to the coroner that had come over with the Royal Police, she'd been positioned after death. There was a gash on her head, but they didn't think that was deep enough to cause her death. Vega had also strangled her, which was a different style of killing for the man. That told Ben he was in a different state of mind. The nothing-to-loose state, he presumed.

"And your girlfriend prosecuted him. So I guess he's after her too?" Uncle Bruce asked.

"Yes, sir. I believe he is," was Ben's response. He knew Victoria was also a target. Vega had made sure of that.

"Devlin and Trent and their men are searching the island now," Linc added. Linc would forever be the leader of their generation. He was the oldest of them all and had naturally assumed the role from the time they'd all begun walking. Nobody really protested because they didn't want the title themselves. Tonight, however, Ben wasn't about to let his cousin stand up for him.

"I've given the Royal Police and the Coast Guard all the information I had on Vega. A few police officers will remain on the island until we're gone," Ben spoke up.

"But how do we guarantee everyone's safety until the wedding is over?" Uncle Albert asked. "Brock is determined this won't effect Noelle's day."

"It won't," Brock spoke up. "Look, right now Noelle is upstairs so upset over this that she couldn't sleep and Aunt Beverly finally gave her a sleeping pill. I know it seems like we should all pack up and go home but I'm not really in the mood to let some coward ruin the moment Noelle and I have worked so hard for. It took us more than a year to come to the conclusion that we were ready for marriage. That wasn't an easy decision for either of us and I'm not about to let some sick bastard take that away from us."

Brandon stood by his brother, a hand on his shoulder. When standing, Brock was two inches taller than Brandon's six feet, with Brock's bronze-toned complexion about two shades darker than Brandon's. Though separated in age by three years and by hundreds of miles as adults, they remained close. "We can't back down. We have to keep going with our plans or he wins. We'll be his hostages, sitting ducks on this island waiting for him to make his move."

Uncle Bernard rubbed a hand over his salt and pepper beard. "Aren't we that anyway?" he asked. He was the biggest brother, with a burly round build, beard and hairstyle that made him look slightly like black Santa Claus.

"We have to think about the safety of all of our families," Uncle Reginald added. "And the other people on this island. We're liable for everyone's safety."

Linc rubbed a hand over his goatee, standing with his feet spread slightly apart. "We're taking every precaution, Uncle Reginald. Trent's working on security. He's confident that with the extra officers on the island, they'll be able to find Vega fairly quickly. We've told the women about his presence so they'll know to travel together and to keep a close eye out for each other. The vendors know about the murder. For now, we've covered all our bases."

"I don't like this," Albert said, shaking his head. He was darker than all his children, his hair having gone completely gray some time ago. He kept it cut low and precise, along with his mustache. "I don't like that we're sitting ducks ready for the plucking."

"Nobody's going to do any plucking with my family," Trent said with a steely voice as he entered the room. "The main house is secure. If he tries to get in, he'll be dead before he recognizes who killed him. The officers are standing guard at Camelot. We found some things in the forest, bags and ropes we think he used. Dev's gonna keep trying to track him through the night. He has no idea who he's decided to mess with," Trent finished icily.

Henry went to his son, patting his shoulder. "You be careful out there. This isn't a war zone and you're not on the government's dime this time."

"I got this, Dad. This bastard has to know he's trying to intimidate the wrong one," Trent continued.

"He's definitely gonna find out," Ben added, his own level of intensity blending with Trent's to fill the room with tension so thick a machete couldn't cut through it.

CHAPTER 13

In Miami, Regan lived in a condo. It had a pool and a gym and all of the most modern amenities. What her building didn't have that the Sansonique main house did was a solarium. Even at night, there was a sort of comfort to the glass-encased room decorated with miniature palm trees, large clay pots of hibiscus, orchids and heliconia and a swimming pool. Along the entrance wall were thick cushioned lounge chairs with mahogany wicker bottoms. In the far left corner was a changing room where extra towels and robes were stored.

It had been an extremely long day and, truth be told, she was still more than a little shaky after learning of the young florist's death. Noelle was understandably upset, especially since she had a personal relationship with Vivi. She'd already made several calls to St. Michaels to speak with the girl's family. Brock wanted the killer caught and so did everyone else. They were both being extremely strong and understanding under the circumstances. Regan wasn't sure she would be the same where she in their position.

The family had returned to the house a little before midnight, sleeping babies in tow. Regan wasn't sure, but she thought Gavin had also returned with them. Since the men had immediately closed themselves in the den, she had no idea who was in there and really didn't want to know. They were most likely arguing over why Trent had kept this from everyone. Regan, on the other hand, was more concerned with why Gavin hadn't told her.

The pain radiating down the back of her neck to her shoulders said regardless of what time it was, she needed to do something relaxing, something that would ease the tension knotting up her body. Diving into the deep end of the pool, she let the water cover her completely and tried to clear her mind. Her stomach lurched at the memory of finding out a woman was dead and that Gavin hadn't really fallen the other night. He could have been that woman. She broke clear of the water, flipping her arms in long, fluid strokes that were failing dismally at calming her frayed nerves.

She touched the rim and tread water for a few minutes, keeping her eyes closed as she tried to catch her breath. Gavin was alive. Her family was alive. She should be thankful. Yes, a woman was dead, but she couldn't bring her back to life. A killer was apparently on the island, but she couldn't climb out of the pool, put a bullet in his head and be done with this whole mess. So she had no choice but to calm down. Bending forward she let her forehead rest on the lip of the pool, mumbling a prayer for peace.

"Are you okay?"

Regan jerked back at the sound of a female voice. With a hand to her throat, her eyes opened wide, she struggled to yet again catch her breath.

"Oh, I'm sorry if I frightened you," Victoria said. "Ace is right outside the door. He told me you were in here."

Regan shook her head, swallowing before getting her words together. "No. No. I'm alright," she told her. "I know about Ace, he was in the hall patrolling when I came out. Trent mentioned that none of us were supposed to go out alone so I knew he'd follow me down here."

Flattening her palms on the side of the pool, she pushed up until she could get out of the water and then padded over to the lounge where she'd thrown her towel.

"What brings you down this time of night?" Regan asked when she'd wrapped a towel around her and used another one to dab at the dripping braids.

"Ben's not back yet," Victoria said with a shrug as she slid onto the lounge chair beside Regan's. "I didn't see anybody in the hallway and I wasn't planning on leaving the house, just maybe getting a snack. I felt silly waking someone just to come downstairs with me."

Regan sat on the side closest to Victoria and nodded. "I know what you mean. I wasn't too keen on Ace following me around the house, but I guess it's safer for all of us this way. Besides that, I was trying not to think of whether Gavin went back to Camelot or not."

"You two been seeing each other long?" Victoria asked.

"We're not seeing each other," was Regan's instant reply. Then she sighed. She'd said she was going to stop fighting the inevitable. "I mean, we are, sort of, as of earlier today anyway."

Victoria tilted her head, her chin-length hair moving slightly with the motion. "I thought it was longer. You two seem much closer than Ben and I."

Regan looked at this women she'd just met a couple of days ago. There was a distinct air of sophistication to Victoria Lashley. It emanated from the way she sat with her shoulders set to the way her knees met comfortably with her elbows leaning on them. For the most part she talked like a lawyer, just like Ben, but right now she was looking uncertain, like only a woman newly involved with a Donovan man could.

"Gavin and I have been sort of seeing each other for about five years now. We didn't tell our families," Regan admitted. It felt good to finally get that off her chest. She hadn't realized how stressful it had been holding that secret to herself all this time.

"Wow. Okay, I didn't think the Donovans had any secrets. When Ben said they weren't telling everyone about Vega being here, I was a little nervous about how that would turn out."

"Oh believe me, that's probably not turning out too well. That's why he's still not back yet. I'm sure my dad and his brothers are not happy about the secrecy," Regan told her.

"I can't say that I blame them," Victoria continued. "I function much better when I have all the facts in front of me."

Yeah, lawyer talk, Regan thought and smiled.

"Was that funny?" Victoria asked her.

Regan shook her head, feeling the quick chill of wet hair falling onto her bare skin as she pulled the towel away. "No. You sound just like Ben though, all lawyerly."

"Oh," Victoria said with a little chuckle, and then sobered suddenly. "What's it like?"

"What's what like?"

"To have this big family that you have to answer to all the time. I mean, I told him I didn't think the secret was a good idea. But it seems like your family is even closer than just this incident. You talk about just about everything, get everyone's opinion."

Regan nodded. "Yes, it can be a bit overwhelming with all the well-meaning opinions coming at you. That's probably why I didn't say anything about my thing with Gavin."

"Are you going to say something now?" Victoria asked. It appeared the woman was full of questions tonight versus the very reluctant attitude she'd taken the first half of this trip.

"I don't think we have a choice. If you just met us a couple of days ago and thought we were close, then I'm sure the others have a pretty good idea of our involvement. It's just that we hadn't really defined what we were doing, so I didn't know what to say before."

"Ben and I haven't defined what we're doing either. Or no, I'm wrong. Ben has defined it perfectly for himself. The jury's still out with me."

"Really? Why? Ben's a great guy. Sure he's arrogant and a little annoying with that perpetual good mood most of the time. But when he loves someone, he's totally dedicated to them."

"Has he loved someone before?"

Regan shook her head. "Not that I know of. And as you already know, there isn't much that goes on in this family that we all don't know about."

"Right. Well, I guess I just never saw myself with a man like Ben. In a family like this." She clasped and unclasped her hands and then looked towards the pool.

Now Regan was confused. "Explain," she heard herself saying, gearing up for the possibility that she might not like what Victoria had to say.

"I don't come from a rich family. My mother worked as an educator all her life and my dad was killed. I spend half my salary helping my mother out and the other half on shoes." She gave a slow chuckle. "The Donovans own their own island." Her arms had lifted to motion the entire space around her.

Now Regan understand. She knew she liked Victoria and would have hated having to curse her back to the states if she'd said something out of the way about her Ben or her family. She sighed with relief and then smiled. Reaching across them, she touched Victoria's hands. "Beneath my skin is warm blood, just like yours. We're all just people, Victoria. And truthfully, most of the money we had was here before any of us were even born, so the money doesn't define us. But I understand how you could easily go with that train of thought. I just hope we've been proving how down to earth we are this week, except for the owning of the island part." She smiled, hoping this would put the woman at ease.

Victoria seemed to relax as she grinned at Regan. "Yeah, I'm having a hard time trying to feel uncomfortable with the snooty rich folk when you're all acting like we've known each other for years and went to the same public schools together."

"Ben and Max did go to public school. Uncle Everette insisted on it," Regan told her. "Don't mess up a good thing with doubts that aren't founded."

Victoria nodded. "Should I be offering you the same advice?" was the woman's next question.

Regan was a little startled by that one. She was just about to tell Victoria that her point was well taken when over her shoulder she saw him approach.

"Am I interrupting?" Gavin asked.

❧

He'd thought of her constantly in the last couple of hours. While talking to the senior Donovans and the men of his generation, Regan had never been far from his mind. If he closed his eyes, he'd see her as she'd looked at him, betrayal quick as a flash of lightening in her eyes. He'd lied to her. She wouldn't take that easily. Not even if he'd done so under the pretense of protecting her.

Victoria, bless her heart, had left them without more than a quick goodbye and a glance toward Regan that he was sure was a "female thing." He hadn't wasted a moment, knew another second would have been too long. Regan had stood with Victoria just before she left so that now she was a few steps from the lounge chair. He went to her, pulling her against him quickly for a hug. To his surprise Regan came willingly, wrapping her arms around his midsection, flattening her hands along his back and holding him just as tightly, if not more so. For endless moments, Gavin relished the feeling. He buried his head in the crock of her neck and simply inhaled the fresh chlorine tinged scent of her.

She broke the connection slowly, looking at him almost lovingly, before shoving him so hard he lost his balance and soon felt the shock of the cold water as he made a splash entrance into the pool.

Coming up for air, Gavin could see her standing at the side of the pool, hands on her hips, face in an angry scowl. He sputtered as he swam to the edge and hoisted himself out of the pool. She took a step back but continued to glower at him.

"You lied to me!" was her first accusation. "You said you fell and hit your head." Which, for a moment made her feel bad about pushing him in the pool. The fact that he'd only sustained a bump on the head coupled with the realization that he'd lied to her made her feel a tad justified.

Gavin shook his head, walking to the lounge, his feet squishing annoyingly in his shoes. "Trent said I fell and hit my head."

"You didn't deny it," was her scathing retort.

Gavin had picked up one of the towels he figured she'd probably used earlier and wiped his face. He took a deep breath before turning back to face her. "No. I didn't," he admitted, because there really was nothing else he could do.

"When they told me you were unconscious, I was worried. I wanted you to go back to the mainland to get checked out. I wanted you to be alright. And you lead me to believe it was nothing but an accident." She wrapped her arms around her body and looked away from him for a second.

"But it wasn't an accident. And the same person that hit you over the head is the one who killed that florist. He could have...," she paused and cleared her throat. "He could have killed you."

Her bottom lip trembled and Gavin was almost certain it wasn't from a chill. Though the cool wet clothes now sticking to him were growing a little uncomfortable, he moved toward her, knowing he was risking another toss into the pool but not caring. She deserved to be angry, but he wanted to make it better.

"I should have told you the truth. But we didn't want everyone to panic about the idea of an uninvited guest being on the island. I wanted to protect you," he told her finally.

Regan shook her head. "I don't want protection from a man, Gavin. I want honesty and respect. If you can lie to me about something as important as this, how can I trust that the next time someone like Raquel comes on to you, you won't take her up on her offer?"

"Whoa, where is that coming from?" He reached for her but she backed away. "Look, Regan, it's one thing to want to keep you safe and not telling you about a possible risk to your life or the lives of others around you. I admit, I was wrong for that. I should have trusted you to handle that situation."

She continued to move away from him as if she were either afraid of his touch or just didn't want it. Not touching her wasn't an option, so Gavin simply reached for her once more, grabbing her at the waist to keep her still.

"But when I'm with you, you can trust with everything I am that I will be true to you. I didn't want Raquel before and I definitely do not want her now. You're the only woman for me, Regan. I've been in love with you for so long, I was just too stubborn or preoccupied to realize it. Please don't pull away from me."

She didn't wrap her arms around him and pull him close. But she didn't turn away either.

"I was afraid for you," she said quietly.

He nodded. "I know and I'm sorry to have put you through that. We weren't totally sure who was on the island when I was hit. I found the overalls when we were together and took them to your cousins. Ben mentioned the ex-con, but he said he was on his way to prison. What were the odds that he'd have escaped and come here?"

"Pretty good odds, I'd say," Regan replied. She took a deep breath and let it out slowly. "This is supposed to be our family reunion. Noelle and Brock are getting married. We shouldn't be prisoners in our house wondering when this madman will make his next move."

"I don't want you to think of that right now," he told her. He pulled her close and she grimaced.

"You're wet."

He smiled. "That happens when you go for a surprise swim while fully dressed."

She grinned, her hands coming reluctantly to his chest. "You deserved that."

Gavin shrugged. "I'll take the fall, so to speak."

"Here, I guess we could share," she said, opening her towel, attempting to wrap it around him as well.

Gavin looked down and swallowed deeply. "What are you wearing?"

"A bathing suit."

So that's what they were calling a few strings and a patch of material here and there. The chill from the wet clothes vanished immediately. "You wear that out in public?" he asked, looking back up at her.

"Only when I'm swimming," was her uncertain reply. "I don't like to swim fully dressed."

His fingers splayed along her bare waist, tingles going instantly through his skin. She was warm and soft and his mouth watered. He'd wanted Regan since the first time he'd seen her, wanted her to be a part of his life. Over the years, as they'd both grown into adults, that want had shifted from just the companionship he desired to something more primitive. Once he'd had her in that way, Gavin thought he'd be content. He thought he'd be satisfied. He'd thought wrong.

He pulled her to him, shushing her when she yelped at his wet clothes pressing against the bare skin of her torso. The towel she'd been holding fell to the floor the moment his lips touched hers. She slipped her arms up, twining them around his neck, flattening her palms to the back of his head and pulling him closer. The kiss went deeper, his tongue delving inside the moment her lips parted. They suckled at each other hungrily, breathing frantically as there did not seem to be enough skin to touch or lips to devour.

"Not here," he murmured against her lips.

"What?" she whispered, pulling her mouth away from his only to latch on to his lower lip and suck.

Gavin groaned, every part of his body going hot and hard at the same time. His fingers gripped her and he cursed inwardly, praying he didn't bruise her with his excitement.

"I want you in the bed," he finally managed to say. "Now!"

"There's no bed here," she said, a tinge of humor in her tone.

With the last shreds of control, Gavin pulled his mouth away from hers, staring down into the puzzled and aroused look in her eyes. "We're going upstairs."

"You're awfully bossy now that I've agreed to this dating thing. I thought I was supposed to be pampered and romanced and all that good stuff."

"Believe me, baby. It's going to be good," he said, bending down to retrieve the towel. On his way up he dropped a kiss at her ankle and one to the back of her calf on the opposite side.

There was a light gasp and Gavin smiled. Towel in one hand, he used the free hand to touch the spot on her calf where he'd kissed. Then he kissed the back of her thigh, rubbed along that spot, kissed the inside of her thigh and let his finger trace the moist heat there. Her breathing was audibly faster now and his own arousal jutted forward, pressing against the zipper of his wet pants. He let his fingers keep moving upward, the soft skin of her inner thigh too alluring to ignore. A thatch of black material covered her mound and he licked his lips. Flattening his palm there, he let his fingers linger and move along what he knew would be tender and moist folds. He was standing then, and her head lulled against his chest.

"I thought you wanted to go upstairs," she said between ragged breaths.

"We are."

She shook her head. "Not if you keep that up. I won't be able to walk."

"Then I'll carry you," he told her seconds before standing and sweeping her off her feet.

Moonlight slipped through the partially opened drapes at the balcony window in Regan's room. She caught its luminescent glow as Gavin lowered her to the bed and eased her back until her head rested on the pillows. On instinct she reached for him, but he pulled away. Standing on the side of the bed, the window to his back, he began to undress. Piece by excruciating piece, Regan watched as the wet clothes were removed and seemingly endless inches of dark chocolate skin revealed.

He was perfection, in her humble and unwavering opinion. Tall and lean, strong shoulders, muscled arms, a chest with all the right ridges and tones, tapered waist, strong thighs and thick arousal. For the first time in Regan's life, she actually ached for this man. When he pressed a knee onto the bed and straddled her, she wanted to open her legs and welcome him inside, but Gavin clearly had another idea.

With movements so slow she wanted to scream for this scene to fast forward, he untied the bikini top she wore, tossing the slight material to the floor. Each hand fit perfectly over her breasts. He closed his eyes momentarily as he held his palms there, as if he were weighing her mounds instead of driving her absolutely crazy with desire. When he looked at her again it was with eyes that were clouded with desire, lips parted slightly as he struggled to breathe. With whisper-like strokes, his thumbs toyed with her nipples until they were hard and aching. She squirmed beneath him and lifted her hands to his chest.

"You've seen all this before," she said, more than anxious to get on with this seduction and a bit confused as to why he wasn't.

"Yes," he said, his voice a low, husky whisper. "I've seen you naked. I've touched just about every part of your body. We've had sex in so many different positions, so many times, I feel like I could write a manual on being intimate with Regan Donovan."

He'd moved down to her bikini bottom, pulling it down her legs and tossing it to meet its counterpart on the floor as he spoke.

"I didn't say all that," she replied, hating that the words had come out a little more breathy than she'd intended.

Gavin smiled down at her and shrugged. "That doesn't stop it from being true."

"I'm just saying that all this seduction isn't necessary. I want you, Gavin," she told him and reached out to wrap her fingers around his length.

She loved touching him here, holding the weight of his arousal in her hands and knowing the warmth exuded there would soon be inside of her. He sucked in a breath as she held him firm, her thumb rubbing along the sensitive tip.

"You feel like you want me, too," she whispered, lifting up from the pillows to touch her tongue to the spot her thumb had just soothed.

"Oh, I definitely want you," he managed to say just before she licked the underside of his length, coming back to the tip to lavish more attention.

Regan knew he liked that, knew he wouldn't be able to keep talking or keep up the foreplay much longer if she continued. She grabbed him at the base and took the tip into her mouth, suckling, applying enough pressure that his hands came to the back of her head, pushing her forward. She pulled back, waited for him to thrust, then moaned as his entire length slid inside her mouth. He would do this only a couple of times before he'd want to sink inside another entrance. She cupped his buttocks, loving the strong feel of his muscles as he stroked her mouth slowly.

Then he pulled out. She fell back against the pillows, tried to spread her legs in welcome, only to be disappointed that Gavin hadn't moved.

"Gavin," she whispered. Regan's mind refused to beg, no matter how much her body needed him right now. She had no idea what was going on, but also had no intention of being made to look like a fool.

Just as she was about to roll off the bed and put him out of her room, Gavin touched her belly. It was such a light touch, if she hadn't been looking at him she might have missed it totally except for the tingles of arousal that soared throughout her body as he continued. His fingertips circled her navel and slipped down her side as if they were liquid falling free. His fingers continued to explore, travelling up her torso to circle her breasts and nipples once more. All the while his gaze had locked on hers. She couldn't look away and she couldn't move. She opened her mouth to speak, but the words were lost as his tongue plunged deep inside, drawing her tongue against his in a slow and torturous duel.

It seemed like eons later when the kiss ended, and then again it really didn't end. His tongue outlined her lips, suckled the bottom one, drawing it inside his mouth until she moaned. His teeth nipped a stinging path along her jawline and she arched upward as he moved to her neck. Long paths of moist heat were drawn over her skin as he traveled down one side of her neck and up to the other. Then he cupped her face, pulling her head slightly so that she looked into his eyes once more.

"Tonight I'm going to make love to the woman I want to share my life with," he told her.

Regan went completely still, the intensity in his tone allowing for nothing less. She'd never seen Gavin look at her this way, never felt every muscle in her body tense at the sight and sound of him.

"I don't want fast and hot. I want slow and simmering. I want this time to last just as my love for you will. Do you understand me, Regan?"

She tried to swallow, but her throat seemed clogged. She blinked but the mood didn't change. She nodded and prayed that would be enough. She should have known better.

"Tell me you want me, Regan. Tell me this is where you want to be, that you need all I have inside for you."

Oh no, that was too much. The logical part of her mind screamed for her to run, to get the hell out of this room and away from this man that was making such a demand on her. The other part of her mind simply melted. He was right. It was what she'd always wanted, what she'd so secretly desired for so long. She could have Gavin and she could have her career and she could be whoever she wanted to be because he wanted her just as she was. It felt good to think it was all a possibility. All she had to do was say the words.

"I want all you have for me, Gavin," she whispered. It was so low she thought maybe she hadn't said it or that he hadn't heard it because he didn't move or speak.

Then his lips were on her collarbone, her chest, her nipples, her torso. He was kissing her everywhere, hot open-mouthed kisses that took each part of her bare skin in heated intervals. She squirmed, moaned, hissed and finally cried out when his hands palmed her breasts once again while his tongue delved into her navel. Her fingers clenched the sheets as her head thrashed, his mouth moving lower. Then his hands shifted, touching her inner thighs and pushing them so far back up she felt like she was preparing to do some type of gymnastics routine. Regan could do nothing but whimper.

Her entire body trembled with anticipation as she waited, needed and prayed for his mouth to touch her nether lips.

"Gavin," she whimpered.

"Yes, baby?" he replied, his warm breath whispering over her moistened center.

"Please."

One word, one request, and Regan closed her eyes in defeat.

"Yes."

One more word, one more second and his lips were dropping soft kisses along the folds of her vagina. He kissed the outside, the inside, up to the hood, over the clit. Tiny pecks were placed in a path of insatiable desire. Her legs began to tremble. Then he licked her, right in the center where she longed for his arousal. He stroked his tongue, pressing inward, pulling outward until the first scream broke free from Regan's lips.

On and on the sweet torture continued as Gavin did everything in his power to simply devour her. The first orgasm came with a rush, her body lifting further off the bed, her eyes squeezing so tightly closed that tears welled in the corners. Regan needed to catch her breath, to gather herself for another moment before…

⟡⟡⟡⟡

Waiting another second wasn't an option and as Gavin lifted up on the bed, letting the heels of Regan's feet rest on the mattress, he entered her with one long, slow, thrust that had both of them trembling.

He'd felt every tremor of her body as her climax had overtaken her, wanted to yell as his own release had threatened to break free. Now he was surrounded by her warmth, cocooned in the tight core of this magnificent woman. He shivered at the thought. Thrusting slowly in and out of her, Gavin leaned forward, pressing his hands into the mattress until they were wrapped around her back. He pulled her to him, let the warmth of her body overtake him. Gavin held tight, thrusting his hips so that he was so deep inside her it was like they were connected. Conjoined. One, instead of two.

"I won't lose you," he whispered into her ear.

She lifted her legs, wrapped them around his waist as her nails dug into his back.

"We've waited so long, so long, baby," he continued, his chest full of an unfamiliar, yet comforting, sensation. He was a professional. He had his own business, his own life, his own family. And right now, at this very moment, all he wanted, all Gavin needed, was Regan.

She pushed against him and Gavin felt himself rolling over, letting his hands fall to the bed as Regan rose above him. Her breasts were high and full, dark nipples pert, primed for his touch. She licked her lips and he moaned, his erection pulsating inside her. The tips of her fingers touched his abdomen, fanning over his skin that was lightly dusted with hair.

"I want you, Gavin," she said, lifting her hips then slowly lowering herself onto his length once more.

His eyes closed, refused to stay shut, and then opened again. "Regan," he whispered.

"This is where I want to be," she continued, and this time circled her hips until the persistent pounding at the base of his spine intensified.

He lifted from the bed, desperately needing to keep this connection with her.

She pulled back until he was almost completely out of her. With bent knees, she balanced herself on her feet, lifting her center away from him slowly.

"I want all," she said softly, relaxing her legs until he was slipping inside her once more, deeper and deeper until they were once again connected.

And then he found his release.

It was blissfully paralyzing, profoundly delicious and more emotional than anything he'd ever felt in his life.

⁂

The door slammed. They'd argued. Again. He hated the fact that he wasn't alone, wasn't taking care of this situation on his own.

That was how Vega normally worked. It was his preferred practice, and yet that plan had been changed. And he'd taken the order. Similar to the way he'd always taken orders from Big Sal. Sure he owed the man a lot, a hell of a lot, but this one was his. Ben Donovan and the pretty prosecutor were his. That other woman, she was just a message, just a way to formally announce his arrival. That was according to his plan.

The man the other night was not. It was premature and put them on guard, alerting Ben to the fact that he was here, he was sure of it. Still, Vega had the upper hand. They didn't know where he was on the island, didn't know what exactly to expect next. He smiled at that, letting the action turn more physical as a low rumble started in his gut. It had been so long since he'd laughed, his body sort of ached with it, the sound echoing awkwardly in the small dwelling.

Rubbing a hand over his face, he reached for the bag and pulled out his camera, cell phone, a knife and a gun. Then he licked his chapped lips and thought of what lay in store for them tomorrow, what they thought they were prepared for. He would finish this and he would win. Vega always won. He had to, because this time his life depended on it.

CHAPTER 14

"There's a hurricane coming," Brynne said with a slight frown. "We don't have hurricanes in Seattle. Sure, we have tons of rain, which does nothing to highlight living on the waterfront with mountains at our back. But we don't have hurricanes. I wonder if we'll have to evacuate."

Brynne Donovan had a curvy figure, long, dark hair and a mouth that seemed to go a mile a minute. She was bubbly and cheerful—that girl that everybody hated in school because she was so bubbly and cheerful. That's how her older sister Keysa described her.

At the moment, Regan couldn't argue.

Brynne lived with her parents, Uncle Bernard and his second wife Jocelyn, in Seattle. Last Regan heard, she was working as a clerk in a jewelry store despite her college degree in art history. Aunt Jocelyn had told Regan's mother and the other aunts that Brynne was still trying to find herself. Uncle Bernard was not happy with that assessment.

"It may pass us by," Regan told her younger cousin as they sat in chairs that reclined back while their face was being covered in a peach scented exfoliating mask that felt like ten layers of mud.

Their hand and foot massage had just been completed and they now wore heated mittens and booties. It was spa day for all the women and the newly hired staff at Camelot happily indulged them. This was the part of Camelot that Jade had a personal stake in. Happy Hands was her day spa in Las Vegas. According to Linc, Jade was excellent at what she did. Becoming a business owner had been her dream and he'd supported her wholeheartedly.

Jade had no idea that the moment she married into the Donovan family, that day spa would grow in its first twelve months to become "the" go-to place for the wealthy and privileged vacationing and/or residing in the Vegas area. Camelot was its first expansion and they were the first clients.

"The weather channel said there's a ninety percent chance Esmerelda's going to blast through the islands. That's what they're calling this one, Esmerelda. A very chilling name, don't you think?" Brynne asked.

Regan had heard the weather reports and was trying valiantly not to let the possibility of the storm making landfall get the best of her. "This storm has changed its course twice in the last week. For Noelle's sake, we've all been trying not to bring it up. I guess this morning's forecast changes that plan." They'd also been trying really hard not to worry about the fact that there was a killer running around the island and that an innocent woman had been killed. But that was just as hard as not thinking about the impending storm.

Their plans for the day were supposed to be a hike around the base of one of the many mountain terrains, and then head back to the main house to start tonight's barbeque. Gavin had told her this morning that while some of them, including Brock, would keep up with the original plans for the week, a small group would stay behind to watch the children and the main house. It was obvious that the mood had changed with uniformed officers standing guard at key points around Camelot and some combing the island. Still, they'd all vowed to keep the festive air in place for Noelle and Brock's sake.

"Are you thinking about the killer?"

Regan's eyes shot open, her head turning slightly to the side so she could look at Brynne.

"What?" Brynne asked, glimpsing Regan from the corner of her eye. "It's not like we all don't know that someone was killed here yesterday. That poor girl who probably had no idea that this lavish wedding was going to cost her her life."

"We're all thinking about Vivianna's death and hoping Trent and his men can catch this lunatic before he tries to harm anyone else. Beyond that, there's not much more we can do. When Noelle talked to Vivianna's parents they even told her that their daughter would want the wedding to proceed," Regan said, returning to what was supposed to be a relaxing position and closing her eyes. "So we all decided it would be best to try not to talk about it as much."

"I didn't decide," Brynne mumbled. "Then again, I rarely get to decide anything."

To Regan, that sounded like an opening. There was something else bothering Brynne, something she obviously wanted to talk about, but felt she couldn't come right out and say. With her body still limber from the nightlong lovemaking Gavin had treated her to, his words of endearment replaying like a tape on loop in her head and the mixed drink she'd indulged in creating a light buzz, Regan did not want the weight of anymore family drama. And yet, she couldn't leave her cousin hanging.

"Is something wrong, Brynne? How's your job going?" she asked with sincere concern.

"Working in a jewelry store is not a job, Brynne. It's a hobby, and you're too old to spend all your time on a hobby. After all, Yale wasn't inexpensive. You have so much potential. It's a shame to waste it selling necklaces and rings."

Regan had chuckled at Brynne's recitation because it had been given in a really good imitation of Uncle Bernard's deep and foreboding voice. Then she felt a pang of sympathy for her little cousin. It was apparent she was trapped, sort of the same way Regan had always thought she was.

"Do you like selling jewelry?" Regan asked.

"I liked finding my own job, just as I liked getting the grades that allowed me a full scholarship to Yale instead of relying on my father's money to pay my way. He tends to forget that fact."

Regan understood even what Brynne wasn't saying. She was also the older cousin and wanted to offer good, solid advice that would keep the already brewing family turmoil to a minimum. "I'm sure he wants what's best for you."

"He wants what's best if it's what he thinks is best." Brynne let out a heavy sigh. "I'm thinking of moving south."

It was probably meant to be a definitive statement, but to Regan it sounded more like a question.

"What will you do there?"

There was a second's pause, then Brynne continued.

"I applied for an internship at the Lakefield Galleries. Last summer, when I went to visit Bailey, she introduced me to the people she worked with. Sam Desdune's wife, Karena, is the head buyer for the gallery in New York. This fall they're opening another gallery in Atlanta. That's where I would be working."

"Really? Karena and Sam are scheduled to arrive this afternoon," Regan stated.

"I know. That's why I plan on telling my parents about the move at dinner tonight. I just hope they don't make a scene," Brynne finished.

"So you want to work in the art industry? That's a good field."

"You know I studied art history, so I think a museum owned and operated by a prestigious African-American family is the ideal place to begin my career. And Monica Lakefield was very impressed by my senior essay, even though I still don't know how she got her hands on it."

"Really? Monica's held in very high regard in the art industry. Aunt Alma works with her mother at the Karing Kidz Foundation. We did an article on the gallery earlier this year, so I had the chance to sit down and talk to all three of the Lakefield sisters. Their father is very proud of the way they're managing the gallery."

"And that's why I want to be there. It's what I love, and with people who can relate to me on more than just a professional level. I just don't know if my parents will approve," Brynne confessed.

The attendants had finished applying the masks, so Regan and Brynne were now completely alone. Regan lifted to sit up in her chair and looked over at her cousin. Brynne turned her head so she could see Regan.

"You're an intelligent woman, Brynne. You're old enough to decide which career path is right for you. I know how it feels to want to do what your parents want, to please them and the rest of the family, but you have to walk your own path. At the end of the day, you have to be satisfied with what you're doing in this world for yourself, not for anyone else."

"Are you satisfied working for the family, Regan? Is being at *Infinity* with your brothers and cousins day in and day out what you've always wanted to do?"

It was a serious question, one that Regan had often asked herself over the years and even more so lately.

"I love working in the fashion industry. I think I was born to be in that place. The fact that I have a family in the media industry that could carve out a special place for me is a blessing. Don't get me wrong, working for family comes with a lot of pressure, some of which I'm sure I put on myself, but it's exactly where I want to be." Regan reached for Brynne's hand.

They both laughed as their mittens got in the way, but Regan managed to hold on regardless.

"We have a great family, Brynne. A very supportive and loving family and they show that support and love in their own way. Your parents love you above all else, so I have no doubt they'll support your decision."

"But they won't like it." Brynne's frown caused her facial mask to crack just a bit across her forehead.

"Only you have to like your decision, Brynne. When you look in the mirror, it's you who has to like what you see, who you are and what you're doing. That doesn't mean you don't love and respect your parents, it just means that you're growing into the woman you were meant to be."

Brynne smiled. Regan smiled. And both their masks cracked.

"Thanks for listening," Brynne said.

Regan shook her head. "No, thank you for being willing to talk."

Regan had never been so open about her feelings, her fears and her ultimate goals. In the time sitting here with her cousin, she'd realized how wrong she'd been in keeping her emotions to herself. Everything she'd just told Brynne applied to her. She'd been so hard on herself about achieving goals that were so high and set by herself, not her family. The struggles she'd faced trying to achieve the goals, the sacrifices she made—they were all her choice. The wrong choice, she finally conceded.

At the end of the day, she had to be happy with what she was doing, even if she wasn't at the top of the fashion game, getting the best stories for the magazine or pulling in the most subscriptions for the month.

At the end of the day, she wanted to smile in that mirror and hopefully look over her shoulder to see a man that also loved what he saw, who she was and what they could be together. With that thought in mind, she lay back in the chair, praying for the spa day to come to a quick end so she could once again see Gavin. Last night he'd admitted to being wrong about keeping things from her. He'd also admitted that he was in love with her. Tonight, Regan had some admissions of her own to make.

But right now she needed to use the bathroom. Signaling for her attendant, she had the face mask and the mittens and booties removed. It took her a moment or so to convince the attendant that she would still reap the rewards of the lavish spa treatment even though she was cutting her pickling time short. Regan had always thought the sitting and waiting that was done at a spa was akin to pickling vegetables—the whole hurry up and wait routine just a bit too restrictive for her nature.

Brynne had been laughing at the exchange when Regan was finally able to leave the area and head down the hallway to the showers and bathroom. Marble in calming neutral tones occupied every surface in the large area. The entrance boasted a vanity complete with three sinks and a wall length mirror on one side along with comfortable and pleasing-to-the-eye couches with plump coral and beige colored pillows.

She rounded the corner to the left where the stalls were located—and that's when she heard it. Not a sound that was often heard by Regan and not one she liked to hear when she did. Still, she moved closer, trying to identify which stall it was coming from, because whomever it was sounded like they needed help.

When she saw the feet beneath the stall, Regan stood at the door and knocked.

"Are you okay?"

Normally bathroom conversations were not Regan's thing. But considering the majority of the people on this island were related to her, concern for their wellbeing overruled.

"Mmm hmmm," was the muffled response, followed by the flushing of the toilet.

Regan took a step back and waited for the door to open. It might have been the last person she expected to see here, but then again, she didn't really expect anyone to be getting sick in the bathroom today.

"I think maybe having a second helping of Gavin's sinful cinnamon waffles and homemade cream may have been a mistake," Victoria said, lifting her hands to tuck her hair behind her ears.

Regan followed her to the sink where Victoria quickly turned on the water and leaned forward to rinse out her mouth.

"They were sinful, weren't they?" Regan asked, recalling Gavin's generous offer to make breakfast after she'd complained about having to get up early to help the women with the task.

The aunts had also been pleased, even though they insisted everyone still remain in the kitchen to help Gavin with any preparation he needed and to help transfer the food from the kitchen to the dining room.

"And you know what else?" Regan continued. "I've never been a big fan of turkey bacon, but even that was delicious. Something about enjoying someone else's cooking just really gets to you."

Victoria was now washing her hands, but she had looked over to give Regan a tiny smile.

"I could use the change in my diet though. Cut out some of the salt, you know. Bacon should definitely be a no-no to me with all the fat and salt from being cured. So I guess it's a good thing I liked the turkey bacon. I won't be able to cut out eggs though. I could eat them every day. Fried, scrambled, boiled, omelettes with tons of cheese and ham. Whew, I think I'm making myself hungry just thinking about it."

Victoria stood up and gave Regan another look. This one, Regan got the impression wasn't a good one. In the next second, Victoria was running back into the stall and slamming the door.

Regan was about to say something to her when she heard voices. Several seconds later the aunts—Beverly, Alma, Janean, Jocelyn—and her mother appeared.

"Why are you hanging out in the bathroom, Regan?" Aunt Alma asked as she moved to the sink, lifting her hand to touch the heavy curls at her ear as if they needed to be fixed.

Nothing about Aunt Alma ever needed to be fixed. The woman was perfectly coifed each and every time Regan had ever seen her, even at 6 a.m., which was the unlawful time she'd insisted they all meet in the kitchen to start breakfast.

"I'm not hanging out, Aunt Alma. Just had to go," Regan said, remembering she still hadn't achieved that task.

She stood at the door of the stall, praying Victoria was finished and that she'd come out soon. The last thing she wanted was for the aunts to pounce on Victoria if she were sick. After their talk last night, Regan sensed that Victoria was still quite nervous being around this many Donovans at one time. The aunts plus her mother would be more than overwhelming to anyone, and most especially Alma since Ben was her youngest son.

Victoria must not have been in the mood to cooperate because there was a loud sound from the stall, one that made Regan wince and instantly caught the attention of the other women.

"Who is that?" Aunt Beverly asked?

Aunt Alma turned off the water. "I don't know but they don't sound good."

"Regan, what's going on?" her mother asked.

"Ah, nothing," she said with all eyes were on her.

Then the toilet flushed and the door to the stall opened and all eyes were on her *and* Victoria.

"Are you alright, child?" Alma asked, moving forward.

She reached for Victoria's hand, but Victoria put it up to her mouth instead and headed for the sink once more. She washed her mouth and her hands while the women looked at her as if she'd grown another head. When her eyes met Regan's, Victoria saw the apology and gave Regan a little smile. They'd forged some sort of bond last night as they'd talked by the pool, and she was glad for it.

Victoria missed her best friend Grace terribly, so being able to talk to Regan had been helpful and nice. She felt herself relaxing around the woman along with the other women her age for that matter. But now, the eyes that were starring quizzically at her through the mirror made her more than a little uncomfortable.

These women were half of the senior Donovans, The Aunts, as Regan and her cousins referred to them. Each one was intimidating in her own right—Beverly with her all-knowing gaze, Carolyn with her kind yet assessing tone, Janean with that motherly smile that very rarely wavered and Jocelyn with her sophisticated aura. They all made Victoria nervous. But none of them compared to Alma, Ben's mother. She'd come to stand right beside Victoria and was at this very moment using a damp paper towel to wipe her forehead. She pushed her hair out of the way, then lifted her chin, staring at Victoria closely.

"Are you ill, Victoria?"

Victoria licked her lips and replied, "I think I had too much to eat at breakfast."

"Gavin was dishing up those waffles as if we were actually paying per plate," Regan added to the conversation.

Carolyn and Beverly both gave her quieting looks and she folded her hands in front of her and looked at Victoria once more.

"I probably just need to lie down. Last night was very stressful. I didn't get much sleep and I've been going and going since sunrise. I should just head back to the main house," Victoria told Alma, then looked around with a weak smile to everyone else.

Beverly stepped forward then, touching a hand to Victoria's neck. She wondered what the woman was doing but didn't dare ask. Beverly looked at Alma and they both nodded.

"Have you been sick every morning since you've been on the island?" Beverly asked.

Victoria blinked and thought about the question. "I don't think so," was her reply.

"Just this morning, huh?" Alma continued with the questioning, turning the back of her hand to Victoria's forehead. "You didn't sleep last night. Well, that was to be expected. I had trouble dozing off myself. How about dizziness? Were you okay walking over here after breakfast?"

"Ah, I think. Yeah," Victoria answered, but remembered as she'd stepped into the spa with its soothing colors and soft aromas her stomach had done a little churn. The world had spun just a bit and she'd grabbed hold of the edge of the front desk to steady herself. But Alma hadn't been near her then, so she couldn't have known.

"You look pale," Beverly added.

Alma nodded. "She probably does need to lie down."

"That always worked for me," Janean chimed in.

"Nothing worked for me," Jocelyn added. "I was sick as a dog the entire time. Threatened to kill Bernard every day until the very end."

Carolyn chuckled. "I know what you mean, Jocelyn. It wasn't a pretty sight."

"But she'll be alright. I'm going to take good care of her," Alma insisted, wrapping an arm around Victoria. "You just come with me, dear, and I'll see that you get all the rest you need."

They were headed out the door before Victoria could open her mouth in protest. A half hour later she was back at the main house, tucked tightly into the bed she and Ben were sharing and given strict instructions from his mother not to move until dinner time.

Of course she didn't listen. She wasn't an invalid and actually felt a little better after getting some air. And after her time spent in the bathroom, she was starving.

CHAPTER 15

The nursery had been designed three years ago, two months after Jade and Linc's engagement. Aunt Beverly had pulled out all the stops with the elaborate design. The walls in the first floor room were painted in blocks of pastel, the dark hard wood floors covered with a matching block rug that encompassed a good majority of the space. There were four espresso colored sleigh cribs, two with yellow bedding and two with light green. Alternating colored blocks on the wall were adorned with hand-made name placards for each child recently born into the family. Torian and Tamala had pretty yellow scripts in diagonal pink blocks. Josiah had his in multi-colored letters set against a lavender block. Trevor's was spread across a U.S. Navy logo, in honor of his father's career, and based in a sky blue block. And Sophia's was a lovely pink and white polka dot in a mint green block. The newest name had been added when they'd arrived last Sunday, a yellow one with happy hot pink letters covered in tiny daisies. It read "Briana"—Tate and Sean's little girl.

There were toys galore, dolls, rocking horses, building blocks, bouncing balls and anything else that made noise. The windows were covered in sheer white curtains that were now tied back, letting sunlight filter inside. From where he stood, Ben could see the trees bending fitfully in the wind, waves rumbling against the shore in angry little bursts. A storm was definitely coming, he thought, and his temples throbbed once more.

Something hit his lower legs, jerking Ben from his thoughts and he looked down to see what it was. Warmth spread in his chest as he watched Adam's son waddle his way toward him, arms extended, smile spread across a face that looked a lot like his father's.

"Hey buddy, you playing ball with me?" Ben said, squatting down so that he'd be on Josiah's level. In one hand, he scooped up the bright red ball beside his feet while extending the other hand to welcome Josiah's chubby little body.

The little boy was the best of Adam and Camille with his milk chocolate complexion, chubby cheeks and laughing eyes.

"Okay. I'll roll the ball to you and you roll it back," he said after he'd nuzzled Josiah's neck, inhaling deeply the smell of innocence.

"Yes! Yes!" was Josiah's reply. "Ball?"

Ben put him down and scooted back a bit. He rolled the ball and watched with elation as Josiah struggled to fit his tiny arms around its circumference. The boy laughed and so did Ben.

"You been placed on nursery duty too?" Max asked.

Ben looked up to see his brother holding his niece, Sophia. The pretty little Brazilian native had instantly become the star and the moon in her daddy's eyes. Ben had never seen Max so relaxed and so enamored in his life. He figured Sophia had even stolen a bit of the love and adoration Max had for his wife Deena. Max had thought his infertility was a life sentence to unhappiness. When spirited and compassionate Deena Lakefield waltzed into his life, all that had changed, and after the foundation that Max's mother and Deena's mother had founded called Karing Kidz, their family had been made complete with the adoption of Sophia.

"All the women are gone. It's either come in here, go hiking with the seniors or walk the perimeter with Trent, Devlin and the others," he said, tussling with Josiah over the ball until the little boy fell back on his bottom, laughing so hard his tiny chest rumbled.

Ben smiled at that, pulling Josiah up for another hug.

"Trent wouldn't let you play with him, right?" Max asked with a chuckle.

Ben looked up at his brother, shaking his head. "I think he's afraid I'll shoot to kill if I see Vega's face."

Sophia loved to play peek-a-boo and was now covering her eyes, waiting for Max to say the words. He did and she pulled her tiny hands from her face with a giggle that was familiar and heartwarming. When they were at home in Las Vegas, Ben made it a point to visit with his niece at least twice a week. She'd brought such sunshine to their entire family, it seemed none of them could stay away from her for two long.

In actuality, all of the newest additions to the Donovan family had brought fresh air to the group. Jade and Linc's twins, Trent's rambunctious son, Sophia, Josiah and even the dainty little Briana with her frilly dresses and infectious smile—all of them had entered this world in the last two and a half years. To say that the Donovans were mightily blessed would be an understatement.

"Will you?" Max asked seriously.

"Will I what?" Ben had drifted back to thoughts of his family and the beautiful children that had been brought into the next generation.

"Will you kill Vega if you see him?"

Ben did not hesitate again. "I will. If I don't, he'll taunt us forever. Victoria and I will never have a moment's peace as long as that man is alive."

Max nodded. "So you're looking to have a future with Victoria?"

"Of course I am. Why would you ask me that?"

Max shifted Sophia in his arms and let her wiggle down when she was tired of being there. He slipped his hands into his pocket as he looked down at his brother. "I asked because you didn't volunteer the information."

Ben stood. "I didn't know it needed announcing," he said with a shrug. Even though he should have figured it did, maybe. The Donovan men weren't known for making commitments to women, so when one did, which had been happening more often in the last couple of years, it did usually require an announcement.

"I was wondering the same thing," Adam said as the twins and Sophia found the three-foot custom built dollhouse and began playing amongst themselves.

Now two married men with children were looking at Ben as if they expected him to give a wedding date and details at any moment. But he wasn't as angered by that thought as he probably should have been. If truth be told, Ben had been thinking more and more about his future with Victoria. He figured it might be more than a little cliché, but he wanted what his older brother had desperately. He wanted the loving wife, the beautiful child, the commitment, the home. He wanted it all and he wanted it with Victoria.

"I'm in love with her," was what he finally admitted to them.

Adam nodded. "And you want to marry her."

Max folded one arm over his chest, lifted the other hand to smooth down his goatee. "But she's not on the same page."

"What is this, a therapy session?" Ben asked, and then tossed the ball to Josiah once more and stood. "Look, we're just starting out in our relationship. We've had some bumps, including a big one by the name of a hired killer on the loose, so we haven't really had time to iron out all the kinks."

It was Max's turn to nod knowingly at Adam.

"What?" Ben asked when the two of them continued to stare.

"Nothing," Adam said with a chuckle, and then looked to Max. "He's done. If she doesn't marry him soon, we'll have to peel him off the ceiling he'll be so crazy."

Max joined him in laughing. "No doubt."

"Whatever," Ben said, dismissing their comments. "Victoria and I are going to be just fine. When the time comes for us to take our relationship to the next stage, we will." Or at least he hoped they would.

❧❧❧

In all the years she'd known him, he'd never looked so good. He had a warm smile, one that touched his eyes and lit up his face to the point whoever was on the receiving end couldn't help but smile in return. He'd filled out a little more since law school. Not at all out of shape, but more defined in the area of his shoulders and the broadness of his chest. In the courtroom dressed in suit and tie he looked formidable and opposing. At home, on a casual level, with jeans and a polo shirt he looked handsome and approachable. Overall Ben Donovan simply had a more mature and distinguished appeal than he had years ago—as if he could have possibly become more attractive.

Victoria eased into the kitchen, taking slow steps, keeping her eyes trained on the spot where Ben stood at the marble topped island. Josiah sat atop the island with what looked like cookies in one hand and a lidded cup of milk in the other. Ben had been talking to the little boy, smiling down at him as if their conversation was the most important thing in the world.

"Am I interrupting?" she asked, feeling like she was intruding on a personal moment.

Her heart skipped a beat as Ben looked up to her, smiling once again. She wondered if she'd ever seen him smile this way before. Definitely not in the last few months.

"Of course not," he told her. "Look Josiah, in addition to that yummy cookie, there's now a very pretty lady joining us."

By then, she'd crossed the kitchen and was standing right beside Ben. Unable to resist, she reached out to touch Josiah's cheek. He tried to say something using the few words he knew, watching her with an observant gaze, probably trying to figure out who she was again. Ben nuzzled Josiah's neck and he giggled. Victoria smiled at the two of them. "Hello, Josiah. Is Uncle Ben keeping your company today?"

In the days since she'd been on the island, Victoria had met all of the Donovan children. She'd even spent some time babysitting them when she felt like Noelle's wedding plans were a bit too personal for her to tag along.

"We were in the nursery, but this little one wanted to explore. We took a tour of the house and ended up here," Ben told her.

"You tend to end up in the kitchen a lot. Don't start pushing your bad habits off on this precious little boy," she joked with Ben.

"If they put a mini-fridge in my room, I wouldn't have to come down here so frequently," he replied.

"You don't have to eat every three hours. You're a grown man, not a pregnant woman," she quipped while helping Josiah lift his cup to his mouth to sip.

She heard Ben laugh and watched as Josiah drank. Victoria replayed the words she'd just said in her mind.

No, she thought with a start. She couldn't be.

"I'm on vacation. I'm supposed to lounge around and eat," Ben was saying.

At the same time, his cell phone was ringing and he shifted a bit to answer it. Victoria tried to keep focused. Josiah was a cute little boy, but he wasn't her son. He wasn't Ben's son. They didn't have any children. Hell, they'd just embarked on a relationship. Children weren't even a thought in their equation. But…

"Bastard!" Ben cursed loud and fluently, effectively jerking her away from her troublesome thoughts.

"What is it? What's the matter?" she asked.

He looked at her, then away, like he was contemplating… "Don't you even think about not telling me what's going on," she warned.

His smiling eyes had turned hard, glittering with anger. His lips thinned and he grit his teeth, then sighed.

"Vega's been in the house," he finally admitted, turning his phone so that she could see the screen.

It was a slide show of pictures: the family at breakfast this morning; the ladies leaving for Camelot; Ben, Max and Adam in the nursery with the kids; she, Ben and Josiah in the kitchen.

Victoria looked around, her skin crawling with the knowledge that they were being watched by a killer. She instinctively reached for Josiah, holding him close to her chest. Ben continued to frown as he wrapped one arm around her and used his other hand to stop the slide show on his phone and press speed dial.

"We've got a problem," he said into the phone. "He's been in the house."

❧❦❧❦❧

It had been a long day. A very long and tiresome day which Gavin would usually end with a slice of pecan pie and a beer. The pecan pie? His mother's recipe and the one part of home he tended to keep with him no matter what. The beer? A necessity to keep his sanity. Tonight, however, he wanted something…or should he say someone else.

The day had started perfectly. He'd rolled over in bed, his eyes barely ready to open, his arm reaching out. And there she was. She'd curled into him, her bottom pressing back into his groin as he happily spooned her. She was warm and accommodating and soon after, satiated. Even after their shower, he'd wanted her again.

"Crap," she'd groaned just as he'd wrapped her legs around his waist. "I've got breakfast duty."

He'd been kissing her neck, loving the little hollow at the base of her throat where her pulse trembled beneath his tongue each and every time. "It's not even six a.m.," he'd complained, his hands gripping the soft curve of her bottom, squeezing until his erection was painfully hard. They hadn't dressed yet, had barely towel dried and their wet bodies were clinging to each other, begging for another round.

"I know, but I've got breakfast duty," she'd whispered in his ear. "Now put me down before I'm late and my mother sends someone up here to get me."

"I've got a better idea," he suggested, one hand still splayed over her bottom while the other maneuvered a little.

This time he put his mouth right to her ear, licked her lobe and whispered, just as his finger brushed past the plump folds of her center, "I'll make you a deal."

She'd bucked in his grasp, only to settle against his touch, sighing her reply, "What's the deal?"

"You give me fifteen minutes and I'll go downstairs with you and fix the entire breakfast." While he talked, Gavin's fingers moved over her moistened center, loving the feel of her soft, warm flesh.

Her answer had been to thrust into his touch, pressing her breasts against his chest. "Hurry," she'd begged when he'd been content touching her, kissing her lobe, down to her neck.

They'd been standing just outside the bathroom door. Gavin took a few steps until they were close to the window. He released her then, groaning as her body slid along his until she was standing in front of him.

He cupped her face in his hands. "I want to watch you come with the sunrise," he told her.

She licked her lips wantonly, her tongue scraping along the pad of his thumb that had been positioned close to her mouth.

"Do you want to come for me, baby?" he asked, letting her have his finger, which she sucked deep into her mouth.

"Yes," she replied when she'd sucked and released him.

With her palms to his chest, Regan pushed him back until he sat on the leather ottoman that was at the foot of the bed. When she straddled him, her back was to the balcony doors. She wiggled her hips until his tip touched her center. He grasped the nape of her neck, pulling her head down for a kiss so desperate and intense they were both panting as his tongue grazed her chin and down her neck. Once again his hands were on the lush cheeks of her bottom. With one quick thrust upward he was deep inside her, warmth and moistness coating his length.

"Ride me," he told her.

"Like never before," she replied, clasping her hands onto his shoulders and working her hips until they were both gasping for breath.

He'd watched her throw her head back on a long, deep moan as her release came. The sunlight amidst a sparkling blue sky framing her naked body and something inside him exploded. It was quick and lethal, the powerful clutching in his chest, the stinging sensations rippling down his spine. Gavin had held onto her so tightly he feared he might hurt her, but couldn't stand the thought of letting go, of losing her. In that moment she was a part of him, an unforgettable connection over which he'd take his own life before breaking.

They'd showered again and he'd resisted the urge to tell her how much he loved her. She'd accepted this new level of their relationship, was willing to work towards something more. He figured Regan would take this quick leap as either a challenge or a threat—to both her reaction would be swift. Gavin just wasn't sure which way she'd go. He'd never believed her to be a jealous woman, and yet she'd been angered by his contact with Raquel. Angered and hurt, and he'd wished she would have just confronted him then so he could have sworn his loyalty to her sooner.

As they'd covered each other in thick soap suds and stood beneath the warm spray of water, he'd looked into her eyes, saw what he hadn't seen in months and wanted to keep that look there. Her brow wasn't furrowed. Her shoulders were relaxed, her eyes clouded with a healthy haze of satiation and contentment. This was how he wanted her to remain, and so he kept his feelings to himself, for the moment.

They'd been fifteen minutes late. but the women hadn't started cooking. They'd all been too busy discussing last night's events. Gavin prepared breakfast and then they'd parted ways, each having events throughout the day. Now, at close to 5o'clock, he'd had about as much space from Regan as he could take.

The spacious main house seemed a bit deserted as he entered through the back door, using the key and alarm code that Trent had given him yesterday. When they'd first arrived on the island, there'd been no need for the alarm system to be activated. The Donovans would do that at the end of the week when they left. The cleaning crews that were contracted to the island had a code they could use when needed. And now, so did Gavin.

Marble floors were throughout the foyer and hallways. The entire house had an open floorplan, so the transition from the rooms on the first level was seamless and lead ultimately to the back terrace. The game room where the men usually met was just beyond the den and, because of its theatre seating and televisions, had a thick oak door to keep the sound inside.

It was from the den that Gavin heard voices and decided to take a chance that Regan might be in there. Unfortunately, by the time he realized she wasn't, it was too late.

"Well if it isn't Chef Gavin," Bruce Donovan said the moment he walked in.

Bruce Donovan was a tall man, surpassing six feet, his hair peppered with gray. He was the impeccably dressed businessman with a keen mind and quick instincts that kept all his colleagues, and more so his enemies, on their toes. So it wasn't out of the ordinary to see Bruce in dress pants, shirt and tie on any given day. For the vacation, he'd traded the shirt and tie for more casual button fronts that matched his dress pants

and leather sandals. It was a smooth but eclectic mixture that
only a man such as Bruce could pull off.

He was sitting at a card table, his brother Reginald—
Regan's father—directly across from him. Savian and Dion
were on either side of him. All of them had a hand of cards and
Gavin quickly tried to use that as an excuse.

"I was just looking for Regan," he said while waving a hand
to everyone. "I'll just check outside to see if she's there."

"They're getting set up for the barbeque," Savian said,
looking at his cards and not at Gavin.

"I thought the guys were taking care of dinner tonight," he
said, knowing instinctively that was a mistake.

"There are some guys out there," Dion told him. "Just not
us." He chuckled and the others joined in.

Gavin smiled. Cooking had never been an issue for him—
that was obvious by his career choice. And while he figured
there was a significant number of men throughout the world he
didn't mind or actually enjoyed cooking, especially
barbequing, there would always be a percentage that did not. "I
hear you. I'll head out there to see if I can help."

"Not so fast," Reginald called to him just as he'd turned to
leave. "Why don't you join us for a game?"

No. He definitely did not want to sit down and play cards
with Regan's father and other members of her family. Sure,
this particular bunch of Donovans Gavin had known for most
of his life, but he wasn't the long-legged teenager Reginald
came to pick up at the rec center to tell him his father had been
killed.

"Cards really aren't my thing," he said.

"Besides," Savian added. "I've got a good hand and I know
the others could use some help outside. Last I heard Brandon
planned to work the grill while Adam, Linc and Brock fixed
the plates. That arrangement has disaster written all over it."

Dion nodded. "Yeah, Brandon may come from Texas but
barbequing is definitely not in his blood."

They were trying to save him, and Gavin appreciated that.
But when Reginald sent a pointed look his way, he had no
choice but to man up.

"I can play a hand or two before I head out," Gavin said, taking steps that brought him closer to the table.

"New deal," Dion said, tossing his cards into the center of the table. "You can take my seat."

He looked apologetic as Gavin passed him. Gavin didn't mind. If he planned to marry Regan, which he did, then having a sit down conversation with her father was expected. Having said conversation with her father, her uncle, one of her brothers and one of her cousins was a bit more than he'd expected, but Gavin had never backed down from a challenge.

Halfway into the first game, Reginald made his move.

"You been chasing around behind my daughter since we've been here," he said to Gavin.

Regan had her father's eyes, dark brown, and the shape of her face was round like Reginald's as well. Her high cheekbones and gut-wrenching smile came from her mother.

"Yes sir," was Gavin's only reply as he played a spade, winning the next book and earning a nod of appreciation from Savian.

"I've known you a long time," Reginald continued, playing a card from his hand. "Since you were about knee high I guess."

"Yes sir," Gavin agreed.

Bruce played a card, and then Savian, who ultimately collected that book with his winning move.

"Known your mother for quite some time too. And your dad was a good man," Reginald told him, hesitating to play his next card.

Gavin spied the older man, frowning down at his cards before throwing one out with a look of disgust.

"Thank you sir," Gavin replied. The thanks was for the compliment and for playing a three of hearts, which Gavin's queen of hearts beat with no problem at all.

By the end of the game, Savian was grinning wildly. Bruce was frowning at his older brother and Dion was clapping his father on the shoulder, a consolatory move that won him a glare from both Bruce and Reginald.

Gavin stood from the table, more than ready to leave when Reginald stood also. Suddenly he was surrounded by Donovan men. Tall, formidable, successful men who were all looking at him as if he could at any moment be put on the chopping block. Gavin swallowed and kept eye contact with Reginald, the one who worried him most at the moment.

"Well, I guess if you love my daughter as well as you play cards, we'll all live happily," Reginald told him, finally extending a hand to Gavin.

Gavin accepted that hand, but didn't release the breath of relief he felt. "I love your daughter a great deal, sir. You don't have to worry about her. I won't let anything happen to her," he vowed.

Reginald nodded as his hand dropped back to his side. "I'm a bit more concerned about what might happen to you should you piss that girl off good one time."

Gavin nodded. "I've known Parker and Savian a long time, sir. I'm sure we could handle it like men."

Reginald shook his head, sharing a knowing glance with Bruce. "I'm not talking about my boys getting after you. I'm talking about Regan taking a chunk out of you herself."

The four men laughed so hard Gavin couldn't help but join in. He had no intention of breaking Regan's heart. Winning it completely was more his goal.

Later that evening, they all sat in the living room enjoying their barbequed meal, following Trent's advice that staying out in the open too long wasn't safe. Sam Desdune and his wife Karena had joined them about an hour ago when the ferry had brought them over, adding to the number of people on the island that needed to be protected.

The last thing Reginald wanted to think about was another killer. Reginald watched Gavin closely, not necessarily because he was presently cuddled up with his only daughter, but because Gavin seemed so much like his father. Anthony Lucas had been a good friend to Reginald and to his family. His death had been a shock to the Lucas family and to the senior Donovan brothers. At that time, Reginald was convinced there had been nothing he or any of his brothers could have done to prevent Anthony's death or the death of their sister-in-law.

Albert had told everyone it was from breast cancer, and yes, Darla had been diagnosed with the awful disease, but that wasn't what had taken her life in the end. The brothers had been adamant they could hold onto the secret.

Now Reginald wasn't so sure.

CHAPTER 16

At 6 o'clock, most of the family had gathered once again in the living room to watch an emergency weather report.

"Esmerelda has officially been upgraded from a tropical storm to a Category three hurricane this afternoon. The tropical wave that developed over the southeastern Caribbean Sea last Saturday morning shifted its course on Wednesday. Aruba is still recovering this evening from its bout with Esmerelda yesterday. On its present course Esmerelda will continue to head west, hitting Jamaica, the Heart Islands and the Cayman Islands some time on Saturday." The weather reporter spoke with a heavy accent but his words were painfully clear.

"Tomorrow evening Noelle will be walking down the aisle in the backyard," Jade said quietly.

Beverly had already begun shaking her head. "We'll have to move it inside. Those winds will shred the tents."

"It still has time to shift," Brandon said hopefully.

He was really happy for Brock and Noelle, happy that his brother had finally found love. Now, his sister was another story entirely. The man that ended up falling for Bailey would have to be someone special, someone along the lines of a saint or an angel equipped to deal with all of God's creations. He'd have to be able to deal with her moodiness and bitchiness, not to mention her thirst for danger.

"It could," Albert added, referring to the storm.

The sound of his voice drew Brandon's attention, and he looked over to the recliner where the man who had raised him sat. This was the man he'd looked up to all his life, the man who could do no wrong. He'd raised his children even after his wife's death. Darla Donovan had died the summer Brandon and Bailey turned twelve. His father had informed them that a car accident had taken the center of their family, and for a while he, his sister and his brother had been lost without her. Albert had been a good father, making providing for his family his uppermost priority even if it had meant being away from home a lot. But after Darla's death, he cut his hours working at Donovan Oil and vowed to be everything his children needed.

Over the years Brandon watched as his father dealt with a range of teenage issues, from Bailey's proms to Brock leaving for college and then deciding not to return to Houston to live. For the most part, Brandon had stayed out of his father's way, doing the right things in school, moving on to college and then securing a good job. Brandon had been the last one to move out of his father's house and was the only one who still lived close enough to see Albert on a weekly basis. Looking at his father now, he knew it was time to talk to his brother and sister about Albert's health.

"Still, we should have a solid backup plan in place," Regan chimed in.

"You're right," Carolyn said, touching a hand to her daughter's knee as they sat together on the couch. "We should gather the vendors and Noelle and work this out before it's time for the bridal shower."

Beverly had already stood. "Jade, you go on up and get Noelle. We'll meet in the kitchen. I'll start calling the vendors."

With that last statement, a silence fell over the room, everyone no doubt thinking of the young life that had been lost. Regan wondered if it were a little morbid, them carrying on with the festivities even though that young woman had been killed. The aunts had said the show must go on, but Regan wasn't so sure. She'd met Vivi briefly the night she'd arrived with her staff and thought she'd seemed like a nice woman. Surely not someone who deserved to die, and especially not someone who deserved to be killed and left on a beach.

"You alright?" Gavin asked, coming over to sit next to her on the couch.

The others had already begun leaving, her mother and the aunts already heading towards the kitchen.

She shrugged. It had been so nice having Gavin here. He'd moved his things from Camelot to the main house yesterday. This morning after breakfast he'd gone over to Camelot to oversee his staff there as they prepared meals for the vendors, and then he'd immediately come back here to be with her. As independent as she was used to being, it was nice to have someone to lean on for a change.

"I'm fine," she said ,turning to look at him.

He still had on his white Spaga shirt and looked like he'd had a long day.

"How are the vendors holding up?" she asked him.

Gavin shrugged. "As good as can be expected, I guess. The caterer they hired is a little flustered that some of his ingredients didn't arrive with that last ferry. I told him we could substitute his seafood dish with one of mine that I have all the makings for, but he wasn't happy with that suggestion."

"I can imagine," she added. "Straying from the plan is not always easy."

Their gazes locked.

"But sometimes you have to be willing to step out of your comfort zone."

"I agree, and that's why I'm willing to miss the bridal party tonight to go back to Camelot with you and help get things together for the wedding tomorrow," she told him.

"The wedding's still on?" he asked.

"Of course it's still on."

"I didn't say anything to the vendors, but I was thinking there would ultimately be a postponement with the storm coming," he said sitting up, his elbows resting on his knees.

Regan had been sitting on the edge of the couch, so now their legs bumped. She shook her head.

"Noelle and Brock have waited a long time for this day. Nobody wants to take it from them."

"Even if it's not safe? Not only is there a killer still on the loose, but there's a hurricane coming this way. Why aren't any of you thinking about evacuating?"

Regan looked confused. "Wouldn't that be like quitting?"

He took her hand, sighing because this was not how he'd envisioned their week together. "Look, I'm the last person that would quit on anything. And if it were just me at stake, I'd say go for it, ride out the storm. But there are at least fifty people on this island at the moment. And if that maniac doesn't kill someone else, the storm just might."

He had a really good point, Regan thought, and was about to say just that when they were interrupted.

"You're absolutely right, Lucas," Devlin said, moving slowly into the room. Even though his pace wasn't quick, the heavy tension that followed him like a black cloud filled the room instantly.

"It is too dangerous for everyone to stay here. It's even more dangerous to try and attempt an outside wedding and huge reception in the middle of a raging storm. Unfortunately, we don't have much choice at this point. Coast Guard's docked all ships. No ferries in or out. The message to us is to lock everything down and hope for the best."

Regan stood. "So we sit and wait and hope the storm doesn't do too much damage?"

"We don't have another choice," Trent said when he entered.

"And what about the killer?" Gavin asked, standing and putting an arm around Regan.

"We wait until he makes his move," Trent began.

"And then I take him down," Devlin finished.

They were like this double dangerous duo, both standing there dressed in all black, Trent's shirt a bit tighter and bulkier than Devlin's because Jade had insisted he put on a Kevlar vest. Guns were at both their waists, a jolting but oddly relieving sight for Regan.

Gavin's arm tightened around her shoulders, but Regan refused to shake. "If the storm's scheduled to hit sometime tomorrow, maybe we should have the wedding now?" she suggested.

Trent and Devlin looked at each other, shrugging.

"I'll go talk to The Aunts."

❧

"There's something you're not saying," Gavin said the moment Regan left the room.

"The others are on their way. Let's just wait until they get here," Trent told him.

"It's not good," Gavin said more to himself than to the two gun-toting men in the room.

"None of this is good," Trent told him. "Absolutely none of it."

It took a few minutes for Ben, Victoria, Brock and Linc to enter the room. When they did, Trent stood in the center of the space and cleared his throat.

"He's been in this house," he said clearly, solemnly.

"Dammit!" Brock cursed.

"When?" Linc asked sternly.

Trent looked to Ben. "Ben got a text earlier with pictures from the nursery and even in the kitchen. The ones from the kitchen were of Ben and Victoria as they were still standing in the kitchen."

"So he's been watching us the entire time we've been here?" Linc spoke again.

Gavin rubbed a hand down his face. This was worst than he'd thought. Being the son of a cop, it wasn't as if he'd never heard about killers and thieves and drug dealers. He'd heard more than his fair share of horror stories from his father. He'd even been on a father/son ride-along sponsored by the police department when his father and his partner received a robbery call. He'd watched his father pull a gun on a man and put that gun to a man's head when he'd grabbed the store clerk and threatened to shoot. Later that night, when Gavin couldn't sleep, his father had been there to explain to him why bad things happened and how good people were always the ones left to deal with them. Gavin had wanted to be one of the good guys then. He'd wanted to be a cop. Then one day the man holding the gun had a different face and the bullet had entered his father's temple from a point blank range. That was the day Gavin's dreams had changed.

Right here, right now, he felt like they might be changing again.

"There are cameras in this house, right?" he asked Devlin, not Trent. Trent was family. He was a soldier and would protect no matter what the cost, but he would also soften the blow for family. He'd assembled the ones he thought he could trust in this room, the ones who could take the worst of the truth and still function to protect others.

Gavin wanted the ugly truth, the words that could only come from a killer with no real connections. He'd seen that look in Devlin's eyes that night when he picked him up off the ground, when consciousness was a room Gavin moved in and out of. He'd seen that look before on the streets his father worked, so he knew exactly what he was dealing with here.

"We found cameras in Ben and Victoria's room and all the main rooms on the first floor. No bugs, so he has no sound. But he's been watching," Devlin told him.

"But today was the first text?" Linc asked. "Why?"

"He's ready to make his move," Ben said. "The message he wrote on that court order nailed to the florist's body was for me to get ready. That means he's coming for me."

No, Gavin thought dismally, the message had specifically said for Ben to get ready to watch Victoria die. He knew why Ben hadn't said that part in front of the women the other night and respected the man for it. He didn't respect this coward ass killer and was tired of playing games with him.

"We need to stick together. Every living soul on this island needs to be in one central location. It's safer regarding Vega and whatever move he plans to make, and its safer regarding this storm," Trent said.

Brock sat down, put his elbows on his knees and dropped his head into his hands. "I don't believe this is happening," he mumbled.

Linc went to his side, gripping his cousin's shoulder. "It's going to work out fine, Brock. You and Noelle are going to be married."

Brock nodded. "In the middle of a hurricane or in the midst of gunfire? None of those choices are what Noelle and I had in mind when we planned this wedding."

"Don't think like that," Linc insisted.

"The wedding's happening tonight, in about three hours," Regan announced a little out of breath as she ran into the living room. "What's going on?" she asked after a few moments of looking around the room.

Gavin moved to her quickly. "Vega's been in the house. We need to all stay in one place together. It's safer that way all around," he told her. He'd held her by the shoulders and looked right into her eyes as he spoke, praying she would remain calm.

Brock spoke then. "We'll go to Camelot. All of us," he said. "The structure there is stronger because we used concrete beams and the windows can be shuttered. We were going to make the same changes to the house during the winter when nobody was down here."

He was trying to sound strong, but Gavin could hear the disappointment creeping into the man's voice. This wasn't easy on any of them, but from what he'd learned of Brock and Noelle, he knew they'd both had a rough time in life. He felt bad that their special day might be destroyed by Mother Nature and/or the spawn of the devil.

"Then we'll have the wedding there," Regan said. She slipped from Gavin's hold and went to stand next to Brock. "The reception was going to be in the ballroom anyway. We can do everything right there. I'm going to go up with Bailey and Jade and tell Noelle. You get the guys together and we'll meet you at the aisle."

Her voice had softened and Gavin watched her touch Brock's cheek a second before going up on tiptoe to kiss him in the same spot.

There was a moment of silence before Brock nodded. "I'll tell Noelle. Everybody else needs to get packed so we can all go at one time. We'll take the vehicles and park them in the underground garage at the back of Camelot."

Fully loaded jeeps, six of them so far, were kept on the island for transportation purposes. So far they'd only been used by the family, but once Camelot was fully up and running, they would be used for taking visitors to other locations on the island, running supplies from the ferry to the resort and taking care of whatever other needs arose.

Regan nodded and went back to Gavin.

"Let's be ready in forty minutes," Linc said.

Trent nodded. "I'll go get Tia and Trevor ready. Dev, you get with Ace and Rio. I want one of you driving the front vehicle and the other at the tail end. Let those cops know what the plan is but do it face to face. No cell phones. We don't know where this bastard is, so none of us can take any messages. Only face-to-face communications so we know exactly who its coming from."

Devlin nodded and left the room. Regan and Gavin followed, heading up the stairs just before Trent, Linc and Brock. With every step he took, Gavin prayed for their safety. He prayed that this time the good people would prevail while trying not to recall the one time they didn't.

At precisely 8:30 on Friday evening, a jazz quartet serenaded the room full of guests with an instrumental version of "A Whole New World," the title track to Walt Disney's *Aladdin* movie, normally sung by Peabo Bryson and Regina Belle. The ballroom had been decorated in royal blue and white, candles illuminating just about every surface—from the small glass vases that outlined the runner going down the center of the room and stopping at the altar to the tall glass vases on each table with cascading flowers. Irises were Noelle's favorite flower, so each arrangement had white irises in its center and were surrounded by roses, some tinted blue and others pearly white.

Round tables were covered in white table cloths. Chairs were also covered in white and tied with royal satin bows. Crystal glasses, china plates and gleaming silverware occupied the tables. The overhead lights had been dimmed to a dull glow that was consistent with the setting sun just beyond the windowed back wall.

The altar was backed up to the windows so that all the guests had an unfettered view of the minister, Brock and Brandon as they stood at the aisle where Noelle and the rest of the bridal party would soon appear. Twinkle lights had been run along each window and the borders of the room. The white runner with royal trim stretched the length of the room and waited for the bridal party's entrance.

Noelle was anything but a traditional bride, so it didn't bother her in the least that her bridesmaids and matron of honor would walk on the runner before she did.

Only a few minutes ago, Tia had lead the bridal party escorted by Trent, who was dressed in an Armani black tuxedo that all the groomsmen wore. Camille had followed with Adam. Karena and Jade, as the matrons of honor, made the walk down the aisle by themselves. Their dresses were different from the other bridesmaids in that they wore halter tops with a thicker apple green sash and no trailing bow in the back. There had been no flower girl since Torian and Tamala were only two years old and in Noelle's opinion, too young to be made to walk down the long aisle and stand perfectly still.

Standing outside the closed ballroom doors, Noelle had taken a deep breath and then looked up into familiar eyes and smiled.

"You ready?" Henry Donovan asked.

He'd been her first and only choice to give her away because since day one of their meeting, he'd taken her in and treated her as if she were his very own daughter. She looked down at herself, taking one last look at the exquisite dress Camille had designed for her. Originally when Noelle had thought of her wedding dress, she'd wanted something spectacular with bling and satin for days. She'd wanted a long train with little girls to carry it behind her. Camille had patiently listened to all her wants and come back with this. The finished product still rendered her speechless.

Material so soft and so sheer wrapped around her body in uniformity, draping off her shoulders to showcase her honey hued skin and the diamond and sapphire necklace Brock had given her as a wedding gift. It was mid-thigh where the tight fit gave way to layer after layer of the sheer material, fanning around her legs like a curtain. The color was white, which her all blue tinted iris bouquet set off like a beacon. She felt beautiful and sexy, but most of all she felt loved. That someone would know her well enough, would care enough to create something so special for her had caused Noelle to get choked up on more than one occasion this week. She would never forget how blessed she was to be a part of this family.

And even though everything wasn't precisely as planned— her other fifty guests weren't here and the menu she'd labored over for weeks was now changed to herbed chicken breasts, wild rice and a seafood surprise that neither Gavin nor her caterer had shared with her—she was still extremely happy. All the planning she and Brock had done these past few months, all the long distance calls and visits to and from Jade boiled down to the next few minutes of her life. A Nothing, whether it be a storm or maniac convict, was going to get in her way.

"I'm ready," she replied with a smile.

Two hostesses dressed in all black but for the blue scarves elegantly drawn around their neck opened the doors. Noelle and Henry stepped through.

She saw Brock the moment her feet touched the edge of the runner and Noelle smiled. In all her years of life, during all the times she'd thought of how far she could go without falling totally on her face, of how many sticky situations she could get in and out of without finally getting irrevocably stuck, she'd never imagined having a man like him in her life. Brock loved everything about her, all her faults and idiosyncrasies. He saw the complete package and tamed her wild spirit with his calm and soothing one. Together they'd built The Gramercy II into a thriving and popular casino and changed Brock's bachelor pad into a cozy and contemporary home where—to Brock's chagrin—they often entertained.

He held her gaze as she walked, each step bringing her ever closer to the moment they'd talked about for the last year. He wore a black Armani tux like the other guys, and yet she didn't see any of them but him. He smiled as she drew closer, his eyes carrying the same joy she felt bursting free in her chest. When the minister asked who gave this woman, Henry spoke up, lifted her veil and kissed her forehead before turning to shake Brock's hand. Then he stepped aside. Brock extended his crocked arm and she slipped her hand through, linking them finally.

"I love you," he mouthed to her.

"I love you back."

CHAPTER 17

"Nobody would have ever known this wasn't the way they planned it," Bailey said, emptying yet another bottle of champagne into her glass.

She'd long since ditched her shoes, claiming all the straps moving up and down her leg gave her the creeps. Regan had laughed as they'd gotten dressed in one of the rooms on the third floor. The ten suites on the second floor were completed and being occupied by the vendors. The entire third floor was still being renovated but would be glorious when it was done. The family didn't mind staying up there in less than perfect circumstances, a fact which Regan thought would have amazed Victoria. Instead the woman had looked on as if her mind were totally someplace else.

As for the shoes, Regan loved the Christian Louboutin's in the festive apple green color, even if they weren't visible beneath the floor length dress. Each time she'd taken to the dance floor with Gavin, Regan had been sure to pull up her dress to show them off.

"It was lovely," Regan commented, twirling her now empty glass between her fingers. She was in a pleasant place at the moment—after four glasses of champagne.

It had just seemed easier to drink and dance the night away while outside the wind and the waves picked up. All the windows had been shuttered and locked. The doors were bolted as well because everyone that was on the island that needed to be inside, was. It was just after midnight and she was sitting in the ballroom with Bailey and Victoria. Regan and Victoria were waiting for their men. Bailey...well, she just seemed to be procrastinating, or getting drunk. Both were worrisome.

"They were a beautiful couple. You could feel the love emanating from them. It was so special," Victoria said, her voice a little dreamy even though Regan hadn't seen her drink anything other than punch.

"It's good to see true love and that happy ever after ending everybody's always searching for," Regan added.

She put her glass down on the table right beside the table card with the Donovan family crest in its center, Brock and Noelle's names at the bottom.

"Not everybody's searching for a happy ever after ending," Bailey quipped, and then frowned into her now empty glass. "Hell, I'm not trying to look forward to an ending at all."

Victoria leaned forward, folding her arms on the table and resting her head there. "I used to dream about my wedding day. I was going to wear a pink dress. It's my favorite color and I didn't want to be a traditional bride. My bridesmaids would wear white. Ha!" She smiled. "Let them see how it feels to be all pristine and virginal."

Regan and Bailey giggled.

"I'm wearing all white from head to toe. A gown that hugs my boobs and fans out like Princess Diana's and sparkles like the moon. The groom and his men will be in black and the guests will be asked to wear black and white, or either. No other colors are allowed. I want it contemporary and chic and so romantic everyone will want to run out and find their own mate when it's over," Regan shared.

She blinked when both Bailey and Victoria were speechless as they stared at her.

"Dramatic much?" Bailey asked and then fell into fits of laughter.

Victoria followed suit and, despite the fact that she was aware they were making fun of her, Regan laughed as well.

They were all laughing until he stepped out of the shadows near the closed windows. He wore all black, so at first Regan didn't register him as a danger. She actually thought for a second that he was one of Devlin's guys. But no, he wasn't. Devlin's guys both had close cut hair and appeared to be a little more buff than this guy. He was big though, broad shoulders, thick midsection...not fat, but not workout toned either. His hair was longer, pulled back from his face. It was the face that sent the first spike of fear through Regan's chest. A scruffy beard, thick eyebrows and as boxed-shaped face wearing a smile that promised nothing but danger.

Regan sat up,. She reached for Victoria, tapping her arm until Victoria lifted her head from the table. Bailey followed their gaze.

"Oh shit!" she cursed and reached for the empty champagne bottle.

She held it just as he approached the table and lifted her arm to swing.

"This is gonna hurt a lot more than a bottle of cheap wine," he muttered, pointing the gun to Bailey's head.

Lights were out on the first floor in every room except the ballroom. All the doors were locked and so were the windows. All they had to do now was go back into the dining room and pick up the women, then they'd all board the service elevator up to the third floor where they would sleep for the night.

"I'll take the first shift," Devlin told the others as they walked through the ballroom doors. "I don't have anyone waiting in bed for me."

Trent paused. He'd been walking in front of Devlin right beside Ben, and Gavin was behind, right beside Devlin. The four of them had been making the final rounds for the evening. He'd long since sent Tia up to bed with Trevor.

"Do I detect a hint of jealousy?" Trent asked his long-time friend.

Devlin scowled. "In your dreams."

The others chuckled.

"The last thing I want is someone wrapped around my neck like a slow moving noose," Devlin continued, his tone gruff and angry as usual.

"Yeah, but they're so warm and soft," Gavin started. "Especially on nights like this."

The wind had picked up tremendously outside. Esmerelda's arrival was now predicted at sometime around dawn. He hoped like hell they could sleep through the worst of it and possibly be having a delicious breakfast during the tail end. Camelot was like a fortress, its highest points reaching upward like arms from the mountains and a plush green forest. Earlier, he'd had a chance to go down to the loading dock where the jeeps were being stored.

"I'll be walking the floors, keeping watch," Devlin replied. "I won't need to be kept warm."

They were halfway across the room when Ben asked, "Speaking of the ladies, where'd they go?"

Trent looked around the room. "Maybe they went up without you," he said slowly and not too convincingly.

"We told them to wait," Gavin added, moving away from the others and going towards the table where the women had been sitting when they left. For the most part, the space had been cleared. Only confetti that had been on the tables was still scattered across the floor.

"That Bailey doesn't listen to a word anybody says," Devlin added. But he too had moved, walking towards the bar. "She doesn't even remember to take her shoes with her." He picked up the green high heels, holding them so the others could see.

"She wouldn't leave her shoes down here," Trent said.

Gavin was shaking his head, a sick feeling forming in the pit of his stomach.

"Victoria would have waited for me," Ben was saying. "She knew how important it was for us to stick...together."

At the hesitation in his tone, Gavin and Trent both turned to Ben, who was reaching into his pocket to pull out his cell phone. Trent had directed everyone to turn off their phones, everyone but Ben. They watched as he pressed a button and then they all cringed as he cursed like none of them had ever heard before. In the next instant, Ben had fallen to his knees, the cell phone dropping on the floor beside him.

"He's got them! That bastard's got them!" Ben roared.

Devlin picked up the phone while Trent went to Ben's side.

"I'm going to kill him! I'm going to put this gun in that asshole's mouth and watch his brains explode," Ben continued, coming back up to a standing position and reaching behind his back to where he had a gun tucked in his pants.

"How did he get in here?" Trent asked with a frown.

Gavin took the phone from Devlin, stared down at the picture of Bailey, Victoria and Regan all tied together in what looked like a shed. His hands shook as he held the phone, his stomach churning with dread. In his mind all he could see was a gun to Regan's head. All he could think about was the bullet that had pierced his father's temple. He wanted to yell with fury, to get his own gun and go out and hunt this bastard down with Ben!

"There's an abandoned little hut deep in the forest," he said. "It's right at the mountain's base."

"What? Why didn't you tell me this before?" Devlin raged.

"You said you searched the entire island," was Gavin's retort. "The entire island would mean the forest and the base of that mountain!"

"We did go through the forest and there was no hut," Trent told Gavin. "How did you know it was out there?"

All three men looked at him suspiciously. Gavin felt their gazes like hot pricks against his skin. He was the outsider here, regardless of the fact that Devlin wasn't a blood relation.

Whatever his station or title, Gavin didn't give a damn what they were thinking. All that mattered to him was Regan's safety and the safety of her cousin and Victoria. The guys could stand here and toss accusations his way all they wanted.

Bending down, Gavin retrieved his own gun, the one he'd kept tucked under his pants at his left leg. He may not have followed in his father's footsteps and become a cop, but he'd gone to the firing range every chance he could, which usually turned out to be once or twice a month, and had a license to carry a concealed weapon. Well, now that weapon wasn't so concealed.

The moment Gavin moved, Devlin drew his weapon and Ben raised his arm, aiming his at Gavin.

"Did you let Vega into our house?" Ben asked him.

Gavin stood up straight. He checked his weapon, even though he knew two others were pointed directly at him. "I'm going to ignore this entire line of questioning because I've known this family all of my life and because I love Regan more than anything I've ever had in my life. Now if you three want to stand here and keep doubting me and my intentions, you go right ahead." He released the safety on his gun, checked the chamber and turned away from them.

"I'm going," he said before heading out of the ballroom.

Ace and Rio had been called from their posts along with two of the officers who had stayed on the island with them. Trent was fuming. The question of how Vega had gotten into the house that was being protected by four of the deadliest men in the world along with police officers was not sitting well with him. They'd locked all the doors, locked the windows and bolted everything down in anticipation of Esmerelda and her Category Three force winds. And Vega had walked in and walked out with three of their women.

He wasn't just fuming. Trent was seeing red and ready to kill.

It had been Trent who stepped forward and grabbed Gavin by the shoulders as the man had headed out of the ballroom.

"Hold on. You can't just go off half-cocked. You have no idea what you're walking into with this guy."

Gavin opened his mouth to speak, his gaze at his gun and then back to Trent's face.

"And that's no match for the storm that's brewing out there. Visibility's going to be a bitch even if you weren't blinded by rage. Just chill. Nobody believes you were a part of this," he told Gavin.

Trent turned back to Ben to reiterate his words. "Nobody believes you were working with Vega."

Ben shrugged. "Trust isn't at the forefront of my mind right now. Vega was in the main house and he's been here. Pardon me if I'm trying to find out how."

"It wouldn't be someone like Gavin," Devlin said, stepping from between where Ace and Rio had entered through a side door. "Vega's a trained killer. If he has an accomplice, it would be someone he thought would easily fit in, someone nobody would question. And since the Donovans are known to be a bunch of arrogant men, he'd most likely choose a woman."

Trent nodded. "He's right. The fact that we have at least thirty vendors that none of us know personally on the island gives him a large pool to select from."

"We're standing here talking about how he got in instead of heading out to find him!" Gavin yelled. "I thought you guys were trained killers. I can't tell from the way you're just standing around."

Trent tossed him a warning glare. He knew Gavin wasn't working with Vega and he also knew the man's father was a decorated officer. But standing right here, right now, Gavin Lucas was a chef, holding a gun, and Trent was the soldier. If he had to tie his ass up to keep him from running off without assistance, he would.

"You're the only one that knows where this hut is, so we need you with us, but you're gonna have to agree to follow our lead. You're not trained to track and kill a murderer, Gavin. Right now you're acting with your emotions. That's the fastest way to get you, Regan and the others killed." Trent had spoken in a calm, decisive tone, the one he'd learned from the SEALs. Then Dev moved closer to Gavin, touching his forearm.

"Stand down for a few seconds. Let us get some things in place and we'll head out to get them." Devlin nodded, waiting for Gavin's answer.

Trent turned to the others, not needing to see Gavin's response. Devlin was a commander, pure and simple. He already knew that Gavin was standing down.

CHAPTER 18

"Bitch!" Vega yelled the moment Bailey's left foot connected with his jaw.

Regan had watched her cousin do this amazing turn and kick thing she was sure she'd only seen on television. For a few seconds, Vegan had stumbled.

But the man was big, tall and solid, so he didn't fall to the ground the way he was probably supposed to. He held firmly to the gun and, just as Bailey was about to strike again, he reached out his free hand and smacked her. She hit the floor of the hut where he'd led them with a sickening thud and Regan fell to her knees to help her.

"Don't you fucking move!" he yelled at Victoria. "Get over there in that corner."Regan looked up to see Victoria shaking as she looked at them then back to Vega once more. Regan nodded, telling her to go ahead and cooperate. They didn't have much of a choice.

"Bastard," Bailey murmured, holding her palm to her cheek as she struggled to sit up.

"Shut up, Supergirl! Next time I'll shoot," he said over his shoulder to Bailey.

Then he threw a pile of rope at Victoria. The action stunned her and she stumbled back a couple of steps. She was still wearing the silver pumps she'd worn with her asymmetric ice blue dress. The shoes were now marred with mud, the dress wrinkled and splotched as they'd traveled through the throngs of the forest to get to the little hut.

The hut sat just below the fall of the cliff where Regan loved to sit and watch the water. She knew this spot very well, could walk out here in her sleep, and that's how she'd known exactly where they were heading. Unfortunately, because this was her favorite spot, she'd never shared this knowledge with anyone. Nobody would know where to look for them.

Regan and Bailey both got to their feet.

"You are such a coward!" Bailey yelled at Vega.

The man looked at her with pure hatred in his eyes. He blinked once, twice, and then laughed. His lips turned in a twisted and gross way that showed off surprisingly straight teeth.

"And you're a dumb bitch," he snarled. "Now we're even."

Bailey would have jumped at him again, but Regan held her back. "Stop it! Are you trying to get yourself killed?" she whispered.

"He's a coward," Bailey retorted. "If he wanted us dead, he would have shot us in the ballroom. This is just a game. His way of getting back at Ben."

Vega laughed. "I'll change that to smart bitch. Now tie them up," he directed Victoria.

"You should just let them go, Vega," Victoria said, holding the rope in both her hands. "They have nothing to do with this."

His head snapped back to her so fast that Regan thought if they were in some sick adult-only cartoon, it might have fallen right off.

"No, they don't have anything to do with this. And neither did you!" he yelled.

Then he took the three or four steps that separated him from Victoria and was right in her face. "All you had to do was work on some other cases, look pretty in some other courtroom. But oh no, you had to come switching your tight little ass into my courtroom. You had to prove you could do what that other prick of a prosecutor couldn't."

Regan could see Victoria swallow, her hands still shaking. But Victoria never backed down, never looking away from Vega.

"I did my job," she told him flatly.

"And I did mine!" he bellowed in reply.

Bailey and Regan jumped at that moment. Their intention was to ambush him, but he turned too fast. His gun arm was stretched forward and positioned right at Regan's forehead this time. Everything inside her shivered and she felt like her legs would give out at any moment. Outside the wind blew harder, shaking the entire structure of the hut. Maybe she was shaking as well because she was scared out of her mind.

Victoria threw the ropes at him from behind, trying to get them over his head, but she was much shorter than he was. He turned on her then and fired.

Regan screamed, moving towards Victoria but stopped by Bailey's tight grip on her arm. She watched in horror as Victoria staggered back into the wall.

"Victoria," she whispered.

Then Vega turned to them. "Get the hell over there and sit your asses down before I burn this house down with all of you meddling bitches inside!"

Regan backed up and felt Bailey right beside her. He approached them both then with the rope in his hands. In seconds, they were tied and sitting on the cool floor back to back. Across the room Victoria moaned, which for Regan was a good sign because that meant she was still alive.

The hut shook against the raging winds again and Regan wondered how long that would hold true for any of them.

⸎⸎⸎⸎⸎

"She's bleeding too much," Bailey whispered to Regan after some time had passed.

"I thought you said she was shot in the arm," Regan replied. They'd been tied back to back and Regan wasn't facing Victoria.

Every now and then, between the howling winds and the start of belting rain, they could hear her moan. But they couldn't get to her. Vega paced the floor, not in a restless or nervous manner, but with sure strides as if he were simply waiting.

"He'll come for you," he said suddenly, and Regan looked to him.

The hut was dark. He had a lantern on the table, but that wasn't emanating much light. He still held his gun and every now and then would point it at either one of them and laugh.

"He could have just represented me for that second case, got me off and then we both would have lived happily ever after." He chuckled. "But he couldn't do that. He couldn't do the job I'd hired him to do."

"He wouldn't represent a killer," Victoria said threw whispered gasps.

"Don't waste your breath on him, Victoria," Bailey told her. "He's a second rate asshole that can't even get the job he's supposed be too good at right. He tried to kill you before and missed, didn't he? Now he shoots you in the arm? What the hell kind of killer-for-hire is he?"

Bailey continued to taunt him and Regan's heart continued to beat a fitful rhythm. She knew what Bailey was trying to do. They'd used this kind of intimidation with their cousins when they'd played as kids. But they weren't in the backyard or at the playground this time. This was for real, and Regan wasn't totally sure it would work. They were tied up. Victoria was bleeding in a corner. How in the world did she hope to get a jump on this guy in their position? Regardless of her questions, Regan worked the ropes.

Parker loved practical jokes and magic when they were growing up. One of his favorite magic tricks was the girl who escaped from the wooden box. He'd tie Regan up good and tight then shut her in a box, locking it from all around. Then he'd open the box again and it would be empty. Three seconds later, Regan would come out with no ropes and a big smile, having untied all of Parker's knots and crawled out the back panel of the box. When she turned ten, Regan figured magic tricks were stupid and refused to play with Parker any longer. But she never forgot how to untie knots.

"I should have shot you in your pretty little face," he said to Bailey.

He came closer and Regan turned so she could see what he was doing to her cousin. The nozzle of the gun ran the length of Bailey's temple and down her jaw to rest over her lips. "Right here, I could shoot you and shut your mouth for good."

"But you won't," Bailey said and Regan bit back a curse. "You won't kill me because you'll need all the leverage you can get to get off this island."

"I'm shooting my way off this damned island," he spat.

Bailey shook her head. "You're going out in a body bag you bastard!"

"Shut up slut!" he yelled, slapping Bailey across the face again.

Bailey jerked at the exact moment Regan freed the knot at her hands. Another minute and both their hands would be free. But before that could happen there was a banshee-like scream from across the room then there was crashing and cursing.

"Hurry up, Regan! She's got him down!" Bailey yelled.

Regan turned to see Vega lying on the floor with Victoria holding a chair over him and kicking the gun that had fallen from his hands out of the way. Regan's hands moved frantically and a very impatient Bailey finally had enough room where she could simply jerk free. The first movement tugged Regan along a little and almost pulled a shoulder out of its socket, but she hurriedly freed her hands as well and scrambled to a standing position to help them.

Bailey grabbed the gun just as Vega lurched upward and grabbed Victoria's arm, the one where he'd shot her. She screamed and dropped the chair, her knees buckling until she fell to the floor.

On a loud rumble the entire hut shook. The shudders that served as shields for the windows were ripped free and glass shattered everywhere. Wind ripped through the tiny space, knocking them all back. Debris flew everywhere as the outside suddenly came in. Later Regan would wonder how she ever heard his voice over all the noise. How through the wild thumping of her heart, Victoria's screams of agony and Bailey's curses to Vega to let Victoria go, all amidst the raging wind and rain, did she ever manage to hear Gavin calling her.

But she did and she couldn't wait to reply, "Help! Gavin! Over here!"

⁂

Gavin had led the way. Ben was right on his heels. Both of them had guns drawn. It had been one hell of a trek moving through the forest in the wind. And then, when it started to rain, they were pelted by shards of coolness. The ground grew muddy and slick quickly. Branches that normally may have cracked beneath their feet were now lodged in mud and served no other purpose than to trip them as they maneuvered their way through.

But nothing could stop Gavin. Nothing could stop any of them, he thought. The others were right behind him, following his lead, all with flashlights and firearms. They'd started out in the right direction and he'd been sure not to stray from the path he'd followed Regan on the other day. The hut sat at the base of that cliff she liked, so he assumed there was a spot he could turn off and head downhill towards it.

With his next step, he found the spot and went tumbling down, his feet lifting upward as his butt hit the ground hard. He yelled for the others "Hill!" and heard a few other grunts behind them. He'd just stood up and taken a second to catch his breath when he looked in the direction of where the hut should be. He couldn't see it. Gavin turned. He still didn't see it. He turned again, until he'd made two complete circles, then he decided to call her.

"If she's out there, she's never gonna hear you over all this," Dev said from somewhere near his right.

Gavin ignored him and called to Regan again.

Then she replied.

"That way! That way!" Ben yelled, pointing his flashlight to the left. They all took off at a run.

The hut was falling apart, the wind grabbing thatches from the roof, the walls and the front door and tossing them around. It was a struggle for Gavin to even walk, so he attempted to run instead. She was in there with a killer and that was all that mattered to him.

The men had just cleared what used to be the doorway, flashlights streaming inside. Water drenched him and Gavin had to blink to try and see clearly. What he saw would forever be emblazoned in his mind. Bailey held a gun. She fired once, twice, three times. Regan lurched forward, reaching for something or someone. A piece of siding ripped free from the wall, smacking into Regan's back and sending her sprawling across the ground. Victoria screamed and screamed and Gavin pulled the trigger.

More loud noise, Victoria thought, and closed her eyes. There was motion all around her as she struggled to keep her eyes open, to not give in to the darkness that threatened to engulf her.

"I love you, baby. Stay with me. Stay with me. Please."

He said those words over and over and at first she wondered why. Then the numbness in her arm jolted a memory. She'd been shot. Ramone Vega had shot her. Breathing was difficult. She felt cold all over. When her eyes fluttered open again, she saw him. It was a blurry vision but she knew it was him.

"Ben," she whispered. "Ben."

He smiled down at her. "Yes, baby, I'm here."

She tried to smile, wasn't sure how it looked, but it felt almost good. "Where am I?" she asked.

"Coast Guard helicopter. We're going to get you to a hospital," Ben told her.

She closed her eyes and this time felt the warmth of tears streaming down her face. "You're always going to the hospital with me," she said with a chuckle that caused pain to radiate from too many parts of her body to continue.

When she winced, Ben's hand tightened in hers. "Shhh, shhh, baby. It's alright. There's no other place I'd rather be."

A few moments went by where Victoria simply listened to the sound of the chopper, thought she felt the chill of the wind blowing and prayed. Or more like gave thanks. Barring the current circumstances, she'd never been happier or felt more alive than she'd been with Ben. She'd been afraid to meet his family, afraid they would be on some unreachable level from her, and she'd been wrong. They'd embraced her and her relationship with Ben long before she'd been able to. Bailey and Regan had fought to save her life as well as their own, as if they were all related and had known each other forever.

And now this man was here with her again. Promising to not leave her side, confessing his love for her. She replayed Regan's advice in her head, "Don't mess up a good thing with doubts that aren't founded." None of the doubts she'd ever had about Ben had been founded. During these last few days and weeks, he'd done everything in his power to make her believe that he loved her, that she and her heart were safe with him.

"Ben..." She called his name slowly.

"Yes, baby?"

"You might be going to the hospital with me again in a few months," she told him, cracking her eyes open so she could see his face.

"What?" he asked. "Why? You planning on getting shot in the arm again?"

He'd smiled and her heart had filled. She loved his smile, his eyes, his strong chin. She loved everything about him.

"I love you," she admitted finally.

His smile broadened as he leaned forward to kiss her. A second before he could touch his lips to hers, she said, "I think I'm pregnant."

CHAPTER 19

"If you keep frowning at me I might get a complex," Bailey quipped.

Devlin had walked into the living room where she'd been sitting after breakfast the next morning. Ben and Victoria had called a couple of hours ago to announce that Victoria was going to be just fine and also that she was pregnant. They were getting married the moment they arrived back in Las Vegas. Aunt Alma was already beside herself with wedding plans. Congratulating sentiments and pats on the back were in abundance throughout the morning. Bailey's head throbbed from all the attention and she'd longed for a few moments alone.

And now Devlin Bonner was here looking at her like she'd just crawled out from under the mud. Truth be told, he'd been looking at her like that since the moment Trent had introduced them. At times she'd thought maybe those looks were different…nah, that definitely was not the case. Right now the scowl he was wearing was saying anything but "I'm into you."

"You're too smart to get a complex," he said, moving with assured steps until he stood directly in front of her.

"Thanks for the compliment, even though I'm sure that's not what brought you in here." She sighed heavily. "Trent's probably upstairs helping Tia pack. The next ferry will be here first thing tomorrow morning to pick us up."

All of the vendors had boarded the first ferry that had come this morning. That's when they were told that because of the cleanup efforts post Esmerelda, there most likely would not be another one out to the island until tomorrow. As that was the day they were all scheduled to leave anyway, the family was

content to stay especially since the killer who had threatened
their trip had been zipped in a body bag and carried off the
island by the Coast Guard last night, just as Bailey had told
him he'd be.

Devlin knelt in front of her, his warm chocolate eyes
glaring. He was bald with a wicked scar along the left side of
his face. Her fingers tingled as she stared at that scar, a knife
wound she'd assessed. And he wouldn't want her touching it,
she was sure of that. That was fine. She really didn't want to
touch it anyway.

"You did good out there," he said through gritted teeth.
"Real good."

Bailey inhaled deeply. Trent had pulled her into him so fast
in that hut that the gun had fallen out of her hands. She hadn't
seen Vega's body, not since she aimed and pulled the trigger.
Trent wouldn't let her. She'd heard other shots around her and
wondered later which one had actually killed him.

"You guys showed up and saved the day," she said while
trying to keep her composure. It wouldn't do any good to fall
apart in front of this guy. It wouldn't do to fall apart at all.

Devlin shook his head. "No. Your shots killed him. Three,
center mass. He was dead before he hit the ground. Our shots
luckily just went into the house and didn't hit anybody else.
Visibility was crap out there."

She nodded, relief, pride, and just a little bit of banked fear
sifting quickly through her. "Yeah, it was."

"But like I said, you did good."

She figured this was his second compliment and she'd look
ungrateful if she didn't acknowledge them both. "Thank you."

"He had it coming, you know. He was going to kill you."

Bailey shook her head. "No. He was going to kill Victoria
and Ben. He was a killer-for-hire. I've seen them before. They
kill who they're told to kill. It's a job, not a hobby. They don't
get any real joy from it, they just do it. He wouldn't have killed
anybody other than his targets." She knew that and had been
more courageous towards Vega because of it. She also had no
doubt that, if pushed to the brink, he would've definitely hurt
her a lot more than the two slaps that had caused both her ears
to ring.

"That's all I wanted to say," Devlin told her.

"Okay. Thanks again," she said.

But he didn't move. And she didn't move. They just sat there, staring at each other like they were in the midst of some sort of communication. When he finally stood up and walked out of the room, Bailey frowned. That was no communication. She was just as baffled by the man that was Devlin Bonner at this point as she was the first day she'd met him.

❧❧❧❧❧

There hadn't been a moment for Gavin and Regan to be alone. From the time they'd returned from the hut, she'd been immediately embraced by her parents, her mother whisking her away for a hot shower and tea. Before that, Gavin had watched Ben boarding the helicopter with Victoria. He'd seen the love and the complete torture on the other man's face and could relate wholeheartedly to what he must have gone through.

"Lucas!"

Gavin heard his name being called just as he'd turned from the helicopter. Ben came running towards him. When the two men were face-to-face, rain still batting at their tired bodies, Ben extended his hand.

"I was wrong to accuse you," he said. "You're a good guy. Unless you hurt my cousin, then I'll have to get my gun again."

The last was said with a smile. But it hadn't mattered. Gavin had appreciated Ben's words, all of them, with or without the friendly gesture of a handshake and a smile. He'd accepted Ben's hand. "You just remember you're not the only one with a gun."

They both laughed then and the Coast Guard called for Ben to come on if he was riding along.

"Take care of Victoria," Gavin said. "She's been through a lot this evening."

Ben nodded. "We all have. I'm just glad it's over."

Gavin had agreed and had gone back to Camelot thinking that he and Regan would spend the remainder of the night together. That hadn't quite worked out the way he'd planned.

At 6 in the morning, there was a knock on his door.

"Storm's passed. We need to get the boards down and assess the damage. You can start in the kitchen," Linc had told him.

No "Good morning." No "How are you doing?" Just get up and get to work. Gavin hadn't argued because he knew Linc wouldn't have come to him unless he considered him a part of the family. It wasn't that Gavin needed another family. No, his mother and sisters were enough. But there had always been something about the Donovans, a connection that had begun with his father, that kept pulling him back in their direction. Now that he'd confessed his love to Regan, he realized how beneficial it would be to have the entire family's blessing for their relationship. This morning was a sign that just might be happening.

Regan had spent most of the day with the other women while Gavin had remained in the kitchen. Windows had been blown out and some of the equipment damaged. He either wrote reports or took new inventories throughout the day. His assistants prepared sandwiches for lunch and took them out to the family. Gavin wanted something more for dinner and so spent some time doing prep work for that.

The meal had gone smoothly, with the senior Donovans thanking him and Regan's mother pulling him to the side afterwards.

"I don't have to tell you that you're a magician in that kitchen," Carolyn said, tucking her hand through his arm as they walked outside.

"Thank you, ma'am," he replied respectfully. This wasn't his first time speaking with Carolyn or being alone with her for that matter. Still, this time felt a little different.

"It's amazing how clear and beautiful today was after the mess it was last night," she said looking out over the back balcony that could be accessed from the dining room.

"Mother Nature has a sense of humor after all," he said lightly.

"Yes, I guess she does."

They continued to look out to the water, now dark with shimmers of moonlight dancing across its surface. It was definitely a beautiful sight, but Gavin was positive this wasn't the reason Carolyn had brought him out here.

"Regan asked for you last night," she began finally.

"I helped Devlin and the others keep water from flooding the basement," he said, thinking how lame that statement actually was.

"I think she's in love with you," Carolyn told him.

"I don't know about that," Gavin replied truthfully.

"What do you know about my daughter, Gavin? I know our families have been intertwined for years now. I've seen you with my boys and in these last few years around Regan more and more. What are your plans where she is concerned?"

And he'd thought Reginald had been blunt and to the point.

"I love Regan, Mrs. Donovan. I've loved her for quite a while now. It just took me a minute to accept it."

Carolyn nodded. "You children believe there's so much time out there. You think you can wait until the next day or the next to do and say the things that are most important." She turned then and grasped his chin between her fingers, turning his face so that he looked directly at her. "Tomorrow is not promised to you. I know you can relate to that considering how things turned out with your father. So you understand what I'm trying to say, don't you?"

Gavin nodded this time. "I think I do, ma'am."

"Regan is my only daughter. She's stubborn and she's competitive and she could worry the hair right off your head." She chuckled after that. "But she's a good girl and she needs a good man to look after her, to make sure she doesn't overdo it, that her competitive streak doesn't get the best of her."

"You're talking about the medication she's on," he said, feeling as if he could definitely trust Mrs. Donovan. Gavin hadn't said anything to Regan about the pill bottles he'd spotted on her dresser, hadn't had a moment to actually, all things considering. But he wanted to know what was wrong with her and how he could help.

Carolyn let her arms fall to the side. "She's got high blood pressure, Gavin. Too much stress going on in her life, too many worries on her mind. I guess it was inevitable since it also runs in our family."

"Regan's a fighter," he said, looking out to the water once more.

"She is, and that's why she's planning to fight this condition the same way she approaches everything else in life— head-on, like a bulldozer." Carolyn gave a quick chuckle.

"Which won't work because that's what got her to this point in the first place," he added.

"You're absolutely right." Carolyn patted him on the arm then. "I knew you were good for her. I told Reginald that year Regan came home from college that she'd changed. And when you came over for her graduation dinner, I could see you were the reason why."

He opened his mouth to speak and Carolyn shushed him.

"You're too young to try and pull something over these old eyes. I could see the sparks between you two even through the battle Regan had decided to create surrounding you. I prayed you two would see it sooner rather than later. I guess fate took control after all."

An hour later Gavin was still reminiscing about that conversation, still hearing the blessing in Carolyn's voice as clear as the day's sky. Now, if he could only find a second to sit with Regan, to hold her hand and tell her how he really felt and what he wanted for their future.

❧❧❧

Pain ripped through her shoulder, radiating down her back where it joined in the pain at her side. She'd been shot. Last night, she'd been about to make her way into the hut to help Vega with those Donovan chicks. Of course, he hadn't picked up the one she'd wanted, the one she'd been waiting to get her hands on, but she was long past caring about which member of this family she hurt. As long as they suffered, she'd be happy, or at least partially so.

Instead she'd been shot and had lay in a cave at the mountain's base, bleeding until the storm passed. It had taken her all day to make her way through the forest she'd come to know well in the last few days until she could finally see her destination clearly. The Donovan house was lit up like a beacon in the night, standing like a mighty fortress with the stuck-up rich folk safely tucked inside. Or at least they thought they were safe. They couldn't be further from the truth.

Sarah laughed.

It hurt like hell, but she laughed anyway.

The wound at her side was just a flesh wound, but damn if it wasn't bleeding like a major artery rested there. Her shoulder was another matter. The bullet had entered from behind, so she couldn't really tell if it had gone through her shoulder or her back. That didn't concern her as much as the period of unconsciousness she'd been experiencing since being shot, and now her limbs were going numb in intervals. She probably wouldn't make it off this island alive. And that was okay.

Salvatore "Big Sal" Pena had owed her a favor. After jumping bail in Miami, Sarah had needed a place to lay low, so she'd called on Big Sal. He'd flown her to Vegas, paid the rent on a tiny apartment and was supposed to hook her up with some money men to get her back in the game. Some thought she was too old, but she could go back to the porn business. Sex didn't get old and as long as she wasn't shriveled up and decrepit, some guy could still get it up at the sight of her on screen—she was sure of it. One of Big Sal's men had mentioned their hit man getting popped for murder and possibly spending the rest of his life in jail all because of some attorney named Ben Donovan who'd shafted him. The name had rung an immediate bell and Sarah thought back to Sean and Dion Donovan, the too-cute brothers who ran *Infinity* Magazine and had ultimately put in a bid for *Onyx* Publications—the company Sarah had built from scratch. She thought about her brother, Patrick, who was still sitting in a federal prison for the schemes he'd run on those dumbass old people and the way his ex-wife Tate had snitched on him and she instantly wanted blood. Tate thought she was all high and mighty now that she was going to marry a Donovan, but Sarah had other plans for her. She had other plans for all of those high society assholes.

She was still on her feet, but the world around her wobbled as she moved. She'd stayed in the trees, waiting until it was dark so they wouldn't see her coming. Their guard would be down now that Vega was dead. That sorry bastard hadn't wanted her around from the start, thought he was too good to be with the likes of her. What he didn't realize was that Sarah was a professional as well, with a resume just a bit more colorful than his. When she was a junior in high school, she'd shot and killed her first man—the liquor store owner who wouldn't give her a bottled water so her brother wouldn't die of thirst. She'd put a bullet right in the center of his forehead and then stole the water and all the money in the cash register.

As Sabine Ravenell, Sarah had been able to clean up, to walk and talk with the rich and famous as if she were actually one of them. But Patrick had always told her trying to fit in was a mistake. He'd wanted them to take their money and go, live high off the hog in some pretty fucking place like this. Now, Patrick could only stare at four cement walls in a nine by nine cell.

Sarah cursed, flattening her back against the wall right next to the patio door. She could hear voices and looked up to the sky to thank whatever deity was up there and watching out for her at the moment. She moved the gun to her good hand, which was her left. She was right-handed but she'd never be able to lift her right arm to get off a good enough shot. Aim didn't matter as long as she killed some of those bastards. Going out with a bang was about to have a whole new meaning.

Regan had just taken Gavin's offered hand into hers. She hadn't seen him all day, but had thought about him constantly. Last night she'd wanted nothing more than to lay next to him, but her mother and father were hovering as if she were an infant. Bailey's dad hadn't had that opportunity since she'd locked herself in her bathroom the minute she returned to the house. Trent had been beside himself with anger about them being taken and felt pride mixed with a healthy dose of fear and pain over Bailey's kill. Brock had also been worried about his sister and how she would deal with the first death at her hands. Brandon had remarked, "After all the years of looking for danger under every rock, Bailey had finally found it."

The brothers and Uncle Albert were afraid she wouldn't deal with it as well as she'd always planned.

Victoria and Ben had headed for the hospital and Regan was the last to be pampered, but not by her man. Yes, she was thinking of Gavin as her man, claiming him as so. That's why she'd happily taken his hand when he'd come into the living room and found her sitting alone on the love seat.

Across the room, Noelle, who had not yet left for her honeymoon—the newlyweds were going to Europe, leaving from Baltimore early Tuesday morning—was at the piano playing tunes she'd just learned. Taking piano lessons had been her idea, thinking it was way past time she had some culture in her life. Of course, Jade and Brock had both laughed at that. But right at this moment Karena and Sam were both leaning over the back of the piano, wine glasses in hand and singing along to the slowest version of "Twinkle Twinkle Little Star" Regan had ever heard.

All of the kids had been put to bed, but the seniors were in the living room sharing in wine and/or coffee. Trent and Tia had turned in with their daughters, along with Camille and Josiah. Sean and Tate had turned in with Briana, while Dion and Lyra had gone to bed just before them. Brynne's announcement to her parents hadn't gone well this morning, so she'd been scarce all day. And Brandon and Adam were off to a corner talking. About what, Regan had no idea, but they looked serious.

Then glass was splattering and crashing, taking her attention away from everything else. For the second time in her life, Regan heard gunshots, and they were too freakin' close for comfort. Gavin almost tore her arm out of the socket as he yanked her to the floor, covering her body with his. There was screaming and more glass and then there was silence, an eerie silence in which Regan thought everybody could hear her racing heartbeat.

The laugh was cold and shrill, bringing to mind instantly the wicked witch in *Snow White*, the book Regan had read to the girls before coming downstairs for nightcaps and hopefully some time with Gavin.

"Got y'all running scared, don't I?" was the question that vibrated through the room. "Or did I shoot you all good and dead?"

Gavin shifted slightly. He was still on top of Regan and pressing down so tightly her shoulder blades felt glued to the floor. But she could turn her head, and when she did she saw legs, wobbling legs covered with mud and leaves. One arm was shaking so much, Regan wondered how the gun in the attacker's hand was remaining upright. The other arm was plastered to the woman's side. There was blood mixed with the mud and the attacker's hair was matted to her dirty face. Regan had no idea who she was, and then she saw the eyes just as the woman opened her mouth to speak again.

"Where are they? Where's Sean and Dion? They thought they'd gotten rid of me. Well tell them I'm baaacckkk!"

"Oh my god. It's Sabine Ravenell," Regan whispered.

"No you're not, bitch!" Noelle screamed just before swinging the lamp she'd picked up, bashing Sabine over the back of the head.

As Sabine hit the floor, gun rolling from her hand, everybody looked at Noelle. Her eyes were blazing with anger, her lips curled as she'd spoken.

"What?" she asked. "I'm sick of everybody trying to wreck my damned wedding!"

Regan wanted to laugh, she really did, but just then Trent and what she now referred to as the cavalry—Devlin, Ace and Rio—had come running into the room.

A few moments later Sabine was cuffed and lifted to her feet and then basically dragged out of the room. Regan had no idea where Devlin would take her since there were no more ferries on or off the island tonight. Maybe he would call the Coast Guard again. Those guys had to be growing tired of the Donovans and coming out to Sansonique.

Gavin pulled Regan to her feet. "Are you alright?" he asked, his eyes searching every part of her they could get to while still in a room full of her family members—members that he should probably go and check on, but she was his first concern.

"Yes, I am," she said while nodding her head. "I'm fine, thanks to you."

She'd cupped his face in her hands to keep him from searching anyplace else.

"I'm fine," he said with a smile. "I'd like one second to be with you without running from killers or fighting hurricanes or getting warnings from brothers and cousins. But other than that, I'm okay."

Regan smiled. "I'd say ditto, but I haven't been getting any warnings. Maybe when you take me home to meet your family, your sisters will have some for me."

His smile spread. "I can't wait to take you home to my family, Regan. But right now I'm more eager to be alone with you," he told her, moving closer so that their bodies were now touching.

"We should stick around to see if we can help in any way. I can't believe Sabine was here too."

"You know her?" he asked, looking towards the door Devlin had carried her through.

"Yes. She was the one trying to buy *Infinity* a few months ago. Then she kidnapped Briana and shot Sean. I guess she figured she wasn't finished yet."

Gavin shrugged and rubbed the back of his head. "I think she was the one who hit me. Her voice sounds awfully familiar."

"Oh really? I wish you would have told me that sooner. I might have been the one to whack her with the lamp," she said seriously.

"You would do that for me?" he asked, rubbing his thumb over her bottom lip.

"Of course," she said, snaking a tongue out to tentatively touch the pad of his thumb. "I have no problem defending my man."

Gavin didn't want to let her go, not again anyway. It seemed like it had taken so long for him to finally find her today. But she wanted to check on Noelle and he desperately wanted to join in on the conversation with Sam, Trent, Dion and Sean.

"I can't believe she came after us again," Sean was saying. "She's crazier than I thought."

"How did she even get out of jail?" Dion asked from where he stood looking through the broken patio door.

"Probably made bail," Sam said glumly.

Gavin looked at the mess, the confetti-like glass splattered all over the floor accompanied by the trail of blood she'd tracked inside the house. "I guess jails aren't as good at keeping criminals inside as they used to be," he mumbled.

"Did you see that jacket she was wearing?" Sam asked.

The moment he'd arrived on the island, Gavin had no doubt Trent had briefed his partner. The man stood now, surveying the scene just like the cop he used to be.

"It has the caterer's logo on the back," Sam continued. "That's who was able to get into the house without being questioned."

"So she was working with Vega?" Gavin asked. "How would the two of them have known each other?"

Sam shrugged. "The Nationwide Criminals Network. I don't know but it's the only thing that makes sense. Vega couldn't have gotten past this security."

"Sabine Ravenell or Sarah Ann Dennison, whatever her damned name is, has crashed her last party," Sean stated firmly. "When I get back to Miami I'm going to make sure they put her crazy ass under the jail!"

"How's Tate taking this?" Dion asked.

Sean ran a hand down his face. "Lyra and my mom are with her now. I'm sure she's upset, probably blaming herself for this lunatic."

"Yeah, it's been like lunatics-r-us around here this week," Trent added. "Bet you'll never come to another Donovan Family Reunion," he directed at Gavin.

Despite the mood and what had transpired in the last twenty-four hours, Gavin chuckled. "Are you kidding? I'm hoping to be at every one from here on out."

To that, Trent tossed his head back and laughed. "If you can handle Regan, we'll gladly have you."

❧❧❧❧

His hands were like heaven, moving over her body with slow, sensuous strokes. The scent of jasmine wafted throughout the room as Regan lay on her stomach in the center of her bed. Gavin straddled her, massaging one of Jade's new moisturizers into her skin. She wasn't sure if it was the herbal ingredients in the product, the bone-tiredness she was feeling after a week of emotional distress and action overload or if it was simply the naked man with the magical hands that made her feel like drifting into a forty-eight hour deep sleep.

Almost two hours after the Sabine incident, the living room was back in some semblance of order, the patio door boarded up as it had been the previous night before the hurricane. Once again, all the women had been concerned about Noelle and once again Noelle had proven she was much more resilient than the average person.

"I'm just ready for my honeymoon. And the minute I get back I'm going to write a book about this week's events," she'd joked to Jade and Karena, who were on either side of her in case Noelle gave in to the stress of the week and simply collapsed.

Regan had gone over to make sure Noelle was okay and could only smile at her words.

"Nobody's going to believe it if you write it," Regan told her. "The truth is often so surreal, it's worse than fiction."

Karena was shaking her head. "You should read some of Deena's books. It's still hard for me to imagine my younger sister having such an imagination, and every time I say that she tells me it's not her imagination, that she and Max are really having sex like rabbits seven days a week."

To that all the women laughed, even Noelle, and Regan thought things might get back to normal for them soon.

Gavin had come to retrieve her soon after whisking her upstairs to her room before anything else could detract them, he'd told her. They hadn't been in that room for ten seconds before they were all over each other. It seemed almost strange to be in his arms, loving the feel of him inside of her, just a couple of hours after a woman had shot her way into their house and even more hours after she'd been held hostage by a hired killer. But the moment her release came, the moment Gavin tensed above her and they took that plunge together, she forgot all that, her mind totally and absolutely on him and, for some reason, rabbits.

"Feel good?" he asked.

"Mmmmm? Oh yes, it feels good," she mumbled as he massaged her shoulders, his thumbs applying pressure to the knot of tension at the base of her neck. "I need to put you on personal retainer."

"What you need to do is take more time for yourself," he said. "Balance your work with your personal life so you won't walk around so tense all the time."

"I'm not tense all the time," she replied in defense. "Not all the time," she reiterated when he was silent. "I just have a lot on my plate right now with Camille's show coming up and it being my first try at producing. Savian and Parker will freak if I mess this up."

"Savian and Parker and the rest of DNT will survive. They've had some shows flop before. Besides, it's Camille Davis Donovan. Who isn't going to want to see the woman behind the designs?" he asked her.

Regan lifted slightly from the pillow, craning her head so she could look back at him. "You follow fashion? You know who Camille is?"

He smiled. The one that made butterflies swarm like bees in the pit of her stomach and her nipples grow hard.

"I follow you, Regan. For as long as I can remember, I've followed everything you've done. From that paper in your tenth grade history class where you talked about Cleopatra's beauty and I silently declared no other woman could rival you in that department, to your first article in *Infinity* where you broke down the reason white after Labor Day was no longer a no-no."

Regan didn't know what to say. He'd been in her history class that day? How was that possible when he'd already graduated? And he'd read her article in *Infinity*, the one that had almost caused her mother to go into cardiac arrest. Carolyn Donovan was never wearing white after Labor Day and she was appalled her daughter would take an entire column explaining why she could.

"I don't know what to say," she whispered.

Gavin shook his head, pressing her back down against the bed. "Don't say anything. I'm just telling you that nothing is worth your health."

"My health is just fine." She waited a beat then lifted up again. "My mother told you, didn't she?"

"She didn't have to," he replied, easing her down once more. "I saw the pill bottles on your dresser and knew something was wrong. Then I overheard you talking that night after the rehearsal dinner. High blood pressure is manageable if you adjust your stress, improve your diet and chill out a little bit."

Regan thought about arguing for her privacy. She knew he'd shown up too fast that night after they'd heard the scream. She could become indignant about him taking the liberty to tell her how she needed to change her life. *Her* life! She was old enough to make her own decisions, to make whatever changes she deemed necessary to remain healthy. She was also smart enough to know when a man sincerely cared about her.

"Next time I have a doctor's appointment, I'll just let you and my mother know. It'll be a lot easier if you hear all the information regarding my health first hand," she quipped.

The sound of Gavin's chuckle relaxed her once more and she closed her eyes to his touch.

"I need to apologize to you, Regan," he said in a serious tone from behind her.

His hands were moving on either side of her spine, applying an intense pressure that made her go as limp as an old dishrag. Her head was turned, her face partially buried in the pillow.

"Apologize for what?" she asked in a voice distorted by the position of her mouth.

"I promised to show you romance, to properly court you like a man does when he's in love with a woman."

Her mind was a haze of sensations ranging from good to goddamn fabulous as he continued to work her tense muscles while they spoke.

"I don't need romance," she whispered.

"Really?" he asked, leaning down closer so that he whispered over her ear lobe as he spoke. "Then tell me what you need, Regan. Anything you want, I'll give you. Anything you desire, I'll make come true. I love you so much."

Regan shifted, turning so that she was now lying on her back, Gavin on top of her. She cupped his face, the way he so frequently did hers, and pulled him down closer.

"All I need is you," she replied. Then Regan decided to go one step further. She'd never been afraid of anything in her life until she'd slept with Gavin. And throughout their entire affair the one thing that had frightened her most was the moment he would decide the relationship had run its course. She thought that moment had arrived the day she saw him with Raquel and it had hurt her far more than she'd ever imagined. And instead of confronting the situation, Regan had done what she was so used to doing—she'd protected herself by walking away. If she could run fast enough, fear would never catch her. Only this time, Gavin had come after her. He hadn't stayed behind, letting her go as far and as long as she needed to.

She could have continued to push him away this week, made her stance perfectly clear and employed the help of her brother and cousins to get Gavin Lucas permanently out of her life. But that would have been running again. It would have been hiding from the feelings that had dogged her heels for so long.

"I love you, Gavin Lucas. I've loved you for so long it feels like I don't even need to say the words." He wanted to say something then, but she kissed him. A slow touch of the lips, a little taste of the tongue, and then she pulled back slightly to ask, "Will you marry me?"

He blinked and for three torturously long seconds she waited, wondering if she'd misread what he'd been trying to tell her all week, if maybe this wasn't what he really wanted. Maybe he'd only meant to reinstate their friends-with-benefits pact, maybe...

He kissed her this time—a soft touch, a gentle swipe of tongue across her top lip and then her bottom one as he leveraged himself on his elbows above her.

"Yes I'll marry you, Regan. And yes, you do need to say the words as often as I plan on saying them to you. I love you," he said, kissing her once more. "I love you." He kissed her again, his tongue delving inside her mouth for a quick taste this time.

She beat him to the punch the next time with, "And I love you."

The last kiss was deeper, filled with moans and whispers as his hands moved over her body and hers over his. The reunion and the wedding was over and hopefully so was the danger. But Regan and Gavin's lives together were just beginning.

EPILOGUE

Their bags were all packed. The reunion was over. It was Monday and the Donovans were all scheduled to leave Sansonique on the next two ferries scheduled to arrive. The Aunts were having their last cup of coffee in the kitchen while most of the younger bunch were in the game room spending their last few minutes together as a family.

The senior Donovans were out on the back terrace, standing in the very spot where Sabine Ravenell had shot her way into their house. The glass had been cleaned and Sabine had been picked up by the Coast Guard early in the morning. Devlin and his men had gone back with her to ensure she was taken to the appropriate authorities.

Albert stood in front of his brothers, doing what he'd hoped he'd never have to do. He'd held this with him all week, waiting for the right time to tell them. That time never seemed to appear as they dealt with one issue after another. But Albert knew he couldn't go back to Houston without warning his brothers, without showing them that a mistake made long ago had come back to haunt them.

"When did you get this?" Henry sat up in the chair, holding the piece of paper in his right hand.

Albert rubbed a hand down his bald head. When he was thirty three, his hair line had begun receding. Darla thought it made him look distinguished, along with the gray that had begun slowly making its appearance at his temples. Three days after burying his wife, he'd shaved his head and had been bald ever since.

"It was hand-delivered to my office last Friday afternoon," he said.

Henry, whose wife Beverly insisted looked like the black Sean Connery, passed the letter to his brother Reginald and looked at the oldest of the Donovan seniors.

"Did you give her money, Al?" he asked, his voice somber.

Al turned away from his brothers. Henry watched the rise and fall of his still broad shoulders, waiting for his reply.

"I thought this was over and done with," Bruce, the youngest, said with a shake of his head.

"I knew she'd never walk away quietly," Reginald added. "All those years ago I just had a feeling we hadn't seen the last of her."

"I thought you'd taken care of this," Henry said. "That's what you hired Anthony Lucas for, Reggie. You said he was going to handle this for us."

"And then Tony was killed!" Reginald replied, guilt still weighing heavily on his shoulders. "And then Darla," he added in a quieter tone. "I figured after all that went down she'd walk away. I thought she'd be too afraid to keep coming at us."

Al turned to them then, his face drawn, eyes a little watery. "Well, she's back and she still thinks we owe her something."

Henry stood slowly, shaking his head. "The only people entitled to Donovan money are the Donovans that worked hard to make it. I don't give a damn what she thinks she has on us. I'm not paying her off."

"That's for damned sure. We don't owe her or anyone else a goddamned thing," Everette added adamantly.

Albert's hands shook as he lifted them to plead with his brothers. "Listen, we need to think about this. We're not those cocky young bucks anymore. We all have children and they have kids and businesses and things attached to the Donovan name. We have to think about them."

He hadn't said anything about their wives, the women that would be most affected by Roslyn and the kind of havoc her returning to their lives could bring. Albert hadn't said that because his wife had already paid that price.

"Nobody's going to hurt our family, Al. I told you that all those years ago and I'm making that same promise to you now," Henry told him. "We stick together, man. We're Donovans."

Henry reached out to touch Al's shoulder.

Bernard's brow was drawn, his jaw set, and when he spoke it was with the booming voice he'd been known for. "That's right, we're Donovans."

Reginald came up on Al's other side, doing the same thing. "He's right, Al. We'll handle this together," he said.

Everette stood with them, his expression dour but determined. Then Bruce joined them, crumbling the letter that Reginald had passed to him and tossing it into the trashcan beside the outside bar where they stood.

"As long as we stick together, nothing can stop us," Bruce said.

It was what they had always said, the Donovan boys who had grown up with money and privilege but still had to fight the same battles as other young black man. They'd been through a lot together, the six of them, and when they'd become adults they'd gone their separate ways. But not even distance could break their bond. And if Roslyn Ausby thought she could change that, she'd better think again.

Do you love The Donovans? Would you like to spend a weekend talking about this intriguing family and their stories of love?

Then you are cordially invited to…

The Donovan Family Reunion
And
Wedding of Brock & Noelle

Special Guests: Celeste O. Norfleet & The Coles Family, Michelle Monkou & The Meadows Family

October 11-13, 2013
Four Points Sheraton BWI
1001 Scott Drive
Baltimore, MD 21240

Reunion Package Includes

Friday: Donovan Welcome & Bridal Shower for Noelle
Saturday: Donovan Family Breakfast and Afternoon at
Maryland Live Casino
and Arundel Mills Outlet Mall
Saturday Evening: Semi-Formal Reception for Brock &
Noelle
Donovan Family Gift Bag w/T-shirt

**TO REGISTER, OR FOR MORE INFORMATION,
VISIT www.acarthur.net
REGISTRATION CLOSES: September 15, 2013**

THE DONOVANS

GETTING SOCIAL...

- For a complete listing of all books by A.C. Arthur and Sapphire Blue visit www.acarthur.net
- For a complete listing of all Young Adult/New Adult Books by Artist Arthur visit www.artistarthurbooks.com
- Follow me on Twitter @AcArthur
- LIKE my Facebook Page AC Arthur's Book Lounge
- Friend me on Goodreads

CPSIA information can be obtained at www.ICGtesting.com
Printed in the USA
LVOW04s2002211114

414978LV00018B/937/P